ADVANCE PRAISE FOR

JK's Code is tense, timely and terrific!
—**Lee Child**, #1 New York Times bestselling author of the Jack ~~

Keen research and high-tech suspense drives Ronald S. Barak's new thriller, *JK's Code;* an incredibly timely political thriller about election fraud and the technology behind it; you'll wonder where reality ends and the fiction begins.
—**Brad Meltzer**, #1 New York Times bestselling author of *The Escape Artist*

If you blended Dan Brown's conspiratorial storytelling with Brad Meltzer's political potboiler, you might end up with Ronald S. Barak's *JK's Code*—but the novel is all its own. Both chillingly topical and as fast as an Indy racer on ice, treat yourself to this thrill ride of a mystery.
—**James Rollins**, #1 New York Times bestselling author of *The Last Odyssey*

Smart, speedy, and suspenseful, JK's Code is a flat out great read. My favorite kind of book: characters you care about, a story ripped from the headlines, and a pace that doesn't let up. The definition of a thriller!
—**Christopher Reich**, *New York Times* bestselling author of the Simon Riske novels

JK's Code is this generation's acclaimed and influential *War Games*. Ronald S. Barak's prescient, perfectly timed, and polished thriller takes current events and somehow makes them even more terrifying than they already are. Chillingly on point in its message and stunningly effective in its execution, *JK's Code* is superb reading entertainment layered atop a cautionary tale. Politics is no fun at all these days, unless Ron Barak is writing about it, and this is a political thriller extraordinaire.
—**Jon Land**, *USA Today* bestselling author of the Caitlin Strong series

Ronald S. Barak's *JK's Code* is both timely and timeless, and did I mention. . . terrific? Timely because election fraud is the heart of the story. Timeless because it's a classic thriller laced with suspense and intrigue. Terrific because it brings back Judge Cyrus Brooks, homicide detective Frank Lotello and attorney Leah Klein to aid Leah's tech-savvy kid brother, JK, who uncovers a chilling conspiracy between the Kremlin and the White House, only to find himself in dire straits. If the raucous runup to the actual 2020 presidential election has been driving you to drink, *JK's Code* will be your perfect nightcap.
—**Paul Levine**, #1 Amazon bestselling author of the Jake Lassiter series

The Brooks/Lotello thriller novels are immediately likeable and pack a bone-jarring punch. In *JK's Code,* an unparalleled real-time election fraud political thriller, Barak swings for the fences and knocks it out of the park.

—**Barry Lancet**, award-winning author of *The Spy Across the Table*

An electrifying blend of political, techno, and international thriller genres, JK's Code is the most-timely adventure you'll read this year. Jake "JK" Klein is Ron Barak's best hero yet, a cool young hacker able to go toe-to-toe and keyboard-to-keyboard with the nastiest and deadliest world leaders. Will JK make it through unscathed? Humorous, often satirical, and always exciting, make JK's Code your next read.

—**William Burton McCormick**, 5-time Derringer Award nominee and author of *Lenin's Harem*

JK's Code draws from the headlines of 2020 to create a political Armageddon scenario that won't be soon forgotten. This suspenseful thriller kept me turning pages deep into the night.

—**T. F. Allen**, author of *The Keeper* and *The Night Janitor*

Holy Sh#t! *JK's Code* is the best damn thriller I've read in a long, long time.

—**Anthony Franz**, author of *The Outsider*

JK's Code is a book that will captivate readers well beyond the 2020 election. With the exception of Stephen King, Barak is now the first three-time "best of the year" *Best Thrillers Magazine* honoree. JK's Code is a really exceptional novel.

The Bottom Line: A timely, compulsively readable political and legal thriller that wryly connects the terrors of the dark web with the fragile state of democracy. One of the year's best thrillers.

In a world where activists like Julian Assange have become famous for extravagant government exposes, Ron Barak's new political thriller imagines what is at stake for the hackers on the front lines. *JK's Code* is named for the text-based key to the mystery that American cybersecurity buff Jake Klein, known as JK, developed to impress his older sister. Little did he know that one day it could be used in an attempt to save his own life.

In the novel's early chapters, a brilliant Russian hacker named Leonid Gradsky takes a meeting with Russian President for Life Alexi Turgenev and demonstrates the power of his new computer program. Turgenev's advisors soon come to the conclusion that the technology will enable them to manipulate the 2020 U.S. election results effectively and discreetly. They also initially assume that they can appropriate Gradsky's election-manipulating solution at any time. Little do they know that the software is dependent on the innovation of a Kazhak developer named Cipher.

Enter JK, who soon discovers Gradsky's real identity, and more importantly, that Turgenev is conspiring with the President of the United States to rig the election.

In the book's early chapters, Barak's burgeoning fan base may wonder what this all has to do with retired U.S. District Court Judge Cyrus Brooks and homicide detective Frank Lotello whose names are the basis for the entire Brooks/Lotello series. The connective tissue is Leah Klein Lotello, the older sister of Jake "JK" Klein, wife of Frank Lotello and stepmother of Charlie Lotello and Madison Lotello (if you didn't get all that, don't fear—Barak has generously added a cast of characters at the beginning). Leah also happens to be an attorney. To say much more about Cyrus and Frank's involvement would add spoilers, but it's safe to say that both play a significant role. Barak has created perhaps his most ingenious plot yet, one that maintains a coherent, suspenseful thread across two continents and the dark web while still carving out a hefty lift for Brooks and Lotello. The dynamic duo's entrance also adds a layer of wry humor to the high stakes political and legal drama.

—*Best Thrillers Magazine*

JK'S CODE

JK'S CODE

A BROOKS/LOTELLO THRILLER

RONALD S. BARAK

Printed and published in the United States of America by:

GANDER HOUSE
PUBLISHERS

Los Angeles, California
www.ganderhouse.com

Hardcover ISBN: 978-1-7345397-1-4

Trade Paperback KDP ISBN: 978-1-7345397-3-8

Trade Paperback IngramSpark ISBN: 978-1-7345397-2-1

Ebook ISBN: 978-1-7345397-4-5

Audiobook ISBN: 978-1-7345397-5-2

FIRST EDITION

Publisher's Cataloging-in-Publication Data
Names: Barak, Ronald S., author.
Title: JK's Code : a Brooks / Lotello thriller / Ronald S. Barak.
Description: Los Angeles, CA: Gander House Publishers, 2021.
Identifiers: ISBN: 978-1-7345397-1-4 (hardcover) | 978-1-7345397-3-8 (trade pbk.) | 978-1-7345397-2-1 (trade pbk.) | 978-1-7345397-4-5 (ebook) | 978-1-7345397-5-2 (audio)
Subjects: LCSH Hackers--Fiction. | Computer security--Fiction. | Elections--Corrupt practices--United States--History--21st century--Fiction. | Presidents--United States--Election--2020--Fiction. | Thrillers (Fiction) | Political fiction. | Legal stories. | BISAC FICTION / Thrillers / Political | FICTION / Thrillers / Espionage | FICTION / Thrillers / Technological
Classification: LCC PS3602.A745 J5 2021 | DDC 813.6--dc23

To my Goosers, forever and ever, whose help to me on JK's Code, and in all other ways, is singular

Those are my principles, but
if you don't like them . . . well, I have others

—GROUCHO MARX

Even if you're on the right track,
you'll still get run over if you just sit there

—WILL ROGERS

I'll probably will do it, maybe definitely

—DONALD TRUMP

My mother and father believed that if I wanted to be
President of the U.S., I could be, I could be Vice President

—JOE BIDEN

CONTENTS

CAST OF CHARACTERS

INTRODUCTION

FOR THOSE OF YOU kind enough to read *JK's Code*, please keep in mind that this novel is pure fiction—meant to entertain and to poke a little fun at our representatives in Washington, D.C. at the same time. Think *Saturday Night Live*, not the op-ed section of your favorite newspaper.

I'm a thriller novelist and a courtroom trial lawyer, not a political scientist. I try to write timely, tense mysteries and suspense novels, with a bit of biting satire and humor thrown in. Timely means what is going on in the world around us today. Tense means readers will want to read just one more chapter before turning out their reading light, but maybe not their night light.

Can I lace tension with a modicum of humor—often at my own expense? I believe so.

Can I call upon my roots as a trial lawyer and as a political junkie following those who *think* they are running our country—without taking myself, or them, too seriously? At least not as seriously as our political "leaders" take themselves? I think I can. At least I try. Some go so far as to recognize that I am trying. Very trying.

I love hearing from my many critics and my fewer fans. You can reach me at: ron@ronaldsbarak.com.

Ronald S. Barak
Pacific Palisades, California
December 2020

PROLOGUE

SOMETHING WAS CRAWLING UP his leg, chewing at his consciousness as well as his skin. He violently slapped at it, heard it scurry away in the darkness, but couldn't see it. It wasn't from the hood that no longer covered his head. When he opened his eyes, it was still pitch black.

He strained for any sounds that might help him get his bearings. Except for his labored breathing, however, there was complete silence.

The cuffs that had bound his arms behind him were gone, although his shoulders still ached. He stood, slowly, felt the lingering stiffness in his body, but was grateful to again be able to move.

He raised his hands in front of his face, pointing outward, and cautiously inched forward. In a few steps, he made contact with a wall. The chill from the stone seemed to penetrate his fingers and travel through his bones as he released a shiver. Pulling his hands back, he could feel dampness remaining on his fingertips. He rubbed his hands together.

He tried stepping out of the dimensions of his indeterminate confines—until his knee banged into something unyielding. He used his hand to trace the shape of the offending object, a john. He reached around it and made contact with an adjacent sink.

After a few more minutes of exploring, he concluded that he was in a cubicle, approximately ten feet by ten feet. He was trembling and he was chilled to the bone.

In his mind's eye, he reconstructed the two emails addressed to Leah Klein Lotello—sent just before the thugs had grabbed him, and roughed him up. As near as he could tell, that was only a few hours ago.

He had written the two back-to-back emails in code—JK's Code—because he couldn't dare let them know what he was actually trying to say. His life depended on concealing the real message of the emails from them.

It had been years since he had used the code he'd devised to impress his older sister and that she'd christened after his own nickname—JK. He wondered whether she would still remember JK's Code, and how it worked.

The first email had read:

> Dear Sis!
> Hope you're well. We need to catch up.
> Hugs,
> Jake

The second email had read:

> BUKAR ABCIM U–

He had been forced to split the message in two parts. As it was, he hadn't had time to finish the second email.

On its face, the beginning of the first email was perfectly innocent. His captors would not know it had a double meaning. He could only hope Leah would, and would apply JK's Code to translate **Dear Sis!** into **Dire SOS!** To tell her that he was in trouble—*serious* trouble. Signing it with his formal name rather than his favored nickname was intended to signal something was amiss.

Jake *hated* having to send the two emails to her, having to be dependent on anyone, especially on his sister, who still treated him like he was a child instead of a twenty-year-old man. The last time he and Leah had spoken—three months earlier—he lost his temper and essentially told her to leave him alone. He didn't think he needed anyone's help. He was wrong.

And he was scared.

CHAPTER 1
July 2019

LEONID GRADSKY HAD WORKED through the long night, applying the finishing touches to his latest electronic masterpiece. Following an early morning walk to clear his head, he returned to his Moscow apartment. He unzipped his fur-lined jacket, removed his gloves, and briskly rubbed his hands together. Recovered from the chill, he descended the steps to his basement office.

Carefully avoiding the jumbled network of cables and wiring that cluttered the room, he was reminded more of a network of tenement clotheslines than the actual high-tech environment of his workspace. He sat down at his desk, stroked his keyboard, and watched the three smaller monitors on his desk and the five larger flat-screen monitors on the opposite wall come to life.

Reading the code displayed across the monitors, the few additional keystrokes he applied caused the images on each of the monitors to instantly respond. Few people could appreciate the transformation Gradsky witnessed. He could. His technical aptitude, skills, and knowledge were second to none.

His new software program was ready. More importantly, Gradsky was ready. In one week, he would share his latest work of art and science combined.

By nature, Gradsky was a self-assured loner. He preferred it that way. He was already independently wealthy as a result of his skill set and his dark web standing. He had developed the vastly upgraded software program on his own. He could certainly fund and implement the undertaking without any third-party support.

In fact, taking on his anticipated sponsor would likely dilute his potential profits. And, more significantly, his autonomy. But Gradsky was conservative and chose to hedge his bets. There was much to be said about the value of this particular patron.

CHAPTER 2
July 2019, Two Days Later

PRESIDENT DUSTIN BAKER REVIEWED what he had been taught. "One and two," he silently mimed to himself as he slowly pulled the driver away from the golf ball, supported on the tee two inches above the turf, and calmly reached—and paused—at the conclusion of his backswing. His left eye was still on the golf ball. Check. His supple left arm and shoulder passed gently under his motionless chin, precisely at the moment his right elbow folded and his right wrist cocked. Check. So far, so good.

Baker also knew all about the downswing that was to come next, barely faster than his backswing. His head was to remain motionless. His right arm and shoulder were to pass gently under his chin, the same as his left arm and shoulder had on the backswing. His weight was to move from his right foot to the side of his left foot, as his left elbow folded and his clubhead ascended over his left shoulder. Check. Check. Check. And check.

And then all hell broke loose! His downswing inexplicably almost tripled in speed over his backswing. His head lunged upward, as if he were trying to follow some airplane passing overhead. His clubhead never cleared his left shoulder, vanishing instead somewhere off into the rightfield hinterland.

And the golf ball. It dribbled off the tee and headed straight down the middle of the fairway . . . for about five inches.

Baker's face was now as orange as the rug barely held in place atop his head—the sole contribution of his golf cap on this overcast day. If one ignored the letters stitched across the front crown of the cap.

There were three advantages to being President of the United States and owning your own golf course: the tee was yours whenever you wanted it; no one recorded anything you said while you were out on the links; and, when you called your swing just a good practice swing, your guests never disagreed.

"Put it out there, Mr. President," the other three members of his foursome said in succession as Baker's golf ball mysteriously reappeared on the tee.

In all fairness, what was dominating Baker's mind these days was quite possibly interfering with his golf. That topic was cryptically addressed when Baker and his guests briefly gathered at the halfway snack bar before making the turn.

"How are our re-election plans coming?" POTUS said to his son, Dustin Baker, Jr., but more for the benefit of the other two members of the foursome.

"Couldn't be better, Dad. Russia is cooperating beautifully, promising to help us with the upcoming election even more than it did in 2016."

Baker listened, and nodded. His mind flashed on the telephone call he was scheduled to have in a couple of days with the newly elected president of Ukraine to make sure he, too, would do his part to help cement Baker's re-election—at least if he expected U.S. aid to Ukraine to continue. *Having trumped the special counsel's so called report, I am more invincible than ever! No reason not to also get Ukraine on board. I can handle this little chore myself. Russia is cooperating with my re-election, at least theoretically, but it definitely requires extra planning and attention.*

"With or without Russia's support, I'm gonna win. Big time. Don't you just love how everyone thinks I'm the moron, the clown, the puppet whose strings are being pulled by Alexi. How little our opponents know. I hate being ridiculed, but we'll see who has the last laugh, who comes out on top—again—with or without Alexi."

Baker glanced at the others. They each smiled and nodded affirmatively. *If they know what's good for them, when I say jump, they damn well better ask how high.*

CHAPTER 3
July 2019, Five Days Later

RUSSIAN PRESIDENT ALEXI TURGENEV was not gloating. Even though he was now well along the way to successfully overhauling the Russian Constitution, and reconstituting and consolidating his cabinet, and strengthening his resulting grip on Russia, he constantly reminded himself of his journey. Today was no exception.

Turgenev got his start in the Soviet Union as a government spy working for the Main Intelligence Directorate, known as the GRU, its Cyrillic acronym. Turgenev went on to become the infamously feared head of the GRU. No longer technically a member, Turgenev nevertheless maintained close ties with the organization, and attributed his present commanding position in, and beyond, Russia to those enduring clandestine ties. He took great pride in continuing to be a feared, and dominating, Russian authority. *People ignore me at their own peril, including that fool, Baker.*

Unlike Turgenev's more famous predecessors—Marx, Lenin, Stalin— who were each primarily content to focus on Russia's internal social and economic principles, Turgenev frankly cared little about such matters. In his mind, his place in history would be assured by one factor and one factor only—international standing and power. In spite of his outward strength and wealth, accumulated on the backs of the Russian working class, Turgenev suffered on the world stage from an extreme but well-hidden inferiority complex. All of his domestic achievements would be to no end if he could not restore Russia to its former Soviet Union glory, on par with—if not ahead of—the United States and China.

Turgenev believed Li Wei's status as General Secretary and supreme "leader" of China was unassailable. U.S. President Baker's tenure, on the other hand, was, at best, precarious. *The man is an embarrassment, a clown, wholly unsuited for the job. Hard to imagine that the "great U.S." could not do better.* Turgenev knew, however, that Baker would continue to effectively do Turgenev's bidding and make his goals easier to attain—so long as Baker remained in office. *And does not forget what I hold over his head.*

It was, therefore, in Turgenev's best interests that he use all his resources to assure Baker's re-election—after Baker first puts down the politically frivolous impeachment attempts his Democratic opponents would certainly be initiating before the year was out, if only as some election campaign strategy.

* * *

Turgenev entered the conference room adjacent to his exterior office used to greet visitors. This visitor's presence had been requested because his reputation had preceded him. Turgenev was curious to see for himself if the rumors were true.

Already seated at the conference table, the man shuffled to his feet. He was tall and lanky. "An honor, Mr. President, thank you for inviting me," Gradsky said.

Turgenev stared at Gradsky's face. It was difficult not to. The scars captured Turgenev's eyes, much as a magnet would attract a nearby piece of iron. He looked away, too late to hide his indiscretion. *Damn my staff for not alerting me.* "Take your seat," Turgenev said to Gradsky after recovering from his momentary unease.

"Please don't be self-conscious, Mr. President; I'm used to it."

Turgenev wondered why Gradsky didn't cover them with a beard. *Perhaps he cannot grow hair over the scars.* "How did it happen?" Turgenev asked.

"An electrical fire years ago, the result of an exploding overheated piece of laboratory equipment."

"Does it hurt?" Turgenev was more curious than sympathetic.

"Not any longer. It's been a number of years. The surrounding nerve endings are long since dead."

Turgenev changed the subject. Pointing to the projector on the conference table, he said, "You've brought something to show me?" He didn't wait for Gradsky to answer. "Proceed."

Gradsky connected his laptop computer to the projector and powered it up. The 120-inch monitor on the opposite wall immediately exhibited the title page of the power point presentation. Gradsky made some opening remarks, and then began flipping through the numbered slides comprising the presentation "deck", stopping on each image to explain what Turgenev was looking at.

Turgenev was not a tech guru, but he fancied himself a pretty quick study. However, ten minutes into Gradsky's slideshow, he found himself totally lost. *This Gradsky is almost as unpresentable as Baker. Not quite, but almost. It's ironic that I'm considering Gradsky to help me with Baker. I can't understand what the hell he's saying. I need to get my staff in here.*

"Wait a second. What am I looking at? I don't understand. Let's take a thirty-minute break and begin again. Take the time to make your presentation clearer." Turgenev stood up and walked out of the room without waiting for Gradsky to reply.

Twenty-five minutes later, Turgenev walked back into the room, followed by two men he did not bother to introduce. "Okay, let's begin again. From the top."

Gradsky teed up the slideshow from the start. This time, there were no interruptions.

When the report concluded, some fifteen minutes later, the two men who had accompanied Turgenev into the room asked Gradsky a number of questions. Gradsky answered, with confidence and without hesitation.

Turgenev wasted few words. "Is your presentation deck preserved in the memory element of the projector?" he asked Gradsky.

"*Da,*" Gradsky replied. "It is."

"Very well. You may leave. And take your equipment with you. *I can always appropriate his technology later should I choose to do so.* We'll be in touch.

* * *

GRADSKY PACKED UP HIS gear and left the room. *Perhaps I give Turgenev too much credit. After all, it was Turgenev who first found and reached out to me, not the other way around. He can achieve far more with my software, and far more effectively, than he realizes. He has more need for me than I do for him. Others will readily buy what I have to sell.*

* * *

"WHAT DO YOU THINK?" Turgenev asked the two men who remained behind after Gradsky had departed. "Boil it down into its simplest terms."

Dimitri Ivanov was the senior of the two engineers Turgenev had convened. At least, he was the one who responded to Turgenev's request. "Mr. President, I believe I can summarize Gradsky's power point presentation in non-technical terms this way:

"One—in 2016, we were able to use our existing technology to alter some of the U.S. election results, and without leaving any obvious tracks or evidence that we had done so.

"Two—on the intervening four years, the U.S. has made significant strides in rendering its presidential election apparatus impervious to our *2016* technology. For the most part, our 2016 technology won't work in 2020, and any failed attempt on our part to use our 2016 technology would be much more detectable by the Americans. They would have proof of what we had attempted to do.

"Three—Gradsky is an absolute genius. There is no denying that. His updated software will allow us to manipulate the 2020 U.S. election results far more effectively and discreetly than we did so in 2016. It works nearly universally on all voting machinery, and will leave behind virtually no trace of what has been done, or how it was accomplished. The Americans think they can prevent their voting machinery from being infiltrated via the internet. They are naïve, and they are wrong. No matter what procedures they employ, those procedures will be exposed to the internet for at least a number of seconds, if not minutes. Gradsky's updated technology needs only a fraction of a second to hack their systems."

Turgenev digested what Ivanov had just said. *Ivanov is able to speak to me clearly, and objectively. Gradsky was unable to do so. Fortunately, however, and more importantly, Gradsky apparently can speak clearly to the voting machines. That's all I need from him.* After a few moments of silence, he asked Ivanov and his colleague to redirect their focus to precisely *what* Gradsky's technology would do if called upon.

Ivanov replied that, without any trace, Gradsky's software could remove registered voters from the public records, fabricate and insert new fictitious registered voters, delete completed ballots, fabricate fictitious completed ballots, and change the votes on a completed ballot from Candidate A to Candidate B.

"You're absolutely sure of this, that these actions can be achieved, and without detection?" Turgenev asked the two engineers.

"*Da*," both men replied in unison. Turgenev noted this was the first word actually spoken by the second technician, Yuri Melchenko. He was a man of few words. Or maybe he was just intimidated by the circumstances.

"But how can this be done," Turgenev pressed further, "when different jurisdictions use different voting equipment and procedures?"

"There are some 8,000 local U.S. voting jurisdictions employing approximately 350,000 voting machines, a patchwork of websites, databases, and hardware systems," Ivanov said. "However, these machines boil down to only a handful of techniques. Gradsky has studied and addressed the most common voting machines. At some stage along the path from pre-usage design and manufacture, to usage, and then to post-usage storage, transmission, and counting, they are connected to the internet and vulnerable to electronic infiltration and alteration. Even if only for a moment. There may be some exceptions which his software may not be able to commandeer, but I am satisfied it will be enough to change the outcome of the election on the basis of what his software can impact," Ivanov added.

"Even if a universal mail-in voting system is used?" Turgenev asked.

"That would require mailing and counting on the order of 200 million ballots. The Americans don't have the capacity to move 200 million *extra* pieces of mail, and they don't have the discipline and the patience to put up with what manual optical scanning and counting would entail. If they succumb to computerized counting and communication, which is likely, Gradsky's software would work on mail-in voting just as well as electronic voting machines."

Turgenev was impressed, but had more questions. "Today, Gradsky *said* what he can do and how he can do it, but he didn't *demonstrate* what he said," Turgenev pointed out. "No proof that I could see with my own eyes, that I could touch and feel. Can the two of you provide me with such a demonstration?"

11

"We can't. At least, not readily," Ivanov said, "but we believe *Gradsky* can."

"If we have his software, can you learn to implement it independently of him?"

"Given enough time, yes, but not likely in time for the 2020 U.S. elections with the limited information we have. However, with Gradsky's cooperation—and his software code, as well as the software itself—we could master his technology more quickly. Perhaps, even quickly enough for the upcoming U.S. elections."

"What is the difference between software and software code?" Turgenev asked.

"Think of the engine in your car as your software and the detailed plans of how to build, operate, and occasionally repair your engine as your software code."

Turgenev nodded. "Got it. Up to me to see that we have *both* Gradsky's software *and* software code within our time constraints. Count on me to assure Gradsky's cooperation. That's all, for now. I trust I don't need to explain to the two of you the importance, and the confidentiality, of these matters."

The uncomfortable looks on the faces of Ivanov and Melchenko told Turgenev all he needed to know—that his priorities were their priorities. Nevertheless, they redundantly nodded affirmatively and left the room.

Turgenev thought about what he had assimilated. He jotted down a few private notes on the pad in front of him.

* * *

No matter how brilliant Gradsky might be, he struck Turgenev as untrustworthy. *My instincts tell me the man's more taken by his own agenda than mine.* Turgenev believed his plan was far too important to have its success riding solely on the likes of this common cybercriminal. *Well, maybe not so common.*

That was why Yvgeny Barovsky, the present head of the GRU and Turgenev's protégé, was seated across from Turgenev in one of the sitting rooms in Turgenev's official Moscow residence. The small table in between the two men held a tray of Russia's finest Beluga Caviar, a bottle of Russo-Baltique Vodka, a bucket of ice, and two glasses.

"*Nazdarovya,*" to your health, each man said to the other, throwing back their heads and draining their glasses. Turgenev consumed the clear fluid in his glass without ice. Two ice cubes clinked in Barovsky's glass.

Turgenev looked at Barovsky. "It is said that iced vodka is bad for one's kidneys," Turgenev said.

"Perhaps so, Mr. President," replied Barovsky, "but the ice allows me to consume our drinks more judiciously, a wise precaution when in the company of one's superior."

"Touché, a very good comeback, which does not surprise me. I have great confidence in your abilities. Otherwise, I would not have entrusted you with such an important position." *Never hurts to remind Barovsky who gave him his status, and who can remove it, and worse, just as quickly.* Turgenev then directed the conversation to the subject matter of Barovsky's new duties.

Turgenev listened with satisfaction as Barovsky rattled off what Turgenev already knew, but did not mind hearing again.

Leading up to the 2016 U.S. election, Russian technocrats had hacked into a number of Democratic websites, capturing and revealing their confidential strategic bounty to the Republican party. They also used thousands of human bots to run a *dezinformatsiya* crusade in Baker's favor. In 2016, these social media campaigns were limited by the need to physically infuse our human agents into U.S. territory. Today, while a smaller complement of elite human bots was still being maintained on American soil, the focus had shifted to digital agents not required to leave Russian space. For much less cost and deployment of human resources, and at less risk of discovery, Russia was generating much more "fake news" on behalf of the Baker campaign than ever before.

Turgenev smiled. "Wouldn't U.S. progressives generally be less accommodating of our international interests than Baker? They would be shocked to know how many of Baker's core constituency are in fact not Americans at all, and not eligible to vote in U.S. elections—at least, not without a digital assist from us."

"But fully able to influence those who are legally registered and able to vote," Barovsky quickly added.

"Precisely," Turgenev said. He went on to recount his meetings earlier that day with Gradsky and his own engineers. "Our cyber capabilities have been greatly enhanced over what they were in 2016. I am very much encouraged by our pending two-pronged attack: your bot program that will convince tens of millions of Americans to vote as we wish before they cast their votes, and our digital programs that will alter the results of tens of millions of voters who your bots are unable to persuade in advance."

Barovsky nodded affirmatively. "Good news indeed, Mr. President."

"Thank you, Yvgeny. That's all, for now." *He may be ready to handle more for me.*

CHAPTER 4
September 2019, Slightly Over Two Months Later

JAKE SAT IN HIS co-ed dormitory, sipping on a Coke with Kelly Moore, his . . . girlfriend? Well, that was part of the problem. Kelly was a girl and she was a friend, but Jake didn't genuinely think of her as his *girlfriend*. He knew Kelly had a different take on the subject.

It wasn't that Kelly wasn't nice, smart, or good looking. She was all three of those. While she was all girl and a great friend—one who came with benefits—Jake just didn't want to be tied down to anyone. *That sounds so cliché, but it nails it.* However, Kelly was only part of the problem.

Somewhere along the way, before he was ten, Jake had learned that his existence wasn't planned. His mom and dad had tried for a second child for a number of years, but had no luck. They gave up. And then, of course, along came Jake. Cancer took Mom shortly after Jake was born, and Dad was never the same. He didn't take well to being a single parent with two kids to raise. His heart finally gave out when Jake was barely eight and still in need of a parent, if not two. So, Sis became Mom, as well as Sis.

Jake knew Leah believed he got the short end of that stick, but he never felt that way. It was her problem, not his, but he was the one who caught the brunt of the backlash. Leah constantly tried to make it up to him, to overcompensate for what he hadn't received as a child, but Leah thought he should have. The result was that Leah smothered Jake, made him feel inadequate.

All of this was complicated. As a youngster, Jake felt he had been an unwanted burden on his parents and his sister, and he felt guilty for resenting Leah's intrusion into his life. The result was that Jake tended to push others away.

He was now beginning his sophomore year at Southern Connecticut State University, not because he wanted to be in college, but because college was what Leah wanted for him. And expected of him.

Why? Because he was "smart", which meant he could pull the grades without having to work at it. It was that attitude, and his mediocre high school grade point average, that explained why he was at SCSU instead of Harvard or Yale, given that his SAT scores were in the 99th percentile.

Simply put, Jake resented those who tried to impose their expectations on him. Leah wanted Jake to behave like her kid, and to do what she wanted him to do—go to college, like all kids should do. Kelly wanted Jake to be her boyfriend.

But it wasn't just Leah and Kelly. It wasn't just feeling suffocated. Perhaps even worse, Jake was bored. He was facing another three years of school just to get his bachelor's degree. And then, Leah would no doubt be harping on him to go on to graduate school for two or three years more. And for what? To end up as a subordinate in some large corporate enterprise that didn't at all appeal to him?

Jake was in SCSU's engineering school, majoring in computer science. That did make sense—sort of—because he was good at it. It was the way Jake was wired, the way he thought. He liked making up problems and then solving them. If 1, 1, 1 was 6 and 2, 2, 2 was 18, then what was 3, 3, 3? *Thirty-six of course. Simple.* He also liked tinkering with machines and technology.

But Jake wanted in on the *real* action, and the money that was there to be made. And he wanted it *now*. He couldn't see putting it off for another three years—or longer. He wanted to get out in the world and make his way—and his fortune—in cybersecurity.

He thought he had some really good ideas he could use to distinguish himself from everyone else, ideas he could promote and market. He didn't want to be just another employee statistic in some large corporation.

So, no, it wasn't really the fault of those in his life that he felt this way. Not Leah, who had it all planned out. Not Kelly, who also had it all planned out. And not Mom and Dad, before Leah and Kelly, who hadn't planned for him at all.

What Jake thought he was after proved to be the beginning of his troubles. He just didn't know it—yet.

CHAPTER 5
September 2019, Two Days Later

GRADSKY'S MOTIVES WERE THREE-FOLD: develop the technology because it was self-gratifying to prove he could do it, and advance his reputation and standing; to make a lot of money by selling it to the highest bidder; and to live long enough to enjoy the resulting spoils. That Turgenev chose to personally meet with him validated his first two goals, but perhaps not the third.

He knew the minute Turgenev's two minions asked him to share his software code with them that he was in a terribly dangerous situation. However, it was by no means anything he had failed to anticipate.

If he capitulated, and provided Turgenev with what he wanted, then Turgenev would no longer be dependent on him to influence the 2020 U.S. elections. Moreover, his knowledge of Turgenev's personal involvement would likely make Turgenev uncomfortable. He was aware that former associates of Turgenev had a habit of disappearing—permanently—once they were no longer needed.

Gradsky had to assure that he *remained* indispensable to Turgenev. But he had to do it in a way that Turgenev would accept. If he offended Turgenev, the dictator's famous temper would take over and prove destructive—to both of them. Turgenev had been known to cut his nose off to spite his face.

If Gradsky was not careful, Turgenev would very possibly lose sight of the bigger picture, his 2020 U.S. election goals. He was used to having his own way, and not being pushed around. Gradsky knew he was walking a very fine line.

He could hack into one of Turgenev's bank accounts and block, say, a billion dollars of his money. Impossible for most, it wouldn't be for Gradsky—if he set his mind to it. He could then explain to Turgenev that the money was locked away to assure Gradsky's safety and would be freed up at some unspecified future date, so long as nothing untoward happened to him.

Such a personal slight—messing around with Turgenev's finances—would be too much to expect Turgenev to abide. He would undoubtedly explode, imprison Gradsky in one of GRU's notorious prisons, torture Gradsky until he released the money, and then kill him. He would give up his 2020 U.S. election objectives before he would allow anyone to extort him in such a personally obnoxious and invasive manner.

Even if Turgenev initially went along with such a personal intrusion, he wouldn't do so indefinitely. After the 2020 election, Gradsky's pending assignment would be concluded, and he would have no continuing basis to hold on to the money. He would have to return it and, surely, Turgenev would then kill him.

Gradsky had been working on a more plausible way out. It was somewhat intricate, but he believed he could sell it to the omnipotent Turgenev.

Gradsky would deliver one encrypted copy of his 2020 software and one encrypted copy of his 2020 software code to Turgenev's designee. Even with the most sophisticated artificial intelligence capabilities presently known or foreseeable to man, no one would be able to crack these encrypted copies of the software and the software code *in time* to manipulate the 2020 U.S. elections without a software digital key and a software code digital key that Gradsky would withhold. The digital keys would randomly reset every 24 hours, and would be housed in an impenetrable electronic vault. Access to the vault would require an electronic digital key that would also be randomly reset every 24 hours.

The encrypted software and the encrypted software code that Turgenev's designee would have would only be functional if the three digital keys were successfully updated without interruption or interference every 24 hours. The only information Gradsky himself would have regarding these arrangements would be the name of the architect of the digital key system, who went by the name Cipher. He would not have the ability to influence or alter the system. It would therefore be pointless for Turgenev to torture Gradsky in an attempt to gain any additional information beyond the description of the arrangements he would voluntarily share with Turgenev, including Cipher's name.

Cipher was well known and respected in dark web circles. The dark web was generally thought to be potentially hazardous to your health, digitally if not physically, and was not trusted by most "ordinary" people. The majority who participated in the dark web did so unlawfully, violating the laws of one or more jurisdictions around the globe, which was to say that many of the underlying dark web activities were themselves unlawful.

For that reason, many dark web activists were commonly described as "ghosts." Not only did they not ever use their real names, but they never physically surfaced at dark web or other events using even their fictitious names, let alone their real names. The explanation for this was simple. Authorities could show up at an event seeking to arrest a well-known alleged criminal, but they would have no idea who their target really was, what the target looked like, or whether the target was actually at the event.

Cipher was unique in that respect. He meticulously complied with all applicable laws of all jurisdictions in which he conducted any business from anywhere in the world. For that reason, regardless of what his true name was, he did not have to be a ghost, and he wasn't. He showed up wherever he chose, and readily identified himself—by the name Cipher, but not by his real name, whatever that might be. For example, Cipher, in person, founded and visibly hosted a highly popular international hacker's convention every year in Kazakhstan.

People knew who Cipher was and what he looked like. They might not know his legal name, but he had no need to be a ghost or to hide his true identity. Cipher was simply part of his brand. That Cipher could uniquely operate in the open as he did helped to explain why his brand was as well known as it was, and why his earnings were as significant as they were.

Gradsky was one who also was comfortable trolling and doing business openly on the dark web—under the *alias* Leonid Gradsky. He also did not operate as a ghost, at least not in any technical sense of the word. People knew what Gradsky looked like. For someone in Gradsky's frequently unlawful business, the dark web provided a reasonably safe platform for him, particularly given that he didn't advertise his physical whereabouts or calendar.

That Gradsky did not hide *certain* aspects of his activities on the dark web did not mean that people knew his true identity, or any of the aliases under which he did business, from time to time. Even Cipher—who generally knew how to contact Gradsky—did not know all of his aliases, or his true identity. This made it difficult for the authorities to attribute any of Gradsky's unlawful activities to Cipher.

For a six-figure, one-time fee that discouraged all but the most serious players, Cipher offered his digital key encrypted security services. Nothing about that required Cipher to know anything about what business his encryption clients were engaged in, or who they actually were, or where they physically were. Turgenev could "encourage" Gradsky to identify and provide access to Cipher, but that would do Turgenev no good because Cipher also had no more access to Gradsky's digitally revolving encrypted keys than Gradsky did.

Central to the encrypted security services that Cipher offered—and of crucial importance to the health and well-being of Cipher and his clients—Cipher posted compelling documentation on his website, demonstrating that there was nothing to be gained by pressuring Cipher or his clients to reveal what they did not know, and could not find out.

In furtherance of Gradsky's personal safety, he had to *personally* log in *every* day to Cipher's online platform in order to preserve the integrity of Cipher's encryption system on Gradsky's behalf. If he failed to do so, the digital keys self-destructed, without the necessity of any further action, and the encrypted software and software code in Turgenev's possession would no longer function. *Ever.* There was no safety valve and no backdoor.

Gradsky might be forced to share his login credentials, but the login system was tied to an unidentified series of intricate biological and biometric characteristics unique to Gradsky that would not work if anyone else sought to use them. Such characteristics included fingerprints, retinal blood vessel size and shapes, breathing patterns, speech habits and affectations, and keyboard typing pressure and cadence. It might be possible to track one or more of these biometric characteristics, but certainly not all of them.

As part of Cipher's website documentation, he invited his clients to share their unique login user name and password credentials, *one time only*, so third parties could verify that the login process was part of Cipher's encryption system personal to one of his clients, but would not work when used by anyone other than the client.

If anyone attempted to use the logins after the one-time demonstration, the digital keys *permanently* deactivated. A second demonstration could be arranged, but it would require the payment of a second fee. Cipher offered no volume discounts.

Gradsky had already paid Cipher's one-time fee. He considered it a form of life insurance, a cost of doing business. Besides, he would be passing on this cost to his client—Russia, or any other party that would elect to acquire a license to use Gradsky's software program, if Russia did not.

The verifiable point, therefore, was that nothing could be gained by torturing either Gradsky or Cipher for information. Turgenev would have access to the encrypted software and to the code, but only on a daily basis, and only so long as Gradsky remained in good health. One day of access would not be enough to alter the 2020 U.S. election results. If Gradsky failed to personally login on any day, the encrypted software and software code would irrevocably self-destruct.

All that remained was for Gradsky to demonstrate to Turgenev that he had rationally engaged and already paid in full for Cipher's services, that Turgenev would have done no less were the roles reversed, and that it was, therefore, up to Turgenev to assure Gradsky's good health—at least through the election. Apart from any threats posed by Turgenev, Gradsky was in good health and was quite willing to submit to a complete medical exam if Turgenev wished to verify that.

After the election was another matter, but Gradsky had by no means failed to take that into account. He had further plans in place to protect his long-term well-being.

CHAPTER 6
September 2019, One Day Later

JAKE'S FIRST THOUGHT HAD been to offer his cybersecurity services to the international business community. Cybercrime was an equal opportunity growth industry that favored no borders. The problem was the number of enterprises offering such services was off the charts. Jake didn't lack for confidence as to his skills, but he didn't have the resources to compete with all those who had already staked their claim and carved out their space. He needed to find a way to narrow the field and distinguish himself.

With the 2020 U.S. elections barely more than one year away, Jake's mind drifted to the subject of election fraud. Opinions of whether Russia, China, Iran and/or North Korea had altered or influenced the 2016 presidential election were rampant. Who, how, and how seriously were being addressed 24/7 by the media—and were the worry of all fifty states and each of the two major U.S. political parties.

As far as Jake could determine, the majority of the so-called election fraud experts were focused more on how vulnerable the elections were to foreign influence and meddling than on how to prevent it. Most of the rhetoric was from academia racing to outdo one another in demonstrating that they knew how to sway one voting mechanism or another, rather than on how to prevent others from doing so. Jake firmly believed that substantially all of the U.S. voting machines in use across the country could be manipulated.

Jake thought the 2020 U.S. elections might provide him with an opportunity to make his mark. All he had to do was to figure out how to *prevent* such universal interference in the upcoming voting processes.

Right, that's all. But someone needs to do it. Why not me?

CHAPTER 7
September 2019, Two Days Later

GRADSKY FOUND HIMSELF BACK in Turgenev's office. He would soon find out if he had misjudged how his client would react to his personal security procedures.

"I'm disappointed," Turgenev said. "I didn't expect you to be so disloyal to Russia, and so disrespectful to me personally."

Gradsky carefully measured his response. *He's angry, but I can't gauge how much. At least he's controlling himself. I hope that's a good sign.* "I'm sorry to hear that, Mr. President. I certainly mean you no disrespect." *To the contrary, I fully respect this man, which is why I've taken the steps I have. How many bodies has he climbed over to get to where he is?*

"Thank you for the clarification," Turgenev said. "I'm not in the habit of doing business with those who do not show my office the proper respect. I will take you at your word. I'm pleased to know we will not have that issue to contend with. However, what about your loyalty to our country?"

As long as I'm secure, I'll blow all the smoke up his ass he'd like. "On the issue of loyalty, Mr. President, I'm afraid my loyalty must run first to my well-being. But I see no conflict in that. So long as my safety is not in doubt, Russia shall enjoy the fruits of my software whenever and wherever you wish. I hasten to add that, while your expressed focus has been on the U.S., my software can be used in any country you wish, and the license I issue is worldwide."

"Let us not equivocate, Mr. Gradsky. I believe we understand one another perfectly. My staff informs me that you have adequately demonstrated the capabilities of your software and your software code. I will wire your fees to the numbered account you have specified before the day is out. As long as your software performs as promised, you will have nothing to worry about. By the way, you should take comfort in the fact that if the tables were turned, I would have done much the same as you have. We are both where we are because we are both cautious. Nothing wrong with that. Good day."

* * *

TURGENEV WATCHED GRADSKY LEAVE his office. The look on his face was not friendly. *His software had damn well best perform as promised.*

* * *

GRADSKY WAS RELIEVED TO exit Turgenev's office under his own steam. That was step one. He would shortly assume a new identity and look. That was step two. He had learned well how to disappear. Gradsky would soon be nowhere to be found. That was of little moment to Gradsky because Gradsky had never existed to begin with.

* * *

LATER THAT DAY, TURGENEV had one more round of drinks with Barovsky. "I think our two-prong influence on the U.S. elections is progressing very nicely. *Nazdarovya.*"

CHAPTER 8
October 2019, Two Weeks Later

BAKER, JR. PLAYED NINE holes of golf at one of his father's private golf courses. His companion was a Russian official stationed at the Russian Embassy in Washington, D.C. During the outing, the official updated POTUS's son about the culmination of Russia's latest developments to alter the 2020 U.S. election results.

As a result of U.S. satellite records leaked to the press before the day was out, the White House Communications Director was asked at a daily White House briefing the next day what the two golfers had discussed during their excursion. In addition to run-of-the-mill chit-chat, she responded that all she knew was that Baker, Jr. was interested in knowing where the Russian official acquired his high-end golf clubs, and the Russian official asked Baker, Jr. for the name of a reputable D.C. dental hygienist.

Further inquiries as to the golf clubs used by the Russian official and the name of the dental hygienist elicited no additional information. "I'm afraid I don't know," said the White House Communication Director.

Before the day was out, Congressional Democrats inquired of the White House staff whether Baker, Jr. would voluntarily appear before a congressional committee wanting to know more about the golf outing. When told the White House would have to seek the advice of White House counsel, the congressional representatives said they were prepared to subpoena Baker, Jr. to provide sworn testimony before the committee.

White House counsel subsequently asserted executive privilege and said that Baker, Jr. would not be permitted to testify. "We'll see what the U.S. Supreme Court has to say about that," said a spokesperson for the DNC.

Baker, Jr. was informed of the DNC's threat. He was upset. He knew what was coming. It always did. *When things go smoothly, he takes the credit. When they go badly, he blames me—even when all I did was exactly what he told me to do.*

CHAPTER 9
October 2019, One Day Later

THE NEXT AFTERNOON, BAKER, Jr. accompanied POTUS on a walk around the White House grounds. The son asked his father for the name of a good local dental hygienist.

More seriously, having created some cover for this meeting, father and son then turned to the real purpose for this confab, a discussion about next year's election. Baker, Jr. reported in detail what he had been told Turgenev had in mind to help Baker. He also filled his dad in on how the elaborate plans of EBCOM, the Executive Board of the Committee to Re-elect the President, were proceeding.

* * *

BETTY BIANCHI LIKED THE power she wielded as Speaker of the House of Representatives, chosen periodically by Democratic members of the House whose party presently held a majority of the House seats. Not only did she exert great influence over the day to day dealings of the House, but under the Constitution, she was next in the line of succession to become President of the United States if both the president and the vice president died, resigned, or became unable to serve before their successors were duly elected. She would also become President on January 20, 2021, the next inauguration date, if the November 3, 2020 election did not result in an official determination of the next president by that date.

Bianchi and several of her Democratic Congressional leaders were sharing one of their weekly working lunch sessions. Nothing fancy, no china and silver, just deli sandwiches and chips. These meetings were becoming more frequent and more intense, given that it was an election year.

Bianchi grew weary of the all too common initial bickering back and forth between the various Democratic factions. "C'mon, folks," Bianchi cut in. "We're all in the same boat here. We have to row together if we're going to defeat Rusty Dusty Baker next year. Enough of all of this intra-party squabbling. I'm a lot more interested in what Rusty Dusty, Jr. was talking about yesterday with that official from the Russian Embassy. A referral to clean his *gums*? Yeah, right. Gimme a break. More like plotting together to clean *house* in the 2020 elections. How the hell do we get some genuine intelligence on what Turgenev and his lapdog, Baker, are doing to control next year's elections?"

One of those in attendance spoke up. "What Baker, Jr. discussed with his golfing companion from the Russian Embassy is something we really should get behind. No doubt, its real purpose was how Russia would interfere with the election. It also wouldn't hurt if we can continue to keep the heat on Baker to produce his tax returns, and anything else that will embarrass him and lead to some more stupid Baker tweets. Anything to give us some more cannon fodder for our coming impeachment vote."

Bianchi listened for a while longer. She had heard enough. The quality of the meeting was deteriorating. She wasn't hearing any more useful ideas. *Don't know about you, boys and girls, but I'm late for a mani-pedi. Otherwise, I might actually have to find something productive to do to earn my salary and benefits for a change.* "Keep up the good fight, everyone," she said with her patented motherly smile as she walked out of the meeting. *Election fraud. What can we dig up on that?*

CHAPTER 10
October 2019, One Week Later

WHEN IT CAME TO the subject of computer science, Jake's aptitude was clearly off the charts. This didn't necessarily mean he knew everything there was to know about computers and related technology, but what he didn't know, he could quickly assimilate, better and faster than most. He knew virtually all the commonly known computer languages. He could write code with the best of them, and had been developing computer games and programs dating back to his early teenage years, but mostly, only for his own entertainment. He also had an excellent command of artificial intelligence software applications.

But Jake had never abused his knowledge or his skill. He could get through most any routine computer firewalls, and he had hacked into the computers of a few of his friends here and there, but only as a matter of curiosity to prove that he could. He had never used, or even looked at, anyones personal information, although he certainly could have had he wanted to do so.

Off and on, Jake had been interested in the subject of election fraud, dating back to its purported use by the Russians to help Baker's ascendancy to the U.S. presidency in 2016. But until recently, his interest was only casual. As he became more and more restless in school, and started thinking about striking out in the field of cybersecurity, he had been doing a lot of reading on the subject.

The most interesting resources he had found were on the dark web. Customary browsers like Edge, Internet Explorer, Chrome, Firefox and Safari couldn't even access the dark web. Of course, Jake knew that the dark web existed, and he had visited it once or twice to see what it looked like, but he hadn't found anything there of special interest to him. The prospect of cybersecurity, in general and election fraud in particular, changed all that.

Because he vaguely knew that lots of undesirable characters frequented the dark web, Jake purchased a cheap dedicated computer and installed a Tor Browser on it that hopefully would allow him to anonymously cross over into the dark web. A Tor Browser not only provided easy access to the dark web and all of its features, it allowed such access without revealing your true digital or real world identity. As Jake examined the dark web more seriously—and cautiously—he found it like a different world, if not a different galaxy. It was full of many anti-social personalities engaged in, and offering the opportunity to participate in, any number of unsavory activities.

Employing such digital anonymity was as important as making sure not to inadvertently reveal your social security number or your bank account information to the wrong people. Whether such anonymity could truly be achieved on the wild frontier dark web of the internet was anybody's guess.

When engaging in nefarious activities through the internet, Jake knew it was also strategic to use the dedicated computer as physically far away from one's home as possible, the further the better. The reason for this was to disguise one's "Internet Protocol Address", generally known as an "IP address", unique to one's computer and one's service provider. While an IP address does not identify the owner of the computer per se, with a great enough effort, one can use the IP address of a computer device to identify the computer device's owner and physical address. When a computer was used for internet activities far enough away from the owner's *physical* address, the connection to the internet would occur by means of a different service provider and would, therefore, reflect a different IP address.

This kind of obfuscation could also be achieved without resorting to the dark web by using a "Virtual Private Network", also known as a "VPN", which would cause the computer to appear to be connecting to the internet from a remote location through a service provider in that location, even though the computer was actually functioning in the home location of the owner. On occasion, Jake had himself been guilty of using a VPN to watch televised sporting events that were blacked out in his home community. If he wanted to watch a Washington Wizards NBA game that was going to be blacked out in D.C., he could simply download a VPN to his laptop and appear to be watching the game from somewhere else in the country where the game was available for viewing.

As Jake became more adept at surfing the dark web, he began to realize its potential, if not its actual role, in election fraud. Tons of chatter existed on the dark web about how election fraud was going to be even more prevalent in the 2020 election than it was in 2016.

If Jake wanted to become an expert in the area of election fraud, it also meant becoming a comfortable frequenter of the dark web. It offered a number of computer hacker conventions and other programs that Jake thought would be fun—and informative—to attend. The more he learned about such illicit activities, the more he could learn about how to prevent them, and to hopefully establish his desired cybersecurity brand.

Most of these events were held in off beaten corners of the world, such as Eastern Europe and Asia. Jake didn't have the funds for that kind of travel, but one of his computer science professors, Matthew Carter, did. More precisely, Carter had some grant money, and course credit, that he had said he would allocate to Jake if Jake would agree to submit a paper on what he learned that Carter could then incorporate in a book he was currently writing. *As long as I scratch his back, he'll scratch mine. Maybe even more so in academia than in the corporate world.*

CHAPTER 11
October 2019, One Week Later

RUPERT AUSTIN ASKED EVERYONE present to return to their seats at the conference table. It was 8:30 pm. He watched the social hour and dinner come and go. The table had been cleared, except for after dinner drinks ordered by him and a few others in attendance. He appreciated the well-stocked, but self-attended, bar available for those who might wish to replenish their drinks as the evening wore on. Just so long as no one was tipsy by the time the meeting adjourned.

This was one in a series of weekly meetings of the Executive Board of the Committee to Re-elect the President, EBCOM for short. All EBCOM meetings were held in the same private dining room of the same hotel, one of many owned by the President of the United States.

Austin glanced around the conference table at the eight other EBCOM members, six men and two women. Austin was the chairman of EBCOM, bringing the total membership to nine.

All nine EBCOM members had one trait in common: they were highly vetted, fiercely loyal senior representatives of POTUS's administration, all thought to be trusted beyond question. Their average age was 67.

Austin had assured himself that all EBCOM meetings were held in complete secrecy. Participants came and went through a private entrance from the underground hotel parking facility. Smartphones and other electronic devices were not permitted in the meetings in order to prohibit the recording of any remarks or discussions. Absolute fealty to POTUS was assumed, but was verified by a full-body scanning machine, through which all participants had to pass in order to enter the dining room. Leaks from the Baker White House were rampant. Austin would tolerate no such disclosures of EBCOM business.

Austin was the only exception to the confidentiality protocols. Famous for his photographic memory, however, he never brought any recording device into the meetings or made any notes of any of the proceedings.

Austin remembered well when the attitude, if not the priorities, of EBCOM changed. It had been almost five months since the long-awaited "special counsel's" report had issued. In Austin's opinion, the title was misleading. He believed special *prosecutor* would have been a more apt label. Without exception, every member of EBCOM had agreed with Austin. Notwithstanding the intervening events, including in particular Baker's foolish telephone call with the rookie president of Ukraine, in spite of the special counsel's report and ensuing public attention, the unanimous vote shortly after the special counsel's vote had sealed EBCOM's pivot from campaigning to re-elect Baker, to protecting his presidency. This was not the kind of determination that was made on less than a unanimous vote.

Austin called the meeting to order. He informed the others that POTUS was reportedly growing impatient. Austin, however, considered one of his most important EBCOM responsibilities knowing when to ignore POTUS, hold him at bay, and prevent him from becoming his own worst enemy. *Like his idiotic* quid pro quo *call to the president of Ukraine.* Being was probably a better choice of words than becoming. POTUS already was his own worst enemy, at least if Austin didn't count those whose mantra in gearing up for the November election was "Never Baker!"

He turned the meeting to the scheduled agenda. In succession, Austin invited each person in the room to summarize the expected progress on his or her respective assignment, subsequent to the immediately preceding meeting. They each did so, resolutely and succinctly. Questions were entertained and answered following each presentation. Any difficulties or problems were carefully scrutinized and addressed.

Austin was pleased with the progress the various EBCOM members reported. He had a timetable to maintain, and he knew he had to stick to it. His life might very well depend on it.

CHAPTER 12
October 2019, Three Days Later

JAKE WORKED THE DARK web on his anonymous laptop without bothering to change his IP address. *Researching unlawful activity is not conducting unlawful activity. I could go watch a murder trial without being guilty of murder.* The more chatter Jake found on the dark web about the likely manipulation of the 2020 election, the more intrigued he became.

Even on the dark web, Jake sensed a prevailing reluctance on the part of most visitors to be all that explicit on the subject of election meddling. Some were more outspoken, but he had no way to know if they were serious players or just braggarts, opportunists, and attention seekers. It was Jake's experience that those who bragged the most about something were the least involved in the subject (sexual proclivity was a perfect example). Those genuinely willing to discuss election fraud seemed more interested in doing so off record and live.

Jake did manage to discover an apparently highly regarded and popular annual four-day hackers conference held every November in Kazakhstan. This year's conference would take place the 19th through the 22nd. Known as KHC, this year's agenda was understandably lacking in specifics, at least in comparison to customary registration materials for less "dark" computer science classes, with which Jake was more familiar, but it was clear that the convention would be heavily devoted to the 2020 U.S. elections.

Going to a conference that would discuss how to commit election fraud would not make me guilty of election fraud. In fact, I would be going there to learn more about how to prevent it.

Jake felt that attending the upcoming KHC event might be the most productive use of his limited Carter generated travel budget. But where exactly was Kazakhstan? Google provided the answer quickly enough. Kazakhstan was formerly a part of the defunct Soviet Union, and located in Eastern Europe, and fairly close to Russia.

The U.S. had no objection to American travel to Kazakhstan, no visa was required by the host country, and the passport he used a few years back to travel around Europe was still good. No inoculations were recommended, which was nice because Jake was not a fan of needles.

He decided to register for KHC, reserve a hotel room, buy a roundtrip airline ticket, pack his bags and get ready to visit his first live dark web event. He would bring along both his regular laptop and his anonymous laptop with the Tor Browser. Somehow, he didn't wonder which device he would mostly be using on this trip.

The more Jake prepared for his journey to Kazakhstan, the more it dawned on him that there was one more resource potentially available to him that he had not yet tapped. He opened the contacts list on his smartphone and found what he was looking for under Abelson, Gali—his college pal on leave from Israel's intelligence agency, Mossad, for some computer studies. He selected Abelson's campus telephone number. After several unanswered rings, the call rolled over to voicemail:

HOME IN TEL AVIV ON A SERIES OF QUICK CHORES. BACK BY THE FIRST. IF YOU NEED ME SOONER, LEAVE A MESSAGE AFTER THE BEEP AND I'LL TRY TO GET BACK TO YOU FROM THE LAND OF MILK AND HONEY. SHALOM.

At the beep, Jake said:

HEY GALI, IT'S ME, JK. COULD USE YOUR HELP AFTER YOU GET BACK TO CAMPUS. LET'S ARRANGE AS SOON AS POSSIBLE. THANKS. SAFE TRAVELS.

He added his cell phone number, pushed all of the right buttons to designate his message as urgent, and clicked off.

Jake decided it was time to call it a day. His mind drifted back to one of his favorite novels, *The Wizard of Oz* by L. Frank Baum. *Hmm, guess I won't be in Kansas anymore either, Toto. Or at least, not in Connecticut.*

CHAPTER 13
Early November 2019, Ten Days Later

THE ANNUAL KHC WAS Cipher's brainchild. He would again be moderating the event and putting together the program and speakers as he did each year. He derived most of his revenues from the hacker visionaries who always attended the conference. Many were repeat registrants who attended every year, and were already well acquainted with Cipher. However, a good 50% of the registrants every year were first-timers, and he focused on them and growing his reputation in the cyber industry.

Many of those who attended the conference fell into the category of "what you saw was what you got". These people were law-abiding information and curiosity seekers who had nothing to hide and registered using their authentic identities. Like those who visited zoos that housed unique and extraordinary animal species, these participants came to gawk and stare. And perhaps learn a trick or two.

Then there were the ghosts—those who made their living skirting the boundaries of society and its laws, and who attended the conference without revealing their true identities. Typically, they had reason to conceal who they were and where they were. They were at the conference, and yet they weren't.

Cipher fell somewhere in the middle. Outwardly careful to follow the law—at least technically—he *generally* did not bother to ghost himself. Which was not to say that many genuinely knew all that much about his private life or his whereabouts.

In addition to heavily showcasing the latest developments in his own digital key-encrypted services programs for those who sought anonymity and security, Cipher also planned to devote a good part of this year's KHC to election fraud. Given the upcoming U.S. elections, this made perfect sense. One of the featured speakers on this subject would be Lars Nilsen, from Denmark. Nilsen was well known in election fraud hacking circles.

For two reasons, Nilsen would be the first speaker following Cipher's introductory remarks:

First, Nilsen was a quadriplegic who could only "speak" digitally. This required special accommodations. It was best to get these arrangements out of the way. By definition, at least when he chose to venture out into the public, he did not do so as a ghost. Like Cipher, Nilsen professed at all times to act within the law.

Second, Nilsen was a user of Cipher's encrypted services program. An implicit endorsement of that program by Nilsen would be financially invaluable to Cipher.

* * *

ABELSON SAT ACROSS FROM Jake, munching on his sandwich outside the dining room in the campus commons. He waited for Jake to explain the reason for their visit. Jake just sat there fidgeting.

"So, what was so urgent that you picked up the cost of my sandwich and extra-large drink?" Abelson finally asked.

Jake laughed. "Are you familiar with something in Kazakhstan called KHC?"

"If you mean the notorious Kazakhstan Hackers Conference, I am," Abelson said. "It's 'da bomb', as they say, whoever they is. Run by a guy who calls himself Cipher, or sometimes C1ph3r when he wants to get cute or a little more exotic. Mossad sends a couple of people to it every year, just to see the latest and who attends."

"I'm going this year," Jake said.

"Why?" Abelson asked.

"An assignment from Professor Carter. I'm helping him with a section of the book he's trying to finish. He's picking up the tab out of one of his grants, and I also get some unit credit."

"Nice gig, but why are you telling me? How can I help? Are you looking for something from me?"

"You've already helped by telling me that KHC is the real deal. I'm wondering if you might be able to . . ." Jake paused.

"C'mon, bud. Spit it out. What is it you want? Don't be shy." Abelson added a mock frown.

"I was wondering if you might be able to help me out a bit. You know, to be as prepared as I can."

"I don't follow. Are you looking for information, introductions, something else?"

"I was thinking maybe something like bells and whistles I might be able to use."

"Holy shit, Jake. Quit dancing all over the place. Are you asking me to provide you with some gadgets you might use while you're in Kazakhstan? To play like James Bond's Q? That's pretty ballsy."

"Well, you could if you're willing, but your answer will sure be no if I don't ask."

"Are you telling me you might want to hack the hackers? That's a lot of risk to take for some unit credit."

"I just want to be prepared for . . . you know, for whatever."

"Well, what's in it for me?" Abelson asked.

"How about I share with you anything I learn that might be of use to Mossad?"

"You mean, in addition to what Mossad will already be learning at KHC?"

"Who knows? Can't hurt Mossad to have another pair of boots on the ground, especially not suspected of any Mossad affiliation," Jake replied.

"Unofficially, you mean?" Abelson asked. "Off the record?"

"Exactly."

I have no idea what my amateur sleuth or hacker is really up to, or for whom, but it probably can't hurt to keep an eye on what he's really after here. "Okay, just call me mini-Q. I'll spot you a couple of widgets." He reached into his briefcase and pulled out a thumbnail drive. "I never leave home without this. Never know when it may come in handy. Put it in the USB drive on any computer for thirty seconds and pull it out. You now have a backdoor into that computer, 'til it's spotted, which ain't easy."

"You're kidding me. That's incredible, but how do I access a computer in Kazakhstan when I'm back here at home in the good old USA?"

That's the second widget I'll share with you. Later today, I'll email you a link to download a remote access software application we use to retrieve files from computers anywhere in the world. It's how we keep tabs on our terrorist enemies. It will access the backdoor you create locally with the thumbnail, and it will copy targeted files on that computer. It will even retrieve deleted files."

"Wow, that's great," Jake said. "I'd heard rumors that a couple countries had this kind of software, but only idle gossip. I had no idea whether this was really true or not.

"Yeah, the U.S., Israel, and maybe Russia, too, have developed this kind of software. Just don't get cocky or carried away. Number one, it won't save your ass if you get caught messing around. Number two, this meeting never happened. The remote access will expire and disappear from your computer in 180 days. I expect you to return the thumbnail as soon as you return home. It's not for domestic use. Don't let me catch you pilfering any answer keys for any of your class exams. By the way, this is a one-time special. I won't do this again, bud."

Jake shook his head appreciatively. "Understood."

* * *

ABELSON SENT AN ENCRYPTED email to his Mossad superior fifteen minutes after he returned to his apartment:

LANDED A NEW RECRUIT. A REALLY DEEP ONE.

He recounted his meeting with Jake and hit send.
He received the following reply:

FULL SPEED AHEAD.

* * *

JAKE RECEIVED THE LINK from Abelson later that day. *With one exception, I'll share with Gali whatever I learn in Kazakhstan. Anything I figure out about countering election fraud is strictly mine. Anything else he can have.*

* * *

NILSEN RECEIVED CIPHER'S EMAIL with the draft copy of the four-day KHC program. Cipher had come through and given him a highly visible stage presence on the first day. He knew the *quid pro quo* for the highly coveted opening presentation would be working a not-so-subtle endorsement of Cipher's encrypted services into his remarks.

Nilsen always walked a fine line in describing his capabilities. That would be particularly true this year. On the one hand, he would love to share how he could use his skills to impact the outcome of the 2020 U.S. election; this would enhance his reputation and generate considerable new business for him. On the other hand, if he were too blatant about this potential, he could very well attract unwanted attention.

CHAPTER 14
November 18, 2019, Two Weeks Later

JAKE'S FLIGHT TOUCHED DOWN at Nursultan Nazarbayev International Airport in the capital of Kazakhstan. He had previously made all of the necessary arrangements. A little groggy from the long international flight and connecting puddle jumper, Jake looked around. He was carrying all of his luggage on him. He walked through the terminal to the exit, and spotted the young man holding a sign with printed block letters that spelled JK.

"I'm Jake," he said to the young man.

The bearer of the sign looked perplexed.

"JK is short for Jake Klein, my full name."

The man's face lit up with understanding. "I get it. Me Amir."

"Hello, Amir. The emails you sent to me were in English. Do you understand spoken English too?"

Amir was slow to respond. "For sure. Yes. Speak good English. Learn in school." Amir reached for Jake's duffel bag and backpack, in which he carried his computer equipment. Jake let him take the duffel, but held onto his backpack.

"Come. Follow me. We go hotel. One with convention. Yes?"

"Yes," Jake said. *Amir's English is a little rough around the edges, but it's a helluva lot better than my Kazakh!*

They walked out front, and Amir directed him to an old Russian Lada. "My friend name Joe. Very good driver." Joe and Jake smiled at one another.

Amir pointed to the back seat, where Jake climbed in, still clutching his backpack. Amir ran around the car and gently put the duffel next to Jake. He then ran back around, and got in the front passenger seat next to Joe.

Fifteen minutes later, the Lada pulled into the entrance of a hotel that said *Hilton International*. Jake smiled. *Even Hilton caters to dark web entrepreneurs.*

"Convention here. Start morning. Tomorrow. Very good Wi-Fi. I check you in now. You sleep, JK. I come morning. Meet you coffee shop. Lobby. Seven o'clock. Tell you everything. Take you convention room. Check you in. Good?"

"Good," Jake answered. In his email, Amir had said he knew 'everything' about the convention. *Does that means Amir is a dark web entrepreneur too?*

CHAPTER 15
November 18, 2019, Later that Same Day

AUSTIN SENT AN ENCRYPTED email to all of the members of EBCOM.

> WE'VE BEEN WORKING DILIGENTLY AND MAKING VERY GOOD
> PROGRESS. FORTUNATELY, THE COMING IMPEACHMENT VOTE
> AND TRIAL, WHICH IS NOTHING BUT A PETTY NUISANCE THAT
> I'M ASSURED WILL BE SUMMARILY DISPOSED OF, IS NOT ON
> OUR PLATE. I'VE POLLED ALL OF OUR MEMBERS. THE PREVAIL-
> ING SENTIMENT IS THAT WE SHOULD ADJOURN AND STAND
> DOWN FOR THE HOLIDAY SEASON. WE WILL RECONVENE NEXT
> ON 5 FEBRUARY 2020 AT THE USUAL TIME AND PLACE. HAPPY
> HOLIDAYS AND NEW YEAR. 2020 WILL DEFINITELY BE A SEM-
> INAL YEAR, ONE THAT WE WILL LONG REMEMBER!

* * *

PERHAPS JUST A COINCIDENCE, only minutes later, Bianchi sent a secure email to all of the Democratic majority party chairs of the House standing committees.

> THANK YOU ALL FOR THE PROGRESS WE HAVE MADE IN 2019,
> INCLUDING THE IMPEACHMENT VOTE THAT WILL BE CONSUM-
> MATED NEXT MONTH. BAKER WILL BE ACQUITTED BY THE GOP

CONTROLLED SENATE, BUT NOT BEFORE WE SCORE HUGE 2020 CAMPAIGN POINTS. WE NEED TO KEEP THE PRESSURE RUNNING ALL THE WAY TO NEXT NOVEMBER, AND WE WILL. WHAT A YEAR 2020 IS GOING TO BE FOR THE DEMOCRATS!! SAFE TRAVELS HOME AND HAPPY HOLIDAYS AND NEW YEAR! WE'LL BE BACK AT IT IN EARLY FEBRUARY. EXCEPT FOR THOSE OF YOU WORKING WITH ME ON THE IMPEACHMENT PROCEEDINGS, SEE YOU ALL IN FEBRUARY.

CHAPTER 16
November 19, 2019, One Day Later

Jake walked into the lobby restaurant at 7 a.m. sharp. He was still a little jet lagged, but ready to go. He looked around the room, but there was no sign of Amir. *So much for Amir greasing the skids for me. Too much to have hoped for, I guess.* The hostess seated Jake and handed him a menu.

Moments later, Amir came rushing up to the table.

"Oh, sorry, sorry," Amir said. "A thousand pardons to be late, Mr. JK! I was making so many arrangements. How was your nocturnal respite? Room okay?"

"No worries, Amir," Jake said. "Everything fine." *Shit. I'm starting to talk like Amir. Everything fine!*

"Worries?" Amir asked. "Something wrong?"

"No, no, everything was perfect, Amir. Thank you very much."

"Oh, I understand. 'No worries.' It's American saying. Slang, yes?"

"Right, yes. An American idiom. No worries means everything is well. Sit down, Amir, please."

Amir sat down opposite Jake. "All very good, JK. Registration in order. We have time for good breakfast. Then take you to meet KHC host. Name Cipher—just one name. Like famous American singers. Beyoncé. Usher. Cher. I like American music. Cipher famous too. Famous in hacker world. I introduce you to Cipher. He make everything good for you."

"Great," Jake said.

"Yes. No worries," Amir said. "Now we eat baursaki and porridge. Famous Kazakh breakfast. Baursaki like American doughnut. Porridge like American porridge. Okay?"

"Sounds good to me, Amir." Jake thought it would be nice to eat in silence, but that probably wasn't going to happen. It didn't.

* * *

No bill came at the end of the meal. Jake thought it might be charged to his room, but neither the waitress nor the hostess ever asked Jake for his name or room number. *Maybe Amir took care of it. Why?*

Amir led Jake first to an escalator, and then to an express elevator. The elevator opened into a large auditorium. "Come, please, JK." Amir led Jake to a reserved seat in the first row with a sign on it labeled "JK." "This your seat, but please to first follow me."

Jake followed Amir up a few steps onto the large podium. They approached a man in jeans and a tee shirt. Amir spoke rapidly with the man in a language Jake could not understand, but he heard Amir say "JK."

The man turned to Jake and extended a closed fist. They bumped knuckles lightly. The man asked Jake, in English, if he spoke *Paruski,* "Russian." When Jake hesitated, the man said "Not a problem, we'll speak English." The man quickly examined Jake, appearing to look right through him. "My name's Cipher. Why are you here, JK?"

When Jake hesitated again, Cipher said, "We're about to get started. Perhaps we can speak later."

* * *

Cipher welcomed the KHC participants. "Greetings, all. If you haven't yet registered, please do so at the first break and pick up your welcome packets, including the schedule of events for the next four days. We're jam packed. As you might imagine, our focus this year will be on just how vulnerable the 2020 U.S. election facilities are likely to be. And if you don't already realize it, the U.S. election facilities are certainly far more vulnerable than many Americans think. They would do well to be here focusing on the subject with you. But for those who aren't, that's their loss. So let's get the show started! Please join me in welcoming our first speaker, Mr. Lars Nilsen. Lars does his thing in Copenhagen. You'll find his bio is in the registration materials, but for most of you, Lars hardly needs any introduction.

* * *

NILSEN WAS TRANSPORTED ONTO the dais by two assistants. To say Nilsen was in a wheelchair was an oversimplification. More precisely, it was a combination wheelchair and a gurney poised between horizontal and vertical positions, much closer to vertical. It was on wheels and silently motorized, able to move forward and back, and rotate clockwise or counterclockwise. There was a lot of equipment strapped into place below the gurney, various cables running here and there. In front of Nilsen, whose body and limbs were also strapped into place, there were two tubes that ran from his mouth into the bowels of the gurney—a larger one that assisted his breathing, and a smaller one that seemed to connect to a keyboard positioned in front of him.

Without warning, in karaoke fashion, simultaneously on a large screen facing the audience from behind Nilsen, and on a laptop-sized screen attached to the keyboard in front of him, appeared the words:

> GOOD MORNING, EVERYONE. IF I WERE MADONNA, OR EVA PERON, I MIGHT SING "DON'T CRY FOR ME ARGENTINA", BUT I'M NOT, AS YOU CAN SEE, SO I WON'T. I'M ALSO NOT A VERY GOOD "STAND-UP" COMEDIAN. GET IT, STAND-UP. HAHA. BUT I DO THE BEST I CAN WITH MY PHYSICAL LIMITATIONS.

The reaction of the audience was mixed. Some were quiet, some turned and looked at one another, a slight murmur noticeable, some laughed at Nilsen's self-deprecating attempt at humor.

> PLEASE BE AT EASE SO WE CAN FOCUS ON THE REASON I'M HERE, AND NOT ON THE SIGHT BEFORE YOU. LET ME JUST SAY, I'VE BEEN IN THIS STATE FOR A NUMBER OF YEARS NOW, IT'S NOT GOING TO IMPROVE, BUT SO FAR, IT'S NOT GETTING WORSE EITHER. AT LEAST NOT AS LONG AS WE DON'T HAVE A POWER OUTAGE THAT PREVENTS THESE MACHINES FROM CONTINUING

TO BREATHE FOR ME. JUST KIDDING. THESE MACHINES HAVE THEIR OWN POWER SUPPLY. I HAVE ACCEPTED MY CONDITION, BUT THAT DOESN'T MEAN I'M NOT CAREFUL.

I ALSO HASTEN TO SET YOUR MINDS AT EASE THAT I AM NOT IN PAIN, AND I HAVE LONG SINCE STOPPED DWELLING ON MY PHYSICAL SHORTCOMINGS. AS SHOULD YOU. I CHOOSE TO CONCENTRATE ON MY MIND. YOU SHOULD PLEASE DO THE SAME.

HOPEFULLY, WE CAN NOW CONCENTRATE ON WHAT I AM HERE TO SHARE WITH YOU, AND WHAT I MEAN TO SAY TO EACH OF YOU, SO TO SPEAK. THAT WILL BE THE LAST OF MY JOKES. MAYBE. IT'S INTERESTING HOW MUCH DIFFICULTY I HAVE USING LANGUAGE THAT DOESN'T IMPLY SPEECH OR MOTION. THERE MAY BE SOME DEEP SEATED PSYCHOLOGY BEHIND THAT. I DON'T KNOW. PLEASE JUST HUMOR ME. LAUGH WITH OR AT ME, IF YOU'D LIKE. WHICHEVER YOU PREFER. I'M HONESTLY FINE WITH IT EITHER WAY.

SPEAKING OF SAYING—SEE, THERE I GO AGAIN—I COULD JUST HAVE PREPARED MY REMARKS IN WRITING AND DIALED THEM IN. BUT THEN I WOULD HAVE NO REAL PURPOSE TO BE HERE TODAY. I PREFER TO USE MY TECHNOLOGY TO SPEAK TO YOU LIVE. TO SHOW BOTH YOU AND ME THAT I AM ALIVE.

I AM GOING TO ADDRESS WITH YOU TODAY THE ISSUE OF ELECTION FRAUD. ELECTION FRAUD COMES IN TWO MAIN STYLES. ONE IS ELECTRONIC WIZARDRY—USED TO ALTER WHO IS PERMITTED TO VOTE, AND/OR TO ALTER HOW THEY VOTE. THE OTHER IS PSYCHOLOGICAL WIZARDRY—USED TO ALTER HOW PEOPLE DECIDE TO VOTE. I WILL CALL THE FIRST TYPE OF ELECTION FRAUD "ELECTRONIC VOTER FRAUD." I WILL CALL THE SECOND TYPE OF ELECTION FRAUD "PSYCHOLOGICAL VOTER FRAUD."

I AM NOT WHAT AMERICANS REFER TO AS A SHRINK. I HAVE LITTLE TO OFFER ON THE SUBJECT OF PSYCHOLOGICAL VOTER FRAUD, OTHER THAN TO SAY THAT IT WAS EXTENSIVELY PRACTICED IN THE 2016 U.S. ELECTIONS. WITHOUT IT, I BELIEVE THE U.S. WOULD HAVE ELECTED A DIFFERENT PRESIDENT, ALTHOUGH I CANNOT TANGIBLY PROVE THAT.

I WILL DEMONSTRATE TO EACH OF YOU THAT THE TECHNOLO-GY EXISTS TODAY TO CARRY OUT ELECTRONIC VOTER FRAUD. IT EXISTED—AND WAS USED—IN THE 2016 U.S. ELECTIONS, BUT THE TECHNOLOGY IS MUCH MORE SOPHISTICATED NOW. I CANNOT TELL YOU TO WHAT EXTENT IT INFLUENCED THE OUT-COME OF THE 2016 ELECTION, BUT I AM HERE TO TELL YOU ELECTRONIC VOTER FRAUD WILL BE USED IN THE 2020 U.S. ELECTIONS, AND WILL INFLUENCE THE OUTCOME.

WILL I PERSONALLY EMPLOY ELECTRONIC VOTER FRAUD IN THE 2020 ELECTION? WHY IN THE WORLD WOULD I EVER CON-FESS TO SUCH BEHAVIOR? WHAT I WILL DO IS TELL YOU THAT ONE OR MORE PERSONS WILL DO SO, BUT YOU WON'T LIKE-LY KNOW WHO THEY ARE, BECAUSE THEY WILL UNDOUBTEDLY USE ANONYMOUS ENCRYPTED SOFTWARE AVAILABLE TODAY TO MAINTAIN THEIR CONFIDENTIALITY. IF YOU ARE INTERESTED IN THAT KIND OF ENCRYPTION, YOU SHOULD SEEK OUT OUR HOST, CIPHER, WHO HAS THE BEST ANONYMOUS ENCRYPTION SOFT-WARE AVAILABLE TODAY.

WHAT I WILL DEMONSTRATE TO ALL OF YOU TODAY, BEYOND A SHADOW OF A DOUBT, IN A MOCK ELECTION THAT WE WILL CONDUCT, IS THAT I HAVE THE TECHNOLOGY TO CHANGE THE VOTES THAT ARE CAST. IF I CAN DO THAT HERE TODAY, THERE IS NO REASON FOR THE U.S. TO RATIONALLY BELIEVE THAT ELEC-TRONIC VOTER FRAUD WILL NOT PERMEATE—AND CONTROL THE OUTCOME OF—THE 2020 ELECTION. TO THE U.S., I SAY, TO BE FOREWARNED IS TO BE FOREARMED.

PLEASE USE YOUR SMARTPHONES AND TABLETS TO SUBMIT ANY QUESTIONS YOU MAY HAVE AS YOU WATCH MY DEMONSTRA-TION. WHEN I FINISH THE DEMONSTRATION, I WILL DO MY BEST TO ANSWER EACH ONE OF THEM. YOU DON'T HAVE TO TAKE NOTES ON WHAT I HAVE TO SAY HERE TODAY. SOMETIMES, I GET INTENSE AND MOVE PRETTY QUICKLY. MY REMARKS ARE BE-ING TRANSCRIBED AND A PASSWORD PROTECTED LINK TIED TO YOUR REGISTRATIONS WILL BE AVAILABLE TO ALL OF YOU.

OKAY, WITH THAT BACKDROP, LET'S TURN TO MY DEMONSTRA-TION OF ELECTRONIC VOTER FRAUD.

Cipher interrupted Nilsen. "It's obvious that Lars is ready to rock and roll, but I think the rest of us could probably use a few minutes break. And for those of you who are interested, I will be demonstrating my anonymity encryption software later this week. Thanks for the plug, Lars." Cipher looked at his watch. "Let's reconvene in fifteen minutes. For those of you who already have questions, be sure to electronically submit them as we proceed. We will get to them at the end of Lars's presentation."

* * *

JAKE STOOD UP AND stretched. Amir magically appeared at his side as soon as he did. "You wish something drink, Mr. JK? Need me to show you washroom?"

"I'm good, Amir," Jake said.

"Good? Of course you're good, JK."

Jake laughed.

Amir smiled. "Another American idiom?" Amir asked.

"Yes. Another American idiom."

"I very funny. See you at lunch break. I have arrangements."

* * *

AFTER THE BREAK, NILSEN resumed his presentation. He pointed out that a ballot booth had been set up on the far end of the stage. He explained that this was the precise voting system used in a great number of U.S. States. Cipher said that he had an advance copy of Nilsen's demonstration, and had personally arranged for the manufacturer of the most commonly used ballot booth system in the U.S. to provide the ballot booth now on the stage. He introduced two representatives of the manufacturer, who verified to the audience that this ballot booth was manufactured and delivered by them, and had been tested for its accuracy.

Nilsen asked for ten volunteers from the audience to come up on the podium. They confirmed that the ballots in the booth provided a choice between voting for mock Candidate Smith or mock Candidate Jones. He asked each of the volunteers, one at a time, to go into the booth and vote for one of the candidates and to write down on a slip of paper provided how they had voted. Afterward, Cipher collected the ten slips and invited the volunteers to return to their seats.

Cipher then scanned the slips and projected them onto the large screen facing the audience. The screen showed that seven volunteers had voted for Smith and three volunteers had voted for Jones, meaning that Smith had won the mock election. He asked the representatives of the manufacturer to examine the ballot booth and confirm the results. They did. Cipher then turned to Nilsen and said, "Lars, you maintain that you can alter these results from your laptop without physically going anywhere near the ballot booth, correct?"

The large screen flashed the words:

> YOU CAN ALL BEAR WITNESS TO THE FACT THAT I CANNOT MOVE ANYWHERE NEAR THE BALLOT BOOTH, EVEN IF I WANTED TO. AND THE ANSWER TO YOUR QUESTION IS, YES, I CAN ALTER THE RESULTS YOU JUST ANNOUNCED.

"How long will it take you to do that?" asked Nilsen.

> IN THIS CONTAINED PROXIMATE ENVIRONMENT, FIFTEEN SECONDS, MAYBE LESS, DEPENDING ON MY KEYBOARD AGILITY TODAY.

"Okay, go," Cipher said. He turned on a stopwatch on his smartphone and began counting out loud.

At ten seconds, the large screen displayed:

> FINISHED.

Cipher asked the two manufacturer reps to examine the ballot booth once again and announce the results. They did so, with some dismay: "Ten votes for Jones, none for Smith."

In less than ten seconds, Nilsen had changed the seven votes for Smith to Jones. Instead of Smith winning the election, Jones was now the winner.

At first, the hush in the auditorium was palpable. Slowly, however, the growing applause overtook the silence, but ceased when words again appeared on the large screen:

THANK YOU FOR YOUR ACKNOWLEDGMENT. CIPHER TELLS ME WE ARE RUNNING SHORT ON TIME. I'VE GLANCED AT THE QUESTIONS YOU HAVE POSTED. I WILL RESPOND TO ALL OF THEM FOLLOWING THE CONFERENCE. HOWEVER, THERE ARE THREE GENERAL QUESTIONS THAT HAVE BEEN ASKED SEVERAL TIMES I WOULD LIKE TO ANSWER NOW.

PARAPHRASING THE MANY VERSIONS OF THE FIRST QUESTION RAISED: WEREN'T YOU ABLE TO ACCESS THE VOTING MACHINE TODAY ONLY BECAUSE IT WAS CONNECTED TO THE INTERNET? AND ISN'T IT THE CASE TODAY, UNLIKE IN 2016, THAT VOTING MACHINES CAN AVOID INTERNET CONNECTION, SUCH AS THE ONE USED HERE TODAY? AND WON'T THAT PREVENT YOUR TECHNOLOGY FROM BEING EMPLOYED IN THE 2020 U.S. ELECTIONS?

THAT'S A TWO-PART QUESTION. PART ONE, YES THE VOTING MACHINE I USED TODAY WAS CONNECTED TO THE INTERNET, AND YES, I AVAILED MYSELF OF THAT CONNECTION.

PART TWO, THE TECHNOLOGY I USED WILL WORK ON ALL DIGITAL VOTING MACHINES AVAILABLE, AND THAT WILL BE USED IN THE U.S. ELECTION NEXT YEAR. THOSE WHO DISAGREE MAKE THE INCORRECT ASSUMPTION THAT THERE ARE DIGITAL VOTING MACHINES THAT CAN AVOID THE INTERNET BY SWITCHING FROM CONVENTIONAL WIFI TO MOVE THE VOTES ACROSS THE INTERNET TO CELLULAR HOT SPOTS AND DIAL-UP MODEMS THAT WILL AVOID REGULAR INTERNET CONNECTIONS.

CELLULAR HOT SPOTS AND DIAL-UP MODEMS ALSO USE THE INTERNET IN THE CHAIN OF TRANSMISSION, JUST FOR MUCH SHORTER PERIODS OF TIME. THE PESSIMISTS WHO THINK THOSE MODES OF TRANSMISSION WILL CONNECT TO THE INTERNET TOO SHORTLY FOR DECRYPTION SOFTWARE TO DO WHAT YOU HAVE SEEN HERE TODAY ARE MISTAKEN. THAT WOULD BE TRUE IN THE CASE OF OLDER TECHNOLOGY. HOWEVER, MY LATEST TECHNOLOGY, IN PART ASSISTED BY ARTIFICIAL INTELLIGENCE SOFTWARE, REQUIRES ONLY SECONDS, AS YOU SAW.

YOU DO NOT NEED TO TAKE MY WORD FOR IT. I WOULD COMMEND TO YOUR READING THE MYTH OF THE HACKER-PROOF

VOTING MACHINE THAT APPEARED IN THE NEW YORK TIMES MAGAZINE ON FEBRUARY 21, 2018. HERE IS A LINK TO THAT ARTICLE:

HTTPS://WWW.NYTIMES.COM/2018/02/21/MAGAZINE/THE-MYTH-OF-THE-HACKER-PROOF-VOTING-MACHINE.HTML

THE SECOND QUESTION RAISED SEVERAL TIMES IS WHETHER MY TECHNOLOGY ONLY WORKS IN THE CASE OF CLOSE PHYSICAL PROXIMITY TO THE VOTING MACHINE—GIVE OR TAKE ON THE ORDER OF NO MORE THAN 150 TO 300 FEET AWAY FROM THE VOTING MACHINE. AGAIN, THAT WAS TRUE IN THE CASE OF OLDER TECHNOLOGY. IN MY LATEST TECHNOLOGY, ACCESS CAN BE ACHIEVED FROM ANYWHERE IN THE WORLD. I CAN ACCESS ANY DIGITAL VOTING MACHINE FROM RIGHT HERE IN THIS ROOM.

FINALLY, MANY OF YOU HAVE ASKED ABOUT WHETHER MY TECH-NOLOGY WILL WORK IN THE CASE OF MANUAL MAIL-IN VOTING. AT THE RISK OF SOUNDING LIKE A LAWYER, MAYBE YES AND MAYBE NO. IF AMERICANS ARE WILLING TO WAIT FOR SCANNED PAPER VOTES TO BE MANUALLY COUNTED OVER WHAT WILL PROB-ABLY REQUIRE WEEKS, IF NOT MONTHS, THEN THERE WILL BE NO CONNECTION TO THE INTERNET UNDER SUCH MANUAL VOTING AND COUNTING AND MY TECHNOLOGY WILL NOT WORK. HOW-EVER, IF AMERICANS DEMAND INSTANT GRATIFICATION, AS THEY ALWAYS SEEM TO DO, THEN THE COUNTING AND REPORTING WILL ENTAIL AT LEAST SOME MINIMUM INTERNET CONNECTIVITY, AND MY TECHNOLOGY WILL WORK. AND THEN, OF COURSE, THERE IS THE QUESTION OF WHETHER THE U.S. POSTAL AU-THORITIES CAN ACTUALLY MOVE 200 MILLION EXTRA PIECES OF MAIL WITHOUT TOTALLY COLLAPSING THEIR DELIVERY CAPACITY, EVEN IF AMERICANS SURPRISE ME AND SHOW THE DISCIPLINE TO WAIT FOR THE RESULTS OF A PURE MANUAL COUNTING SYSTEM THAT AVOIDS ALL INTERNET CONNECTIVITY.

THANK YOU LADIES AND GENTLEMEN FOR YOUR ATTENTION AND INTEREST. PLEASE ENJOY THE REMAINDER OF THE CONFERENCE.

Once again, the auditorium lit up with applause.

* * *

JAKE HAD NO WAY to know for sure if the demonstration he had just watched, and Nilsen's answers, were for real. The demonstration could easily have been rigged, but that would have required either that the manufacturer reps were fakes, or were in on a possibly rigged show. However, Jake could see no reason why the manufacturer would be motivated to disclose that its technology was vulnerable to corruption.

Even if Nilsen's answers were self-serving and exaggerated, Jake was still fascinated both by the answers and the underlying questions. This was a highly sophisticated audience. While nothing Jake heard or witnessed suggested that Nilsen's ballot box demonstration was not legitimate *as presented*. It was also clear that Nilsen was not giving away any of his "how to" secrets. At least, not for free.

After the buzz calmed down, Cipher announced it was time for lunch, and some networking opportunities. He added that the auditorium would be secured during the break, and it would be safe to leave one's personal effects in the room. At least the lunch, as opposed to whatever it was that Cipher and/or Nilsen were really at the conference looking to sell, was free, meaning it was included in the cost of the program registration.

CHAPTER 17
November 19, 2019,
Midday And Afternoon Same Day

JAKE FINISHED ENTERING SOME notes on his customary laptop while the auditorium emptied out. He expected Amir would appear at any moment. His anointed "personal assistant" was nothing if not predictable. He wondered just how much in the way of a tip would be required at the end of the week.

"Please to follow, Mr. JK. You have lunch with Cipher. It's okay?"

"Sure, Amir, thank you, that's very nice," Jake answered. He followed Amir to one of the elevators. Pretending he had a sudden afterthought, he stopped and said, "Shit, I forgot to make a note on my laptop. Please go ahead and I'll meet you in the dining room."

Sensing that Amir was about to say he would wait for him, Jake gently pushed the somewhat puzzled Amir through the open elevator door. "I'll see you downstairs." He turned and headed back into the auditorium before Amir had a chance to protest.

From his front row seat, he had seen Cipher leave his laptop up on the dais when he headed out of the auditorium, perhaps due to sloppiness from all he had on his plate with the conference. *This may be my only chance.*

The laptop was chained to the table, powered down, and no doubt password protected. Neither of those constraints presented any obstacle. Jake pulled the Mossad thumb drive from his coat pocket, stepped up on the dais, as if he were admiring the large flat screen and, making sure no one was watching him, he quickly inserted the thumb drive into the USB port on

Cipher's laptop and turned back to the large flat screen when he heard it snap into place. *One thousand one, one thousand two. Oh my God, this is the fucking longest thirty seconds ever!* He kept counting until he reached one thousand thirty.

He turned around, and was still the only one in the large room. He returned to the laptop and deftly removed the thumb drive. He hopped off the dais, grabbed his backpack, and hurriedly walked out of the room. Unlike Cipher, he chose not to leave his backpack and two laptops behind. He summoned an elevator and rode it down to the banquet floor of the hotel.

Amir was waiting for him at the banquet room entrance, and dutifully escorted Jake into the large dining room and to a round table with eight seats. Five of the chairs were already occupied. The other three chairs were tilted forward against the table, the universal sign that the seats were reserved. At least this custom was the same in Kazakhstan as in the U.S.

Amir directed Jake to the middle vacant chair, and took one of the other chairs. Jake introduced himself to the five table guests already seated, three women and two men. All were around the same age as Jake, give or take a few years. In introducing himself, Jake gave his name and said that he was from the U.S. The five recipients responded in kind, but said nothing more. All were from Europe; none seemed to speak much English, at least not that they were willing to admit. Amir did not introduce himself, and no one acknowledged his presence. For the next few minutes, the conversation was confined to those at the table who already knew one another, or were able to speak in a common language. Jake felt left out.

Moments later, Cipher appeared and took the last empty chair, greeting each of the individuals at the table. He seemed to know them all, and was able to speak their native tongues, at least superficially. Jake was impressed—and envious. *Americans sure can't do that.*

For the next few minutes, Cipher was engrossed in his smartphone. Lunch was served, and people ate mostly in silence, Cipher included. Finally, he turned to Jake and asked, "What do you think of our little event so far, JK?"

"I'm impressed," Jake said. "The morning session was over the top. I think it's safe to say I've never attended anything quite like your convention before."

"Yes, I think over the top is a good way to put it," Cipher responded. "Nilsen always creates quite a reaction, not only because of his physical presence, but even more so by the controversial things he says and does. I always like to begin our events with him."

"I'm also amazed by the international flavor of your audience," Jake added. "They seem to come from everywhere."

"Everywhere except the U.S. You are our only American guest. I think that is because few in the States are familiar with the dark web, the only place on the internet where we're active. Earlier today, I asked you what brought you to us, but there was no time for you to answer. Perhaps you'll now tell me why you are here."

Jake thought about how best to respond to Cipher's inquiry. The image he decided to present was that of a naïve young puppy dog, who posed no threat to anyone. People like puppy dogs, especially ones that are quiet and don't bite. He figured this approach was his best shot at endearing himself to Cipher, persuading him to let down his guard, and possibly offer Jake something useful. *One generally catches more flies with honey than with vinegar.*

He said he wanted to pursue a career in cybersecurity, in particular the prevention of election fraud. "I just assumed the dark web was the place for me to hunt around. I found a lot of discussions on the subject, including mention of you and your convention. Lars Nilsen was also mentioned in several instances. I decided this was the place for me to come. Fortunately, one of my college professors had some grant money he would provide to cover my expenses, in exchange for my agreeing to share my experiences here for a book he is writing."

Cipher stared at Jake, but didn't say anything. There was a bit of an awkward silence.

Jake felt he needed to keep the conversation going. "I also saw a bunch of chatter on the dark web about a man by the name of Leonid Gradsky. He seems to be highly respected in the field of election fraud. Do you know him? Will he be here at KHC? I'd really like to meet him."

Cipher continued staring at Jake, as if he were deciding how to reply. Jake could almost see the wheels turning behind Cipher's eyes. Finally, he said, "Yes, of course, I know Gradsky. He's quite extraordinary, but very private. He seldom attends events like this. I don't believe he's registered for our program this year. Still, he always manages to stay at the forefront of computer technology. I would not be surprised if he is in high demand, and very busy leading up to next year's elections."

"I'm sorry you don't expect him to be here. I really was hoping to meet him. I'm also hoping to meet Mr. Nilsen. Could you provide me with introductions to these gentlemen?"

"Lars will be staying overnight because he is on the program again tomorrow. I'll see if he would be willing to meet with you. I'll reach out to Leonid and see if he might be willing to speak with you as well. I'll let you know, but you shouldn't get your hopes up. He's pretty reclusive."

"Thanks. I appreciate whatever you can do, on both counts."

Cipher suddenly stood up, said he had things to do, wished everyone well, and departed.

Amir leaned over to Jake. "Cipher like you, Mr. JK. Not usually talk so much with strangers. Come, return to auditorium for afternoon talk show."

There were a lot of useful technical presentations in keeping with the general subject of hacking activities in the afternoon, but nothing quite as exciting as the morning session had been. And his possibly budding relationship with Cipher as well.

CHAPTER 18
November 19, 2019, Late Afternoon—Same Day

TURGENEV PONDERED THE ENCRYPTED email he had received from Ivanov and Melchenko, the two engineers he had assigned to the Gradsky project. While he was very satisfied with the Gradsky arrangements, as a matter of completing his due diligence, he had sent Ivanov and Melchenko to attend the KHC now underway, just in case they might pick up something the three of them had possibly overlooked. In their email, they reported about an impressive presentation on election hacking, made by one Lars Nilsen—a severely physically challenged individual from Denmark. Unfortunately, they were not provided the opportunity to vet Nilsen's technology, but his election hacking demonstration seemed every bit as exciting as Gradsky's.

Turgenev wanted to discuss this live with the two engineers on their return to Moscow. As far as he knew, the Gradsky program was in place, but Gradsky, to his credit, had placed himself beyond Turgenev's control. That was not Turgenev's style. This Nilsen provided a possible backup alternative. And Nilsen, because of his physical limitations, could not readily run and hide. A fundamental issue would be whether the two technologies would be complementary, or contradictory.

Turgenev sent an encrypted reply, asking Ivanov and Melchenko to set up a meeting with Nilsen.

* * *

IN THE COMPANY OF Amir, who always seemed to be at Jake's side, Jake approached Cipher at the end of the afternoon session.

"How did you like the afternoon session, JK?" Cipher asked.

"Very good." *But nothing like the morning session. Absent finding a way to make contact with Gradsky, I'm guessing the remaining three days of the KHC will be anti-climactic, at least for me.*

"I have good news for you. Lars is a bit fatigued, as you might understand, but he has agreed to visit with you for a few minutes in his room at six o'clock this evening." Cipher gave Jake Nilsen's room number.

"That's great. And Gradsky? Were you able to reach him for me?" Jake asked.

"I was. But I'm afraid the results were not as favorable. As you will recall, I speculated it might be the case, Leonid was not interested in meeting with you. He said he's simply too busy at the moment. I made the point that you are barely an hour's flight away from him at the moment, and that you and your teaching sponsor might offer some worthwhile visibility for him, but that didn't seem to make any difference. I'm sorry. I did try. Maybe another time."

"I understand. Thank you for trying."

I wonder just when he did try. Between my request at lunch and his negative report to me now, he's been totally preoccupied with his conference. "I think I'll run and get a quick shower before my visit with Mr. Nilsen."

"You're welcome. Enjoy your visit with Lars and your evening. See you tomorrow.

* * *

IT TOOK SOME DOING, but Jake persuaded Amir that it might be best for him to visit Nilsen by himself, and that he was tired, wanted to skip dinner, and turn in after the visit with Nilsen. Amir looked disappointed, but acquiesced. They agreed to meet for breakfast the next morning in the hotel coffee shop.

* * *

JAKE KNOCKED SOFTLY ON the door of Nilsen's hotel room at precisely six o'clock. The door was opened by one of Nilsen's assistants. "Mr. Klein?"

"Yes," Jake answered.

"Please, come in. Professor Nilsen is expecting you. However, this visit will have to be brief, as the professor is laboring after his travels here yesterday and his presentation this morning."

"Of course, I fully understand."

The assistant brought Jake into the living room of the large suite and introduced him to Nilsen, who was arranged in the same life support equipment as he was during the program. This time, however, the laptop screen in front of Nilsen was turned around so it faced outward, as the assistant positioned Jake in front of the laptop screen.

Almost immediately, the following words appeared on the computer screen:

HELLO, JK. IT'S A PLEASURE TO MAKE YOUR ACQUAINTANCE. CIPHER SAID SOME VERY NICE THINGS ABOUT YOU. I UNDERSTAND YOU ARE FROM THE U.S. YOU HAD A LONG JOURNEY TO GET HERE. HOW WERE YOUR TRAVELS?

"The pleasure is all mine, professor. My flights were uneventful, as I always like them to be. I'm still not quite on local time, but I'm managing. I must say, I was completely blown away by your presentation today."

THANK YOU SO MUCH. WITH MY TECHNOLOGY IN PLACE, THE RESULTS ARE ACTUALLY QUITE EASY TO ACHIEVE. MAY I ASK, WHAT IS YOUR INTEREST IN MY TECHNOLOGY?

"I'm trying to launch a career in cybersecurity. It would really help me to understand the inner sanctum of your technology as much as possible."

I SEE. THAT MEANS WE ARE POTENTIAL OPPONENTS. NOT IN THE SENSE THAT YOU WISH TO DEVELOP A TECHNOLOGY TO COMPETE WITH MINE, BUT RATHER, THAT YOU WISH TO DEVELOP A TECHNOLOGY TO DEFEAT MINE. THAT'S PERHAPS EVEN MORE THREATENING TO ME. AM I NOT CORRECT?

"Well, I would hope not. Today, when asked if you intended to use your technology to interfere in the 2020 U.S. elections, you seemed to answer in the negative. In that regard, I was hoping you might have no objection to joining me in putting together a capability to prevent any fraud in the upcoming U.S. elections."

Nilsen seemed to be losing his patience:

> FORGIVE ME, JK, BUT THAT DOES SEEM A TRIFLE NAÏVE ON YOUR PART. I ANSWERED AS I DID TODAY BECAUSE IT WOULD NOT BE ADVISABLE FOR ME TO SAY OTHERWISE PUBLICLY. THAT IS NOT TO SAY THAT I WAS COMPLETELY CANDID IN MY RE-MARKS. WHILE I DON'T DIRECTLY INTERFERE WITH ANY ELEC-TIONS FOR MY OWN ACCOUNT, I DO HAVE CLIENTS WHO OF-FER ME A GOOD DEAL OF MONEY TO ASSIST THEM IN DOING SO. MEANING, LICENSING MY TECHNOLOGY TO THEM AND TEACHING THEM HOW TO USE IT. WHAT THEY DO WITH THE TECHNOLOGY IS NONE OF MY CONCERN, BUT IT COULD PROVE HAZARDOUS TO MY HEALTH IF I WERE TO DO ANYTHING CON-TRADICTORY TO THEIR USE OF MY TECHNOLOGY AS THEY SEE FIT. AS YOU CAN SEE, MY HEALTH IS ALREADY AS COMPRO-MISED AS I CAN AFFORD. PLEASE NOTE MY CAREFUL CHOICE OF WORDS. WHAT I SAID WAS OFFER. I DIDN'T SAY PAY. I MAKE NO SUCH ADMISSIONS, EVEN IN PRIVATE.

Well, you can't blame a fellow for trying. "I had hoped for another answer, professor, but I do follow your thinking, and your choice of words."

The assistant stepped forward and explained to Jake that they needed to wrap up the visit.

Nilsen made one more statement on his screen:

> THANKS FOR COMING TO VISIT, JK. PERHAPS WE'LL SEE ONE ANOTHER AGAIN IN THE MORNING. IF NOT, I WISH YOU A SAFE JOURNEY HOME AND THE BEST OF LUCK IN YOUR CAREER.

"Thank you for seeing me, professor. Please be well." Jake noticed Nilsen had closed his eyes before Jake finished his final remark.

The assistant showed Jake out of the hotel room and closed the door—perhaps in more ways than one.

CHAPTER 19
November 22, 2019, Three Days Later

JAKE FOUND THE REMAINDER of the KHC relatively fruitless. It was full of awesome gimmicks, gadgets, displays, and exhibits that would round out Jake's skill set and laptop content, but it offered Jake nothing tangible in terms of election fraud. The conference was over. Jake had checked out of his hotel and settled up with Amir, who was now with Jake at the airport.

"You very nice man, Mr. JK. Miss you already."

"Me too, Amir. Perhaps you will come to America and visit me. Then *I* can show *you* around."

Amir said that he would. Little did Jake know how soon that would be.

* * *

JAKE'S SHORT CONNECTING FLIGHT to Frankfurt landed a little more than one hour ahead of the scheduled departure of his Lufthansa flight to D.C. He needed to switch terminals and caught an airport shuttle, checked in, got his boarding pass, and cleared security with forty minutes to spare. He walked the half-mile to his gate. He was hungry, but there was no time to get something to eat at one of the many inviting restaurants he spotted in the terminal. He'd wait until he could get something on the plane.

He had barely found a nearby seat and set his duffle bag and backpack on the empty seat next to him when he saw the message on the overhead digital screen. His flight was delayed one hour. All passengers were invited to freshen up in the complimentary Lufthansa VIP Lounge normally reserved for first and business classes. *Might as well check out the lounge not typically available to this economy traveler.* He picked up his gear and found his way to the lounge. He was impressed with the complimentary food and drink, and filled a plate.

He was half dozing when he heard the page: "Passenger Klein, please report to the nearest terminal phone and announce yourself. Passenger Klein, please report to the nearest terminal phone and announce yourself." He picked up a nearby phone. "I heard the page. This is Jake Klein."

"It seems we have overbooked your flight. Your seat is no longer—"

"You're kidding me, right?"

"—available. But not to worry, we were able to upgrade you to business class—at no additional charge, of course. Please check in at the gate before the flight is called for boarding, and you will be given a new ticket and boarding pass."

"Great. Thanks very much."

"Have a good flight, Mr. Klein."

Jake decided to take advantage of the free Wi-Fi in the lounge to check his email. He deleted all the unsolicited junk mail and texts, and quickly replied to a couple of friends, including one from Kelly. *Have to deal with that, but not long distance.* That left two more emails—one from Professor Carter, and one from Leah.

The one from Carter was brief:

> HOPE TRIP WAS PRODUCTIVE. HOW ABOUT AN UPDATE?
> MATT.

His reply was equally short:

> VERY. DETAILED WRITTEN REPORT FOR YOU ON MY RETURN.
> JK.

The email from Leah was in typical Leah fashion:

> HEY BABY BRO, HAVEN'T HEARD FROM YOU IN A WHILE. ARE YOU JOINING US FOR THANKSGIVING? YOUR ROOM AWAITS YOU. LET ME KNOW. HOPE ALL IS WELL. LOVE YOU, SIS.

Jake fired off a quick reply:

PERFECT TIMING. YES. JUST BOARDING LUFTHANSA FLIGHT 6743 FRANKFURT TO DULLES. CAN SOMEONE PICK ME UP WHEN I LAND? I KNOW, I KNOW—WHAT THE HELL AM I DOING IN FRANKFURT? FLIGHT BEING CALLED. WILL EXPLAIN IN PERSON. JK.

* * *

JAKE HAD STOWED HIS bags in the overhead bin, fastened the seat belt in his aisle seat, and closed his eyes when he heard the soft voice: "Excuse me. I believe that's my seat."

Jake opened his eyes. "I'm sorry," Jake said. "Perhaps I misread my ticket."

"No, no," she smiled. "I mean the seat next to you, by the window. I'm sorry to disturb you."

"Not at all." Jake unfastened his belt and moved out into the aisle. "Can I help you store your wheelie?"

"How kind, but I can manage it. Thank you, though." The young woman stowed her bag and stepped through to the inside seat."

She was quite an eyeful—long blonde hair, bright blue eyes, and dressed in tight jeans, boots, and a sweater that showed off her features. "Hi, name's Jake. Jake Klein. Friends call me JK."

She nodded slightly, but didn't say anything.

Jake wasn't prepared to give up that easily. "It's nice to meet you," he said. "What's *your* name?" he asked.

"My name's Anya." That was all she said. No last name. Nothing else. She didn't seem interested in making conversation.

Jake reminded himself this was a long flight.

* * *

JAKE STOOD UP AND stretched after the "Fasten Seatbelts" lights were turned off. He pulled his laptop down from his stowed backpack and tried to outline the report he would be writing to Professor Carter. It was no use. He couldn't concentrate.

After a while, he gave up, closed the file, and clicked on the ebook reader on the laptop to a novel he had started on the way over to Kazakhstan. It was easier than trying to work on his report.

"May I ask what you're reading?" Anya said to Jake.

"*The Eighth Sister,*" Jake replied. "Do you know it?"

"I think I do. It's by Robert Dugoni, right?"

"Yes. Have you read it?"

"I have, because it takes place both in my home country, and in the country in which I am now going to study for a year. I think Mr. Dugoni is a good writer. *The Eighth Sister* is an exciting story."

"Oh, I think he's an okay writer," Jake said. *Actually, I really like Dugoni and know the sequel will be released next year.* "But I'm more interested to know how you speak English so well if your home is Russia?"

"That's very kind of you to say, but my English is not very good at all. I am a language major. I have been in Germany the last year practicing my German. I will now be in the U.S. for the next year working on my English. Then I will return home to Russia."

Jake wanted to ask her how she financed her studies, but he knew it was none of his business. Their meals came and they ate in silence. The momentum was lost, at least for the time being. At a minimum, he wanted to somehow get her contact information and find out where she would be spending her next year in the U.S.

At one point during the flight, when Anya excused herself to use the lavatory, Jake thought momentarily about inserting his magic thumb drive into her laptop—which she had left behind on her seat—but he quickly came to his senses.

Gross! That thumb drive is a damn elixir, like having the genie give me three magic wishes. That's not why I have it.

* * *

THE FLIGHT LANDED AT Dulles. Jake gave Anya his contact information, and she reciprocated. Mission accomplished. He now had her last name: Lebedev. Better still, Jake learned she would be in a graduate program at Harvard, but said she would be spending a few days with friends in the D.C. area before going on to Boston. He also managed to learn that all of her expenses were covered by the Russian government. At the end of the year in Boston, she was expected to return home and spend one year for each year of financing she had received working for the Russian foreign service.

As they walked toward the terminal exit, he asked her if he could drop her off somewhere, but she politely declined. He saw Leah standing in the arriving area, and said goodbye to his flight companion, after doing his best to keep the door open. "Please give me a call if there's anything I can do for you during your stay in the U.S."

CHAPTER 20
November 23, 2019, One Day Later

JAKE HAD ALREADY GIVEN Leah a summary of his trip to Kazakhstan on the ride home from Dulles—in typical JK fashion, very short. "I was helping one of my professors with a book he's writing. I attended a computer science convention in Kazakhstan for him, and now I have to write it up for his book." In passing, he also mentioned he was thinking of taking one year off from college to explore developing a cybersecurity business platform. That went over like a lead balloon. He did not connect the two subjects, the relationship of his trip to Kazakhstan and taking a year off from school—if not longer.

Leah was worse than unhappy, but at least she hadn't become hysterical. He assumed she didn't want to put a damper on the upcoming family Thanksgiving weekend, and the December holiday season. What she said was, "Young people need a college degree today more than ever. You can always take a year off between getting your bachelor's degree and going to graduate school."

Jake didn't argue. He didn't want to spoil the family visit either. He said he hadn't fully made up his mind, but was just giving the idea some thought.

* * *

JAKE WAS SITTING AT the food court in one of the nearby local malls with Leah's step-daughter, Madison Lotello, and Madison's best friend, Cassie Webber. They had all gone for a jog, and were now enjoying lunch. Jake had the feeling that Cassie had politely refrained from outdoing Madison and Jake during their run.

Madison and Cassie were high school seniors, and Jake knew all about Cassie's background. On the light side, she was a golf superstar and generally an over-achiever. On the darker side, she had been very fortunate to survive a harrowing week-long kidnapping ordeal at the hands of a psychopath who meant to pressure her grandfather, a Supreme Court justice, to fix the decision in a landmark courtroom battle.

"How's your golf game doing?" Jake asked.

"You're a little bit behind the times, *Uncle* Jake," Madison said. "I'd say her game's okay. She joined the LPGA tour four years ago, and is fast becoming one of the top money earners on the tour. She's now winning two to three professional tournaments a year."

"Wow. I was going to ask you if we could get in a round together while I'm visiting, but maybe that might not be so good for my self-esteem," Jake said.

Cassie smiled. "Sure thing, any time. We can play at my parents' club. It's a nice track. I'm the touring pro there now. Give me your cell phone number. I'll let you know when I have an opening in my golf schedule."

* * *

"OMG, WHAT A HUNK," Cassie said to Madison later that day, obviously referring to Jake.

"Cassie! What are you saying? Jake is my uncle! You can't talk like that!"

"He's just your step-uncle. It's not like he's a blood relative of yours or anything."

"That doesn't matter," Madison said.

"It doesn't matter to me either," Cassie smiled. She knew that she and Madison were speaking at cross-purposes, about very different "matters."

CHAPTER 21
November 25, 2019, Two Days Later

JAKE STAYED MOSTLY TO himself for the next two days. First of all, he had slept most of the day before, recovering from the jet lag. By today, Monday, most everyone else in the Lotello/Klein household were preoccupied with their own weekday agendas. Niece Madison and nephew Charlie had gone off to school. Dad Frank had work, protecting all the D.C. denizens from the criminal element. Leah was pulling double duty between her law practice and getting ready for the big Thanksgiving dinner on Thursday. They all said how much they loved having Jake there with them, but they all were busy too.

Anya had popped into his mind several times. He wanted to call her, but every time he thought about doing it, he chickened out. He convinced himself it would be best to wait until the following week. The truth was, he was afraid she wouldn't be the least bit interested.

He also owed Professor Carter a report and was struggling with exactly what to give him. He and Carter had different objectives. He knew Carter had to publish his work-in-progress book on computer hacking and cybercrime, and would like to cherry pick everything that was on Jake's mind. Jake simply wasn't willing to reveal to Carter everything he was intending to pursue—even though Carter's grant money had really given Jake a big boost.

He was going to send Carter some kind of a bare bone's report, giving him something he could use for his book—and then be done with him. But no way Jake was going to allow Carter to become part of Jake's plans.

The first thing Jake needed to learn was more about the three primary characters he had identified: the quadriplegic, Professor Lars Nilsen, the ever elusive Mr. Leonid Gradsky and, of course, the single-named dark web celebrity, Cipher. And what the connections were between Cipher and Nilsen, and Cipher and Gradsky. The second thing he needed to figure out was how any of them were planning to be involved in the election. Based on his visit with Nilsen, Jake had little doubt that the integrity of the election was in jeopardy, and that some combination of his three individual targets were at the root of it all. To topple that was an opportunity that Jake could not pass up.

The starting point for Jake was to head back to the dark web. That would be the easy part. He would begin digging in the morning.

It was what would come next that worried Jake. But he knew that was what held the key to everything. *No risk, no reward.*

CHAPTER 22
November 26, 2019, One Day Later

GIVEN HIS EXTRAORDINARY APPEARANCE at the KHC last week, Jake decided that Nilsen was the logical starting point of his investigation. He was not disappointed. Tons of people who attended the KHC and watched his presentation had already posted comments on what they had witnessed, but Jake was more intrigued by what he hadn't seen.

Apart from similar posts about when Nilsen had publicly appeared at other events, dating back to 2015, Jake found hardly anything on Nilsen—especially prior to 2015. Nilsen had authored a few earlier papers, but not all that many. Where did Nilsen come from? What exactly was the affliction from which he suffered? An injury? Some kind of debilitating illness? Aside from a couple of superficial references to his extreme physical condition, there just wasn't much of anything.

One of Nilsen's assistants had referred to him as "Professor." Jake traded in the dark web for the customary internet, and went in search of universities located in Copenhagen. He found no mention of Nilsen in any of his conventional browsers. No Copenhagen based institutions of higher learning listed Nilsen as a faculty member. He expanded his search to all of Denmark. That finally produced one solitary hit.

As Jake was about to give up, he stumbled across DTU, the Technical University of Denmark. Located in the town of Kongens Lyngby, seven miles north of central Copenhagen, it was founded in 1829 as Denmark's first polytechnic institution, specializing in vocational and technical subjects. In other words, a trade school. DTU's website listed a "Dr." Lars Nilsen on its faculty. Apart from saying that he taught courses in computer science and technology, little more information was provided.

At least, and at last, Jake had "found" Nilsen. Jake felt a tap on his shoulder and jumped. "Whoa, sorry JK, didn't mean to startle you," Madison said. "Mom asked me to let you know dinner's in fifteen."

"No problem, guess I was deep in thought," Jake said.

"Whatcha working on, anything interesting?" Madison asked.

"Not really, just some stuff for school. What's for dinner?"

"Don't know, but it smells good. Mom must be making something special for you."

"Great. I'm gonna take a quick shower, freshen up my foggy brain. See you in a few." *Gradsky will have to wait for a couple more hours.*

* * *

JAKE WAS BACK ON the dark web later that evening. Gradsky apparently hailed from the former Soviet Union, but not the part that encompassed Russia. He found a couple of stories about Gradsky being involved in a laboratory explosion that burned his face, but nothing else. The man really was kind of like a ghost. As with Nilsen, there was very little known or reported about him.

Jake powered down his password protected alternative laptop and stuffed it away in his backpack. *Tired. Tomorrow's another day.* The last thing Jake remembered as he drifted off to sleep was not Cipher, Nilsen, Gradsky, computers, thumb drives, or election fraud . . . it was Anya.

CHAPTER 23
November 27, 2019, One Day Later

CIPHER'S MIND KEPT WANDERING back to the two Russians who approached him at the end of the second day of the convention, Ivanov and Melchenko. They said they were enjoying the program, and wanted to know if he could arrange for them to meet with Dr. Nilsen.

His antenna had immediately skipped onto high alert. He needed to divert their attention, but at the same time, he wanted to curry any favor he possibly could with Russia. "Nilsen's good. You guys are the second request I've had this week to make such an introduction." He was curious to see if his remark would pique any interest. It did.

"No kidding. Do you recall who the other request was from?"

"Jake Klein, a first-timer here from America. Goes by the moniker JK."

"Can you tell us how we can get in touch with this JK?"

"Do you have an iPhone?" Cipher asked.

"*Da,*" one of the two Russians said.

"May I have it, please," Cipher said.

The Russian handed Cipher his phone. He took his own iPhone and held it up to the Russian's phone, head to head. "You now have a copy of Klein's registration for our convention on your phone. I'll check with Nilsen and get back to you on whether he is willing to meet."

This morning, Cipher sent an email to the Russians that he had passed along their request to meet with Nilsen, and that Nilsen had replied that he unfortunately had no time at the moment. He added that Nilsen asked for their contact information and said he would contact them when he had some free time. Cipher confirmed that he passed along their email addresses to Nilsen. He also asked them if they had been in touch with Klein.

Cipher received a prompt email reply from Melchenko. It thanked him for his assistance. He said nothing about Klein.

* * *

JAKE WAS BACK AT his two laptops. Today was Cipher day. No surprise, he found no mention of Cipher on any of his customary browsers, so he returned to the dark web on his anonymous laptop.

There was plenty of chatter, most of it about the KHC, but there was more. Cipher clearly had a presence and a reputation in the digital underworld. He seemed to mysteriously have his finger in all entrepreneurial things involved in hacking. It was not just that he seemed to know everything there was to know about hacking. It was that he also seemed to be *the* market maker when it came to the subject. Need an introduction? Cipher was the one who could make it happen. For a price, of course. Or anytime there was possibly something else in it for him.

Who had dealings with Cipher and *who* he put together with *whom* was another matter. There was nothing beyond some useless gossip. And whether Cipher ever crossed over the line and himself did anything unlawful was also nothing more than speculation.

This was now the creepy part that made Jake kind of anxious. The part where he struck out, unless he was prepared to do what his targets did—*hack*. Jake was up against a wall unless he was prepared to hack into Cipher's computer, the one in which he had installed a "backdoor" during that harrowing thirty seconds on the dais in the Kazakhstan Hilton ballroom. Thanks to Abelson, Jake knew *how*. But *doing* it was another thing.

* * *

JAKE EXHALED, NOT REALIZING he had been holding his breath. "Enter," he said. "It's open." It was Leah. *How could I ever have known?*

"Hey, baby bro," she said. "Wanna make a run with me to the market while I get some last minute stuff for tomorrow's Thanksgiving bash? Maybe you'll find something special you'd like."

"Sure," he answered, powering down his laptops. *Can't put the inevitable off forever.*

Leah drove. "Still planning on staying with us through New Year's?" she asked.

"I am. Looking forward to some quality family time before next year gets underway. 2020's going to be very busy for me. And the country, too, I suspect."

"Made a decision yet about school?"

"Not really," he lied. He turned the tables on her before she could push the matter further. "How's your budding law practice doing?" After he milked that one for all he could, he moved on to married life and what it was like to be a *real* mom. He managed to keep up his cross examination until they returned home, and he was back at his anonymous laptop—the only one he would need for his next step. *Wonder why I just don't tell her.*

* * *

JAKE DECIDED HE COULDN'T be too vigilant, so he purchased a brand new cheapie laptop computer. He took it out of the box, but did not set it up. Instead, he drove across the border into the small nondescript town of St. Michaels, Maryland, approximately 75 miles away from Leah and Frank's home in D.C.

Once there, he opened his smartphone and found a nearby Starbucks. He checked it out on Google and confirmed that it offered free internet, as he knew most Starbucks did. Minutes later, he pulled into the St. Michaels Starbucks and went inside with his new anonymous laptop. He used the Starbucks Wi-Fi to set it up, including installing a Tor Browser.

Next, he found Abelson's email with the Mossad software link. The link allowed Jake to download a zip file to his pristine new computer. When he opened the zip file, it contained the remote access and retrieval file, as well as several "how to" manuals and other "white paper" files explaining in detail how to use the Mossad software. He quickly skimmed the Quick Start file, figuring that would do for now.

When he opened the downloaded Mossad software, the first thing it did was display a list of all computers accessible through the thumb drive backdoor. In this instance, there was only one computer displayed—Cipher's. He recalled that, had he been less honorable, it would also have listed a backdoor access to Anya's laptop.

Jake "pointed" the software at Cipher's laptop and held his breath, as if someone were watching him. *Holy shit, I'm in!* He expected to be confronted by an encrypted password, and he was. A few keystrokes on the Mossad software, and he was able to remotely bypass Cipher's password as well. *Scary how easily the world of hacking works—if you are armed and know what you're doing.*

And then, shocking him out of his reverie, the facetime alert on his iPhone sounded. He opened the app. *Oh my God, there she was, staring right at me.*

"Anya! What a nice surprise."

"Hi, JK. My GPS says I'm nearby you. I've been doing some shopping. Wondering if you might like to grab some, *chai*, tea?"

Duh! Play it cool, dufus! "Great idea. Sounds very nice. There's a delightful spot close by, for a spot of tea—haha, my English upbringing. It's called Gentry's. It's at Elm Street and 19th Avenue Northeast. Do you think you can find it? Or I can come to you."

"Hold on a minute," Anya said. After a pause, "I've found it. It says I'm only 15 minutes away from there. I have some more shopping to do, but I can be there in about an hour. Will that work for you?"

"Just finishing up some work myself. I can meet you there in about an hour and a half. Is that okay?"

"Sure. It looks like there's a bookstore next door. Come find me in there when you arrive."

"See you then," Jake said, as low key as he could muster. He almost forgot to shut down his laptop. But he didn't.

* * *

CIPHER HEARD THE TRIPWIRE alert on his laptop computer. *What the fuck! Someone's trying to hack into my computer?* He was immediately torn as to how to react.

The cautious part of him said he should instantly destroy the computer. It was all backed up elsewhere. Why let anyone possibly poke around and perhaps attempt to retrieve what he had previously deleted from the hard drive? If the computer no longer physically existed, nothing could be accessed through it.

The curious part of him, however, wanted to know who was messing with him. So he could teach them a lesson they would not forget. He looked to see what he could, whether he could identify any obnoxious presence. Nothing.

Might have been a random accident, but not likely. If intentional, my uninvited intruder will be back. Gde raki zimuyut. *I will find and punish you severely for this.*

His curiosity—and rage—got the better of him. He was too incensed to recognize that curiosity *sometimes* killed the cat. But not *this cat!*

* * *

JAKE WAS OUTSIDE THE entrance to Gentry's in less than eighty minutes. He located the bookstore next door, but Anya was nowhere to be found. He sat at a table near the entrance and waited. She walked in ten minutes later.

"Sorry to be late," Anya said. "I was told growing up that the girl always has to be fashionably late. But not *too* late." She smiled.

"Oh, you're perfect," he responded ambiguously. They were both dressed in jogging suits, her's a bit more chic than his. "Looks like great minds think alike. Do you actually like to run?"

"Nothing serious, but a little, just when I'm feeling like I need some exercise," she answered.

"There are some very scenic running paths nearby," Jake said. "Perhaps we can give one of them a try sometime."

"If you're not too forward for me. Wait, I mean too fast for me." She blushed. "If you don't run too fast for me. You can see why I need to study my English."

"I understood what you meant the first time. I promise not to be too forward or too fast for you." Jake smiled. So did Anya.

They had tea and talked—in English, and perhaps in some other unspoken dialect. Certainly not in German or Russian.

Abruptly, Anya looked at her watch. "I'm late. I have to go. The people I'm staying with are leaving for the holiday weekend."

"Are you going with them?" Jake asked.

"No. I'm not included. They weren't expecting me to arrive here so soon."

"That's too bad. Are you going to be alone for our Thanksgiving holiday?"

"I am, but it's not a problem. I'll be able to keep myself occupied."

Jake paused. "Would you like to join my family and me for our Thanksgiving dinner? Nothing formal, but we have a nice time."

"That's a very nice offer, JK, but I couldn't possibly intrude."

"You wouldn't be. Our family is very easy going. They love making new friends, like I do."

"Are you sure?" Anya asked.

"I am. I have the address you gave me where you are staying. How about if I pick you up tomorrow at three o'clock?"

"That's very kind, but not necessary. I'm actually quite independent, you know. I have a car and my GPS. Please just give me the address and tell me what time I should arrive."

Jake gave her the address and suggested she arrive anytime fashionably late—around 3:30 pm. Anya smiled. She seemed to smile easily. Jake paid for the tea, gave her a quick kiss on the cheek, and they headed off in their separate directions.

* * *

JAKE SAILED HOME. HE bumped into Leah as he entered the house.

"Where've you been?" Leah asked.

Can't keep taking a steady diet of all these questions. "Just having tea with the girl who sat next to me on the flight here from Germany."

"Tea? I've never seen you drink tea," Leah said. "Very proper of you. You must like this young lady quite a bit."

More questions, even if veiled. "Well, she's very nice, and she's a visitor from a foreign country. It was the least I could do. By the way, she was going to be by herself on Thanksgiving, so I invited her to join us. I hope that was okay." *Leah would never say no. Besides, now she'll be able to satisfy her motherly curiosity for herself. She never trusts what I say anyway.*

"Well, of course it's okay. By the way, what's your friend's name, and where's she from?"

"Anya. She's from Russia," he added in passing. He headed off to his room—and his next date with Cipher—before Leah could ask more questions.

* * *

JAKE SLIPPED OUT AFTER dark and headed straight for the St. Michaels Starbucks. He wondered if his nighttime absence would be noticed by anyone at home. He wouldn't be gone that long, three hours tops. If asked where he was, he'd think up something to say.

Traffic was light, and he reached his destination in short order. Were it not for Mossad's software, he would have needed to have actual physical access to Cipher's computer. In that event, he had his own software that could have copied whatever was on the computer, and also retrieved whatever might previously have been deleted from the computer. While there was no way he was going to get his hands on Cipher's computer, thanks to Abelson and the Mossad software, actual physical possession of Cipher's computer was no longer necessary. It was as if he did have physical possession of the computer. One might call it virtual possession.

Once again, he was back inside Cipher's computer in a matter of seconds. Once again, he easily circumvented Cipher's password. He spent the next hour scouring the computer—just as if he were sitting right in front of it—but to no avail. There were folders with a number of names—more precisely, initials. Unfortunately, all the folders were empty. One of them was identified as "GL." After a moment's hesitation, the possibility occurred to him: Gradsky, Leonid. But who was represented by the other sets of initials?

He made good time on the drive back home as well, during which he reaffirmed his prior tentative decision on what he was and was not going to report to Professor Carter. He would tell him everything that was publicly available from the KHC, nothing more, nothing less.

That meant he would effectively summarize the Nilsen presentation. He would also report what Nilsen had alluded to in their personal meeting. Professor Carter would be able to report in his soon to be published manuscript that technology capable of manipulating the 2020 U.S. election results definitely existed, and that there were those who intended to apply that technology to the election.

He would not speculate in his report to Carter who that might be, or how they might be stopped. To the extent he might be able to put that together, that was his and his alone.

It was a long night, one that would be short on sleep, but Jake finally put his Carter report together, attached it to an email addressed to Carter, and hit send.

CHAPTER 24
November 28, 2019, One Day Later

JAKE HEARD THE DOORBELL. "I'll get it," he said. He opened the door, smiled, and told Anya how nice she looked. He invited her in as she returned Jake's smile.

Leah and Madison had followed Jake to the door. "This is my sister, Leah, and my niece, Madison," Jake said.

"Welcome to our home, Anya," Leah said. "It's so nice to meet you."

"Hi, Anya," Madison added.

"Hello. Thank you for inviting me, or allowing JK to do so. I wasn't sure what to bring. I hope this will be okay." Anya handed the gift wrapped bottle of wine to Leah.

"How sweet of you, we'll drink it tonight."

"Your accent is cool," Madison said.

"Thank you for saying so."

"Please come in and let me introduce you to everyone," Leah said. She took Anya gently by the arm, and led her into the living room. "Everyone, I'd like to introduce our special guest, Anya Lebedev. Her family name means 'the swan.'"

"Oh, I see you know Russian," Anya said.

"I don't, but Google does." Leah smiled.

Everyone in the room stood.

This is my husband, Frank Lotello. He's Madison and Charlie's father, and a homicide investigator with the D.C. police. You've already met Madison. This is Charlie."

"Welcome," Frank said.

"Thank you for including me," Anya answered.

"Hey," Charlie said.

Madison intervened. "This is my friend, Cassie Webber, and her parents and grandparents." Names and smiles were exchanged. Anya and Cassie looked like they might have been sisters, but Cassie's smile didn't quite match Anya's when the two were introduced.

"And," Leah resumed making the introductions, "these are our very dear friends, retired Judge and Mrs. Brooks. Judge Brooks may be retired from the bench, but he is anything but retired—or retiring. He has been professionally involved with Frank and me for years."

"Hello, Anya, I'm Eloise Brooks. Please call me Eloise.

"*Dobryj dyen Anya, menya zovut Cyrus,* Cyrus Brooks said. *Rad vstreche,*" he added.

"*Spasebo*, thank you, Judge Brooks. Your Russian is fantastic."

"Nonsense, but thank you for saying so. I only know a few words. Please call me Cyrus."

"Anya, come sit here next to me," Leah said. "How was your flight? Have you been here before?"

"My flight was fine. Thank you for asking. This is my first time in America."

The conversation continued for a few minutes, most of it directed toward Anya since everyone else knew each other. Anya tried to keep up with a few polite questions of her own.

After a few minutes, Leah invited everyone to move to the dining room. "It's buffet style, everyone, so fill your own plates and sit anywhere."

The dinner conversation was pleasant. Anya was deferential, but politely held her own. Only once was she completely silent. That was when Leah tried to enlist Judge Brooks in her attempt to keep Jake in school. Leah struck out.

Brooks said to Leah, "I am reminded of the story about two youngsters, a brother and a sister, a couple of years apart in age. The younger one was already talking and walking more than the older one. The mother spoke to the children's doctor about it. He responded that she should not worry about it, that you soon won't remember which one was the first out of the gates. In this case, the older slower one became the captain of his high school debate team and went on to become an Olympic athlete." He softly added, "I have no doubt that Jake will find his own best way in his own time."

"Cyrus, I think you may have made that story up for my benefit, or for Jake's," Leah said. "I don't necessarily agree with you, but I get the point." Leah told Anya that Cyrus rarely lacked for a point—or two or three.

Brooks didn't quibble.

"However," Leah continued, "speaking of the Olympics—Anya, you might be interested to know that Cassie is a world-class golfer, and is a shoo-in to be on America's next Olympic Team."

"Wow, that's incredible," Anya responded. "I love playing golf. Do you get to travel a lot?"

"A little," Cassie said. "I've already been to Russia once, and I will be there to play in a tournament again next year. Maybe you could come watch the tournament as my guest?"

"That would be very nice, but I'm afraid I'll still be here in the U.S. working on my English. Perhaps another time."

The evening ended after lots of sweets and coffee and tea, as nicely as it had begun. Anya made her excuses and was the first to leave. "I have many chores to take care of tomorrow. Thank you all for a lovely evening, and for making me feel so welcome."

Jake walked Anya to her car. "I'm glad you were here. I hope to see you again soon."

"Thanks for inviting me, JK. I had a really nice time."

Before she got in her car and drove off, it was Anya, this time, who gave Jake a kiss on his cheek.

* * *

CARTER PUT DOWN THE printed copy of Jake's report. Even though it was not everything he was hoping he might get, it would definitely make a superb addition to his manuscript. He would complete the inserts within the next two days and make the submission deadline imposed by his publisher with a few days to spare.

His book would be finished, but that didn't mean he was.

* * *

CIPHER CLOSED HIS COMPUTER. As he expected, the hacker had returned for a second bite at the apple; "like the insect helplessly drawn to the spider's silky web by its electrical pull," he softly muttered to himself. *How apt, thinking of myself as the spider attracting this foolish insect into my electronic web.* As near as he could tell, the intruder hadn't stuck around for very long, and had not yet likely found his way to anything particularly useful. So far, he was just dipping his toe in the water, feeling his way, experimenting. His appetite not yet satisfied, he would be back. And then I will capture him, this intrepid insect. He re-read the short encrypted message:

> NAME'S JAKE KLEIN. I THINK YOU KNOW HIM. WHAT YOU DON'T KNOW IS THAT HE MIGHT BE TROUBLE. BIG TROUBLE. BETTER GIVE IT SOME THOUGHT.

CHAPTER 25
December 3, 2019, Five Days Later

JAKE HAD ENJOYED A lazy Thanksgiving weekend with the family. Mostly, he had watched football and basketball games on television with Frank and Charlie. Madison was out and about with Cassie, doing whatever it was that teenage girls did on school holiday. Leah was catching up on client work she had let slide, which gave Jake some respite from her continuous hammering on him to stay in school. He and Frank also shared a few buckets of balls at the local driving range. *Definitely was not ready for a prime time round of golf with Cassie.*

In between television and Thanksgiving dinner leftovers, Jake's mind vacillated back and forth between his Mossad classmate, Abelson, back at school and Anya, but not necessarily in that order. He called Anya a couple of times, but she didn't answer, and he didn't leave any voicemail messages. *Gutless wonder!* He managed to do a little research on long-distance remote retrieval of deleted computer files. This definitely was cutting edge stuff. He hoped the Mossad software would help him out, save him a bunch of time.

He also read some online news sources, mostly politics, something he usually didn't have time to follow. It looked like Baker and the Democrats were on an impeachment collision course. He was not a politician; he couldn't appreciate why. To him, Baker looked guilty as hell, mostly because of the *quid pro quo* call to the Ukraine president, and his subsequent attempt to conceal the transcript of that call. On the other hand, why would the Democrats waste time and resources when there was no chance that the GOP-controlled Senate would convict Baker? Most objective media pundits said it was nothing more than a clear attempt to jump start the 2020 presidential campaign.

Jake agreed; it wasn't like it was rocket science. What annoyed him most was that the politicians were just wasting time and taxpayer money on all this nonsense, instead of doing their jobs—working on immigration reform, homelessness, tax restructuring, saving the planet, lowering the cost of health care and prescription drugs, redoing highways and other infrastructure, and cleaning up the "swamp" and other white-collar crime, to name just a few important topics that seemed obvious to him.

He knew he didn't have the patience to become active in the political scene, at least not directly, but he might be able to do his part if he could assure the honesty of the 2020 election. *Good for me* and *good for the country.* When he first began this journey, it was all about himself. Now, he was beginning to recognize that there was a more noble cause he might *also* serve.

Until after the first of the year, however, with most of the country shut down for the holidays, he thought things were largely going to be a matter of hurry up and wait. He decided to enjoy the respite while he could.

CHAPTER 26
December 4, 2019, One Day Later

BIANCHI HAD MIXED VIEWS. She personally believed that impeaching Baker would be a mistake. Baker would be acquitted by the GOP-controlled Senate. He would then send out tweets for the entire world to see that he was innocent, a mere political victim of the Democratic Party. Not only would he get to play the martyr card, but many of those on the fence about how to vote might well be persuaded that he was the righteous candidate. They might decide to support him in his bid to win re-election. The whole charade could end up backfiring.

But there was no convincing the outspoken progressive extremists in her party. And she needed their support to hold on to her coveted position as House Speaker. If the Democratic Party defeated Baker and maintained control of the House, she would be only two heartbeats away from the presidency. Given the age of the likely Democratic nominee, she could easily become only one heartbeat away from the presidency. Stranger things had happened. Stranger things *could* happen.

Against her better judgment, and in spite of the fact that Baker would be acquitted, she would have to clear the way for Baker to be impeached. She would make sure the country knew the impeachment was due to Baker's increasingly deplorable conduct and fell squarely on the shoulders of the progressive wing of the Democratic Party.

If I play this right, I will come across solely as the loyal soldier, and not the one to be blamed for initiating this patently political waste of the country's resources.

CHAPTER 27
December 7, 2019, Three Days Later

AMIR HAD EYES IN the back of his head. Or so it seemed to him. It had been more than three days since he first gleaned that someone was following him. Actually, there were two of them, although they were not always together. When he was on foot, so were they. When he was driving around town, he noticed the same dark SUV in his rearview mirror.

The first day, he thought it might be his imagination. Not the second day. *Do they think they're fooling me? Do they think I don't see them?*

What he didn't know was why. Why were they following him? And why now? Why not earlier? Who were they? Was he in danger? In Kazakhstan, one could never be sure. One could never be safe. Certainly, he couldn't. It was not unusual for things like this to happen in Kazakhstan. No longer part of the Soviet Union, but was it really so different? The Soviet Union no longer existed, but Russia did.

Again, he wondered, why now? Was it something to do with Cipher? Or the American JK who he had guided through his city?

The real question was what to do about it?

* * *

JAKE WAS BERATING HIMSELF. Okay, wuss, no more excuses. Two days dead time. Call Anya. *Now! She may still be sleeping. I'll give it another couple of hours. Maybe we can go for a jog.* Have lunch. He waited two hours and tapped in her number. Anya didn't answer. He got a default recording.

> THE PERSON YOU HAVE CALLED HAS A VOICEMAIL BOX THAT HAS NOT BEEN SET UP YET. PLEASE TRY YOUR CALL AGAIN LATER. GOODBYE.

I have her address. Should I just drop by her place? No way! Way *too pushy. I'll call again this afternoon.* He did, but he got the same result.

Hmm. I'll try again in the morning. If I get this message again, I'll have a decent excuse to stop by her place. If nothing else, I can leave a note for her, let her know that I've been trying.

No one was home at the Lotello/Klein household. *No one's paying me any attention.* He borrowed Frank's clubs and went to the local driving range and hit a few buckets of balls. *Not great, but improving.* He left the range, unsatisfied, and went to the park down by the lake and jogged a 5K—by himself.

CHAPTER 28
December 8, 2019, One Day Later

AMIR LOST THE TWO men who were following him. He went to Cipher's apartment. Cipher didn't advertise his location, but that was no problem for someone as resourceful as Amir.

He knocked on the door. No answer. He knocked again. This time: "*Da?*"

"Cipher, it's Amir. Can we talk? *Pozhaluysta*. Please."

The door opened, but Cipher didn't invite Amir to enter. He was not particularly friendly. Perhaps Amir was interrupting something.

"What do you want?" Cipher asked.

Amir explained that for the past few days he was being tailed by two men. He didn't think they were being all that discreet, so he spotted them easily. He wanted to know if Cipher knew anything about who they were, what they wanted.

Cipher stared at Amir as if he were wondering what to say. Finally: "*Psikh*! You are crazy. Why are you bothering me. Go away!" Cipher slammed the door in Amir's face.

* * *

CIPHER WONDERED IF THIS obnoxious little twit could have something to do with the insect hacking into his laptop.

* * *

JAKE HAD CALLED ANYA again with the same result—the default greeting. He was now at the address where she said she was staying. He realized he wasn't sure she had told him the truth, although he couldn't imagine why she would have misled him about that. He rang the doorbell, and a middle aged man opened the door. "Yes? Can I help you?" he said.

"Hello, my name's Jake Klein. I'm a friend of Anya. Is she here? May I talk to her, please?"

"Sorry. She's not here. I don't know when she'll be back. May I give her a message?"

"Yes, please," Jake said. "Please tell her I stopped by to say hello. Her phone doesn't seem to be set up. Please ask her to call me. Again, my name is Jake Klein. She has my number."

"Why don't you give it to me again, you know, just in case."

Jake felt a little reluctant, but gave the man his cell phone number.

* * *

AMIR RETURNED TO HIS car. As he did, two men approached him and asked him to come with them.

"I don't wish to," Amir said.

One of the men pulled a gun from inside his coat. "That was not an invitation," he said to Amir. "Your wishes are of no concern to us."

Amir hadn't misunderstood, but he thought it was worth a try. Resigned, he was accompanied by them to the black SUV he had previously noticed following him around town. One of the men, the one with the brandished gun, joined him in the rear seat. The other man hurriedly got behind the wheel and drove them away. Amir had known it was not an invitation. What he didn't know was where they were headed.

* * *

DISAPPOINTED, AND A BIT UNSETTLED, Jake returned to the family home. Everyone was back in the roost.

"We were about to have a late lunch. Care to join?" Leah asked.

"Sure." Jake was worried that Leah was about to have at her favorite subject again, but she didn't say a word about it—Jake and school. Instead, they talked politics.

"What do you think about the upcoming impeachment vote?" Leah asked him.

"I don't know really," Jake said, "but it sure seems like a wasted exercise to me."

"My sentiments exactly," Frank said.

Charlie didn't say anything, his head buried in his smartphone.

Madison said she thought Baker was a jerk and had it coming.

"I'm kind of with Madison," Leah commented.

"Why bother?" Jake asked. "We all know what the outcome's going to be."

Leah said she thought it was important for Congress to uphold its constitutional oversight responsibility, even if the outcome was a given.

"Probably because you're a lawyer," Jake said. "Personally, I think our taxpayer dollars could be put to better use than playing politics in the name of our Constitution."

Frank smiled. "How 'bout them Washington Nationals?" Frank said, diplomatically changing the subject. "Think they can repeat?"

* * *

BIANCHI AND HER HUSBAND were sharing a sandwich at their D.C. townhouse. "Are you resigned to it?" her husband asked. "And when's the vote?"

"Not much of a vote," she said. "It'll pretty much be Democrats in favor and Republicans against. Maybe a few exceptions, but straightforward and anti-climactic. And yes, I'm resigned to it. I just hope it doesn't blow up in our faces."

* * *

ANYA'S RED-EYE FLIGHT TOUCHED down at Domodedovo International Airport in Moscow early the next morning. She was met by a driver and whisked away. *I don't see why we couldn't have done this by telephone. It's always all about him.*

CHAPTER 29
December 9, 2019, One Day Later

AMIR CAUGHT NOT ONE, but two lucky breaks. One, the two men who kidnapped him were cocky and lazy. Two, they were in Kazakhstan and not Moscow.

They took him to an old office building downtown, and didn't bother to blindfold him. Amir knew Kazakhstan backward and forward, so he knew exactly where he was, and how to find his way to safety—if he ever got the chance.

They tore a bedsheet into strips and tied him to a chair they positioned in the center of the otherwise empty room—a far cry from chaining him to one of the walls or standing him on the chair and hanging him from the ceiling. He assumed they were GRU henchman, away from their home turf and assigned to get what they were after without the delay required to transport him to better equipped GRU facilities in Moscow.

To his dismay, they were prepared to make do with what they had.

* * *

ANYA SAT IN THE well-appointed office for approximately thirty minutes. She could have fallen asleep after the long sleepless flight, but she didn't dare. She was not the least bit surprised when he entered the room. He took the seat to her right, facing both her and the empty chair opposite her.

"I trust you had a nice flight, Lieutenant," her handler said. "Not everyone is treated to first class flight accommodations. I hope this reminds you of the importance of your mission."

Anya was feeling a bit chippy. "I knew that when you felt the need for me to travel halfway around the world when we could just as easily have accomplished whatever we are about to accomplish by a scrambled telephone call."

"That decision wasn't mine to make. Nor yours. Besides, not even our embassy telephones are reliably secure. Our American colleagues will not be able to intercept these in-person discussions."

She was entirely surprised by the next person to enter the room. The two of them immediately stood and faced the newcomer.

"Keep your seats," Turgenev said. "We will be brief. You have a return flight to catch in just two hours. I wanted to discuss a few things with you in person, but I don't want your absence to draw attention." He looked straight at Anya, and spoke as if she was the only one in the room with him.

"When you were abruptly assigned to engage with the American, I believe his name is Jake Klein, you were told merely to cultivate a relationship with him and report back to us on his activities and proclivities. You weren't told anything more. In particular, you weren't told why. You have done well so far. What I will now share with you is extremely sensitive and confidential. It is of the utmost importance to Russia." He paused.

"I understand, Mr. President," Anya said without further prompting.

"*Ochen khahrahsho.* Very good. What I am about to tell you now must never leave this room." Turgenev then explained to Anya Russia's interest in the 2020 U.S. election, what steps he was personally taking to assure the outcome of the election, and his concern that Klein represented a possible threat to that outcome. "He must be stopped at all costs. I am counting on you to develop the kind of *personal* relationship with Klein that will allow you to keep us informed of what he is going to do *before* he does it. Do you understand what I'm saying?"

Anya paused. "I am not naïve, Mr. President. You are perfectly clear. You can count on me to do what you expect of me. For Russia."

"*Bolshoi spasebo.* Thank you. Your country is in your debt. You will be rewarded. Have a good flight." Turgenev stood and left the room.

"Come, Anya, your driver will take you back to Domodedovo," her handler said.

* * *

JAKE WAS UP EARLY, showered, dressed, on his second cup of coffee, and studying the "how to" Mossad manuals on his new computer. As the files were now locally resident on his computer, he did not have to connect to the internet to view them, and so it didn't matter that he was using his computer at Leah and Frank's home.

CHAPTER 30
December 10, 2019, One Day Later

AMIR WAS BANGED UP, bruised, and hurting. It had been a long day. The two thugs had assured that. They wanted to know what Amir knew about the American, Jake Klein. He kept telling them he didn't know anything, that the American was just a customer referred to him by a travel agent to usher him around Kazakhstan during hisfour-day stay. He told them where he drove him, and what arrangements he made for him at KHC. He said that was all he knew. They "encouraged" him not to leave anything out. Over and over.

After too many hours, and too much encouragement, Amir told his captors that he needed to use the bathroom. "Please, hurry, my stomach is very bad. I can't hold it much longer."

They untied him from the chair and freed his hands so he could use the latrine at the end of the hall. One of the men, gun in hand, accompanied him. Amir entered the washroom and the stall. He spotted the window he was hoping for—the third world's air conditioning system. He wanted to close the door to the stall, but the man wouldn't let him. He relieved himself in plain sight.

Amir was a good actor. He had exaggerated his condition. He knew his life depended on it. As he slowly started to exit the washroom, hunched over, swiftly reached forward, and grabbed the exposed gun from his assailant, instantly slamming it across the man's skull. One more time for good measure, and the man dropped to the floor, unconscious. Amir turned back into the stall, jumped up on the toilet, forced open the window, and climbed out.

* * *

THE GRU AGENT STRUGGLED back to his feet. But Amir was now the one with the gun. He spun around and raced back to retrieve his partner and reestablish the odds. They rushed out the door and looked up and down the street. It was too late. Amir had disappeared.

* * *

THE HOODLUMS RAN TO their SUV. Amir was on foot. Given his appearance, it was unlikely that he could flag down a ride. They'd beat him back to his apartment, if Amir even went back to his apartment.

* * *

AMIR DID NOT RETURN to his apartment. He had a different plan. When you grew up on the streets of Kazakhstan—and when you were in Amir's line of work—you had to be prepared at all times. He had associates who had disappeared at the hands of the government—permanently. So Amir was prepared.

For starters, Amir went straight to the safe house he maintained. It wasn't much, but it had what he needed—a few changes of clothing, a roller bag, some toiletries and cosmetics, a bundle of money, and several travel documents. He used one of his precious bottles of water to clean himself up as best he could and then changed his clothes. He had a schedule to maintain. It was time to leave, and he wasn't coming back.

CHAPTER 31
December 11, 2019, One Day Later

JAKE SPENT THE DAY further studying the files pertaining to the remote retrieval component of the Mossad software. It was as powerful as the manuals were thorough. He digested the user guide for the software, and a number of "how to" videos, and white papers that illustrated various tasks the software could be used to accomplish that he didn't yet appreciate.

Every now and then, Jake wondered about Anya. As much as it pained him, the next move had to be hers. Her host had said she was doing some traveling. He promised to let her know Jake had stopped by when she returned. Either she'd call him on her return, or she wouldn't. He had too much on his plate. He couldn't allow Anya to slow him down.

CHAPTER 32
December 12, 2019, One Day Later

AMIR HAD SPENT THE day before in a youth hostel near the airport. He cut and dyed his hair to match the identical picture in the three meticulously forged passports he had kept in his safe house. He was now Daniyar Aronov in his Kazakhstan passport, and Dhruv Bhakta in his Barbuda and Bermuda passports.

He had carefully selected Barbuda and Bermuda. It wasn't because of the tourist board island images in his mind. It was all international treaty arrangements. Barbuda was one of the few countries that a citizen of Kazakhstan could travel to as a tourist without the necessity of a visa. Bermuda allowed citizens of Barbuda to travel to Bermuda as a tourist without any requirement of a visa. Citizens of Bermuda were permitted to enter the United States as a tourist without having to obtain a visa. This was the only way Amir could get from Kazakhstan to the United States with nothing more than the three false passports already in his possession.

In his preparations, Amir had learned that the Caribbean island of Barbuda had been substantially destroyed by Hurricane Irma in 2017, including its international airport. However, he also knew the airport had been restored by dubious investors earlier in 2019, and was once again operational. The flight to Barbuda would be the long leg of Amir's journey. From there, it was only 1,000 miles to Bermuda. The flight from Bermuda to the U.S. was just a few hundred miles.

Amir used some makeup to cover up his bruises and replicate the complexion in his passport photos as much as possible. It wasn't perfect; he hoped it would do. It would have to.

He watched the Kazakhstan airport for the better part of the day, but saw no signs of his opponents. Buying the ticket to Barbuda and boarding the flight this afternoon would be his Achilles heel, but if he got out of Kazakhstan, the rest of his long planned journey should be smooth sailing.

* * *

ANYA SLEPT ON THE flight back to Dulles. She was reasonably well rested when she arrived. Walking through the terminal, she opened her contacts and tapped on Jake's number.

"Anya, did you have a nice trip?" Jake asked.

A nice trip? What does he mean? He couldn't possibly know where I was. And then it dawned on her, what her local associate would have said to him. "It was nice. I just decided to spend a couple of days sightseeing along the coast. But I'm back now. I remembered you said there are some nearby scenic jogging trails. I have some chores to take care of today. How about tomorrow? And lunch should be my treat this time."

"Sounds great," Jake replied. They decided on a place to meet at eleven o'clock.

Progress. The President should be pleased.

* * *

JAKE WAS STRUGGLING SOMEWHAT with the remote retrieval details of the Mossad software. He was generally in full command of all things technology, but this software was a bit foreign to him—literally. The manuals were not written to be read in English as well as Hebrew. It was tough sledding. He put a call into Abelson that afternoon. He was able to make a video conference call date to connect with Abelson the next morning at eight o'clock. That would give him ample time to square everything away in time to meet Anya for their outing.

CHAPTER 33
December 13, 2019, One Day Later

JAKE AND ABELSON WERE right on time for their video conference.

Jake put Abelson through his paces with tons of questions about the Mossad software. He made a point, however, of not opening the software across the internet because he was speaking from Leah and Frank's.

"Hey, sport, I wasn't expecting all this," Abelson said. "Do you want me to come on board your computer to illustrate some of the answers to your questions?"

"Nah, I don't think we need to do that," Jake answered.

"You mean, you're avoiding triggering your IP address, right? You really are being pretty careful. We ought to put you to work for Mossad."

Jake paused.

"Just kidding. Besides, you've come up the learning curve pretty quickly. I think you understand the software now better than I do."

"Not really, but I'm getting there. It's incredible. Wish I didn't have to give it up so soon."

"Yeah, well, that's the way things work. Cinderella had to be home from the ball by midnight. I don't want you to get too comfortable with all this stuff, Mr. Hacker."

Jake made a point of looking at his watch.

"Something on your mind?" Abelson asked.

"Actually, I have a date soon with a lady I met on a recent flight. I don't want to keep her waiting. How about if I play around with the software a bit and get back to you if I'm still having any difficulties?"

"Sure thing. Don't want to keep that hot lady waiting. Call me anytime."

Jake powered down his laptop and returned it to his backpack.

* * *

JAKE WAS BREATHING HEAVIER than he wanted Anya to realize. "I thought you told me you were worried you wouldn't be able to keep up with me," Jake said. "Seems like you were playing me."

"Playing you?" Anya asked. "Should we do one more lap around the lake?" she said.

"Fool me once," Jake replied.

"Fool you once," Anya repeated. "What does that mean?" She asked.

"There's an English saying: 'Fool me once, shame on you. Fool me twice, shame on me.'"

Anya thought about that a moment. "Very clever. We have a similar saying in Russian: '*Umnyz celovek dvazdy na odni i te ze grabli ne nastupit.*' 'A clever man won't step on the same rake twice.'"

"Ah, yes, exactly the same meaning. There is sort of another English saying, 'Quit while you're not ahead.' He added, "not."

Anya smiled. "Then I think it's time for us to have our lunch," she said. "What do you think?"

"I think that's a great idea," Jake answered.

* * *

ANYA AND JAKE WERE seated at the smallest table. Anya could sense Jake's eyes on her. What woman didn't enjoy being admired? *Even if I'm working it, playing the innocent coquette.* From his backpack, Jake produced a small gift wrapped package when they were first seated.

"For me?" Anya asked, displaying excitement.

Jake nodded affirmatively.

"That was so kind of you. Thank you. May I open it now?"

"Yes, of course."

She made a spectacle of removing the ribbon and the paper wrapping. She opened the box and eyed the four round chocolate bonbons. "I love chocolate. I have to taste one," she said. "But just one, I don't want to spoil my appetite." She delicately lifted one of the chocolates and allowed it to pass slowly through her lips. "Hmm, cherry centers, my absolute favorite. But you shouldn't have gone to the trouble," she lied. "Would you like to have one too?"

Jake declined. "They're for you. And it was no trouble at all," Jake said. "I was picking up a computer cable at a store on the way here. The candy store was next door, and the sales lady was kind enough to offer to gift wrap the box for me."

"Well, it was very nice of you just the same. I will enjoy the other three this evening all the more because of the source and the thought behind them."

"How did you know to pick this place?" Jake asked Anya.

"Mr. Google helped me. It was actually quite easy. In Russia, we have the same kind of search engines. The one most popular is called Yandex."

After they had ordered and were waiting for the food to arrive, and perhaps to break the silence, Jake said he liked to read suspense thrillers and asked Anya what kind of books she most enjoyed.

"Well, I like mysteries, too, but romance novels are my number one favorite," Anya replied. "I am particularly fond of *The Lady With The Little Dog* by Anton Chekhov. I have read it several times." On the heels of her tacit reference to romance, Anya conspicuously allowed her hand to settle on the table where Jake could not help but see it. Would he notice? Would he take the bait?

If the placement of her hand had registered, Jake didn't show it.

After their meal, Anya ordered tea and Jake followed suit.

There was another lull in the conversation. Jake filled the silence. "This has been really nice, Anya, thank you for suggesting it, but I'm afraid I have a boatload of work waiting for me this afternoon."

"Boatload?" Anya said.

"It's an English expression that means a lot. In this case, a lot of work."

"Oh, I get it. But you haven't told me what kind of work you do."

"That's a bit complicated," Jake said. "Perhaps we can save that for our next visit. But I do have another English saying for you. Would you like to hear it?"

"By all means," Anya smiled. "I think I just shared one with you first—'by all means.'"

"Yes, you did, very good. Here's mine: 'Parting is such sweet sorrow.'"

Oh, that's an easy one—William Shakespeare, *Romeo and Juliet*. Do you know what it means?"

"Sure, Romeo and Juliet were about to part, and they were sorry about that."

"Yes, but why did Juliet say the sorrow was sweet?" Anya asked.

"Well, because . . ." Jake paused. "I guess I don't really know."

"Because," Anya explained, "Juliet observed that their parting reminded her that they would be meeting again. And to her, the thought of meeting again was sweet. So, she meant to say that their sorrow was . . . sweet."

Jake nodded in agreement.

The waiter brought the check and set it down on the table next to Jake. He reached for it. Anya playfully slapped his hand and took the check away from him. "This was my invitation, and my treat."

"But a lady always lets the gentleman pay," Jake said.

"What makes you think I'm always a lady," Anya replied, hoping Jake got the message.

Jake smiled and let Anya take the check.

* * *

AUSTIN AND BAKER, JR. sat nursing their drinks in the nondescript Georgetown bar. "With the impeachment vote due out of the House next week, I thought it wouldn't hurt to go over our stories one more time," Austin said to Baker, Jr. *Hard to arrange an off record with the old man. Unfortunately, the apple doesn't fall very far from the tree. Have to make sure that father and son understand how POTUS needs to play his response.*

"I get it, and so does my dad," Baker, Jr. said. "Fake news, outrage, political chicanery on the part of the Democrats, an insult, a waste of taxpayer money. Yada, yada, yada. Am I missing anything?"

"You are," Austin said, trying his best not to show that he was losing his patience. "It's not *what* POTUS says, but *how* he says it, how he *sells* it. Not angry, not returning fire with fire, but playing the martyr card. POTUS has to rise above the fray, come across as the victim here."

"I understand," Baker, Jr. said, "but you know as well as I do that there's no controlling my dad. He has a mind of his own. He doesn't listen very well. When he's sitting there with his smartphone keypad in his hand early in the morning and gets himself all worked up, there's just no controlling what comes out of his fingers."

"I can't emphasize this enough, Dustin," Austin said. "If we're going to pull this off, POTUS has to tow the mark. He has to exude reasoned leadership, that he is the chosen leader. This is not about convincing those in your dad's core constituency—that's the easy part. It's a matter of convincing those who are on the fence that they should accept our plans. You've got to impress this upon your old man."

"I'll do my best, but don't ever let my dad hear you refer to him that way."

* * *

JAKE DROVE STRAIGHT BACK from his lunch date with Anya to the sanctity of his Maryland Starbucks. Slowed down by the Friday early weekend traffic, he didn't arrive until shortly after dark. He would need at least two hours of practice time to be sure he had the Mossad technology down pat.

Leah had weekend plans for the family, himself included, a command performance. He would return on Monday for his next visit to Cipher's computer. He booted up his pristine new anonymous laptop and opened the Mossad software. It was good that he had allowed for this dry run.

Mossad's engineers seem to have thought of everything. It works beautifully, but it takes some serious practice and getting used to. Good that I thoroughly get my arms around it before primetime with Cipher.

* * *

LEAH WAS DOZING DOWNSTAIRS with a book in her lap when Jake entered the townhouse. She looked at her watch. It was after ten o'clock. "Nice evening?"

"Wow, Sis, can't remember the last time you waited up for me to get home. Good thing I made curfew. Just catching up with some friends. And it was okay, nothing special."

"Anyone I know?" Leah asked.

"Nope, don't think so." Jake hated the nosey third degree. "See ya in the morning." He went off to his room before Leah could continue.

* * *

AMIR HAD MADE IT safely out of Kazakhstan as he had wisely researched and planned some years in advance, and was now resting in Barbuda. He would give himself two days to adjust to the time change before taking the short flight into Bermuda, where he would allow himself a few days' vacation. *When have I last had a vacation?* He was beginning to relax for the first time in days. After that, he would fly to Dulles and find Jake. *JK will be very surprised to see me, yes?*

CHAPTER 34
December 15, 2019, Two Days Later

CASSIE READ THE TEXT over one more time.

> HEY, JK. COACH HAD TO CANCEL SCHEDULED PRACTICE
> ROUND TOMORROW. WANT TO MEET FOR 18 AT MY PARENTS'
> CLUB AT 8 A.M.? CASSIE.

She added the club's name and address and hit send.

* * *

JAKE'S TEXT ALERT SOUNDED. He opened his cell phone and read Cassie's text. He knew he had a date at the Maryland Starbucks, but hell, it could wait a day. *Not really, but how often do I get a chance to play a round of golf with a pro?*
He fired back a reply:

> SURE THING, CASSIE. THANKS. SEE YA THEN. BETTER BRING
> YOUR A GAME. JK.

Better bring your A game? Ridiculous. Might work with one of my buds, but a pro?
Jake found Frank sitting in the family room. "Can I borrow your clubs tomorrow?"

"Sure. Just a work day for me. They'd just be sitting in the closet, gathering dust."

"Thanks. I'll take good care of them. *Good thing I didn't have to ask Leah. I would have had to fill out a questionnaire, in triplicate.*

CHAPTER 35
December 16, 2019, One Day Later

JAKE ARRIVED AT CASSIE'S parents' club at seven o'clock, and carried Frank's bag out to the driving range. Cassie was already there hitting balls. *Oh shit! What'd I get myself into?* "Morning, Cassie. I see you're taking this seriously."

"Hey, JK. Out on the course is the easy fun stuff. This is where the real work gets done."

"I see. So, how many strokes are you going to spot me?" Jake asked.

"How about a stroke a hole, match play, and I'll play from the tips with you. A $1 Nassau to make it interesting? Two down, automatic press?"

My God, being hustled by a high school kid? Guess ya grow up fast out on the tour. "Uh, sure," Jake said. *Too late to back down now.*

Cassie smiled. They shared a cart and played the 18 holes in three hours. Cassie drove, probably because she knew the course. What a treat to play a great course, and in only three hours. All Jake ever got to play was poorly maintained public links that usually required between five and six hours a round.

Turned out, that one stroke a hole wasn't nearly enough of an edge for Jake because Cassie almost never made a mistake, and Jake almost always did. Still, conveniently for Jake, he finished down only one hole a side. That meant he owed Cassie $3. He paid up. *Geez, first Anya busts my balls jogging, and now this. Not sure how much more my male ego can take. To make matters worse, I think Cassie was carrying me. She's sure good. And she's as polite and fun as she is talented.*

He wasn't sure what Cassie had in mind for the afternoon, but he didn't want to leave it to chance. He decided to strike preemptively. "I have some chores to run this afternoon, but I have time for lunch if you do. My treat."

"Lunch is great, but you can't spend your money at the club. It'll have to be my parents' treat this time. Is that okay?"

Man, I've been had all the way. A free round of golf, let down easier on the course than I deserved, and now a free lunch. "I guess, just as long as I get to reciprocate while we're both still in town."

"Anytime," Cassie answered.

* * *

JAKE CARRIED FRANK'S CLUBS into Leah and Frank's townhouse mid-afternoon. Just as Madison came out of the kitchen with a soft drink in hand.

"Hey, JK, you've sure been practicing a lot of golf. I saw you heading out early this morning with Dad's clubs."

Something told Jake he really didn't want to get into his golf outing with Cassie. Something else told him he might get into more trouble if he didn't. "I had a last minute chance to play 18 this morning with Cassie. You were right, she shellacked me. It wasn't even close. Plus, she emptied my wallet."

"Sick, but don't say I didn't warn you," Madison quietly said. She put on a light face, but Jake was puzzled, especially when she disappeared without wanting to know anything more.

Damned if I do, damned if I don't? And Jake hadn't mentioned anything to Madison about his lunch with Cassie after their match—or what Cassie had told him.

* * *

MADISON WAS ON THE phone as fast as her legs carried her to her room. "Rat Stinker!" she said.

"What?" Cassie answered.

"Don't you 'what' me," Madison said. "I told you to stay away from Jake. He's my uncle, for God's sake! Actually, he's more like my brother. And you don't even tell me that you guys are now dating."

"Don't be silly. We already hashed that out. Besides, all we did was play golf." Cassie paused. "And have lunch."

"That's all! You better tell me all about it, right now, and don't leave out a single detail!"

"Well, he parred the first hole. I birdied it. Then—"

"You know that's not what I mean, Ms. Webber," Madison said.

"Well, I'm sorry to disappoint, *Ms. Lotello*, but that's all there was. Times seventeen more holes and a couple of cheeseburgers. Oh, and we did share an order of fries. As sexy as you could imagine! But I'm sorry to say he was a perfect gentleman. What did you expect?"

"You have that backward, Ms. Webber. What did *you* expect?"

Actually, the thought of Cassie and Jake together is kinda dope, just as long as she doesn't know I think that.

* * *

THE ENTIRE CLAN HAD dinner together that night, the Lotellos and the Kleins. The big topic of conversation was Jake's round of golf with Cassie. More accurately, it was the big topic of conversation among the men. Frank and Charlie wanted to know all about it—the golf. Madison didn't say much, but Jake thought she was dialed in, in her own way. Leah was also kind of quiet—for Leah.

"I didn't think I was that bad of a golfer," Jake said. "Cassie showed me how wrong I was. But it was just great to get to play with someone that good."

After dinner, Jake helped with the dishes and then sidled off to his room—where he thought long and hard about what Cassie had told him about Anya toward the end of their otherwise pleasant lunch. *Why had Anya lied at Thanksgiving when she said to everyone that she loved playing golf? Worse still, why did she lie to Cassie later that evening about her family? Could Cassie have misunderstood Anya? She must have.*

CHAPTER 36
December 17, 2019, One Day Later

JAKE WAS FEELING BEHIND schedule. *Enough slacking off.* While Leah was still asleep and unaware of his absence, by nine o'clock, Jake was already ensconced in "his" Maryland Starbucks, sipping on an Oatmeal Cookie Protein Shake and focused on his dedicated anonymous laptop.

Jake booted up his new laptop, the one with the Mossad software installed on it. Employing the protocols he had previously used, he was shortly hacked into Cipher's computer and past his password once again. He quickly found the outwardly empty folder labeled "GL." He opened it. It still looked empty.

He "pointed" the retrieval component of the software at the target GL folder. He confirmed to the software that this was the folder he wanted to restore. He was asked to specify a beginning date, and chose "Inception." The software activity light changed from red to green, and showed approximately ninety-three minutes remaining until completion.

This was what worried Jake. That the software was not stealth, no surprise, given the long distance remote nature of the process. There was no way to speed up the operation, and nowhere for Jake to hide while the recovery was doing its thing. The good news was that there was data to be restored, or the software would have estimated much less time remaining, down to zero if it detected no retrievable data.

This was precisely why it was imperative that Jake made the drive to Maryland in order to hide his true IP address. Jake's anxiety was still on high.

He ordered a Carmel Latte decaf in the hopes of quieting his nerves.

* * *

CIPHER WAS ALERTED THE moment the hacker was back on his machine. *This time, the bastard was not in and out as quickly as before.* Cipher went to work. If the perpetrator remained on board long enough, Cipher would have a chance to trace the hacker's whereabouts, perhaps even the culprit's actual identity. *Two can play at this game.*

Forty minutes elapsed—the hacker was still on board. Cipher's software told him the intruder was somewhere in the United States. *Why am I not surprised?* The culprit was still engaged. So was Cipher's tracing software.

Another thirty-five minutes went by—the trespasser remained on board. Cipher felt vulnerable. He wasn't used to the feeling of not being in control. He didn't like it. *What the hell can he possibly be doing? As soon as I identify him, his ass will be mine, wherever the fuck he is.* Cipher's software continued searching. His location was narrowed to the eastern seaboard of the United States.

Another eighteen minutes—the prowler was gone. Cipher's software had narrowed the his location to Maryland. *Shit! Not good enough. I needed another ten or fifteen minutes.*

Cipher immediately sent a text:

> HACKER BACK! ON MY COMPUTER NINETY-THREE MINUTES. TRACKED HIS LOCATION TO SOMEWHERE IN MARYLAND. I NEEDED HIM ANOTHER TWENTY MINUTES TO LOCATE HIM PRECISELY. NO IDEA WHETHER HE WILL RETURN.

He heard back in less than five minutes:

> YOU DON'T KNOW WHO HACKER IS, BUT HE KNOWS WHO YOU ARE. HE'S OBVIOUSLY INTERESTED IN YOU. THINK OF WAY TO ENTICE HIM TO RETURN.

Cipher sent one more text:

> WILL TRY.

* * *

Jake replicated the folder identified as "GL" on his anonymous laptop. It had a fair amount of data, but it was in a foreign language. *Of course. What did he expect?*

Using Google, it took only minutes to identify the language as Kazakh, and to translate it into English. The translation was not perfect, but that was not the problem. What *was* the problem was that the language was in some kind of code. With other decoding software Jake had, he could break Cipher's code, but it would take time. He would need one or more further "visits" to Cipher's computer, but not until he first broke the code being used in the folder.

Jake didn't know how long that might take. Complicating matters even further, one of the baristas in Starbucks had pointed out his extended stay to someone who looked like he might be the store manager. The manager came over to Jake. "Hi, name's Neil. Something I can do to help you?"

"Nope, I'm good, thanks," Jake said. "The Oatmeal Cookie Protein Shake and the Carmel Latte were both great."

"Good to hear. It's just that, you've been here doing whatever on your laptop for over two hours. You're starting to draw attention to yourself and to make people nervous."

"Oh, I'm sorry," Jake said. "I had some work to get done, and the Wi-Fi in my apartment building was down for maintenance. I didn't mean to cause any problems. I'll pack up and be on my way."

"No worries, man," Neil said. "The Wi-Fi goes down in my apartment all the time. Didn't really mean to run you off. Was just curious, I guess. Take as long as you need. By the way, I didn't get your name."

"Gerry," Jake answered. "Gerry Ross." *Guess I've worn out my welcome here.* Jake tossed his laptop in his backpack, placed two large cups of ice water in a cardboard container to see him through the drive back to D.C., and headed out the door to his car.

* * *

Jake joined Frank and Charlie for dinner at the local pizzeria. Leah was stuck on some project at her office, which spared Jake from having to explain his whereabouts all day. The conversation was pretty much constrained to sports and politics—more sports than politics. Madison was having dinner with Cassie and her family. Someone's birthday, it seemed. Cassie's grandparents were there too. *The grandfather, Supreme Court justice who was the target when Cassie was kidnapped.*

When the boys got home, Jake excused himself, saying he had some work to do. He spent the night exploring software used to break codes. From what he found and read, such software was first developed during World War II. Today, it was being used by countries as part of their anti-terrorist operations. *Lot more sophisticated today.* He stayed with it until his eyes and his mind gave out. *Tomorrow's another day.* He showered and was asleep before his head hit the pillow.

CHAPTER 37
December 18, 2019, One Day Later

JAKE HAD A BIG day ahead of him—so did the country. Jake had spent a few hours breaking the coded files he had retrieved from Cipher's computer. Three hours into his work, the headlines flashed across his laptop. The House had voted to impeach President Baker. Jake made himself a sandwich and read the details.

Remarkably, there weren't that many details, and there weren't that many surprises. The vote was mostly along party lines. Only one Republican voted to impeach. *Now, that was a surprise.* Just a couple of Democrats voted against impeachment. *They must be in districts that vote red.* The overwhelming consensus of the media was that the Senate would quickly vote to acquit, and all that would remain would be the political fallout—on both sides of the aisle.

Jake wondered what impact all of this would have on the election, now less than a year away. He returned to his decoding. *Hmm, trying to decipher Cipher. Hah!*

Actually, Jake had made a fair amount of progress. Most importantly, he had discovered an extraordinary number of files in the GL folder on Cipher's computer, pertaining to an individual identified solely as MC. He guessed those two letters probably referred to a person whose first name began with C, and whose last name began with M. He wasn't far enough along with his work yet to know just exactly what there was to make of the mysterious MC. In particular, until the occasion of his next visit to Cipher's computer, Jake would remain curious to know if MC would prove to be the subject of still another seemingly deleted folder.

* * *

EVEN TOWARD THE END of this busy and eventful day, Jake's mind wandered back to Anya. He opened up his phone and sent her a text:

> THINKING OF OUR NICE LUNCH THE OTHER DAY. I HAVE LOTS GOING ON, BUT I HAVE ONE OF MY FAVORITE LOCAL SPOTS I'D LOVE TO SHOW YOU ON SATURDAY IF YOU'RE FREE. PICK YOU UP AT 1 P.M.? NO JOGGING, BUT WEAR YOUR JOGGING SHOES, AND A WARM JACKET. EARLY DINNER AFTER. JK.

A few minutes later:

> HI JK, I WAS THINKING MAYBE YOU FORGOT ABOUT ME. :-(SATURDAY SOUNDS LOVELY. 1 P.M. IS PERFECT. ANYA.

Jake fired off one more text:

> SEE YOU THEN. JK.

And one more even shorter from Anya:

> :-)

* * *

ANYA THEN SENT AN encrypted text of her own. But it wasn't an afterthought, and it wasn't to Jake. It was just one word:

> PROGRESS.

CHAPTER 38
December 19, 2019, One Day Later

Baker's EYES SHIFTED BACK and forth between Austin and Baker, Jr. "Okay, so I've been impeached. Who gives a shit. Not the first president to be impeached, won't be the last. The stupid DNC is just playing right into our hands. *My* hands. The GOP will acquit me in no time flat, and I'll be able to tweet that I was innocent, like we said all along—that the impeachment was nothing more than 'fake news' politics. When will the trial be concluded? How are you guys doing with EBCOM?"

"Apart from making sure that your summary impeachment defense is in place, EBCOM's plans are right on schedule," Austin said. "The trial should begin mid-January, and be over in two or three days tops. Nothing else for us to do until then, and until everyone is back in D.C. following the holidays."

"Will EBCOM be meeting by phone between now and then?" POTUS asked. He was surprised by the confused look on Austin's face. "What?" Austin glanced at Baker, Jr., but said nothing in response to Baker's inquiry. Baker, Jr. fielded his father's question. "Hey, Dad, EBCOM doesn't act by telephone. Too much risk. We've been over that."

"I know that. I was just testing the two of you. Besides, your mom and I are going to our Florida home through New Year's. I have some guests joining us for some rounds of golf and a couple of parties. If anything comes up that needs me before I'm back, just plan to come on down." It never occurred to

Baker that either of them might have any plans of their own that might have to be canceled on a moment's notice.

Austin and Baker, Jr. nodded their understanding to the uncaring POTUS.

* * *

BIANCHI SAT AROUND THE table with the impeachment trial managers she had selected. "Of course, we know the outcome—that Baker will be acquitted by his cronies. There's nothing we can do about that. Our goal is simply to take as much time as we can putting on the strongest case we can. Baker will argue the acquittal means he was innocent, as he has said all along. Our job is to see if we can get a couple of Republicans to break ranks and vote guilty, and to be able to argue that we discharged our constitutional responsibilities as we were required to do, and that Baker was in fact guilty of impeachable offenses. We'll make as much of that as we can, and also attempt to make the GOP look bad for handing Baker a free pass." She gazed at Ralph Sylvester, Chair of the House Intelligence Committee, who would be acting as the lead trial manager in the Senate.

"We understand, Madam Speaker," Sylvester said. "Baker's lawyers think they will be able to force a quick vote in a day or two. We believe we will politically milk the trial for all we can, using every trick we can, in the Senate and in the press, to drag the trial out for at least three weeks. Every day, we plan to hammer Baker over and over. He'll get his acquittal, but we'll make sure that as much of the country as possible will see how guilty he is. He'll get to tweet up a storm about how innocent he is, but hopefully this trial will help us in November when the election takes place, and when matters really count."

"I hope you're right, Ralph," Bianchi said.

* * *

THE ALERT ON JAKE'S smartphone sounded. The words "Unidentified Caller" appeared on the screen. Ordinarily, he let calls he didn't recognize go to voicemail. More often than not, they were spam calls and didn't leave a message, even if they were a live caller. Legitimate callers left a voicemail message, and he could decide whether and when to return the call. Perhaps it was just the holiday season. He was feeling undisciplined and answered the call. "JK."

"Mr. JK," the voice said. "Big surprise. Amir is."

"Amir! Nice to hear your voice. It sounds like you're right here next to me. How is everything in Kazakhstan?"

"Not in Kazakhstan. Am here in D.C."

"Here? In Washington? Are you okay?"

"Things very bad in Kazakhstan. Had to leave fast. Here now. You help me, please, Mr. JK?"

"Where are you, Amir?"

"Staying in Dulles Youth Hostel near Dulles Airport." He gave Jake the address.

Jake looked at his watch. He punched the address into his phone. He looked at the route and time estimate. "I'll be there in an hour, maybe a little less. Where will I find you?"

"Coffee shop off lobby. Like restaurant in Kazakhstan Hilton. I wait for you there, Mr. JK."

"Okay, Amir, I'll see you as soon as I can get there."

* * *

JAKE WALKED INTO THE coffee shop. It was almost empty, but he didn't see Amir. Suddenly, he felt a menacing hand from behind tugging on his shoulder. Startled, he quickly turned and raised his hands to protect his face from the stranger confronting him.

"Not to worry, Mr. JK. Am Amir."

"Amir. Yes. Oh my God. You look so different than you did in Kazakhstan. I hardly recognize you. What happened? Are you okay? What are you doing here? How did you get here?"

"Am okay now. Very long story. Please to sit. I explain."

More than an hour later, Amir had described everything that had happened to him after Jake left Kazakhstan, and how he barely managed to escape and make his way to the United States. He showed Jake a Bermuda passport that identified him as Dhruv Bhakta. Given the change in the style and color of his hair, his looks more or less resembled the photo in the passport, rather than the Amir he remembered. He also showed Jake a series of selfie pictures on his phone that displayed a badly beaten Amir. The bruises were almost fully healed, but his gait was somewhat awkward, as if he still felt the discomfort of the fading marks.

More significantly, there were holes in Amir's story not explained by his English deficiencies. Amir said he hoped Jake would help him to obtain asylum in order to remain in the U.S., but he was vague when Jake asked who did this to him, and why. He was even murkier when Jake questioned how he was able to put together the resources to flee Kazakhstan so quickly, and journey to the United States on a passport supposedly issued to look-like Dhruv Bhakta in Bermuda, and why he was perceptive enough to take and save those selfies? For that matter, how did this seemingly naïve and inexperienced street urchin from Kazakhstan have a smartphone that was getting cell service here in D.C.?

Jake thought there was a lot more Amir was holding back than he was sharing. He felt sorry for him and wanted to do what he could to help, but he wasn't quite comfortable with the thought of bringing him to Leah and Frank. "Of course, I will try to help you, Amir," Jake loosely said. "But for now, you need to stay here at the youth hostel until I can get the right information for you. I will call or text you, but it will probably not be until tomorrow."

* * *

JAKE ARRIVED BACK AT Leah and Frank's to find an empty home. *Makes sense. It's a weekday and it isn't dinnertime yet.* He had thought about what he was going to tell them on the way back from the youth hostel. He reviewed his thoughts one more time.

Leah walked in a few minutes later. "Hope you're hungry," she said. "Frank's on the way home. He stopped to pick up some takeout. Knew I had too long a day to think about cooking. Charlie and Madison are at a friend's, so it's just the three of us."

"Sounds good to me," Jake said. He decided he would wait to tell them about Amir at the same time so he didn't have to go through the saga twice. "I'm gonna grab a quick shower."

By the time Jake came back downstairs, Frank was home, and Leah was putting the food out on the table. "C'mon guys, get it while it's hot, or cold, as the case may be."

The food was good. So was the small talk.

"I had an unusual experience this afternoon that I think you will find interesting," Jake said. He then told them about Amir, and what Amir had relayed to him.

"That's quite a story," Leah said. "First Anya and now this Amir. I'm surprised you didn't bring him home to meet us."

Frank smiled but didn't say anything.

"Actually, I met Amir before I met Anya," Jake answered. "I thought about bringing him back here with me, but something about Amir is nagging at me. His story is all a little too pat. And not. Both at the same time."

"You think?" Frank said. "Besides, whatever might be nagging you about Anya is probably a little different."

Leah chortled.

"Right," Jake said. "If we're done with the jokes, can we talk about what we can actually do to help Amir?"

"I'm no expert on the subject," Leah said, "but Amir is correct that what he needs to do is apply for asylum. I once helped someone pro bono with the asylum process. As I recall, you have up until one year from entering the U.S. to file the application with the U.S. Citizenship and Immigration Services. People usually apply at the port of entry because they have to pass through the authorities to enter the country. Because Amir entered on a Bermudan passport that required no visa, he just passed right through and isn't under any short-term pressure. His situation might be a little more complicated because he entered on a false passport."

"That being the case," Frank said, "if I were Amir, I'd lie low for the time being, until I figured out exactly what I wanted to do. In this case, I'd say don't do today what you can put off until tomorrow. It might also be a good idea for you to speak to Judge Brooks. He usually has a worthwhile idea or two about almost everything. He also knows a lot of people."

"I think talking to Cyrus is a great idea," Leah said. "I have something else I need to discuss with him tomorrow. I can ask him about this as well."

"Thanks, guys. I'll tell Amir. Let me know what Judge Brooks says."

"In the meanwhile," Frank said, "it's fine to be supportive, Jake, but you seem to have a lot on your plate. Might be a good idea not to make Amir too much of an additional project."

Jake didn't answer.

* * *

LEAH WAS NOT HAPPY. *Damn, if it's not one thing, it's another. The thought of Jake sticking around "boring" college is looking grimmer and grimmer.*

CHAPTER 39
December 20, 2019, One Day Later

LEAH FILLED JAKE IN on her conversation with Cyrus. "He said lying low for the time being was good advice, that speaking randomly with some low-level representative of the U.S.C.I.S. was more likely to complicate matters than help. He added that he has a friend there who might be able to help. He put in a call, but he's away for the holidays. He said he'd be happy to try him again after the first.

"Okay, thanks, Sis," Jake said. "I'll let Amir know what Judge Brooks said."

"Aside from the fact that no one useful in any federal agency is likely to be focused and on hand during the last week of the year," Leah added, "there is one thing I recall that is odd about the way our immigration laws work. Amir may wish to obtain permanent residence in the U.S., or even U.S. citizenship, but that is much more complicated than obtaining asylum, and asylum allows the asylee to stay in the U.S. indefinitely. If one applies for a green card, or permanent residence, it may be necessary, depending on the timing of the application for permanent residence, to leave the country while that application is pending, even though open-ended asylum has already been obtained."

"Sure sounds complicated," Jake said.

"Anything involving the U.S. government typically is," Leah replied. Little did she know how those words would come back to haunt them.

* * *

JAKE SENT AMIR A detailed text explaining everything he had learned. He said he would call Amir to set a date to get together. With Leah's permission, he also gave Leah's contact information to Amir.

Moments later, he received back the following reply:

THANK YOU. DHRUV BHAKTA.

* * *

LATER THAT DAY, JAKE called Amir on his cell phone. He received a message that the phone number was no longer in service. He called the youth hostel and asked to speak to Dhruv Bhakta. He was told that Mr. Bhakta had checked out. He did not leave a forwarding address.

* * *

THAT EVENING, JAKE TOLD Leah and Frank what had transpired with Amir.

"All for the better," Leah said.

Frank didn't say anything.

Jake wondered about what Leah said. *All for the better for whom, Amir or me? At least I didn't shine him off. Did what I could.*

CHAPTER 40
December 21, 2019, One Day Later

JAKE WAS FEELING SERIOUSLY restless. He had promised Leah that the next two weeks would be devoted to quality time for the family—no work and no computers, not even cell phones. Not for any of them. It was going to be movies, television, jigsaw puzzles, and board games, book stores and restaurants. She and Frank had both taken the coming two weeks off from work to be with Jake, saying they knew it might be the last such occasion. Even Charlie and Madison had promised to go along. The least he could do was cooperate.

Cipher and his computer would just have to wait, much as that thought disturbed him. *What might the rat do in the interim?*

But the "no-fly zone" applied only to work and computers. *Doesn't mean Anya is off limits.*

CHAPTER 41
December 22, 2019, One Day Later

Jake had to get special dispensation from the family. Frank, Charlie and Madison were easy. Leah was tougher. She first suggested that he simply include Anya in the family movie and dinner outing planned for that afternoon and evening. Jake prevailed when no one backed Leah's suggestion.

* * *

Jake pulled up in front of the home where Anya was staying at exactly one o'clock.

Anya must have heard Jake's car arrive. She opened the front door of the house and met him at his car. True to his instructions, she was clad in a warm coat and jogging shoes. He wondered what she was wearing under the coat, and whether and under what circumstances he might have the opportunity to find out before the day—or night—was over. "You look wonderful," he said to her.

"Thank you. You clean up pretty well yourself."

How could she possibly have command of such an idiomatic expression? "I try," he replied. "Every once in a while."

They drove to Georgetown and parked in a lot near the entrance to the Chesapeake & Ohio Canal, more commonly known as the C & O Canal or simply the Grand Old Ditch. The canal runs alongside the Potomac River. Jake retrieved a blanket and picnic basket from the back seat of the car and they walked to the canal entrance. "The canal runs from here to Cumberland,

Maryland," Jake said, "almost two hundred miles. In the mid-1800s, it functioned as a towpath canal trail, hauling coal mined from the Allegheny Mountains. Today, it's a tourist attraction, a reminder of days gone by. People can ride one of the refurbished original canal boats. They can also use the towpath trail for hiking, jogging, and bicycling."

"You are quite the tour guide, Mr. Klein," Anya said.

"The canal is definitely one of my favorite spots when I'm home in D.C. I thought we would begin by taking a ride on one of the canal boats. Would you like to do that?"

"I would, but are we going to ride all the way to Cumberland?" Anya asked. "I didn't bring a change of clothes." She laughed.

"Haha! No, not quite. There's a place we can get off after a couple of miles and then walk around a bit. I know a private area where we could spread out our blanket and enjoy a nice picnic. After, we can hail a carriage bicycle to bring us back along the towpath."

"That sounds like a wonderful plan. I'm guessing you may have done it before," she teased.

"Just once or twice, but never with someone quite so charming," he replied.

Anya grinned, but demurely bypassed the remark. "What is the meaning of the word towpath? I have not heard it before."

"As you will shortly see, the canal boats do not have their own power. Instead, mules are tethered to the boats by long ropes and they tow the boats from the paths. For this reason, the paths came to be known as towpaths."

"I see," Anya said. "A very good choice of words, even if not in any of my English books."

"That's why I'm here."

"I hope my language instructors at school will be as accomplished as you are." They boarded one of the canal boats and took two seats next to one another.

Forty minutes of picturesque views later, they disembarked. "Follow me, but watch your step. These trails can be a little bumpy. That's the reason I suggested jogging shoes."

Ten minutes later, they came upon a private cove where they could still look upon the water through thin reed-like trees. "We have arrived," Jake said. He spread the blanket on the ground, setting the picnic basket down on the blanket and removing its contents: two sandwiches, two bottles of water, a bottle of wine, fruit, cheese, cookies, napkins, cups, condiments, and silverware.

"Wow, you thought of everything," Anya said. "I'm really impressed."

"Precisely what I had in mind."

For a while, they took in the surroundings, the good views, the good food and drink, and the good company. They traded questions, anecdotes, and stories about their respective families and histories, just getting to know more about one another.

As the sun and the temperature began to drop, Anya rubbed her hands together to offset the mounting chill. Ever observant, Jake took advantage of the opportunity to slide closer to Anya and put his arm around her. She didn't resist. After a few moments, the conversation gave way to the sounds of their setting. Anya turned to face Jake and their eyes met. While Jake hesitated, wondering exactly what to do next, Anya didn't. She leaned in and brought her lips to Jake's.

* * *

ANYA PACKED UP WHAT was left of their meal in the basket and folded up their blanket. She allowed Jake to take the basket and guide her leisurely out to the towpath. They found an available carriage bicycle that returned them to Jake's car.

Anya sat close to Jake as they rode, mostly in silence, back to the home where she was staying. She thought about how things had gone. When they arrived, Anya turned and thanked Jake for a lovely day. She found herself wanting to kiss him again. She brought her lips gently to his and closed her eyes. She felt his hands in her hair, pulling her closer to him. She was pleasantly surprised at the intensity of his response. And hers. The gentle kiss became more aggressive. Just as quickly, however, she recovered her composure and pulled away. She did not invite him into the house.

"We'll talk," was all she said as she got out of the car. *Less is more.*

* * *

LATER THAT EVENING, ANYA sent an encrypted text to Moscow:

MORE PROGRESS, BUT NOTHING SPECIFIC TO REPORT.

In a matter of minutes, she received an encrypted reply that was less than pleasing:

LACK OF SPECIFICS DISAPPOINTING. PREPAID TICKET AT DULL-ES. RETURN HOME TOMORROW MIDDAY FOR ADDITIONAL PLANNING AND TRAINING.

Again? Are they seriously going to tell me how to do my job? She sent an encrypted reply:

REALLY NECESSARY? ADVISE SCHEDULE. I NEED TO EXPLAIN ABSENCE TO SUBJECT. ALSO, HARVARD CLASSES BEGIN MON-DAY, 6 JANUARY.

She did not have to wait long:

FOLLOW INSTRUCTIONS. DO NOT MISS FLIGHT. YOU WILL BE IN MOSCOW THROUGH YEAR END. YOU WILL RETURN TO U.S. IN TIME FOR CLASSES.

She had no choice:

UNDERSTOOD.

* * *

JAKE WAS GREETED BY the family tribe when he came through the door. They were watching something on TV. "So, how was your date?" Madison asked, losing all interest in whatever it was they were watching. "Tell us all about it." Leah pretended not to be interested, but casually looked up from the TV. Frank and Charlie continued watching the program.

"It was fun," Jake said. "We had a nice time."

"That's it?" Madison continued. "That's all you're going to tell us? Discerning minds want to know all of the salacious details."

Without moving his head away from the television, Charlie said, "A gentleman never tells."

Frank laughed.

"What are we watching?" was all Jake said. He sat down. A few minutes later, he stood up and said, "Lots of walking and hiking today. Think I'm gonna turn in. See you in the morning."

CHAPTER 42
December 23, 2019, One Day Later

JAKE HAD RETURNED FROM an early morning run. Everyone else was still sleeping. He had showered and was munching on a bagel and sipping a glass of orange juice.

It was bad enough that his election fraud pursuits were on a two-week hiatus. He was also pondering how to tell Anya that his priority for the next two weeks was going to have to be his family.

He would explain that he wasn't happy about not having more time to spend with her, but this was the last time he would likely have a block of time to spend with his family. He hoped she would understand—and be as interested as he was in reconnecting when he was back at SCSU and she was at Harvard, just a two-hour train commute.

He didn't know how to word all of this, because he really didn't know how she felt about him. He was making assumptions that might not be valid. He kept wrestling with exactly what to say, and how to say it, when his phone alerted him that he had a text. *I know I agreed no devices, but that's just when the others are around. I can certainly do as I please when they're sleeping in and I'm the only one up.* He opened his text app:

GOOD MORNING, JT. THANK YOU AGAIN SO MUCH FOR THE LOVELY DAY YESTERDAY. I WILL REMEMBER IT FOR A LONG TIME. I WAS LOOKING FORWARD TO OUR SPENDING MORE TIME TO-

GETHER OVER THE NEXT COUPLE OF WEEKS BEFORE YOU RE-
TURN TO SCSU AND I BEGIN MY LANGUAGE STUDIES AT HAR-
VARD. I DON'T KNOW IF YOU WILL HAVE TIME FOR ME THEN. IN
THE MEANWHILE, MY PARENTS SURPRISED ME LAST NIGHT WITH
A ROUND TRIP TICKET FOR ME TO RETURN HOME TO MOSCOW
TO SPEND CHRISTMAS AND NEW YEAR'S WITH THEM. THESE
ARE TRADITIONAL BIG HOLIDAYS IN RUSSIA. I CANNOT SAY NO
TO THEM. I HOPE YOU UNDERSTAND (AND CARE). MY FLIGHT
LEAVES IN JUST A FEW HOURS. I HAVE AN UBER COMING TO
TAKE ME TO THE AIRPORT. I HOPE TO SEE YOU AGAIN. HAPPY
HOLIDAYS. ANYA.

Jake didn't know how to feel. He no longer had to worry about how he would explain to Anya that he had his own family commitments for the next couple of weeks. However, Anya's text may have been a way of her saying she didn't care as much about him as he did about her, or that she wasn't interested in moving the needle as far or as quickly as Jake was.

There was hopefully one other thing inherently positive in Anya's text: Cassie's suspicions about the ambiguity of Anya's family must have been mistaken.

CHAPTER 43
January 6, 2020, Fourteen Days Later

JAKE'S FIRST CLASS WAS not until the next day. Charlie had driven him to pick up a rental car. He got underway while everyone was still sleeping. It was easier that way. He was now en route to his Maryland Starbucks for one more run at Cipher's computer. He would then turn his rental in and take the train from there to New Haven.

Leah had wondered why he wasn't just taking the train from Dulles to New Haven. He explained that he had some friends to visit along the way, and the rental would be more conducive.

The extended family had given Jake a send-off dinner at one of the nicer local restaurants the night before: Leah, Frank, Charlie, and Madison. Judge and Mrs. Brooks had joined as well. So had Cassie. She had told him she thought all he needed was a little more practice with his golf game and gave him a sleeve of balls. She also told him she would be playing in the Connecticut open in a few months, and hoped he would come watch. He assured her that he would.

When they returned to the townhouse after dinner, Frank, Charlie, and Madison gave Jake hugs and left him and Leah for a few private moments to themselves. Leah teared up and told Jake she hoped he wouldn't do anything rash about school. He told her not to worry. Whatever I do won't be rash, and you'll be the first to know. He wasn't sure that would be true.

* * *

BAKER, JR. AND AUSTIN each struck a few more balls. It was evident that Baker, Jr. spent more time on his golf game than Austin did. "By the way," Baker, Jr. said, "when I mentioned to Dad that you and I were meeting this morning, he asked me to bring something to your attention. Top secret, this goes no further. He would like your take as soon as possible."

"Okay," Austin said, returning his club to his bag.

"Seems Dad's intelligence people are picking up some noise about some kind of supposedly very contagious, very deadly virus coming out of China. Reportedly, people in some town over there called Hunan are dying right and left."

"Uh, I think Hunan is a style of Chinese cuisine. Do you perhaps mean the city of Wuhan?"

"Whatever," Baker, Jr. responded. "Meanwhile, White House medical advisors are telling Dad they're afraid this bug has already spread to the U.S. and if we don't quickly nip it in the bud right now, we could have a pandemic on our hands."

"Fuck. That's terrible. You mean people possibly getting sick and dying all over the country?"

"Well, yeah," Baker, Jr. continued. "But even worse, that could put a serious dent in our economic numbers and hurt Dad's chances for re-election. He wants to know what you think, how we need to handle this, keep a lid on it."

"Hmm, gotcha. Let me think about it."

* * *

AUSTIN WALKED OFF THE driving range. *A possible pandemic that could quickly kill God knows how many people across our country, and all that's bothering POTUS and his son is how it may affect POTUS's re-election chances.* He just shook his head as he put his bag of clubs in the trunk of his car. *Hunan and Wuhan, all the same to them. This apple really doesn't fall very far from this tree.*

* * *

JAKE WALKED INTO "HIS" Maryland Starbucks for what he expected to be the last time. He looked around for the manager, Neil, but didn't see him anywhere, and figured it was safe to set up shop.

Jake booted up his laptop. He hacked into Cipher's computer and easily passed the encrypted password, once again. *The Mossad software is just incredible.* This time, he headed straight to the folder labeled "MC", and double clicked on it. As he expected, it was empty—or so it looked.

Like before, he chose the retrieval component of the Mossad software, but this time, he pointed it at the MC folder, confirmed that it was the folder he wished to restore, and again chose the start date "Inception." Just as the software did when he was targeting the GL folder, its activity light changed from red to green, but this time, showed approximately 117 minutes remaining, 24 minutes more than it had estimated for the GL folder. *Hmm, more MC data than GL data. This will leave me naked for almost two hours. No choice. Nothing I can do about it. I need that MC folder to make sense of what I saw in the GL files.*

* * *

ONCE AGAIN, CIPHER WAS alerted the moment the hacker was back on his machine. *Took your sweet time. Thought maybe you'd given up. Game on, motherfucker!* Cipher activated his tracing software. *Hopefully, the bastard will stick around a little longer this time, so I can precisely pinpoint his location.*

He watched the tracing application do its thing. Forty minutes went by—the hacker was still on board, and Cipher's tracing software had him somewhere in the United States. *Same as last time.*

He gave it another thirty minutes and checked again—the hacker was still on board. His location was narrowed to the eastern seaboard of the United States. *Either bold or stupid. Is he in Maryland once more?*

Another twenty minutes—the hacker was still there. *And right there in Maryland again. C'mon, you SOB! Stay with me. Just another ten or fifteen minutes and I've gotcha!*

Cipher watched the second hand on his wall clock slowly grind out another ten laps. *Damn, it's taking forever.* Finally, another ten minutes transpired. He checked again. *Gotcha! Right there in a local Starbucks near St. Michaels, Maryland, wherever exactly that is.*

* * *

JAKE HAD WATCHED THE Mossad software do its thing. Almost two hours later, the MC folder was now replicated and on his laptop. He closed up his

Starbucks office, and turned in his rental car near the train station, where he would catch the train that would take him to New Haven. He was sitting on the train and had five hours to see what he could learn about MC.

He had a pile of data, even more than in the GL folder. Once again, the contents were in Kazakh. He correctly used freeware to translate the MC files from Kazakh into English. Again not perfect, but good enough. As with the GL files, the data was coded. Unfortunately, it was not the same coding Cipher had used with the GL files. He would have to use his decoding software from scratch to find out what he had. It would be slow trekking, but he had almost four hours to go before he would arrive in New Haven. *A lot more interesting than streaming a bad movie.*

* * *

Cipher's tracing software had served him well, but he knew his hacker opponent still had a significant advantage over him. Somehow, his adversary was able to hack into his computer from almost six thousand miles away. That required highly sophisticated software, which very few people had. *He's damn good, or resourceful. Even I don't have that kind of software.*

He now knew the *location* from which he had been hacked, but he didn't know *who* had hacked him. Anyone could have come after him from that Starbucks. He had to somehow find out who was in that Starbucks when he was hacked.

No doubt, he speculated, Starbucks had surveillance cameras in its café and saved its surveillance tapes for at least thirty days, maybe even longer, on its computer. He could readily access Starbucks's computer, but not from six thousand miles away. He didn't have the software that his rival did.

He had two choices. He could reach out to Turgenev, who no doubt would have the kind of long-distance hacking software he didn't himself have, or he could take a trip to St. Michaels, Maryland, and use his own routine software to hack into Starbucks's surveillance records from its adjacent parking lot.

* * *

Austin thought Potus's thinking about sitting on the pandemic was too dangerous to keep another day. He called Baker, Jr. "I'm going for a power walk along the river. Join me?" Power was code for urgent.

"Sure. Thirty minutes?"

"Perfect. See you there."

They were each in sweatsuits and jogging shoes when they joined along the river bank. "What's so urgent?" Baker, Jr. asked.

"POTUS's thinking that he should play down this threat of a pandemic out of Wuhan. After giving the matter some thought, as you requested, I think it would be a really terrible mistake if your dad doesn't take the potential pandemic public loud and clear at the earliest possible moment, and then transfer the responsibility to the medical experts and local government. Otherwise, I think this could come heavily crashing down on his shoulders if it ever comes to light that he was slow to act. And lead."

"Understood. I didn't express my view because I didn't want to influence your thinking, but I'm totally with you. I'll let Dad know how you feel right away. Thanks."

* * *

POTUS WASN'T HAPPY AS he and Baker, Jr. convened in the Rose Garden. "What was so fucking important that it couldn't keep until tomorrow?"

"You asked me to get Austin's view on this virus business." Baker, Jr. repeated what Austin had said, "After giving the matter some thought, as you requested, he said he thought it would be a terrible mistake if you don't take the potential pandemic public at the earliest possible moment, and transfer the responsibility to the medical experts and local government. Otherwise, he thought this entire pandemic could come heavily crashing down on your shoulders if it ever came to light that you were slow to act. And lead."

"What the fuck's the matter with you? What I asked was for you to get him on the record agreeing with my position. Not contradicting it."

"I told him, Dad. He just didn't listen."

"You let the son of a bitch know if he doesn't get with my program, I'll find someone else who will. Besides, my medical experts are telling me that this virus business is nothing. It's going to vanish as quickly as it appeared. I'm hearing that all you need to do is gargle with Clorox."

"No worries, Dad. I'll tell him. Again."

CHAPTER 44
January 14, 2020, Eight Days Later

JAKE WAS SITTING IN one of his classes. Even after almost two months away, he was already bored. How could he not be given his recent life. He had traveled to Kazakhstan, met several incredible people, and was using extraordinary software in pursuit of his cybersecurity ambitions. Ambitions that might also render a valuable public service.

He hadn't yet cracked the MC data code, although he was getting close. But school was getting in the way, really slowing him down. He could manage the work quickly enough, but his professors expected him to be in class. That was time consuming, and there was no way around that. Real time was real time. *Why am I procrastinating? Maybe it's time to just make the decision and cut the school cord?*

Kelly was another problem. After almost two months away, she wanted to make up fast for lost time. She expected his attention, but when he was with her, his thoughts were on Anya. He knew he needed to end things with Kelly, but he wasn't sure where he was with Anya.

The text alert on his phone sounded. He opened his text app:

HELLO, JK. ARE YOU BACK IN SCHOOL? I'M AT HARVARD. IT'S VERY EXCITING. AND ALREADY VERY DEMANDING.

I HOPE YOU HAD A NICE COUPLE OF WEEKS WITH YOUR FAMILY. AND A BIT OF A REST. WHAT DID YOU DO WHEN YOU WEREN'T SOCIALIZING WITH YOUR FAMILY?

I HAD A VERY NICE HOLIDAY SEASON WITH MY FAMILY. IT WAS THE RIGHT THING FOR ME TO DO, BUT I DID MISS YOU.

I'M NOT SURE HOW OUR SCHEDULES ARE GOING TO MESH, BUT I HOPE WE WILL FIND TIME FOR ONE ANOTHER.

LET ME KNOW HOW YOU'RE DOING. HUGS, ANYA.

Damn. If it wasn't one thing, it was another. Anya was at the head of the list. Excitement? Undeniably. More distractions? For sure. Whatever Professor Sanchez has been saying for the past ten minutes, Jake sure hadn't heard any of it. *Shit. Now I'll have to borrow someone's notes. More distractions.* He sent Anya a short reply:

YES, BACK IN SCHOOL AFTER SPENDING TIME WITH FAMILY. BORED WITH SCHOOL ALREADY, BUT VERY BUSY. GLAD YOU HAD A NICE VISIT WITH YOUR FAMILY AND HARVARD IS EXCITING FOR YOU. MISSED YOU TOO. HOPE WE CAN MAKE OUR SCHEDULES MESH. LATER, JT.

She said "Hugs." *I wanted to say something better than "Later." Wasn't sure what to say. I'm so lame, damn it. Sanchez, what did he just say?*

* * *

ANYA CLOSED HER PHONE. *"Later?" That's all he could say? He really didn't say much of anything. Busy with what? I'm expected to find out. Pressure from home. To get them what they want. Hoped Jake would come to me. Guess I'll have to take the lead and visit him. Soon.*

CHAPTER 45
January 24, 2020, Ten Days Later

AMIR WALKED OUT OF the U.S.C.I.S. offices in downtown Manhattan. He still had the three passports he had used to reach the U.S., but now he also had a card that said "Authorized Stay."

He had to wait in line for almost a full hour. "Passport, please," the agent first said to him.

Amir reached in his bag. He pulled out only his Bermuda passport and handed it to the agent.

The agent kept looking back and forth at Amir and then the photo in the passport. He had a puzzled look on his face. "You are in the line to file an application for asylum," the agent said. "Why are you seeking asylum?"

"Life in danger," Amir said. "Go home, surely be killed."

"You would be killed in Bermuda?" the agent said. "By whom?"

"Not in Bermuda, in Kazakhstan," Amir answered.

"Kazakhstan?" the agent repeated. "I don't understand."

Amir then produced his three passports and explained his circumstances, that what he did was the only way he could escape Kazakhstan and reach the United States.

"So you entered the U.S. on a false passport. That's not good at all."

"Only way, not do, dead. Please not to send back to Kazakhstan. Will be killed." He showed the agent the photos on his phone of his bruises. "Please to looking." He pointed to his face. He also lifted his shirt to show what remained of his bruises.

The agent grimaced. "Well, this is highly unusual, traveling with multiple passports not issued by your claimed country of origin. I will leave it for the hearing officer on your asylum application to evaluate how you entered the country, and to decide what to do."

He helped Amir fill out and file his asylum application. He gave Amir a copy of the "Authorized Stay" card. "Retain this card. Don't lose it. It's very important." He allowed Amir to retain his three passports. He gave Amir a date in six months to report back for the hearing of his asylum application, and wrote the date on his copy of the asylum application. "Bring all three passports to the hearing," he said to Amir. "You can now stay and work in the U.S. until your asylum application is decided. If it's granted, you can remain and work in the U.S. indefinitely, and can apply for a green card—permanent residence—after one year. If you are granted a green card, you can then obtain a U.S. passport and will be required to surrender your three existing passports."

"Work now anywhere in U.S.?" Amir asked.

"Yes. How will you get by until you find work?"

"Have American dollars cash."

"You can use your Authorized Stay card to open a bank account and obtain checks. It's dangerous to walk around with more than a little cash for short-term use."

"Even in America?"

"Even in America."

Amir was surprised how easy it actually turned out to be. *Photos of bruises did trick. Especially when show bruises remain. Lift shirt, agent afraid have weapon. Agent keep saying unusual story is.*

Amir now had some time, but he had to find a job to live in America. He was afraid to go to the Kazakhstan consulate in New York because his enemies might learn of his whereabouts. For the same reason, he didn't think it would be safe to reach out to the Kazakhstan expat community in New York.

He thought more about how and where he could best find a job and make a living. All he knew was how to drive a taxi, but New York was too complicated and too expensive for him. He thought maybe he would go to New Haven and get a job driving for Uber. He was surprised that it was not necessary for him to own his own car. *Google say many foreign persons from many countries in New Haven. Call melting pot. Can hide self well. Can also watch what Mr. JK in New Haven is doing. Why came to Kazakhstan to learn hacking.*

CHAPTER 46
January 31, 2020, One Week Later

JAKE HAD FINALLY MANAGED to decode the duplicate MC folder residing within the Mossad software on his anonymous laptop—the one he never used to access the internet other than to hack into Cipher's computer solely from the Starbucks café in Maryland.

Decoding the MC data had proved far more arduous than decoding the GL data. *Why did Cipher go to even greater extremes to hide the contents of the MC folder than he did with the contents of the GL folder?* He began reviewing the multitude of files now housed in the duplicate MC folder on his computer. It would take him the better part of a day. He needed to get through it today because Anya was coming to spend the day with him tomorrow, Sunday.

And, finally, there it was, the answer to Jake's question, hiding right there in plain sight. Or there *he* was. Any number of emails interspersed among other less elucidating material in the MC folder made clear that the true author of the sophisticated software Turgenev planned to use to control the outcome of the 2020 U.S. election was none other than MC, short for Cailin Molloy. Unfortunately, however, the MC folder contained no specific details regarding the software.

Partly derived from Cipher's decoded MC folder, including inexplicably Cipher's own research into Molloy's background, and Jake's additional research as well, Jake had been able to patch together at least a preliminary sense of who Molloy was, and what his motives were:

Molloy, whose descendants, along with thousands of other Irish immigrants, had emigrated from Ireland to Windmill Point, a small neighborhood village in Montreal, Quebec, to escape the Irish period of mass starvation and disease between 1845 and 1849—known as the Irish Potato Famine. Rampant poverty, disease, and death in the Montreal surroundings unfortunately followed these immigrants on their flight in search of a better life. One of the dwindling line of his all but destitute family, Molloy never made it past high school. All he had was a mathematical aptitude, a love for all computer toys and games, and a burning desire to make a mark—some kind of mark—that his family had never been able to do.

But to do that, even if known only to himself, he had to survive. *Kind of like those art collectors who steal famous art and then have to keep it locked up in their basement vaults, known to and enjoyed only by themselves in order not to lose what they wrongfully accumulated—and worse still, perhaps end up in jail.* Similarly, Molloy chose to conceal his identity and live vicariously as a ghost through his two charades—Leonid Gradsky and Lars Nilsen. *Guess it works for him.* Gradsky and Nilsen were well thought out and carefully created figments of Molloy's boundless imagination. Unlike his aliases, Molloy suffered no physical ailments whatsoever.

Only Cipher and Molloy previously knew the truth. And now so did Jake. He wondered if that knowledge would threaten his well-being.

CHAPTER 47
February 2, 2020, Two Days Later

JAKE HAD SPENT THE day with Anya after he picked her up at the train station. He showed her around New Haven in the early part of the day and they had lunch at one of his favorite coffee shops—nothing extravagant at all.

At lunch, Anya asked Jake to explain to her the goings on of the Baker impeachment trial. "Why do they bother?" Anya asked Jake. "Almost three whole weeks. It seems like such a waste of time and resources."

"Yes and no," Jake answered. "While there is no doubt about the outcome, that Baker will be acquitted in a vote along party lines having nothing to do with his actual guilt or innocence, each side, Democrats and Republicans, will have played American politics to the hilt, posturing for any possible edge in terms of the coming November elections."

"I'm not sure I follow," Anya said. "Maybe I just don't have the necessary background. Nothing like this could ever happen in Russia."

"By the time of the vote this coming week, the Democrats will have enjoyed major daily visibility for almost three straight weeks in their quest to paint Baker as a corrupt and dishonest individual who should never have been elected in 2016, and certainly should not be reelected this time around. That they will have expended millions of taxpayer dollars for that possible benefit is of no concern to them. It won't be as if they had to spend their own money on this frivolity."

"And what about Baker?" Anya asked. "Is he just an innocent victim of all these theatrics?"

"Only Baker's strongest core followers consider him an innocent victim. As you can see on the daily news reports, Baker is constantly tweeting that the impeachment trial is nothing more than a "witch hunt" and that he will be totally "vindicated" by the acquittal vote—as if it were an impartial vote, which we all know it will not be—and that the Democrats should be rejected by the voters in November. Not only in the presidential election, but in the downstream congressional elections as well."

In the afternoon, they visited the Yale campus and finally his own SCSU campus, which didn't compare all that favorably to Yale, but it did include his apartment. The day had gone nicely. He had some thoughts about showing Anya his apartment, although unfortunately his roommate had some friends in. *So much for that bright idea.*

He had to settle for a hug and a whiff of her vanilla perfume when he saw her off for her train ride back to Harvard. *The next visit will probably have to be on me. At least I'll get a sense of what I missed out on by not getting better grades in high school—Harvard. Leah would have been so proud. Maybe my parents too.*

* * *

ANYA THOGUHT THE DAY had gone well. While she didn't yet have any information of what Jake was pursuing, she was growing her relationship with him. Hopefully, that would in due course lead Jake to confide in her. She had mixed emotions, but she knew her optimistic report home would be required and well received. *I hope JK'll now be motivated to make a visit to me in the next week or two. If not sooner.*

* * *

MIKHAIL OBLONSKY CLEARED CUSTOMS at John F. Kennedy International Airport in New York. He obtained a B-2 visitors visa at the U.S. Consulate in Moscow. All he had to say was that he would be traveling to the U.S. to attend a one-week international studies conference at Harvard, but the paranoid Moscow authorities spent two weeks making sure that Oblonsky wasn't actually seeking to defect to the West. Human assets were increasingly valuable and not to be lost under the guise of a short academic exercise.

The B-2 visit was good for six months. He would not need that long. At JFK, the customs officer asked him why he was there. He gave his pre-arranged answer, and the agent stamped a form and handed it to him, and told him to have a nice day. He went to Hertz and picked up the rental car that was waiting for him. All he had to do was show his international driver's license and insurance certificate. He plugged his destination into the GPS on his smartphone and drove out of the airport.

* * *

AFTER JAKE LEFT ANYA at the train station, his mind returned to Molloy. *Work before pleasure.* He needed to get into Molloy's computer and see what more he could learn. The emails in the MC folder on Cipher's laptop made clear that Molloy still made his home in Montreal. Montreal was much closer than Kazakhstan, but it might as well be Kazakhstan because he had no backdoor into Molloy's computer, like the one he had planted on Cipher's.

Somehow, he was going to have to get physically close enough to Molloy's computer so the Mossad software could hack into it without needing the Mossad thumb drive sourced backdoor. The problem with that was that such an approach was a one shot affair, unless Jake was going to repeat it periodically as needed. Otherwise, Jake would have to come up with a more elaborate and permanent solution. Such a long-term solution was Jake's only prospect at present to sufficiently identify Molloy's election hacking software to design a software anecdote or barrier.

This was going to be tricky, both in terms of planning and execution. Tricky in a way that did not fall within Jake's skill set.

Jake thought about the possibilities. From the MC folder, and Jake's own research, he had the address of Molloy's upscale home outside Montreal. As a matter of curiosity, he had also found that Molloy's cover story for having such a grand home without any tangible means was that he had done well timing the market over the years when the real explanation was his dark web consulting revenues.

A big stumbling block was that while Jake had pictures of Molloy from the MC folder, Molloy—aka Nilsen—also knew exactly what Jake looked like. Unless Jake was going to involve an accomplice, which did not at all appeal to him, he was going to have to develop a blueprint that did not require his physical presence in Montreal to be known to Molloy.

It was over the top, right out of a spy novel, but Jake slowly conjured up a game plan. He would fly to Montreal, rent a car, drive close enough to Molloy's home at a time when he knew Malloy would be away—but that his computer would be there—and use the Mossad software to disarm the computerized security alarm and cameras Molloy undoubtedly employed at his home. He could research when Malloy left his home on chores and didn't have other staff around.

Jake would then break into the home and use his Mossad thumb drive to plant the backdoor into the USB port of Malloy's computer, just as he had done with Cipher's computer in Kazakhstan. He would then have to get out of the house, drive a safe distance away, hack into Molloy's computer using the Mossad software and the now established backdoor in Molloy's computer, copy the contents of Molloy's computer onto his own laptop, and leave Molloy's computer content intact. After all that, he would also have to re-arm the home security system before Molloy might subsequently discover that Jake had copied the content of his computer while the home security system had been offline during the few minutes Jake was in Molloy's home.

This assumed that the Mossad software could hack the re-arming instructions on the home security system before deactivating it so that the Mossad software could then be used to re-arm the system once Jake had left Molloy's home. If not, Molloy might ultimately suspect that he had been hacked, unless he assumed it was some random power outage that was not protected by any backup generator at his home. *I've never seen a backup generator that reliably performs all the time as they are "guaranteed" to do.*

Jake concluded that the one to fear, so long as he safely made good his escape from the Molloy home, would not be Molloy but rather his client—Turgenev—who was seeking to control the 2020 U.S. election, ostensibly on Russia's behalf. Realistically, however, he concluded that it would be in Molloy's best interests to keep his client in the dark about any such breach.

Jake would have to sleep on all of this and go through it again. Not just once, but several times. He wanted to make his way in the world, and his fortune, but was this really the way? *My God, I'm a computer guru, not a home invasion burglar!*

CHAPTER 48
February 3, 2020, One Day Later

MONDAYS WERE JAKE'S BUSIEST days of the week at school. He thought through his approaching gambit on his morning run. The more he thought about it, the more it seemed like it could work. And he couldn't think of any other way to meaningfully hack into Molloy's computer long term.

But he had to return to Monday's real world. He had to shelve his planning for at least one more day. On top of everything else, Carter had sent him a text early this morning requesting his presence to go over his portion of Carter's pending manuscript. He got through it fine; it just took more of his precious time.

* * *

CARTER THOUGHT ABOUT HIS meeting with Jake. *I was hoping for an opening to go further into what Jake is up to, but he just played it so close to the vest. Didn't give away a damn thing. I couldn't be any more obvious than I was. I need to come up with some other tactic.*

* * *

OBLONSKY WAS PARKED IN his rental car, immediately behind the Maryland Starbucks. His laptop was, fittingly, open and sitting on his lap. He expected to find the Starbucks Wi-Fi connection to the internet fully unsecured. Were that not the case, the multitude of Starbucks customers who sipped on their posh coffees while they checked their email and did some of their work would not be possible.

After briefly updating himself on the status of the silly Baker impeachment trial, Oblonsky was into the Starbucks computer. It was password protected—but as was a poorly guarded secret, the password used on most Starbucks computers was "PASSWORD." *How fucking dumb is that?*

From his laptop, he hunted around the Starbucks computer. He found it quickly enough, a folder entitled "Surveillance Tapes", another not so brilliant name. *I guess the Starbucks IT folks are not that well compensated.*

There were subfolders for inside the café and for the surrounding parking lot. He first tried the videos inside the café.

He found the surveillance tape that bore the date his predator last hacked into his laptop. He calculated back from the Kazakh time the hacker was on his computer to what the local time then was in Maryland. He fast forwarded the video to that time and started watching as the camera rotated around the café. It took only a few minutes. He froze the video and backed it up several frames and froze it again. He didn't really need a copy of the video, but he was there, and it just required a few clicks and he had it saved on his laptop. *Never know when it might come in handy.*

Oblonsky, more commonly known in his circles as Cipher, sat staring at the frozen image of his predator. *Why am I not surprised?* He was looking at none other than the infamous intermeddling Jake Klein. *The question is what to do with him now that I know it's him?*

CHAPTER 49
February 4, 2020, One Day Later

THE GRU LIAISON IN the D.C. Russian Embassy reported to Turgenev every day by diplomatic pouch for his eyes only. By custom, if not law, these pouches were the property of Russia, as if an extension of the country itself and the Russian property on which the D.C. Russian Embassy stood.

One week before the January 16, 2020, commencement of Baker's impeachment trial in the U.S. Senate, Turgenev's daily pouch included a copy of the supposedly confidential opening brief of the DNC trial managers. *Confidential, my ass. What a joke.* He had ordered the opening brief leaked to the media because it was the safest way for him to make sure that Baker's lawyers had plenty of advanced notice of what the DNC's case would be without the intelligence being attributed to him.

Turgenev knew there was no chance that Baker would be convicted tomorrow, but the DNC had compiled quite the case against Baker as a form of early election campaigning to damage Baker's bid for re-election in November, and to embarrass Russia at the same time for *allegedly* using its resources on Baker's behalf. The result of the trial would be exactly as everyone knew it would be before Baker was impeached in December, but to the DNC's credit, the trial had been drawn out way longer than he thought the GOP should ever have allowed.

He had a *lot* of money invested in Baker's re-election. He had wanted to do everything he could to undermine the credibility of the impeachment trial. Every day for the past month—once it became apparent that Bianchi had reversed her original position out of her own political necessity, and was going to allow the impeachment trial to proceed—tens of thousands of social media comments and print journalism op-eds were posted every day from one end of the U.S. to the other by Russian bots posing as Americans highly critical of the Democrats for their obvious political mischief.

Ironically, Baker constantly tweeted about all of the "fake news" being directed *at him*, but it was only a fraction of the *pro-Baker* fake news Turgenev was mounting on Baker's behalf and there was not a damn thing the Democrats could do to stop it. When they put out one fire, two more cropped up. *Why not? The Democrats were guilty of the very same chicanery. At least here in Russia, we are not such hypocrites as the American politicians are.*

Turgenev's assistant entered his office and handed him a printout of a text that had just arrived and was marked "urgent." He accepted the printout and read to himself:

> IT HAS COME TO MY ATTENTION THAT AN AMERICAN WHO ATTENDED MY KAZAKHSTAN HACKERS CONFERENCE LAST NOVEMBER, AS DID TWO OF YOUR REPRESENTATIVES, HAS BEEN HACKING INTO MY COMPUTERS. THIS AMERICAN'S NAME IS JAKE KLEIN. AS I HAVE PREVIOUSLY ASSURED YOU, THERE IS NO POSSIBLE WAY HE CAN UPSET YOUR PLANS, WHICH ARE PROTECTED BY MY ENCRYPTION SERVICES. I HAVE THE MATTER UNDER CONTROL, BUT I THOUGHT YOU WOULD WANT ME TO LET YOU KNOW. YOUR FAITHFUL SERVANT, CIPHER.

The only one he faithfully serves is himself, and he has a big mouth to boot. If he had the matter under control, Klein would not be inside his computer. Nor does Cipher seem to recall that he foolishly mentioned Klein to my comrades when they attended his conference in November. Does this imbecile truly believe that I would entrust my interests to him to protect? I suspect I know more about Mr. Klein than he does. But perhaps not as much as I should.

Turgenev did not respond to Cipher's text. *Let him worry about what I'm thinking.* But then, he remembered his investment in Gradsky—and Cipher—and that they had him at their mercy. *Up to a point!*

* * *

JAKE WATCHED THE NEWS that the impeachment trial was expected to conclude the next day, February 5, 2020. He had watched snippets of it on the news every day, but it had been hard for him to take it very seriously. As he had explained to Anya during the course of their preceding weekend visit, he was convinced that it would be nothing more than political playacting, and so it appeared to him to have been. Still, only two presidents before Baker had ever been subjected to an impeachment trial—Andrew Johnson and Bill Clinton. Guilty or innocent, it was obvious that Baker would be acquitted. The GOP controlled the Senate, and that was that. He had paid attention to the trial as much as his time permitted, and he would watch the formal vote tomorrow, but only because it might well impact the November election, and his own future destiny.

This brought Jake's mind back to Molloy. He revisited the decision he had recently made.

* * *

CIPHER HAD DELIBERATED BACK and forth. He had wanted to send Klein an unsigned anonymous text to shake him up. He had even drafted it:

I KNOW WHO YOU ARE. I KNOW WHAT YOU'VE BEEN DOING. I'M COMING FOR YOU.

But to what end? Maybe, if they were still in Kazakhstan together, but here in the U.S., they were on Klein's turf. The words were empty. They might even violate some U.S. laws for all he knew—something he studiously avoided doing. He had decided long ago not to have to function as a ghost. He enjoyed his open goodwill. No, he had accomplished what he came to the U.S. to accomplish, and he electronically documented what he found.

He had informed Turgenev of what he learned, but he had not shared his digital records with him—the time stamped surveillance tapes of Klein at the precise time someone had hacked into his computer. At least not yet. He would wait and watch to see how Turgenev might deal with Klein. His records weren't going anywhere. He could always produce them later if it proved beneficial.

Oblonsky boarded his return flight to Moscow. On arriving, he made the short trip from Moscow to Kazakhstan.

CHAPTER 50
February 5, 2020, One Day Later

JAKE WAS CHOMPING AT the bit. He had previously made up his mind to chase down Molloy's computer contents, but had decided it would have to wait until after today's anticipated verdict in Baker's impeachment trial. Jake had known the trial was going to be a daily media circus, literally on television 24/7, live coverage during the day and replays at night. Given Molloy's presumed stake in the November elections, Jake assumed that Molloy would stick around his home and closely watch and record all of the hoopla and goings on.

If Jake chose to make his Montreal journey during the course of the impeachment trial, he would very likely have had to hang around north of the border for an undefined period of time before he achieved a reliable window of opportunity during which to execute his break-in strategy—if he received any such opportunity. That was not possible.

He might have been able to head to Montreal today, following the announcement of the impeachment verdict, but Anya had invited him to be her guest at a special weekend Harvard open house this coming Saturday and Sunday. He had been forced to decline several of her recent invitations to visit her—he hadn't had the heart to say no once again. If he flew to Montreal today, it would only leave him two days in Montreal before he had to get back to Harvard. That was not enough time.

Given his current school schedule, he would now have to wait still another couple of weeks before he could create a block of time sufficient to pull off the trip north, including travel time and time required in Montreal. *Have I just been a gutless wonder, conjuring up one excuse after another not to make my home invasion debut? Aarrgh!*

Just as all of the news pundits had predicted, notice of the announced verdict flashed across his smartphone screen. Baker was acquitted. With a couple of minor exceptions, the vote was strictly along party lines, the culmination of run-of-the-mill politics at the huge expense of "we the people."

* * *

TURGENEV WATCHED THE VOTE on his television monitor. *Maybe we can finally get on with things now. About fucking time.*

* * *

CIPHER WATCHED THE RESULTS of the vote. *Kinda wished Baker had been convicted. Would have made all the stress about Klein moot. Wonder if Molloy has already reached out to Turgenev. If not, he probably will now.*

* * *

MOLLY TURNED OFF HIS large-screen monitor. *Game still on. My software is still needed. It might have been a nervous time if Baker was convicted and Turgenev had no further need for me. Time for me to talk to him now about Klein.*

CHAPTER 51
February 9, 2020, Four Days Later

JAKE SAT LOST IN thought on the two-hour train ride back from Boston to New Haven. Anya had met him on Friday evening when his train arrived in Boston. She drove them the short three and a half miles to her Cambridge apartment on the edge of the Harvard campus.

He had wondered whether he would be staying with Anya or at a nearby hotel. Anya had apparently not given that question a second thought, nor did she make any pretense about his staying in the spare bedroom in her apartment. It did strike Jake as a natural evolution of their relationship, but it was an exciting beginning to the weekend nonetheless.

They had a nice dinner out and walked around parts of the town, chilly as the night air was, before retiring for the evening. A cozy fire in the apartment and some very pleasant recreational activity on the inviting rug in front of the fire made up for the chilly night air outside.

The rest of the weekend was divided between Harvard's open house events, sightseeing around Cambridge, and more downtime in her apartment.

Anya filled Jake in on her language studies. He could see firsthand her growing command of the English language. He imagined that she would be quite fluent by the end of the school year.

She said the thought of returning home to Russia when her time was up would now be quite difficult, if not impossible, given their blossoming relationship.

Her curiosity about Jake's career plans for the future seemed quite natural, and Jake did not hesitate to share *some* of his thoughts about his future. It had been a fantastic weekend, but somehow, he just wasn't quite ready yet to share *all* of his most intimate plans—including his pending trip to Montreal.

CHAPTER 52
February 10, 2020, One Day Later

ANYA SAT IN FRONT of her keyboard, struggling with exactly what to report:

> KLEIN SPENT THE WEEKEND HERE IN CAMBRIDGE WITH ME. I INVITED HIM TO STAY AT MY APARTMENT AND HE DIDN'T HESITATE TO ACCEPT. WE DID THE TOWN, BUT WE ALSO SPENT CONSIDERABLE TIME IN THE APARTMENT. I AM GETTING CLOSER TO HIM, BUT HE STILL SEEMS RELUCTANT TO SHARE HIS FUTURE PLANS WITH ME, IN SPITE OF THE FACT THAT I CONTINUE TO PROBE AS MUCH AS I CAN.

The reply was even less favorable than she had expected:

> WE NEED MORE RESULTS. WE ARE RECEIVING CONSIDERABLE PRESSURE FROM ABOVE. ARE YOU PERHAPS ENJOYING YOUR ASSIGNMENT TOO MUCH?

That last suggestion had angered her, but she had to be careful and not forget who she was talking to:

> WHAT MORE DO YOU EXPECT OF ME? I'M DOING EXACTLY WHAT I WAS ASKED TO DO. YOUR SUGGESTION IS INSULTING.

How am I supposed to further demonstrate my loyalty?

The reply came more rapidly and more tersely:

Watch your tongue, Lieutenant. My job is to expect— and obtain—the results that you have been ordered to deliver, not to tell you how to do your job. That's for you to determine. As you have been trained to do. And as you have agreed to do. Stop talking. And start delivering. Soon.

She said nothing further. She knew from experience when it was best to let her handler have the final say.

CHAPTER 53
February 17, 2020, One Week Later

TURGENEV RETURNED FROM A short trip to the Mideast, and he was not in a good mood. *Do I have to do everything myself? Things in Syria are a fucking mess. Baker had allowed his impeachment trial to drag on forever, instead of just ending it. And now, this report about Lieutenant Lebedev's lack of results. What is it about this American Jake Klein? First, he seems to be having his way with Cipher, and with Gradsky as well for all I know. Now, he's having a wonderful time with one of my best agents, and I'm getting no useful results. Other than reports that she's trying. Whatever the hell that means.*

He fished the olive out of his drink and swallowed it down. The vodka flavor was soothing. *Maybe I need to take this into my own hands. It would not be difficult to arrange a simple car accident to take care of Klein. I have to keep Gradsky and Cipher alive. But I don't have any need to keep Klein alive. To the contrary, his continuing presence is proving to be a considerable nuisance.*

He finished off his drink and thought a bit more about the troublesome Klein. *Yes. I think that might work.* He reached for his phone.

* * *

CIPHER WAS INCREASINGLY RESTLESS. His recent text to Turgenev hadn't technically called for a response. *Still, I had hoped.*

And then there was Klein. He wondered what Klein was doing. He hadn't seen any sign of him since his most recent hack into his computer. *His quietude may be even more worrisome than Turgenev's.*

And then his phone rang—the number very few people had.

CHAPTER 54
February 19, 2020, Two Days Later

TURGENEV WAS PACING ABOUT his office when his secretary escorted Barovsky into his oversized office. Turgenev took his seat. "Good morning, Barovsky."

"Good morning, Mr. President. I understand you have been waiting for an update of the effectiveness of our social media and print propaganda campaign relating to the—"

"Yes, yes,—"

"—November U.S. election?"

"Of course, but I have something of more immediacy to discuss with you."

"Yes, certainly."

"Let me first say, I read your daily reports and know our U.S. impeachment trial and election efforts went well, even though Baker and his compatriots allowed the trial to drag on much longer than it should have. I also see that your election promotions are proceeding as expected."

"Thank you, Mr. President," Barovsky replied.

"However, on a different subject, does the name Jake Klein mean anything to you? He's an American college student in Connecticut studying computer science. He seems skilled beyond his years."

"I'm sorry. I don't believe I've ever come across that name."

"No reason to think that you had, but I didn't want to waste time on background if you already knew of him."

"I'm confident I do not. May I be of some assistance, Mr. President?"

"As you know, we have two separate and distinct programs concerning the U.S. election, the program you are heading to influence how Americans choose to vote, and a second program—a digital program—to control actual votes. The purpose of this meeting is to discuss how you might help us with our electronic objectives."

"I'm happy to help in any way I can, but I'm afraid my technology skills are rather limited."

"That will not be an issue. It has come to my attention that Klein is becoming uncomfortably close to—and possibly familiar with—the software we will be using to control the electronic results of the election." Turgenev stood and walked to the windows that looked down on the Moskva River. The view always helped him organize his thoughts.

Barovsky waited patiently.

"Klein needs to be stopped," Turgenev said, "before he can possibly endanger our efforts. There—"

Turgenev was interrupted by a knock on the inner door to his office. "Yes?"

One of Turgenev's deputies stepped through the door and signaled to him. Apologies, Mr. President."

Turgenev was annoyed. "Excuse me a moment," he said to Barovsky, and stepped through the open door, closing Barovsky off behind him.

* * *

BAROVSKY WAS LEFT SITTING in Turgenev's office. *Why in the hell would he possibly want to discuss with me stopping some American who is proving an irritation to him? I may be the titular head of GRU, but such physical tactics are hardly within my expertise. Or anything I want to be involved in.* Barovsky was still pondering his bewilderment when Turgenev finally returned twenty minutes later.

* * *

CIPHER ANSWERED THE CALL. "*Da?*"

"Gradsky, here." No social amenities, he came right to the point. "Around the end of November, I sent you an encrypted message about an American by the name of Jake Klein. You had met him at your annual conference. I said I thought Klein might prove troublesome. I asked you to give the matter some thought. It occurs to me that you have never responded. I pay you a lot of money. I expect better."

Cipher was caught off guard. Not because Molloy identified himself as Gradsky and spoke Russian. He always did that—it was part of his paranoid ghost cover of his true identity. More to the point, he wasn't sure he wanted to admit to Molloy that his Kazakhstan computer had been remotely hacked long distance by Klein. Or that he had reached out to Turgenev and shared that information. He wasn't sure which might prove more unsettling to Molloy, that he had no action plan to offer Molloy at the moment, or that he might *appear* closer to Turgenev than he truly was.

"I have someone here with me. I cannot talk now. I'll get back to you." He clicked off without waiting for Molloy to respond.

* * *

TURGENEV RE-ENTERED HIS OFFICE and found Barovsky right where he had left him. "Apologies," Turgenev said, without much conviction. He also offered no excuses for his absence. "We were talking about the need to dispose of the American, Jake Klein. As I was about to say when we were interrupted, there is the obvious way, of course, but it occurs to me that there may be a better way." He outlined his thinking to Barovsky.

Barovsky nodded. "Very clever, Mr. President. I understand completely. I know what you want me to do. Leave it with me. I will take care of it, and I will, of course, keep you informed."

CHAPTER 55
February 21, 2020, Two Days Later

JAKE SAW ABELSON EYEING him from the other side of the room as they walked out of one of their shared classes. He didn't want to stir things up with Mossad, but he didn't dare pretend he hadn't seen him. He put a smile on his face and walked over. "Just the guy I was looking for, Gali," Jake said. "I know I owe you an update. Sorry, I've been spread really thin between classes, Carter's manuscript assignment, and my extracurricular activities. Got time for a cup of coffee?"

"Sure, let's do it," Abelson said.

Jake knew he had a fine line to walk. Abelson had generously provided Jake with two Mossad toys that were proving invaluable to him. He had to let him know at least something about what he had been doing with the technology, enough to show his appreciation, and to make sure Abelson would have no second thoughts or regrets about having loaned it to him.

He had been procrastinating on feeding Abelson's obvious curiosity for any number of reasons, but lack of appreciation was not one of them. Most of all, he wasn't about to share any of his proprietary interests with *anyone*. The fame and fortune he was after was going to be his, and his alone. He wasn't taking the risks he had just to have someone beat him to the punch, or even share his thunder.

He also didn't want to burden Abelson with any more detail than necessary, only to have him perhaps ask for the return of the technology before he could complete his pending mission to Montreal. The more Jake thought about it, the more convinced he was that he had to make that trip, and there was no way he could pull it off without the Mossad technology. If he had been skirting any laws up until now, he was soon going to be heading way beyond skirting. There was no way he was going to reveal any of his Montreal plans to Abelson.

After they filled their cups and settled into a corner booth in the commons cafeteria, Abelson said, "Okay, bud, spill it, and I'm not talking about the coffee. What exactly have you been up to? Don't forget your deal with the devil—you promised to share. I have to explain myself back home."

"I know, I know," Jake answered. "This spy stuff is kinda new to me. On the one hand, I don't want to waste your time on what may already be common knowledge to you. On the other hand, I don't want to involve you in anything you might not want to know. To make sure I protect your plausible deniability."

"Wow, all them cute words. I just love it when you talk dirty to me," Abelson said. "Tell ya what. Why don't you let me be the judge of all that stuff. You start sharing, and I'll let you know anytime I need you to stop. Work for you okay?"

How can I say no? "Sure, that works," Jake answered. He started off by mentioning Nilsen's demonstration at the conference. He figured that would be boring because Abelson had previously told him Mossad had people at the conference. He would already know all about Nilsen.

"Remember, we had folks at the KHC," Abelson said. "Nothing new there. We know all about Nilsen and his technology. If they have boots on the ground at the right places here in the U.S., they can mess a bunch with the election results, but that takes a lot of manpower. Don't know that they can make a significant dent with Nilsen's technology."

"What if it's not necessary to have boots on the ground?" Jake asked. "What if they can do it long distance, kind of like the technology you've been sharing with me?"

Abelson's eyes perked up. "What are you saying, Jake? Are you telling me there are some private hackers out there who have something comparable to our long-distance technology? Spit it out, man."

"Well, I'm not really sure," Jake said, "but I think Cipher is working on something like that with some individual by the name of Gradsky."

"Yeah, we know about Gradsky too," Abelson said.

"Well, that's about all I know right now," Jake lied, "but I'm still working on it. Give me another couple of weeks and maybe I'll have something more for you."

"Fair enough," Abelson said. "Just remember our deal. Don't be a stranger. I gotta run. Talk soon." Abelson stood, gave Jake a pat on his cheek, and walked out of the cafeteria.

* * *

THAT NIGHT, ABELSON SENT a brief encrypted text:

> ONE THING INTERESTING. HE MAY—REPEAT MAY—BE ON TO SOME PRIVATE HACKERS DEVELOPING LONG DISTANCE HACKING CAPABILITIES. NOT SURE, BUT I THINK HE MAY BE HOLDING OUT ON ME. HAVE THE FEELING HE'S NOT SHARING EVERY-THING HE'S GOT. THINK HE MAY BE TRYING TO PLAY COWBOY.

Two could play at that game of being less than totally forthcoming, Abelson thought to himself. He wasn't surprised by the encrypted response he received:

> NO WORRIES. JUST KEEP AN EYE PEELED AND LET US KNOW IF HE STUMBLES ACROSS ANYTHING INTERESTING.

Abelson smiled.

CHAPTER 56
February 26, 2020, Five Days Later

CIPHER TELEPHONED MOLLOY ON their rerouted telephone arrangement that would leave no record of their call.

"Gradsky," Molloy answered Cipher's call. "You sure took your sweet time getting back to me. Did you use our established calling protocols?"

Molloy drives me nuts when he uses his Gradsky alias with me. He knows I know who he really is. "I did."

"Okay. So what's your plan? What are we going to do to stop this guy, Klein, before he messes up our plans?"

This ain't gonna be pleasant, but I'm gonna have to put an end to this right now. Look, Molloy—"

"Stop calling me that. My name is Gradsky."

"Whatever," Cipher said. "The point is, this is *not* about what *we* are going to do about *our* plans. Whatever *you* are doing with Turgenev is *your* business, not mine. You hired me to provide you with certain encryption services. That's all I was supposed to do, and I've done it, lived up to my perfectly lawful end of the bargain. If Klein is making you uncomfortable for some reason, that's *your* problem. And Turgenev's. *Not* mine." Cipher paused to catch his breath.

"Are you done?" Molloy asked.

He hasn't started yelling and screaming or interrupting me. That's a good sign. "I'm not," Cipher answered. "I don't know about you, but I'm not some kind of common thug. I don't go around beating people up, or worse. Maybe you do, but I don't. Unless you have some sign that Klein has penetrated my encryption system, any problem you have with Klein is *your* problem. And unless you are some kind of gangster, I'd suggest the one *you* need to address *your* concerns with is Turgenev, not me. The relationship with Turgenev is *yours*, not mine, and he's probably the best one to address your concerns with—especially if he shares them. He is the one who has an identity of interest with you, not me, and I suspect he's the one who has the resources and ability to take care of any problem Klein represents. *Now, I'm done.*"

"If you are that disloyal to me after all I've paid you, perhaps I should express my present dissatisfaction with you to my client and see how *he* feels about that."

Sounds to me like Molloy is getting weaker and weaker. How could someone so good with computers be so bad with humans? I don't have any choice. I have to keep the heat on. "Now you're threatening *me*? Have you forgotten that if anything happens to me, Turgenev's access to your software terminates. I doubt that Turgenev has forgotten that. Or will be very pleased if you mess up his plans. The ones for which he paid you a small fortune."

The line went dead. *Did that asshole hang up on me?*

* * *

ANYA THOUGHT ABOUT JAKE. *Time to make sure I'm still on his mind. But not be too cloying.* She thought about sending him a selfie or two, but decided that would not be dignified. She settled on a tempting text instead:

I MISS YOU. WHEN CAN WE SEE EACH OTHER? THIS WEEK-
END? ANYA.

* * *

JAKE HEARD THE TEXT alert on his phone. He read Anya's text and was pleased. He had too much work during the coming week, this weekend would be much better. *Shit! Kelly told me her parents are coming into town this weekend and I have to spend time with her and her family. She's acting like we're engaged or something and need to set our wedding date. I don't want to hurt her, but I have to quit procrastinating and end things with her. Just as soon as her parents leave.* He texted Anya back:

> BAD WEEK, INCLUDING PROJECT THIS WEEKEND. MISS YOU. HOW ABOUT IF I COME VISIT YOU ONE DAY NEXT WEEK? I'LL LET YOU KNOW WHEN I CAN GET AWAY. JK.

Two hours went by and no reply. *Did I blow it?*
And then, finally:

> DID YOU THINK I WAS PLAYING HARD TO GET? I THOUGHT ABOUT IT, BUT NO. I WOULDN'T DO THAT. I JUST FELL ASLEEP WAITING FOR YOUR REPLY. LET ME KNOW WHEN YOU CAN COME. SOONER THAN LATER, PLEASE. ANYA.

CHAPTER 57
March 1, 2020, Four Days Later

TURGENEV TURNED OFF THE television. *When are all of these U.S. political theatrics going to come to a halt? First, it was the impeachment trial. Now that's over, but there's still no let up. I can't stand Baker, but I can't stand Bianchi and her Democrats even more! And besides, I have no leverage on them.*

* * *

MOLLOY TURNED OFF THE television. He was tired watching all of the political nonsense going on in the U.S. *Another few months, and hopefully I will bring all this noise to an end.*

His mind drifted back to his conversation with Cipher. *Let the bastard sit and stew about my hanging up on him and what that meant. Truth be told, that pompous ass was probably right. Like me, he's a computer scientist, not a political scientist. The one I really do need to discuss Klein with is Turgenev. He's the political scientist, and the one with the resources to handle Klein.* But picking the right time to talk to Turgenev about anything sensitive is very difficult to figure out. He was such a prima donna. And then, a knowing smile crossed his face. *I was spot on to provide myself with an out in case I need it.*

CHAPTER 58
March 2, 2020, One Day Later

JAKE WAS ON HIS way to the first of his Monday classes. He thought about the past weekend with Kelly and her family. They had really pressed him about his feelings for Kelly. It was all he could do not to end it while they were all there with him. But he thought he owed Kelly better than that. He had to at least let her be the one to orchestrate the breakup.

This week was off to a better start. He had finally cleared enough time on his calendar to fly up to Montreal and accomplish what he hoped to accomplish. He had even managed things so that he could spend a couple of days with Anya along the way. He had traded confirming texts with her last night. He was going to rent a car and drive to Cambridge early tomorrow morning, spend the day with Anya on Tuesday and Wednesday, and then *supposedly* head back to New Haven.

In fact, he was going straight to the airport and taking a flight to Montreal. It was time. No more delays. No more excuses.

He had to rent a car because if he came by train, Anya would want to see him off on his return train to New Haven. This way, they would say their goodbyes at her apartment. He had mentioned in his text that he was driving because he had some chores to handle on the way back to New Haven, and it was easier if he drove.

I hate all this lying. Is this the cost of trying to be a successful businessman?

CHAPTER 59
March 3, 2020, One Day Later

JAKE WONDERED IF IT was perhaps the calm before the storm. He had rented his car, driven to Cambridge, and spent a romantic evening and morning after with Anya. They had taken a midday walk, and had lunch in their favorite local café near Anya's apartment.

Their short visit had been all that Jake had hoped, but his mind was now drifting to the storm that lay ahead—his impending trip to Montreal. *No risk, no reward.* "I'm afraid I have to get on the road," he reluctantly said to Anya.

"So soon?" Anya asked. "Can't you stay a little while longer?"

"I can't. It was hard for me to fit this in, but it was worth every second."

It was less than a block to Anya's apartment. They held hands and silently walked back to Jake's car. He had put his duffel bag and backpack in the car earlier that morning.

Anya looked sad.

"No need to be sad," Jake said. "Remember how you explained to me, what now seems like years ago, the meaning of 'parting is such sweet sorrow?'"

"Yes. My turn next to come to you. This weekend?"

"We'll talk," Jake said. "The rest of this week is tough for me. One of my professors has a project that may take most of the weekend."

"I don't mind. I can read and practice my language exercises while you're working. If you get too busy, I can always hook up with your roommate," Anya kidded.

"Right," Jake said. "Very funny."

A lingering embrace, and Jake drove off.

* * *

BAROVSKY FINISHED PACKING. *AMERICA awaits. It would be a short trip, but an important one—one that I sure need to get right. Might prove hazardous to my health if I don't. Working for Turgenev has its rewards, but the stress is relentless. Maybe I should just stay in America. Now that's a thought.*

* * *

MOLLOY HAD TO WAIT a long time, but his scrambled call was finally put through.

"Gradsky, to what do I owe this unexpected pleasure?" Turgenev asked. "I trust you saw the results of the Baker impeachment vote?" he added.

"*Da.* That's why I'm calling, Mr. President. I think we may have a problem."

"I don't like to hear about problems, Gradsky. Only solutions."

"Well, I'm hoping we might come up with a solution together. I am concerned about an American by the name of Jake Klein." Molloy detailed his worries about Klein to Turgenev.

"Stop!" Turgenev interrupted.

"*Da.*"

"Does your software do what it's supposed to?"

"*Da.* Of course."

"Is it encrypted and secure as you have assured me?"

"*Da.* Cipher has assured us both."

"Then you and Cipher have nothing to worry about, and Klein is not *your* problem. You leave Klein to *me.* Have a nice day. *Paka, paka.*"

Molloy wasn't sure what Turgenev had in mind, but he had done all that he could.

* * *

JAKE'S FLIGHT LANDED IN Montreal. Clearing customs in Canada was a snap for a U.S. citizen. He rented a car and drove the short distance to the nearby hotel where he had made a reservation while waiting to board the flight.

He checked in, went to his room, unpacked his duffel bag, and ate the light dinner he had stopped to purchase in the ground floor snack bar. He went through his plans again, as he had done on his flight. *Can't be too careful.* His adrenaline was already on high.

Using the maps bundled on his laptop, he had already studied and had a pretty good feel for the neighborhood in which Molloy's home was located. Still, he decided it would be a good idea to make a dry run and canvass the home and the neighborhood in person. The drive took him less than half an hour. His smartphone app was accurate to the minute. *Very cool how the algorithms adjust for fluid traffic patterns.*

On the way, he noticed a hotel on the perimeter of the residential neighborhood. According to his car odometer, the hotel was approximately one mile from Molloy's residence. He drove past the home without stopping. It was a large two-story contemporary structure with lots of glass and steel. *Maybe three stories if there's also a subterranean basement. I could get used to digs like that. Is that why I'm taking the chances I am?*

He made two passes through the neighborhood, focusing on the different ways in and out of the community. All of the homes were pretty well sized. He wondered why there was a hotel so close by. *Maybe these folks don't all like sharing their private space with guests.*

This was not a new neighborhood. Most of the homes were older than Molloy's seemed to be. He must have remodeled his. *Maybe for his cyber toys and his security?*

He parked his car one door down and across the street. He pulled his dark web laptop out of his backpack and booted it up, opening his Wi-Fi app. In seconds, the app displayed no less than six neighboring household Wi-Fi networks, all of them password protected. He would have expected no less in an upscale neighborhood like this. One of those networks read GLNet. *Gradsky Leonid?*

On the fly, Jake made his first change of plans.

* * *

Austin was surprised to hear from Barovsky, and that he was here in D.C. Usually, Barovsky would give him some advance warning when he was going to be in town.

"Sorry for the short notice, Rupert," Barovsky said. "It was short notice for me too. I've got something I'd like to run by you, if you can fit me into your schedule."

"Actually, your timing is impeccable, Yvgeny. I have a pair of tickets for the Wizards- Mavericks game tonight. Susan just begged off. Would you like to join me? Also, it's a great place to visit away from prying eyes and ears. Lots of people and lots of yelling and screaming."

"Delightful. We don't have any NBA teams in Moscow—yet. I miss seeing those games when I was stationed here. Tell me where and when to meet you this evening."

In between hot dogs and fries at the arena, smothered with chili, cheese, and onions, Barovsky said, "Jake Klein. He's American. Ever run across him?"

Austin spilled some chili in the cardboard box and wiped his mouth. "Don't think so. Do I want to?"

"Yes," Barovsky answered.

Halftime was over. They returned to their seats. The Wizards won the game by one point on a shot at the buzzer. Austin barely noticed.

* * *

JAKE REALIZED THAT IF he could use the Mossad software on his laptop to hack into Molloy's Wi-Fi network and any other device passwords from out here in his car, he might be able to copy the contents of Molloy's computer without having to first get inside his house. If so, the only reason to break into Molloy's home in the next day or two—if he could find a time when Molloy would be out of the house—would be to plant the backdoor on Molloy's computer for future long distance . . . visits.

He scrunched down in his car so hopefully none of the residents would see him from their homes. If his luck held, no one out walking their dog would spot him and become curious, or alert the authorities.

His luck seemed to hold. One teenager walked by with her dog, but she was wearing ear buds and looking at her smartphone. She seemed oblivious to her surroundings. *Kids are the same in Canada, or at least here in Montreal, as back at home.* The next hour proved very efficient and productive for Jake.

Molloy's home had a sophisticated security system connected to his home Wi-Fi network. Foolishly, in Jake's opinion, the security system had an online operator's manual. *Might as well say here's everything you need to know to get around me.* Jake was able to quickly peruse the Read Me First file to see how the system worked, including how to activate, deactivate, and reactivate the system.

The security system included surveillance cameras throughout the house and all around the grounds. So long as the security system was on, each camera was activated whenever there was any motion in the corresponding zone. The resulting surveillance tapes were saved on the system until deleted.

It also included an alarm feature. If armed, opening any of the home's windows or doors would trigger the alarm, no doubt setting off some kind of loud siren. And also alerting Molloy's security service, and the local police as well. The alarm also had a motion detection component.

As Jake had anticipated, the property also included a backup generator. If there was a power outage that lasted more than sixty minutes, the generator automatically came on and provided power to the entire home, including reactivating the security system. Jake did not see any way to disconnect the backup generator. This meant he could allow himself no more than fifty minutes to break into the house, install the backdoor entrance on Molloy's computer, and get the hell out.

Using the Mossad software, Jake next hacked into Molloy's main computer. Given that he was just across the street, he was able to decrypt the computer password in short order, and copy and download the contents of Molloy's computer to his own dark web laptop in just around fifteen minutes. He would wait to see what kind of a score he had made until he was back at his hotel. Right now, it was time to depart the charming Molloy neighborhood for the evening.

* * *

BAKER, JR. ANSWERED HIS private line. "Kind of late for a social call, isn't it?"

"I was thinking of hitting a bucket of balls in the morning," the voice said. "Say, around seven o'clock. Care to join me?"

"Sounds good to me," Baker, Jr. said. "See ya there."

* * *

JAKE WAS BACK AT the hotel in slightly less time than it had taken him to drive to Molloy's home. He opened his laptop, and started examining what he had copied from Molloy's computer.

A lot of the material he had lifted from Molloy's laptop was interesting, but two things were of immediate benefit. One, he had Molloy's digital calendar. He had a two-hour dinner meeting scheduled tomorrow evening with a new investment banker at the Downtown Dinner Club. He assumed that "Downtown" meant downtown Montreal, which the maps on his laptop confirmed. *That should give me more than enough time to get in and out of Molloy's home.*

Two, and he couldn't believe his eyes, and although the file was obscurely titled, it looked like Molloy had an extra copy of his voting manipulation software on his own computer. *Son of a bitch doesn't trust Cipher! Or Turgenev. He maintains an extra copy!* The contents of the file were password protected, and no doubt coded, but he would ultimately be able to get past that and reverse engineer the software.

I'll do it when I get back home. Don't have the equipment I will need here. Productive day. Adrenaline worn off. Tired. Time to get some sleep.

CHAPTER 60
March 4, 2020, One Day Later

BAKER, JR. WAS ALREADY hitting balls when Austin arrived. Austin grabbed a wedge from his golf bag, looped it behind his back, and held it in place in the palms of each hand. He slowly rotated left and right, stretching both his shoulders and his hips. He emitted a sound like something between deep breaths and a series of groans. He then bent forward at the hips and bobbed slightly, as if his head might come close to his toes. "I swear, I get stiffer every day," he said to Baker, Jr.

"Tell me about it," Baker, Jr. answered, striking another ball.

Austin took the iron and hit a few soft wedge shots. "I can feel the rhythm—in my head. I just can't produce it," he said, to no one in particular.

Baker, Jr. smiled, but only to himself. He didn't stop his own hitting to watch Austin struggle. "Another request from the Russian Embassy for a good dental hygienist?" Baker, Jr. asked without turning to Austin.

"Haha," Austin said. He hit a few more balls, and then told Baker, Jr. about his dinner date the night before with Barovsky. And what Turgenev was suggesting.

Austin now had Baker, Jr.'s attention. He stopped hitting, turned to face Austin, and leaned on his club. "You're shitting me, right?" he said.

"Nope. It's what he proposed," Austin answered.

"Okay, then," Baker, Jr. replied. "I'll pass it on to POTUS and get back to you."

Each man struck a few more balls. It was evident that Baker, Jr. spent more time on his golf game than Austin did.

* * *

Jake was dressed in a black hoodie sweatsuit—he looked like a Ninja warrior. *Unfortunately, I don't function like one.* He parked where he had the night before, and hoped his luck would continue to hold up. He donned his gloves and double checked that the Mossad thumb drive, the glass cutter, the roll of masking tape, the small canister, and the tube of crazy glue were all in the money belt around his waist, and that the pouch was zipped closed.

He started the stopwatch on his smartphone and watched the tenths of seconds speed by. He had fifty minutes tops to disarm the security system, break into the house, find Molloy's computer, allow the thirty seconds necessary to install the backdoor on the computer, retrieve the thumb drive, get the hell out of the house, glue the glass back in place where he broke in, re-arm the security system, and get the hell away.

* * *

Potus and Baker, Jr., took a walk around the White House grounds. They were accompanied by two secret service agents, but they were out of earshot.

Baker, Jr. told his Dad what Turgenev had in mind.

"I have a slightly better idea." POTUS mapped it out to his son. "Pass it on to Austin, and get him cracking on it. You know this is actually very cool. I never cease to amaze myself."

* * *

Jake used his laptop to disarm Molloy's security system. He looked at his stop watch.

07:02.32

Already used up seven minutes. Damn! As best he could, Jake looked in all directions out of the windows of his car—the coast seemed clear. He jumped out of the car and locked the door with his key fob to secure his laptop, which he was not taking with him. He hooked the key fob on his money belt. *Can't afford a single mistake.*

He sprinted across the street and up the steps toward the front door of Molloy's home. He stepped around to the large window on the side of the house, out of sight from the street. If he had successfully deactivated the security system, then his footsteps wouldn't set off anything.

10:07.05

No blaring sirens, but look at the damn stop watch. Already ten minutes gone. He found the roll of masking tape and tore off four strips, each about four to five inches in length and applied them to the window in the shape of a square just below the inside window latch. He tore off four more two-inch strips and applied them in two pairs to the strips already attached to the window, so as to create a pair of handles.

He put the roll of masking tape back in the money belt. He removed the glass cutter and traced out a square on the window, just outside the four square strips of tape now firmly stuck to the window. He held two of the tape handles in one hand and tapped on the glass inside the traced lines with the large knuckle of the index finger of his other hand, held his breath, and gently pulled on two of the tape handles near one another.

The square piece of glass dropped out of the window. *Just like Google described it, and I had practiced it.* As the glass square dropped free of the window, Jake caught it and set it down on the ground a foot or so away from his feet. *I sure don't want to step on it!* He returned the glass cutter to his money belt pouch and zipped it closed.

17:02.17

Shit! Look at the time. I'm not gonna make it! He cupped his hand, palm up, reached hurriedly through the open window, turned the latch, and opened it. He climbed into the dining room, stood up, and momentarily stretched his back.

19:08.09

He turned around to get his bearings, unzipped the money belt purse, and removed the small spray canister. He tiptoed out of the dining room into the hallway. He had to find Molloy's computer. He made a lucky guess it would be in a ground floor office opposite the dining room. *I sure hope Molloy's off at his meeting, like his calendar said.* He inched forward from the hallway to the foyer.

22:48.31

He saw what looked like an office opposite the foyer. There was a chair and a glass table in the center of the room. He saw the computer sitting on the table, and moved gingerly toward it.

26:27.04.

And then he heard the high-pitched cry. His luck had run out. He raised the canister and spun around, hoping the mace would do the job.

* * *

BAKER, JR. CALLED AUSTIN. "Tit for tat." Sorry to now be calling you so late. It took me a while to get Dad's attention."

"No worries," Austin replied.

"Another bucket of balls in the morning, same time, same place?" Baker, Jr. asked.

"See you there," Austin answered. "You know, if we keep this up, our handicaps are going to drop. We won't win any more tournaments."

* * *

JAKE STARED STRAIGHT INTO his eyes. The stare was returned with equal animosity and trepidation—both parties were frozen still. The other eyes blinked first. Suddenly, the cat turned and bolted out of the office, and down the hallway toward the rear of the house at lightning speed. Jake took several deep breaths to settle himself. He wiped the sweat from his forehead with the back of his hand.

28:07.24

Hurry! Jake sat down in the chair facing the computer. He set the canister on the glass table next to the computer. He opened the money belt and quickly inserted the thumb drive in one of the USB ports on Molloy's computer. He counted down the thirty seconds, which seemed to take forever. He pulled out the thumb drive and returned it to his money belt.

29:32.09

Mission accomplished. Time to get the hell outta here. He stood and raced out of the office toward the dining room window through which he had entered. He came to a screeching halt. *Shit.* He turned and flew back to the office. *Goddamn canister!* He grabbed it off the table and ran back to the dining room window.

32:45.17

He climbed out the window and set the canister down next to the glass square. He took the crazy glue out of his money belt and applied it to the edges of the glass square. He waved the glass square back and forth for a minute in the night air and let the glue dry a bit. *This stuff sets fast. More of it on my gloves than the glass.*

Holding the glass square by the masking tape handles, Jake inserted the square back into the window. He waited another minute for the glue to take hold and meld, and then another minute for good measure, and gently peeled the used tape off and returned it to his waist belt. The glass square held perfectly.

He could hardly see the cut lines, but the glass was a bit smudgy where the tape had been. He became creative and swooshed a little of the contents of the aerosol canister on the window and gently rubbed it out with the one finger of his glove that didn't have any crazy glue residue on it. He returned the small canister to his money belt and zipped it closed.

38.22.49

He walked carefully to the front of the house and looked up and down the street and at the houses on the other side of the street. No one in sight. He moved swiftly across the street to his car, and used the key fob clipped to his money belt to unlock the car door. He removed his gloves and tossed them on the front seat next to his laptop. He was about to get in when he noticed someone looking at him.

40:45.19

Son of a bitch! It was the same girl he had seen the night before, walking the same dog, holding the same smartphone and wearing the same ear buds. "Hi, I'm Jamie," the girl said. "We're your new neighbors, we live a few doors down the block. My parents and I, and our dog, Geoffrey, just moved in last week. Geoffrey's named after our goldfish. He died. We flushed him. Your sweats are sick, by the way. What's your name?"

Stop talking! Jake was flummoxed. He wondered what to say his name was. *Gradsky? Molloy? What would my nemesis say if Yakety Yak was talking to him? Ah, fuck it.* "Molloy. Cailin Molloy. You can call me Cail. Everyone else does. Gotta run. Stop by anytime, Jaime." He climbed in the car and watched Jaime and Geoffrey continue their walk.

45:23.27

He reached over and opened his laptop. He re-armed Molloy's security system, closed the laptop, and drove off. *Nothing to it. Plenty of time to spare, even with the Jaime factor.*

49:32.16

CHAPTER 61
March 6, 2020, Two Days Later

JAKE WAS BACK HOME in his campus apartment. He had preliminarily revisited Molloy's coded copy of his election manipulation software. The coding Molloy had employed was like none other than Jake had ever seen before. He could see that cracking the Molloy code was going to take a considerable amount of time and effort. With the help of his decoding software, he was confident he would get there, but when remained to be seen.

His mind drifted to Molloy, the man. *What a strange fellow. I wonder if he knows yet that someone has broken into his home. Has he discovered the time lag in the security system? Would he write that off as just an aberrational power failure? He could eliminate that possibility by speaking out to the local power company, which presumably would advise him that there had been no power failures of late. Is my glass patch of his dining room window holding up okay? If not, would he have spotted it yet? Even if it's still in place, might his housekeeper have spotted the patch in the course of their cleaning duties? And my friend Jaime, has she paid a visit to him? If he has discovered, or suspects, my break-in, what would he do about it, besides fret? Would he dare contact Turgenev?*

Between the technology challenges now confronting him, and decompressing on his return from Montreal, Jake had not noticed one collateral benefit: he hadn't time to think about the ladies in his life, Anya, Kelly or even Leah, and whatever they might be doing or thinking about him right now.

It occurred to him that there were a couple of men in his life he also hadn't thought about. Carter, and what more he might be after from Jake, and even that strange little man, Amir, who mysteriously showed up in the U.S. out of the blue, and then disappeared just as quickly.

CHAPTER 62
March 8, 2020, Two Days Later

TURGENEV REFLECTED ON HIS debriefing of Barovsky. *How dare that ingrate Baker reexamine* my *designs of how best to use Klein to our advantage? I get him elected president, and this is how he repays me? I've created a damn monster. Do I have to remind him what I hold over his head?*

Turgenev reviewed his two pertinent objectives:

First, reestablish Russia as a singular first tier world power—not the case since the Sputnik era. Its standing suffered, along with the subsequent collapse of the Soviet Union. He had to assure that Russia was once more recognized as the equal of—if not superior to—the U.S. and China.

Second, his personal reputation had to rise above the reputations of those at the helm of the U.S. and China. An essential ingredient to any country's perceived greatness was the greatness of its leaders.

Ironically, Baker, who fashioned himself the ultimate salesman, was inept when it came to selling himself outside of his core followers. The reputation of China's Li Wei was suffering because of China's increasing aggressiveness on the world stage. The pandemic spread of COVID-19 beyond China would also impair Li Wei's standing.

In most international circles, Turgenev was regarded as little more than a mean-spirited GRU spy. To rise above Baker and Li, Turgenev had to position himself as astute, impeccable, and most of all, stately. He had to rise above the common and ordinary.

If the media—without tangible evidence—loosely painted Turgenev as behind Baker's election, that actually added to his stature—so long as he plausibly denied any personal involvement. However, if he were caught red-handed controlling the outcome of the U.S. election, that would personally be catastrophic for him, and Russia.

Turgenev's strategy, therefore, was to let it be seen that someone other than him—anyone other than him—was advancing the election of Baker, his perceived U.S. choice, and supposed puppet. It could be another country. It could be an individual possessed of extraordinary know how—such as the loner, Jake Klein

The advantage to having Klein appear to be behind the manipulation of the election in Baker's favor was that it made Turgenev look crafty enough to get what he wanted without having to sully his own hands, or anyone associated with him.

But Baker was unwilling to appear—even tacitly—to be the beneficiary of any outside influence. He wanted the use of Molloy's software come election time, and he was all for having it appear to be at the hands of some treasonous American—Jake Klein—but he wanted to re-script Turgenev's strategy to instead make it out that Klein was actually trying to steer the election not in favor of Baker, but in favor of the Democratic nominee.

I have to hand it to the twit. He wants what I have to offer, but he doesn't want to pay to play my *way. Maybe Baker's not quite as dumb as I think he is. We'll just have to see whose will is greater, Baker's or mine.*

CHAPTER 63
March 11, 2020, Three Days Later

JAKE READ ANYA'S TEXT:

> MY DEAREST JAKE,
>
> I AM SENDING THIS TEXT TO YOU WHILE I'M WAITING TO BOARD MY FLIGHT HOME. MY MOTHER HAS SUFFERED A STROKE. MY FATHER NEEDS ME TO HELP TAKE CARE OF HER. I'LL TEXT YOU FURTHER WHEN I KNOW HOW LONG I'LL HAVE TO REMAIN AT HOME WITH MY FAMILY.
>
> I'M SO SORRY THAT WE COULDN'T SEE EACH OTHER IN PERSON BEFORE I HAVE TO LEAVE, BUT THERE'S NO TIME. I ONLY LEARNED ABOUT WHAT HAPPENED HOURS AGO.
>
> LOVE,
> ANYA.

Jake was in shock. He had no idea what or how to feel. He replied:

> MY HEART IS WITH YOU AND YOUR FAMILY. BE SAFE. UPDATE ME MORE WHEN YOU CAN. JK.

* * *

ANYA SENT STILL ONE more text, this one encrypted:

> I HAVE SENT KLEIN THE TEXT YOU PREPARED FOR ME TO SEND.
> I WILL NOW DO AS YOU HAVE INSTRUCTED.

CHAPTER 64
March 14, 2020, Three Days Later

JAKE WAS STEELED AWAY in his campus apartment. He had not heard anything further from Anya, and he was afraid that might not be a good sign. He was torn between sending her another text to display his concern, and not imposing on her at the moment. *Maybe I'll wait another few days, and then text her, if I still don't hear anything further from her.*

Progress on cracking Molloy's code was proving extremely difficult, but Anya's situation made it hard for him to concentrate. He had been at his desk, chipping away on Molloy's code, for several hours when he heard the knock at his door.

"It's not locked. C'mon in," he said. *Probably should start keeping it locked.* The door opened. Jake couldn't believe his eyes.

* * *

AUSTIN FILLED BAKER, JR. in on the two customary off record items on their agenda, in addition to the buckets of balls each was exhausting, sort of. "Turgenev is insistent that his anti-Klein campaign be carried out without modification, as he put it together. I side with your dad if he's prepared to take Turgenev on over this."

* * *

Jake looked at his long-lost friend. "Amir! I was wondering why you vanished like you did. Come in! What's going on? How are you?"

"Mr. JK, nice see you. Amir fine. You too?"

"Yes, I'm fine," Jake said, "but I want to hear about you."

"Little to say, Mr. JK. Didn't mean to disappear, but not want to be more burden on you. After you explain immigration here, went to take care myself."

"How did it turn out?"

"File application for asylum. Am legal now. Allowed to stay and work until application hearing." He showed his official asylum papers to Jake. "If approved, hope can stay in America permanently. Not want go back Kazakhstan. Danger for Amir there."

Jake really wasn't clear what Amir's problem was in Kazakhstan, but if he's allowed to stay here, and wants to, he thought that would be great. "Amir, where are you staying now, and what are you doing? Are you working?"

"Decide stay in New Haven. Nice town. Many people from different countries. Making some friends. And near where you are. All good. Buy used car. Working for Uber. Making enough for small apartment with other Uber driver. Hoping fix my English and maybe get job as campus guide at Yale."

"Wow. Seems like you're doing very well." Jake wondered how Amir had the money to buy a car.

"Like to have lunch, Mr. JK? My treat. I drive us to favorite coffee shop in my Uber car."

"Sounds good. Let me grab my jacket. But maybe we could go dutch treat."

"Not understand. Restaurant not Dutch food. Maybe another U.S. saying?"

Jake explained the meaning of dutch treat—where each party pays their own way—as they walked to Amir's car. He was surprised to see the car—a small four-door sedan—but only a couple years old and very clean. It drove very well. They had a nice lunch. Amir treated.

Amir dropped Jake back at his apartment. "Amir very busy now, working many hours and studying to become campus guide. Maybe we have dinner in one month. Go dutch treat."

* * *

BAKER TURNED RED IN the face. "Fuck him!" he shouted. "Both of them."

"Dad, ease up, I'm just delivering the mail, and you don't need to blow a gasket."

"I don't need any mail I don't want, and my gaskets are just fine. Time to let Turgenev know that when we're in America, we do it my way and not his. I may have to kiss his ass to get the okay to develop a hotel in Russia, but here, it's my way or the highway—for him. He can huff and puff, but there's not a damn thing he can do about it. He doesn't want the Democrats taking control and investigating the hell out of him. He has no choice but to quietly do everything he can to get me reelected. He figures, after another four years in partnership with me, he won't have to worry about the Democrats."

"I get it. I'll make sure he gets the word."

CHAPTER 65
March 16, 2020, Two Days Later

AUSTIN CALLED THE EBCOM meeting to order. Each member reported on his or her area of responsibility. Things generally seemed to be progressing as anticipated. "Unfortunately, I do have a bit of distressing news to report," Austin said. "This couldn't be more confidential, as will be obvious."

He then revealed to the members the early reports about the virus that was now starting to pop up around the country, and the fact that POTUS was *still* refusing to address it. "He is in denial. He seems to insist that he can ignore anything he doesn't want to hear and it'll go away. He's used to getting his way, as we all know, but he doesn't seem to understand that he can't intimidate this virus."

They went around the table. There were no dissenting opinions. Baker was going about this all wrong, but there was nothing they could do. They were stuck with him. He might not be great, but he was better than the Democratic Party that has totally been taken hostage by the progressive left wing of the party.

Austin adjourned the meeting after all views had been shared. *The die is cast.*

CHAPTER 66
March 18, 2020, Two Days Later

JAKE HAD FINALLY RECEIVED a text from Anya:

> SORRY NOT TO WRITE SOONER. THINGS HAVE BEEN DIFFICULT HERE. AT FIRST, WE WEREN'T SURE MOM WAS GOING TO MAKE IT. I WAS AFRAID TO WRITE WHEN THE NEWS SEEMED SO GRIM. BUT SHE IS NOW SHOWING SOME IMPROVEMENT. MY DAD CAN'T BEAR THE THOUGHT OF MY ABANDONING THEM NOW, AND SO I CAN'T. I HOPE THAT I WILL BE ABLE TO RETURN TO MY STUDIES AT HARVARD—AND TO YOU—IN ANOTHER COUPLE OF MONTHS. I MISS YOU. LOVE, ANYA
>
> P.S. HOW ARE THINGS COMING WITH YOUR STUDIES AND WORK?

He was pleased that she hadn't forgotten him, and that her mom was recovering. He sent her a short reply:

> SORRY, THINGS ARE SO DIFFICULT AND THAT I CAN'T HELP YOU, BUT HAPPY TO KNOW THAT YOUR MOM IS IMPROVING. STUDIES AND WORK HERE ARE FINE, SAME 'OL, SAME 'OL. MISS YOU TOO. WRITE WHEN YOU KNOW MORE. JK.

Jake was modestly intrigued by the fact that Anya had inquired about his work. Given that what he was doing was very anti-Russia, it seemed wise to him not to possibly put Anya on the hot seat, given her heritage and presumed loyalty. That was why he had decided to side step her inquiry.

At least he had simplified his love life during Anya's absence. He had finally forced himself to make a clean break with Kelly—she didn't seem to be surprised. She said that they would still be friends, just without benefits. He hoped she meant it—that they would still be friends.

Jake was also beginning to make some serious progress with decoding Molloy's software. It wasn't easy—Molloy was a tech beast—but Jake was gaining some traction. It was like trying to build one of those several thousand piece jigsaw puzzles. First, you have to find the four corners. Then, you have to find all of the pieces that have straight outsides that make the perimeter. Then, you just have to keep working from there, as best you can. As you work toward the center, it becomes tougher and slower.

He thought he might have a full handle on it in another couple of weeks. He was confident of his abilities, but he was beginning to be mindful of the clock.

He also had an exciting software thought, but that would have to wait until he had finished the decoding.

CHAPTER 67
March 24, 2020, Six Days Later

JAKE HAD JUST FINISHED one of Carter's classes. As they were walking out of the lecture hall, Carter told Jake they needed to meet, and they were now seated in Carter's office. The professor had made a point of closing the door, which he didn't usually do.

Jake sensed things weren't quite right. "Anything wrong, Professor?" Jake asked.

"Yes, but it certainly isn't your fault, no problems with either your classwork or the extracurricular work you put together for my manuscript."

Carter paused. Jake figured it was Carter's meeting, so he waited for him to continue.

"I should have known," Carter finally said. "With these damn publishers, it's always hurry up and wait. You bust your ass to get your manuscript finished, and then you have to sit and wait, and then wait some more. The publish or perish principle only makes this tedium all the more aggravating, although I can't blame that on my publisher."

He sure is taking his sweet time coming to the point. "What's on your mind, Professor?" Jake asked.

"My publisher was just acquired by one of the big five publishing houses. And wouldn't you know, they have some different ideas about my manuscript. They think it's too bland. They want me to rewrite it, make it more . . . progressive."

"I don't get it," Jake said. "I thought tech books are just that, techie, not political. What do they mean by progressive?"

"The new publishing house is very anti-Baker. They think the publishing industry will do better under the Democrats if Baker is defeated this November. They want to do whatever they can to help achieve that result. They've given me one month to edit my manuscript, and turn it into more of an intellectual piece. One that is very progressive, to boot. Leaving very little doubt as to who I think should win in November."

Jake's antenna was rising. So was his blood pressure. "And how does this have anything to do with me?" Jake asked.

"I'm gonna have a tough time turning this manuscript around in four weeks, but I have no choice. Our university here is even more progressive than my new publisher, with whom they side."

Jake sat opposite Carter, waiting for the other shoe to fall.

"I'm up for tenure in the coming school year. I need to read the tea leaves. As the saying goes, I have to publish . . . or perish. And what I publish has to ring progressive—ultra-progressive. If I don't appease the university, and the new publishing house, I could end up out on the street. I'm hoping you might be able to help me with the rewrite, redoing the chapter you wrote about KHC to make it more of an advocacy piece than the existing neutral tech report you originally submitted?"

"Wow. That's a tough ask, Professor. I'm not at all a political creature. My thing is computers, not politics."

"Yeah, I get it, Jake, but you need to get it too. Shit flows downhill."

He started out kinda using honey. Seems like he just pivoted to vinegar. "Let me give it some thought, Professor, and see if there's anything I might be able to do," Jake said. *Maybe I'm being more political than I realize because I know damn well I'm not gonna do what he's asking, and I'm not at all being candid or honest about that.*

CHAPTER 68
March 26, 2020, Two Days Later

TURGENEV SAW NO CHOICE but to concede. *I can't devote any more time to this bullshit. I've got bigger fish to fry, including this new pandemic business, which is taking a ton of my time—and is going to get a lot worse before it gets any better. Baker just doesn't give in. I have to let him win this round, agree to take Klein out by marrying him to those damn progressive American Democrats. I hope Baker knows what the fuck he's doing. I sure as hell don't want to spend the next four years fighting a number of goddamn progressives who certainly aren't my friends.*

I'm also amazed that Baker doesn't seem to be paying the least bit of attention to the pandemic. Not a word coming out of his administration as of yet. Boggles my mind.

CHAPTER 69
March 30, 2020, Four Days Later

JAKE CAME UP FOR air. He had finally managed to fully decode Molloy's software. He now understood exactly how it worked, and how it was going to be employed to help Baker gain reelection. *Time for me to see if I can now turn my conjecture that I can block Molloy's software into reality. It's gonna take me even longer than it did to decode Molloy's software because I have to design and write it from scratch. Not a lot of time until the election. Have to really haul ass.*

He also stopped by to see Carter and break the news to him. There was no way he was going to do what Carter wanted. He wasn't a politician, and he wasn't going to become one.

He expected a full on collision. If so, he was prepared to deal with it.

Carter surprised Jake and just reversed course: "Don't worry about it, JK. It was wrong of me to ask you what I did. The problem is mine, not yours. I'll deal with it."

CHAPTER 70
April 11, 2020, Twelve Days Later

AS A YOUNG ISRAELI, Abelson remembered when he was first recruited out of the Israeli army to join the Mossad. It was one of his proudest moments. The Mossad enjoyed a reputation as one of the most sophisticated intelligence agencies in the world. As far as he was concerned, no other country's intelligence agency held a candle to them, including the American CIA, or the Russian GRU. The Mossad earned its reputation because of its technology, its commitment, its discipline, and its worldwide networks of underground moles.

It wasn't often that Abelson was invited to participate in one of the daily intelligence briefings of Mossad's upper echelons held in Mossad headquarters in Tel Aviv—this was one of those rare occasions. In this instance, by scrambled telephone from his apartment at Southern Connecticut State University where he was on leave studying computer science. Abelson didn't know whether to be pleased or concerned.

"Thanks for joining us, Gali," said his handler. "We have a piece of intelligence we wanted to bring to your attention."

"That was a great way to get my attention," Abelson responded. "Anything I should be worried about?"

His handler ignored Abelson's question. "As you know, we are well aware of the not-so-secret Russian efforts to assure Baker's reelection in November. According to intelligence from a well-positioned mole in Moscow, there is some kind of joint campaign afoot between Turgenev and

Baker to attribute Russia's actions to a young Jewish American computer expert by the name of Jake Klein."

No shit! Abelson now knew why he was invited to this briefing. He figured it would be best to listen until he was asked to say something.

His handler continued. "Turgenev is reportedly worried that Klein is getting too close to what Turgenev and Baker have been orchestrating, and how they are going about it. Turgenev and Baker want to discredit Klein, and make him the source of the upcoming U.S. election manipulation so Baker can arrest Klein for treason and get him out of the way, making it appear that Klein is a progressive trying to assure that the Democrats will win the election."

Abelson continued to listen without remark.

"I reminded our colleagues that you and Klein are classmates and that you have cultivated a relationship with Klein. I also reminded everyone that, with our permission, you have loaned some of our technology to Klein in furtherance of his cybersecurity career objectives, and with the informal understanding that he would share with you—with us—anything he learns that might be of interest to us. Klein presumably does not appreciate the extent to which you are following his pursuits. Have I summarized that about correctly?"

"As you always manage to do, boss, yes you have," Abelson answered.

"Obviously, Israel cannot take sides in the U.S. elections, but we'd like to be in a position to prevent the future use of Turgenev's technology to manipulate elections in other countries—including Israeli elections. This was the reason we authorized you to help Klein. We now find ourselves in an awkward position, Gali."

"I think I get it," Abelson replied.

"On the one hand, we want—and almost feel a sense of duty—to protect Klein as much as we can, in light of the fact that we may potentially benefit from his efforts. On the other hand, if we come to Klein's rescue in any noticeable way, Turgenev will likely figure out where our information came from, and our Russian mole will be exposed, and no doubt captured, tortured, and terminated. Our asset must be our first priority."

"I understand," Abelson said. "First things first. It pains me, but blood is thicker than water. I trust that I can give Klein a heads-up?"

The answer of everyone in the room was unanimous: "Absolutely, just so long as Mossad—and Israel—do not otherwise tangibly surface or become involved in domestic American politics."

* * *

JAKE WAS WAITING FOR the other shoe to drop. Every day now, the news was riddled with stories about the COVID-19 pandemic. Jake was trying to follow it all, to stay informed and responsible, but he couldn't tell who to listen to, or what to believe. He figured Baker and the federal government would be taking the lead and offering reliable science-based data and advice. But all Baker seemed to do was to make light of it—buy some Clorox—before there was a run on it—gargle and rinse with it, and just wait for the virus to vanish. Which he said would happen as quickly as it had appeared.

The Democrats were making much more of the situation, and blaming Baker for being so cavalier. What should have been science was turning into politics. *What else could happen in this election year?*

He was waiting to see how SCSU would tackle the issue. He just finished reading their email missive, issued jointly by the University President, and the Director of the Campus Health Center:

MEMORANDUM

APRIL 11, 2020

FROM: OFFICES OF THE UNIVERSITY PRESIDENT AND THE CAMPUS HEALTH CENTER DIRECTOR

TO: ALL STUDENTS, FACULTY, OTHER UNIVERSITY EMPLOYEES, AND THEIR FAMILIES

BY NOW, YOU ARE ALL AWARE OF THE POTENTIAL COVID-19 PANDEMIC THAT IS FACING OUR COUNTRY, AND THE ENTIRE WORLD. WE WANT YOU ALL TO KNOW THAT WE ARE VERY CAREFULLY MONITORING THIS SITUATION, AND THAT YOUR HEALTH AND SAFETY IS OUR FOREMOST CONCERN. WE

WILL UPDATE THIS COMMUNICATION FROM TIME TO TIME AS APPROPRIATE. YOU SHOULD ALL SHARE THIS MEMORANDUM WITH YOUR FAMILY MEMBERS FOR THEIR PEACE OF MIND.

FOR NOW, WE ARE CONTINUING ON-CAMPUS CLASSES, BUT ALL STUDENTS SHOULD USE THEIR BEST EFFORTS TO DISTANCE THEMSELVES FROM ONE ANOTHER. WE ARE LOOKING INTO THE POSSIBILITY THAT WE WILL SOON NEED TO SUSPEND IN-PERSON CLASSES AND REPLACE THEM WITH ONLINE VIRTUAL CLASSES. WE REPEAT: CLASSES ARE STILL OPEN, BUT STUDENTS SHOULD EXERCISE COMMON SENSE AND GOOD JUDGMENT.

IF YOU EXPERIENCE ANY SYMPTOMS SUCH AS: FEVER, EXTREME FATIGUE, WEAKNESS, DIFFICULTY BREATHING, OR LOSS OF SMELL OR TASTE, YOU SHOULD IMMEDIATELY REPORT TO THE CAMPUS HEALTH CENTER. OUR STAFF ARE TRAINED TO ASSIST YOU. IF YOU NEED HELP GETTING TO THE CAMPUS HEALTH CENTER, PLEASE CONTACT THE TELEPHONE OPERATOR BY PICKING UP ANY CAMPUS TELEPHONE AND DIALING ZERO (0).

FOR THE TIME BEING, ACCESS TO THE CAMPUS WILL BE CONFINED TO STUDENTS, FACULTY, AND OTHER UNIVERSITY EMPLOYEES. GUESTS WILL NOT BE PERMITTED. YOU WILL NEED TO PRODUCE YOUR UNIVERSITY IDENTIFICATION IN ORDER TO BE ADMITTED TO THE CAMPUS.

FOR THOSE OF YOU WHO RESIDE IN CAMPUS HOUSING, SUCH HOUSING WILL REMAIN OPEN AND CAMPUS FOOD SERVICES WILL CONTINUE.

PLEASE KEEP CALM, EXERCISE GOOD SENSE AND COMMON JUDGMENT, BE WELL, AND STAY SAFE.

Jake read the memo a second time. He figured the smartest thing for him to do was to remain in his campus apartment where he was close to any medical attention he might require. Hopefully, that would not prove necessary.

Jake attached a copy of the memorandum to a text he sent Leah saying he would be remaining put in his campus apartment for the time being.

She called him immediately. "Are you sure you wouldn't be safer here with us?" she said.

"No," he answered. "I don't want to skip my classes as long as they are still being conducted. I'll be fine. I'll call if anything changes. Take care of the family."

"I will," Leah said. "Please let me know if anything changes. If there's any doubt, please come home."

He knew Leah. If he didn't end the call, she'd just keep talking, in spite of the fact that there was nothing more to add. He ended the call.

CHAPTER 71
April 14, 2020, Three Days Later

FRANKLIN KELSEY WAS ONE of the country's wealthiest arch conservatives. He supported any number of right-wing causes and organizations, both directly and as the founder of the companion *Red Crier Magazine* and *Red Crier Online*. He was one of President Baker's five largest donors. Without any byline, the following identical "news" bulletin copy appeared in the April 14, 2020, weekly and daily issues of *Red Crier Magazine* and *Red Crier Online*:

> IN AN EXCLUSIVE FROM AN ANONYMOUS SOURCE NOT AUTHO-
> RIZED TO SPEAK BECAUSE OF THE SENSITIVITY OF THE MATTER,
> IT WAS CONFIRMED TO RED CRIER TODAY THAT JAKE KLEIN,
> AN ACCOMPLISHED COMPUTER SCIENCES MAJOR AT SOUTH-
> ERN CONNECTICUT STATE UNIVERSITY, HAS REPORTEDLY DE-
> VELOPED SOPHISTICATED SOFTWARE TECHNOLOGY THAT HE
> PLANS TO USE TO ALTER THE UPCOMING NOVEMBER ELECTION
> RESULTS IN FAVOR OF SEVERAL DEMOCRATIC CANDIDATES,
> INCLUDING LOGAN SULLIVAN, EXPECTED TO SOON LOCK UP
> ENOUGH PRIMARY DELEGATES TO BECOME THE DEMOCRATIC
> NOMINEE FOR PRESIDENT. ONE OF KLEIN'S PROFESSORS AT
> SCSU, MATTHEW CARTER, WHO HAS CLOSELY MENTORED
> KLEIN AND IS KNOWN TO BE A LEADING PROGRESSIVE MEMBER

OF SCSU, TOLD RED CRIER THAT KLEIN, WHOSE COMMAND
OF COMPUTER TECHNOLOGY IS UNPARALLELED, IS SOMEWHAT
OF A LONER, BUT HAS SHARED WITH CARTER HIS STRONG
OPPOSITION TO THE REELECTION OF PRESIDENT BAKER. "IT
NEVER OCCURRED TO ME THAT HE WOULD DO ANYTHING LIKE
THIS," CARTER SAID. THE OFFICE OF STUDENT AFFAIRS AT
THE UNIVERSITY SAID THAT THE PRIVACY RIGHTS OF ITS STU-
DENTS PRECLUDE IT FROM COMMENTING ON A STORY LIKE
THIS. KLEIN HIMSELF HAS REFUSED TO COMMENT.

The wire services declined to carry the unsubstantiated news bulletin. However, the story was trending on Twitter and Facebook, and comments were running two to one against Klein. Some of the comments against him were quite inflammatory, but were not removed by either of the social media platforms. Facebook explained that in the absence of clear and immediate threats of bodily injury, the right of free speech of all members must be respected.

When asked about the story in his press conference this afternoon, President Baker said, and shortly thereafter repeated on his Twitter account, "I know all about this guy. It'll take a lot more than Jerky Jake to stop me from being reelected, but that doesn't lessen the seriousness of his treacherous and treasonous conduct. Nothing is more important than the right of our citizens to know that the elections of our public officials are carried out with integrity and without fraudulent and undue influence."

* * *

AUSTIN'S SECRETARY HANDED HIM copies of the *Red Crier* "news" bulletin and the resulting social media posts and comments. He read it all and smiled. "Make sure copies are sent to all members of EBCOM."

Austin promptly put in a call to Louis Tenenbaum, Director of the FBI. "Did you see the *Red Crier* news bulletin published today?" he asked the director.

"A copy of it was brought to me. I just finished reading it. I was about to task a couple of our special agents to pay a visit to this radical fellow, Jake Klein. These progressives are just getting worse and worse."

"That's why I'm calling, to let you know that POTUS would like you to just let it be, to let you know that he's got it handled."

"Really? Isn't that a bit out of his field?"

"Really," Austin said.

"Okay, Rupert, if you say so, the FBI will stand down, but it'll be on POTUS to explain why if we're asked how we came to look the other way about this."

"Thanks, Lou."

* * *

TURGENEV ALSO READ THE *Red Crier* bulletin and social media posts. *Maybe Baker had the right idea after all.*

* * *

CARTER MORE OR LESS knew how the bulletin would read. He fully anticipated the onslaught that Klein would soon bring down on him. He was ready.

* * *

GRADSKY SHARED AN ENCRYPTED call with Cipher within minutes after the *Red Crier* bulletin went public.

"Did you see the social media coverage too?" Cipher asked. "I guess Turgenev knew how best to handle this after all. Our software is now covered and good to go."

Gradsky focused on Cipher's characterization of Gradsky's software. *Our? Since when is* my *software* our *software?*

* * *

ANYA RECEIVED A SCRAMBLED call, informing her about the *Red Crier* bulletin and related social media posts and comments. She was instructed how to respond when Klein reached out to her.

"When?" she asked. "Don't you mean 'if?' Do you expect him to reach out to me about this here where I *supposedly* am? In Russia?"

"Just be prepared."

* * *

JAKE ANSWERED THE KNOCK on his campus apartment door. He looked at a very somber Abelson. "Gali, I don't recall ever seeing you look so serious,"

Jake said. "I also don't recall you ever showing up at my door unannounced like this. What's up? Where's your usually cheery self?"

Gali handed the *Red Crier* and social media printouts to Jake. "I take it you haven't seen any of this yet," he said.

Jake looked at the papers. He couldn't believe his eyes. He couldn't breathe. He wasn't sure what to do. He sat down and looked at Abelson. "Are you able to explain this to me?" he asked. "I trust that's why you're here."

Abelson gave Jake the background. Most of it. He didn't tell Jake the part about Mossad knowing more about what Jake had accomplished than Jake realized. "Look, JK, I'm really sorry about this. Mossad would like nothing more than to jump into this fray with you, but we can't. We just can't. We have an asset to protect in Russia. And we are also prohibited from taking sides in U.S. politics."

Jake seemed to recover. Maybe. It might have been bravado. Or an adrenaline burst that had not yet been overtaken by panic. "I get it, Gali. I'm on my own."

"Look, I understand," Abelson said. "Obviously, you have to take this seriously and you have to figure out how you're going to deal with this. While Mossad cannot come out of the shadows, I want you to know it will be whatever kind of quiet resource it can. You're not alone, even though it may feel like you are. I've been your point of contact to date, and I will continue to be your point of contact."

Jake was breathing again—a little. "Trust me. I'm not about to roll over. My biggest worry is how I'm going to explain this to my family, especially my sister. And how I'm going to protect them from all of this."

"Maybe you'll get lucky. Maybe they won't see this shit and maybe you won't have to explain it. If your sister doesn't raise it to you, I wouldn't raise it to her, if I were you. If she does raise it, and asks you why you didn't come to her, just play her macho brother, tell her it was just a bad joke, that you'll handle it, that it'll go away. Tell her to stay out of it. That otherwise, she'll only make it worse."

"Good advice, I guess. All right. I need some alone time to process this. I also have a girlfriend, but she's at home in Russia helping her father nurse her sick mother. So maybe she won't see this, and I won't have to talk to her about it either.

"A Russian girlfriend?" Abelson asked. "Have I seen her before?"

"No. She's new on the scene, but we've become pretty close." Jake gave Abelson the G-rated short version.

"Hey, I don't want to be paranoid and I don't want to make you paranoid, but Russia seems to be all over your life. I would be lying if I didn't tell you this girlfriend—what's her name?—makes me more than a little nervous."

Jake hesitated, but he did give Anya's name to Abelson.

"All right then, bud, I'm outta here, but I won't be far away. You know how to reach me, 24/7."

Jake closed his apartment door. *Well, at least he still called me bud.*

CHAPTER 72
April 15, 2020, One Day Later

JAKE BURST THROUGH CARTER'S unlocked office door without knocking, and squarely faced off a startled Carter. He grabbed Carter by his shoulders, yanked him out of his desk chair and shoved him up against the rear wall of his office. "What the hell did you do to me! And why?" It was a good thing I gave it the night and counted to ten before coming over here. What would I have done to him yesterday!

"Hey, man, calm down, back the fuck off. I didn't have any more to do with this than you did."

"Like hell you didn't. I suggest we go through this so-called 'news' bulletin, line by line, while I'm still reasonably open to what you have to say. You'd better make sense—a lot of sense. And fast." Jake pulled out a copy of the news bulletin from his jacket and slammed it down on Carter's desk. "I'm listening."

"Am I allowed to sit?" Carter asked.

"Quit being a wise ass and get to it."

"Okay, first of all, I'm not the source mentioned in the bulletin, and I have no idea who is. Nor, smart guy, do I know anything about any software you've supposedly developed. All you ever said to me is that you learned about election software developed by others. Why would I attribute it to you?"

"And the rest of it?" Jake asked.

"They did contact me and ask about you. All I said was you're extremely savvy. And that I couldn't believe you'd do what they said you were planning to do."

"What about you quoting me as being against Baker?"

"I didn't say anything like that," Carter said.

"Well, they say you did," Jake responded.

"Let me ask you something," Carter said. "They say you refused to comment. Is that true?"

"Of course not," Jake responded. "They never contacted me."

"My guess was they hadn't," Carter said. "And that was a lie. A lie you know about. If you know about that lie, does it not occur to you that they may have lied about quoting me saying you're against Baker being reelected?"

That slowed Jake down considerably. He didn't know what to believe right now, but he still had the feeling that Carter had used him to his own undisclosed benefit. To Jake's detriment. "I'm not finished with you, Professor," he said, but he closed Carter's office door with less force than he'd used to open it.

* * *

It DIDN'T TAKE JAKE very long to realize the notion that Leah might somehow miss his sudden infamy was wishful thinking. With the events of the past few hours, he had overlooked his smartphone, usually glued to his hip, if not in his hand. When he returned to his apartment, he reached for the phone on automatic pilot. He thought about turning it off and closeting it away somewhere out of sight. *Who am I kidding?* He spotted all of the texts and voicemail messages, almost all of them from Leah.

He called her back. How could he not? He would follow Abelson's advice—and his own instincts—and hold her at bay. In spite of everything that was going on, he couldn't help but smile—sort of—when he thought back about how the call had gone.

No, I'm fine. No, I had no idea this was coming. No, there's no truth to it whatsoever. Are you kidding, asking me that? No, I have no idea who did this, or why. No, you will not get involved. I'm a big boy. I'll take care of it myself. This is just some kind of prank, some kind of a sick joke. If I don't feed it, it'll blow over in a few days. The last thing I am is newsworthy. Don't you do anything to make me newsworthy!

Reluctantly, Leah promised him she would leave it be. That didn't mean that Jake would. With Leah hopefully under control, Jake sat down and tried to organize his thoughts, decide what to do next.

It was useless. His mind was a jumble. His head was splitting. He took a shower, three extra strength Tylenol, and went to sleep. It was ten hours until he came to.

CHAPTER 73
April 16, 2020, One Day Later

BIANCHI HAD NEVER HEARD of this Jake Klein character. At least not that she could recall. She had just finished meeting with Simon Lefevre, the chair of the DNC. Klein's name did not appear anywhere in their database or computer system. He was a non-entity, as far as the DNC could tell. Lefevre had assured her that he would promptly put out an appropriate release. He had. Bianchi read it:

DEMOCRATIC NATIONAL COMMITTEE HEADQUARTERS
APRIL 16, 2020 FOR IMMEDIATE RELEASE

THE DEMOCRATIC NATIONAL COMMITTEE DISAVOWS ANY
SUGGESTION THAT ANY INDIVIDUAL BY THE NAME OF JAKE KLEIN
HAS, OR EVER HAS HAD, ANY DEALINGS OR RELATIONSHIP WITH
THE DEMOCRATIC PARTY. AT NO TIME HAS THE DEMOCRATIC
PARTY ENGAGED IN ANY COMPUTER MISBEHAVIOR TO CONTROL
THE OUTCOME OF THE PENDING ELECTIONS. NOT WITH MR.
KLEIN, NOR ANYONE ELSE. THE DEMOCRATIC PARTY WILL BEAT
PRESIDENT BAKER FAIR AND SQUARE THIS COMING NOVEMBER.

THE NEWS BULLETIN RELEASED EARLIER THIS WEEK BY *RED
CRIER* IS WHOLLY UNSUBSTANTIATED AND PURE FABRICATION,

SOMETHING THAT OUR OPPONENT WOULD LABEL "FAKE NEWS." WE NOTE THAT RED CRIER IS A CONSERVATIVE PUBLICATION FOUNDED BY FRANKLIN KELSEY WHO IS ONE OF PRESIDENT BAKER'S LARGEST DONORS.

THE DNC HAS NO IDEA WHO MR. KLEIN IS, BUT SUSPECTS THAT HE IS A CO-CONSPIRATOR IN THIS INSIDIOUS SCHEME, OR IS ANOTHER ONE OF ITS INNOCENT VICTIMS. THE DNC NEITHER HAS, NOR HEREAFTER WILL, ENGAGE IN ANY COMMUNICATION OR DEALINGS WITH MR. KLEIN, OR ANYONE CLAIMING TO BE MR. KLEIN, OR TO BE ACTING ON HIS BEHALF.

* * *

BAKER READ THE DNC press release and laughed. "Perfect. The more attention they give this, the more traction it will gain."

* * *

JAKE'S MIND WAS STILL whirling. Turgenev. Molloy. Gradsky. Nilsen. Cipher. Now he had more to add. Carter. Baker. And Baker's supporters. The list was endless. And growing. The DNC. Abelson. Anya. *Are they all my enemies? Is there anyone I can trust?*

He thought about Anya. He wanted to reach out to her. Find out if she was friend or foe. But how could he bring himself to confront her? Especially if she was what she seemed to be, and was home dealing with her parents. What if Anya was not back in Russia with her family? What if she was here, spying on him? *Geez, I remember when I was starstruck and afraid to approach her because she might not be interested. Now, I'm afraid to approach her because of why she might be interested.*

He decided to reach out to the only ones he knew for sure he could trust. His computer. And himself. And to ignore all of the other noise for as long as he could.

CHAPTER 74
April 23, 2020, One Week Later

AUSTIN CHAIRED THE EMERGENCY meeting of EBCOM. The discussion focused on POTUS's reaction to the pandemic, the stock market's reaction to the pandemic, the economy's reaction to the pandemic, and how EBCOM should react to the pandemic.

The consensus was that POTUS's and the stock market's reaction to the pandemic were much the same—irrational—and the economy and POTUS's position in the polls were much the same—dropping, sort of. As for EBCOM's position, the consensus was Katy bar the door, full speed ahead, and man the torpedoes.

As one of the members put it, less than eloquently, "What choice do we have? There ain't no such thing as being a little pregnant."

* * *

JAKE WONDERED IF A computer could have writer's block. Actually, he remembered when one of his favorite high school teachers brought a guest panel into his English class one day. The subject was "blocking"—what it meant to suffer a block, who all could suffer one, and how did you get past it.

The panel consisted of two bestselling authors and two computer programmers from IBM. Each of the authors acknowledged that all authors suffered from writer's block at one time or another in their careers, often more than once. Jake's class seemed to buy into that because writer's block was a well-known phenomenon. Jake recalled experiencing writer's block himself when he had to write a short story for an English class.

Less well received, the programmers professed that the same was true for them. The fact that a programmer knew what he was out to accomplish didn't necessarily mean he knew how to do it, or that it would be easy. Programmers often suffered what they referred to as programmer's block. They knew what they wanted to do, to get from Point A to Point Z, but it didn't mean that it just fell into place because they wanted it to.

They all agreed on the solution: don't panic, be patient, change the subject, think about something else, and wait for it to come. Relief. It always did. For most.

Jake was trying to apply the advice he had heard that day. He now understood Molloy's software, backward and forward. His interest was more in the backward than the forward. He was working on it, but so far, it just wasn't happening.

He wasn't panicked. Yet. He was trying to be patient. But his patience was starting to run short. The problem was that time was also starting to run short.

He needed to change the subject. Wait for it—the code he was trying to write.

He tried to think about different things—Anya came to mind. He thought maybe he should send her a text. But then he remembered what Abelson had said. He pushed Anya to the back of his mind. The next move had to be hers.

CHAPTER 75
May 7, 2020, Two Weeks Later

MOLLOY WAS RESTLESS. SOMETHING had been bothering him since he had first discovered it—the one-hour gap in his security system surveillance tapes. It had never happened before.

And one hour later, just as it was preset, his backup generator test kicked in and reactivated the computerized security system. The only problem was that when he checked with the local utility authorities, there had been no power outages on the date and at the time his computerized system had shut down.

Sometimes, things just happen without any rhyme or reason. *Not so. There's always an explanation, even if you can't figure out what it is.*

Until she knocked on his door.

"Hello," she said. "Is Mr. Molloy here?"

"Who are you?" Molloy asked. "And why do you want to know?"

"My name is Jaime. My family and I, and our dog, Geoffrey, moved in down the street a few months ago. One night, when I was walking Geoffrey, I met Mr. Molloy out in front of his house here. He was very nice. I just wanted to stop by and say hello to him."

"You don't say," Molloy said.

"No. I do say. I just did say. That's exactly how it happened, but it wasn't any biggie. I just thought I'd say hello."

"What I mean is that there must have been some misunderstanding. *I'm* Mr. Molloy. You must have met my housekeeper and misunderstood."

"No kidding," Jaime said. "Well, he still was very nice. Could I say hello to him, please?"

"Oh, he doesn't work for me anymore. He moved back home to Vancouver. I don't expect to hear from him any further, but if I do, I'll be sure to tell him you came by and said hello."

"Cool. Thanks."

"Have a nice day," Molloy said and closed the door.

One hour later, after a meticulous inspection, Molloy found the tiny seam in his dining room window. He called a local glass company and arranged to have the window replaced.

*　*　*

JAKE COULDN'T BELIEVE IT. It happened just like he had heard back in high school. How people got past blocks. He hadn't been thinking about it at all. It just popped into his mind. Out of the blue.

CHAPTER 76
May 14, 2020, One Week Later

TURGENEV WAS LOSING HIS patience. All he wanted was to assure Baker's reelection. He assembled a team of experts to make it happen. He paid their fees, and that was it. He didn't need—or want—to keep hearing from them. Yet, here they were, again. Gradsky and his weird middleman, Cipher.

Worse still, the reason for their call was to alert him that Jake Klein had apparently broken into Gradsky's home in Montreal. And, undoubtedly, Gradsky's personal computer. Enough was enough.

Back in November, when Klein was first brought to his attention, his initial thinking was to arrange for this nuisance Klein to be terminated. As his thinking ultimately developed, months later, he decided on a slightly different course of action. Instead of having Klein killed, he'd orchestrate a campaign to make him out to be the one who was going to rig the election. He would in essence *kill* two birds with one stone—stop Klein's continuing interference, and deflect attention away from Russia as the true source of the election fraud.

He and Baker quarreled about the details, but the fake news campaign seemed to have worked very nicely. However, in order to make the deflection work, he had to recall Anya Lebedev back to Russia. If Klein were to draw attention away from Russia, it wouldn't do for him to have a girlfriend who was a Russian foreign exchange student. It meant he'd no longer have Lebedev to spy on Klein, but that was a small price to pay.

Nevertheless, Klein continued to be a nuisance. He had fulfilled his deflection purpose. While Turgenev was forced to tolerate—indeed preserve—the well-being of Gradsky and Cipher, the same was not the case with Klein. It was now time for him to address Mr. Klein in a more permanent manner, whether Baker liked it or not.

CHAPTER 77
May 21, 2020, One Week Later

JAKE WAS CORNERED BY Abelson on the way into one of their classes. He was all business, and said they needed to talk.

"Can't it keep until after class?" Jake asked.

"It can't," Abelson answered. "When you hear what I have to say, I think you'll agree."

Abelson was silent, until they retreated to a small table and two chairs in the remote park-like area adjacent to the classroom building. Abelson then unloaded. "I thought I told you to lie low. What the hell have you been up to?"

"Nothing. I have been lying low. Just going to classes and working on a computer program I've been designing. I swear, that's it. What's going on?"

"You remember our asset, the one in Moscow who has been passing information to us in Israel? That Turgenev and Baker were planning to make you out as some perverted computer mastermind out to interfere with the November election in order to conceal the real culprit behind all of this—Russia?"

"Are you kidding me? Do you think I would forget what they have done to me, and my family?"

"Well, according to our source, you've done something to further piss Turgenev off, and now he has decided you have outlived your usefulness to him. He wants *you* terminated."

"You're kidding me, right?" Jake asked.

"Do I look like I'm kidding?" Abelson answered.

"Other than it being kinda scary," Jake said, "this seems like something that would only happen in some kind of an international spy novel."

"Turgenev kind of is out of an international spy novel. In that vein, let me tell you something even more scary," Abelson said. "We decided things were getting too hot, and that we needed to bring our mole home to Israel. We have a fail-safe procedure to reach him every day. We've not been able to reach him now two days in a row. It looks like he's been compromised. Seems he's completely vanished—either gone underground, or worse. You need to stay put."

CHAPTER 78
May 23, 2020, Two Days Later

JAKE STEPPED OUT OF the shower, looked in the mirror, and wiped the shaving cream from his cheeks. He barely recognized the face that stared back at him.

He had grown his now former beard to make himself look older, more . . . worldly. To cover up his youthful face where it had struggled to belong in the first place. In spite of his six-foot-plus wiry frame, whenever Jake tried to cultivate the coeds in his college classes, he had to overcome the impression that he was just some junior high school adolescent trying to score on the older ladies. The sandy-colored beard had definitely helped "age" him.

Ironically, where he was now headed, he would be better served if he looked like a harmless adolescent who couldn't possibly pose any threat to those he would be pursuing.

He finished toweling off, donned his youthful blue jeans, tee shirt, knitted hoodie, and cross-training shoes, and double checked the contents of his duffle bag and backpack. He wouldn't need more where he was heading. If he did, he had a wad of cash hidden in the false lining of his backpack. He calculated he would be gone about two months—ten weeks tops. Although, the campus "bubble" quarantine might preclude a return indefinitely. That was a chance he would have to take. He reread the note addressed to his roommate and left it on the desk, along with his keys to their apartment and his Honda Civic.

He threw the backpack over his shoulder, grabbed the duffle bag, and donned a face mask. He stopped momentarily to double check that he had a box of extra face masks in his duffle bag, as well as a couple of bandannas if he ran low on masks. He took one last look around the apartment, sighed, brushed aside his second thoughts, and walked out the door, closing it behind him. He wondered how much more he might be closing behind him.

* * *

TURGENEV BROKE THE SEAL and read the contents of the unusual envelope, the one that bore the handwritten words that had been brought to his attention:

> TO: PRESIDENT TURGENEV
> PRIVATE AND CONFIDENTIAL
> CONTENTS FOR YOUR EYES ONLY
>
> FROM: JAKE KLEIN
> ADVISE ALERTING KREMLIN OF SENDER
> BEFORE POSSIBLY FAILING TO FORWARD
> AT EMBASSY'S PERIL

Turgenev's assistant had been informed of the existence of the sealed envelope and the strange cover message. The assistant scoffed, but knew better than not to bring the message to Turgenev's immediate attention. With no outward show of emotion, Turgenev directed his assistant to instruct the embassy to determine the safety of the envelope—if possible, without opening it—and to then pouch it overnight. No one was to read or copy the contents of the envelope.

The envelope arrived with the seal intact—his assistant also knew better than to disobey orders. He handed the unopened envelope to Turgenev and asked whether he should remain while Turgenev opened it.

"*Nyet,* no, that won't be necessary."

The assistant departed from Turgenev's office.

Turgenev had examined both sides of the envelope, it contained no other words. He confirmed to his own satisfaction that the seal was original and unbroken. He could not see what was inside the wrapper, but it wasn't heavy. Even though it had been tested in the embassy before being placed in the pouch, he had wondered if the package might still contain anything physically dangerous—an explosive, or some form of deadly gas or powder.

Turgenev knew that anyone else in his position would summon security personnel to unseal and open the object for him. Some leaders of other countries required that every one of their meals be sampled in their presence before eating—but not Turgenev. He would not allow himself to be intimidated in that fashion.

He had put on a fresh set of his pandemic protection—a gas mask, a face shield and a pair of gloves. *They won't protect against an explosion, but perhaps some microscopic poison gas or powder.*

He had taken a razor blade and carefully preserved, but opened, the seal. No explosion. No gas. He turned the packet upside down. No powder spilled out. He removed the only contents, a single sheet of paper containing handwritten words that matched the handwriting on the envelope:

5.21.2020

Mr. President:

This is between you and me. One on one. Mano-a-mano. If you can find and take me down,—I repeat me— then more power to you, and your secret intentions that I have unraveled will remain your secrets—assuming none of your staff have violated my seal.

However, should you, or anyone on your behalf, harm—or attempt to harm, contact, or even approach—any member of my family, or any of my friends or acquaintances, I have taken irreversible steps to assure that your secrets, and your personal involvement, will be immediately released to the world, including a copy of this letter.

If you keep our contest where it belongs, strictly between the two of us, then your objectives will not be defeated, unless I personally accomplish that which is

MY CLEAR INTENTION. IF YOU ARE ABLE TO PERSONALLY DE-
FEAT ME IN ANY WAY YOU CHOOSE BEFORE I SUCCEED, THEN
YOUR OBJECTIVES WILL REMAIN SECRET AND WILL, NO DOUBT,
PROVE SUCCESSFUL.

IT SHOULD BE BENEATH YOU TO STOOP TO THREATENING MY
FAMILY OR FRIENDS TO EXTORT ANY UNFAIR ADVANTAGE OVER
ME. AGAIN, THIS SHOULD BE BETWEEN YOU AND ME—YOUR
INTELLECT AGAINST MINE.

I'M WILLING TO PLAY. ARE YOU? ARE YOU UP TO THE CHAL-
LENGE?

JAKE KLEIN

That mother fucking son of a bitch! How dare he think he can talk
to me that way? Actually, in his position, he was damn clever, and perceptive. Exactly what I would have done. He's cut me off at my knees.
Preemptively extorted me before I could extort him. Kudos to the bastard.
Let the games begin!

CHAPTER 79
May 28, 2020, Five Days Later

JAKE COULDN'T BELIEVE HIS eyes. Just when he didn't think things could sink any lower. But there it was, all over the news: the brutal May 25 death of George Floyd—and all of its aftermath. The protesting and public firestorm growing out of the infamous eight minute and forty-six second video came as no surprise to Jake, but its depth and magnitude did.

Maybe in death, Floyd will serve a public benefit he certainly never did in life. At least if we can overlook those obnoxious looters disingenuously rationalizing their misdeeds in his name. And those who seek to justify such unlawful behavior with catchphrases such as "Social Injustice" and "Black Lives Matter". Don't all lives matter? The pendulum typically overreacts. Hopefully, it will ultimately settle and come to rest in a good place.

"Amazing Floyd video and pictures," Amir said to Jake. "Would expect in Russia, not U.S."

"There are bad people all over the world, Amir," Jake said, "not just in your homeland. We have to try and focus on the good ones."

Jake's mind wandered to the fake destination he and his roommate had conjured up for Turgenev and his thugs: Minneapolis, where Floyd coincidentally was killed. *The thought of those goons searching for him in Minneapolis among the hordes of demonstrators marching in the streets at this historic moment in time complaining about bad cops is rather ironic, if not downright laughable—genuine bad cops, so to speak, right there in plain sight, among all those who were protesting all cops—the good with the bad.*

CHAPTER 80
May 31, 2020, Three Days Later

TURGENEV WAS FURIOUS. JAKE Klein was nowhere to be found. Not at his college campus, not at his family's residence—his agents couldn't find Klein anywhere.

But that was them. There was a reason they worked for him, and not the other way around. He hadn't accomplished all he had in life because he couldn't outsmart his opponents. Plenty of them.

In fact, in recent months, he had been working on more revisions of the Russian Constitution that would further consolidate his authority and position, and pave the way for him to become President for Life.

And Turgenev thought he had figured out how to deal with Klein, just as that smart-ass invited me to do. *We'll see who's up to the challenge.*

CHAPTER 81
June 1, 2020, One Day Later

JAKE READ THE TEXT:

DEAREST JK,

WONDERFUL NEWS. THE DOCTORS HAVE SAID MY MOTHER'S HEALTH HAS IMPROVED ENOUGH FOR ME TO RETURN TO MY ENGLISH STUDIES—AND TO YOU. I WANTED TO SURPRISE YOU. I CAME TO SCSU, BUT I HAVE BEEN CONFRONTED BY NOTHING BUT OBSTACLES.

FIRST, I WAS NOT ALLOWED TO ENTER THE CAMPUS BECAUSE ONLY SCSU STUDENTS, FACULTY, AND EMPLOYEES WITH OFFICIAL IDENTIFICATION CARDS ARE ALLOWED ON THE CAMPUS BECAUSE OF A PANDEMIC LOCKDOWN INSTITUTED BY THE UNIVERSITY.

I CONTACTED CAMPUS OFFICIALS. WHEN I EXPLAINED TO THEM WHO I WAS, THEY INFORMED ME THAT YOU HAD LEFT THE CAMPUS AND THEY HAVE NO KNOWLEDGE OF YOUR WHEREABOUTS.

PLEASE TELL ME WHERE YOU ARE SO I CAN COME JOIN YOU. I WANT TO BE WITH YOU! I MISS YOU SO MUCH.

LOVE, ANYA

He froze dead in his tracks.

CHAPTER 82
June 2, 2020, One Day Later

TURGENEV ALWAYS DID ENJOY a good fight. It kept him on his toes.

"I wrote the text for her, just like you and I discussed," her handler said to Turgenev. "She sent it to him."

"And?" Turgenev asked her handler, who sat across from him in his office.

"He hasn't responded," the handler said.

"This Klein seems to have pretty good instincts," Turgenev observed, as much to himself as his aide. "Let me ask you something. How do you know she sent the text?"

"Three reasons: one—she told me she did, and I trust her not to take a chance by lying to us. Two—because she blind copied me on the text. And three—most significantly, because we have a hidden monitor on her smartphone. The text she sent is there."

"Three reasons *should* be enough," Turgenev said, "but I'm still not convinced. Keep an eye on her, and keep me informed."

* * *

AFTER THE MAN LEFT, Turgenev paced about his opulent office. He stared out the floor-to-ceiling window at the flowing river below that always helped him to relax and organize his thoughts. Finally, he sent an encrypted text of his own:

> WE CANNOT REST WELL UNTIL WE HAVE DISPOSED OF THIS
> JAKE KLEIN ONCE AND FOR ALL. HE TROUBLES ME. I THINK IT
> MAY BE TIME TO IMPLEMENT OUR PLAN B.

Of course, he didn't mention his own Plan B.
The recipient promptly replied:

> UNDERSTAND AND AGREE.

* * *

JAKE THOUGHT IT SEEMED like such a good strategy at the time, back before the *Red Crier* smear campaign made him *persona non grata*. There was only one consideration then: find a way to validate and implement his new software program. But now, there was a second concern: find a way to stay alive long enough to carry out his first objective, if that first objective remained possible post *Red Crier*. And post COVID-19 as well. *Planning is definitely a lot easier than doing.*

He wondered why lately his mind kept going back in time. Perhaps it was more comforting—and less frightening—than looking forward at all that confronted him. And the world.

First, he had dwelled on his high school English teacher and her panel of experts on getting past hurdles and blocks. The ones who had helped him push through his new software program.

Now, oddly, he found himself continuing to recite some old slogan, *"the enemy of my enemy is my friend."* Kind of like an old song he couldn't get out of his mind. Why this mantra? What did his subconscious know that he didn't? Where, somewhere, had he learned this phrase?

Finally, it came to him. An old history teacher had spent an entire class session on that catchphrase one day. Turned out, it had been around forever, but Winston Churchill had reportedly updated it during World War II when he said, *"If Hitler had invaded Hell, I would've introduced the Devil to the English House of Commons."*

More recently, he tried to recall his thoughts when he first read the *Red Crier* phony news bulletin about him: "Turgenev. Molloy. Gradsky. Nilsen. Cipher. Amir. Carter. Baker. Baker's supporters. The DNC. Gali. Anya." *Are they all my enemies? Any among them I can actually trust?* Anyone?

He had decided to reach out to someone he hoped he could count on—his computer, with himself at the helm. He had said "for as long as he could." Was he now past "as long as he could?" *The devil you know . . .*

He couldn't put it off any longer. It was time to respond to Anya's text. He bought a burner phone with some prepaid minutes with cash. He sent her the following text:

> HAPPY TO HEAR YOUR MOM IS IMPROVED. ON A JOURNEY NOW
> I MUST FACE ON MY OWN. WILL BE IN TOUCH WHEN I CAN. JK.

After hitting send, Jake removed the SIM card from the burner phone, cut the card in half with one of the spare razors in his toilet kit, and then crushed the burner phone into several pieces, depositing each piece into a number of isolated shallow graves here and there. *Not likely the phone can be reconstructed. Or used to trace me.*

He had another call to make. But he would use his own smartphone for this one. All he had to do was power it back up.

* * *

ANYA READ JAKE'S TEXT. She was frightened that her handler might view this as a sign of failure on her part. She immediately tried to reply, but received only the following response:

> THE NUMBER YOU HAVE TRIED TO REACH IS NO LONGER IN
> SERVICE. IF YOU THINK THIS MESSAGE WAS RECEIVED IN ERROR,
> PLEASE TRY AGAIN.

* * *

TURGENEV LISTENED TO THE news quietly. He was not surprised. "Pending further instructions, tell her to try him again once every other day."

* * *

JAKE WATCHED THE DRIVER pull up to the confirmed pickup point. He hopped in the passenger seat and closed the door. His missing beard and the mask covering much of his face didn't matter. It must have been his eyes.

"Mr. JK!" Amir shouted. "Look young."

CHAPTER 83
June 3, 2020, One Day Later

ABELSON HAD BEEN INVITED to telephonically attend another one of the daily meetings of the senior Mossad officers which was in session. Mossad had received confirmation that its Russian asset had been identified—and eliminated. Even halfway across the world, Abelson could see—and feel—the cloud of sadness and anger that hung over the room. He could relate. Not only because he was now an Israeli, but also because his family had emigrated to Israel from Russia when he was still an infant.

"Considering the alternative, it may be best for him," one attendee said. "However bad it was at the end, at least it's over. He isn't hurting anymore."

"Do we still feel we must remain hands off where Klein is concerned?" another officer asked.

"We still can't operate *on* U.S. soil," said another at the table.

"Our asset must not be allowed to have died serving no good purpose," said his handler. "There are things we can do to help protect Klein without violating international or Israeli protocols. We must do what we can."

"But how do we avoid meddling in the election or any other U.S. domestic matters?" asked the meeting chair.

"I don't give a flying fuck who wins their election," said the deceased asset's handler. "All I care about is doing whatever we can to assure that the election is conducted honestly. And that the life of our fallen colleague is well-honored."

The sentiment in the room was unanimous. The only question was how best for Abelson and the others to carry it out.

* * *

JAKE HAD EXPLAINED TO Amir why he had tracked him down, and what he somehow hoped to accomplish—with Amir's help. "Your life will be in danger if you decide to help me," Jake warned Amir.

"Give minute think," Amir said. Ten seconds later: "Okay, think. Amir enemy of your enemy. Russia. We do together. Very pleased help. I drive. Register in motels using name in fake passport. No one know. Travel from Kazakhstan here using fake passports. Very safe. No problem use fake passport here. Do all time. Where go first?"

"Thanks, Amir. I don't know where we need to go first, but what I do know is we have to leave New Haven right now—because this is the first place Turgenev's gangsters will look."

One hour later, they were on the road. New Haven was a speck in the rearview mirror of Amir's car. And, as it turned out, none too soon.

* * *

TURGENEV KNEW HE WAS technically butting up against the deal, but he decided to take a chance. *I'm not threatening anyone, and I don't think Klein will forfeit his own ambitions so easily.*

* * *

THE TWO "HARVARD" OFFICIALS, compliments of the Russian Embassy, had no problem getting through SCSU security and to Jake's campus apartment. All they had to do was produce their forged Harvard Medical Center identity cards, and explain that Jake Klein had recently been together with a Harvard foreign exchange student by the name of Anya Lebedev, and that Lebedev was now testing positive for COVID-19. They produced a supporting statement signed by Ms. Lebedev. They were tracing and testing everyone who recently came in contact with her, and they had to locate Mr. Klein as quickly as possible.

They were escorted by SCSU campus police to Jake's campus apartment, and knocked on the door. Jake's roommate was a bit more daunting than the campus police.

"Just a minute. I need to put a mask on." A moment later, the door was opened by a nondescript male student wearing a mask who backed six feet away from the door after opening it.

"Are you Jake Klein?" one of the Harvard officials asked him.

"Nope. He's my roommate," the young man answered.

"Can you please show us some identification?"

"Sure. Just a sec." The student went to a table, opened his wallet, pulled out a driver's license, and flashed it to the visitors.

One of the men, wearing a mask and gloves, reached for the driver's license.

The student quickly pulled his driver's license away.

"I need to inspect your license. I'm masked and gloved, for Pete's sake. And I'm tested every other day. All of my tests have been negative."

"Nice to hear. Please ask the other three with you to move back." They did. Only then, the student stepped forward, and handed his license to the masked and gloved individual, who remained at the door.

The official examined the license and handed it back to the student. "Do you have any idea where Mr. Klein is?" he asked the student.

The student again backed away from the door. "I don't. He told me he was working on a project of some kind, and was heading to Minneapolis for a few weeks."

"Did he leave any kind of note?"

"Nope."

"Any kind of forwarding address or contact?"

"Sorry."

"What if you need to get hold of him?"

"I have his cell phone."

"Seems like you might be holding back on me," the official said.

"Hey, man, I'm his roommate, not his mother. And not his keeper. Are we done? I got stuff to do."

"Just another moment," the Harvard official said. "Do you mind if we come in and look through the apartment?"

"Are you kidding me?" the student asked through his mask. "That doesn't feel right to me. Do you have some kind of paperwork authorizing you to do that?"

The official turned to the campus police. "Can you help us with this?"

"Not unless you have a warrant," one of the officers responded.

"We'll be back!" the official said and they stormed off.

"Hold up!" one of the officers said. "We need to escort you off the campus. And you'll need to have a warrant to get back on. We care about our students here."

* * *

JAKE'S ROOMMATE CLOSED AND locked the apartment door. *Interesting that they didn't ask to test me since I had been in JK's company.* He posted a three-word message on his Instagram account:

IMPRESSIVE CLOUD FORMATION!

The three-word post was accompanied by an image of a breathtaking cloudy sky.

CHAPTER 84
June 4, 2020, One Day Later

TURGENEV SCOWLED AT NO one in particular.

His aide took a step back. He had no difficulty reading the mood blanketing the room in spite of the mask blanketing Turgenev's face.

"Minneapolis my ass!" Turgenev exclaimed. *If the roommate said Minneapolis, to the west, we can be sure he's headed somewhere to the south because he can't get very far going north or east.* "This punk kid is messing with me. We'll see just where that gets him."

He had decided not to take a chance approaching Klein's sister as he had done with his roommate. There was too much chance that Klein would feel Turgenev was violating Klein's conditions, even though he hadn't balked when Turgenev's agents approached his roommate—which Turgenev guessed Klein knew by now.

"Let's not send anyone to call on Klein's sister," he said to his aide. "She's an experienced lawyer. We're not likely to fool her. It'll be a waste of time." *And I'll be damned if I'm going to give Klein the satisfaction of embarrassing me again.*

"Yes sir, Mr. President," the aide said. "Anything else I can do for you?"

"Did I ask you to do anything else?"

"No, Mr. President!"

"Then you have your answer. For now."

* * *

JAKE CLOSED HIS INSTAGRAM account. He explained to Amir what the cloud formation meant. "They're after us," he said. "Well, they're after me." *Technically, Turgenev violated my ground rules by approaching my roommate. He was smart enough to know I have a dog in this hunt, and wouldn't pull the plug on my own goals over something that tacky. It wasn't like he threatened my roommate. But if he tries something like that with my family, I'll have no choice but to blow the whistle on him. I think he's smart enough not to press his luck with my family, though.*

"No worry, Mr. JK. Okay to say us. We are team. Amir not afraid."

Jake selected a cheap local bed and breakfast in Raleigh, Virginia. Amir sought to register for the room because Jake figured his pursuers would not know of Amir or be able to connect Amir's identification. Jake was concerned that Amir's heavy accent and poor English and the dark color of his Muslim skin might prove problematic. However, fifteen minutes later, Amir opened the locked door at the end of the hallway opposite the lobby where Jake had remained outside while Amir went to register. "Any trouble?" Jake asked when they went up the back steps and were safely in "Amir's" room.

"Man at counter not friendly," Amir answered. "Amir's looks and language not help." He ask for identification. Amir show fake passport, Connecticut driver's license same name, credit card same name, and cash want use to pay because afraid robbers might take cash. That worked. Man take photo of papers and put credit card in machine, but say only use credit card if not pay in cash when leave."

"This is a nuisance, I know. The problem is that we had to run before I was really organized and ready. I have another week or two of work to do on my computer program before I'll be geared up for our destination."

"No worry, JK. Handled registration. And have English schoolbooks and famous literary novels. Will work on English while you work on computer. Can also be tourist and walk around town."

"English yes, tourist no," Jake said. Turgenev has people looking for me. They don't know you're with me, or your fake name, but they may know what you look like."

"Yes. Good thinking. By the way, what is destination when computer ready?"

Fortunately, Jake didn't know yet. He didn't want to lie to Amir.

CHAPTER 85
June 7, 2020, Three Days Later

ABELSON HAD TRIED REPEATEDLY for three days in succession to reach Jake. He even used his phone on the Sabbath—an orthodox Jewish taboo. He tried Jake's smartphone. He tried each of his three computers. No luck. Jake had shut everything down. *The man obviously wants to be off the grid. Period.* After three days of getting nowhere, he reported to Tel Aviv. Everyone agreed, there was nothing more to be done unless Jake reached out to Abelson. *If* he did.

CHAPTER 86
June 17, 2020, Ten Days Later

JAKE AND AMIR MOVED every two days. They had traveled as far south as Myrtle Beach, South Carolina. They were now back in a little area outside of Charlotte, North Carolina. Jake thought it wise not to move in a straight line toward their first destination. He was finally almost finished with his software program, just a few more finishing touches and tests to work through. Of course, the real test would not come until they reached that destination.

He now had more devices than an electronics store. He had shut down his three computers and his smartphone so no one could possibly track him. Or even reach out to him because he wasn't ready to talk with anyone. Not yet. He had bought a fourth computer with cash to safely do his work. There was no way anyone could track him on that device. He had also bought five more cheapie burner phones.

He felt terrible about leaving Leah in the dark, although she knew he didn't call very much, if at all, when he was away at school. *Maybe I need to hear her voice more than the other way around.* He had tried calling her on one of the burners, but only got voicemail. *Probably doesn't pick up unknown callers. Can't blame her for that.* He didn't dare leave a message. As it were, just to be safe, he completely destroyed that burner and its SIM card.

He thought about Anya, but there was no way he could call her right now. *Maybe after. Hmm, after what?*

That left Abelson. He really did owe him a call. Surprisingly, the Mossad agent on school leave answered the unknown caller in his phone screen on the first ring. "Shalom."

"Shalom, Gali, it's me, Jake."

"Tell me something I didn't know. What the hell didn't you understand about 'Stay put?'"

"Sorry, couldn't do that. If I had, Turgenev would have gotten me. As it was, I *barely* got away."

"I know. Your roomie told me. And I'm not talking about Anya. I guess you knew best, but the least you could have done was call me, asshole."

"You want me to call you an asshole?" *I wonder why Gali and I make light of things that aren't light at all. Maybe it's a way of releasing anxiety. Or just falsely trying to out macho one another.*

"Haha, very funny," Abelson said.

"So what the hell are you doing? Where are you?"

"Better that I not tell you, at least not for now."

"Are you saying you don't think you can trust me?" Abelson asked.

"C'mon. I wouldn't insult you by harboring such a thought. And you shouldn't insult me thinking I would. Given that Turgenev somehow tied Israel to my activities, and was willing to kill your mole, I don't think it's such a stretch that it will occur to Turgenev to look for an Israeli connection at SCSU and find his way to you."

"Not a bad thought. Well, it's actually a terrible thought—that Turgenev might come after me and not just you—but good thinking on your part nonetheless. However, you do know that the Mossad trains its operatives to defend themselves quite well, don't you?"

"Yeah, right, Mr. Neanderthal. You can take out one or two of Turgenev's agents, maybe even three, but if you do that, he'll just send more."

"Well then, what do you suggest I do?" Abelson asked Jake.

"I thought you'd never ask," Jake said. "Here's precisely what I'd like you to do if that happens." Jake explained what he was thinking to Abelson in intimate detail.

"Very clever," Abelson said. "I think even I can handle my end of that."

"Well, it's close, but I'm guessing you can, Gali."

"Uh huh. Well, glad you're at least back to calling me Gali instead of asshole. But, unfortunately, I do have some news for you as well." He told Jake that their Russian asset had been terminated. "The good side of that, if there is a good side, is that Mossad is now willing to come to your rescue long distance so long as it isn't required to favor either party in the coming U.S. elections."

"Sorry to hear about your colleague but otherwise much appreciated. I really do mean that, Gali. I probably could ultimately use some help, but not yet. How 'bout I let you know when I'm ready?"

"Nice way to look a gift horse in the mouth, bud. As they say, don't be a stranger. I guess."

Jake promptly destroyed still another burner phone. He felt all alone again. He modified his thinking. He was thankful to have Amir.

* * *

ABELSON PLACED A SCRAMBLED call to Tel Aviv. He summarized his conversation with Jake.

"Guy sure knows how to look a gift horse in the mouth," his contact said.

"Funny you should say that," Abelson replied.

CHAPTER 87
July 1, 2020, Two Weeks Later

Turgenev turned off the television monitor in his office. The image of all those Black Lives Matter protesters marching in the streets across America warmed his heart. *Those hypocritical U.S. officials never hesitate to jump all over me every time some former Russian agent somewhere in the world dies under mysterious circumstances. Wonder how they like it when they are getting a taste of their own medicine for the ill treatment of blacks in America. I just love it, that common criminals breaking into small businesses across the country are being excused for such behavior because of unjust treatment of blacks by the U.S. government. Such a beautiful sight.*

Watching the results, or more accurately, the *lack* of results of several of the U.S. primary elections conducted on June 2 had also pleased him. *It shows that our plans for the November election are right on track.*

His glow, however, was short-lived. His mind soon returned to Klein. He was incensed that his dispatched army of agents were still unable to find their elusive target. And then, it occurred to him. *Maybe I'm going about this all wrong.*

* * *

Jake had read about all of the primary election debacles that had occurred two days earlier. Bottlenecks had occurred right and left. Why? Because voting authorities across the country were scared to death that electronic voting, rather than mail-in voting, was going to be manipulated. They were overwhelmed by the resulting massive in-person and mail-in ballots they were trying to achieve. He had taken his software testing as far as he unilaterally could. It was time for him to head for his first destination. Perhaps the first destination of several.

* * *

TURGENEV THOUGHT OF A smarter way to find Klein. *The kid is a Jew. Jews are* always *the cause of our problems. Even young ones like Klein.*

He thought about the Zionist Israeli mole the GRU had recently discovered, and put to death—after first extracting from him all information he possessed. *So, well deserved. But as fast as we get rid of one, another seems to pop up and take his place!*

It finally occurred to Turgenev: if Klein was at the center of his problems, there was a good chance that Israel was also in the picture, and not very far away. *All I have to do is find the Israeli tentacles, and let them lead me to the head.*

CHAPTER 88
July 6, 2020, Five Days Later

FYODOR GANCHAROV WAS A sophomore foreign exchange student at Southern Connecticut State University on a student visa. His family ran a modest co-op farm owned by the Russian government one hour outside of Moscow. His father never finished high school—he had barely started it. His father was not familiar with computers or any other forms of technology, including cell phones. His parents were very pleased that Fyodor would be the first member of their family to attend college.

Gancharov was more than surprised to receive an email from his father. Until he read it. Then he understood, and knew what he had to do. He had no choice.

CHAPTER 89
July 8, 2020, Two Days Later

POTUS AND BAKER, JR. were just finishing breakfast in a private setting in the Rose Garden.

"The pandemic is playing out just as we wanted," son said to father. "The BLM 'I can't breathe' campaign couldn't be going better than if we had incited—"

"What do you mean '*if*?'" POTUS interrupted his son. "Of course we incited *all* the protests, precisely as *I* designed them to happen, in order to facilitate my law and order crusade."

"Just a figure of speech, Dad, sorry. Of course the protests have grown exactly as you planned. And our recently elevated Russian President For Life, Alexi Turgenev, is cooperating beautifully. Not just helping us with the upcoming election, even more than he did in 2016, but also with other schemes—such as the bounty program he has recently offered the Taliban for each American soldier in Afghanistan they assassinate."

"Refresh my recollection," POTUS asked his son. "How long does Turgenev now hold office as President For Life of Russia?"

"The term of his office now runs through 2036," Baker, Jr. answered.

POTUS shook his head in admiration and envy.

* * *

GANCHAROV DONNED HIS MASK and gloves, and set out on foot across the SCSU campus. Already within the SCSU "bubble", he was free to move about, so long as he remained inside the campus. He knocked on the door of the apartment identified in his "father's" email.

"Yes?" sounded a voice from within the apartment.

"My name is Fyodor Gancharov. I'm a student here."

"Are you wearing a mask and gloves?" the voice inside the apartment asked.

"Yes, of course," Gancharov replied.

The occupant opened the door, also clad in a mask and gloves. He examined Gancharov. "My name is Abelson, Gali Abelson. Do we know each other? Are you sure you have the right place?"

"Unfortunately, I am," was all Gancharov softly said in reply, almost swallowing his words.

* * *

JAKE AND AMIR WERE on the move.

"Where to, Mr. JK," Amir asked.

"Harrisburg, Pennsylvania."

"Why there?" Amir asked further.

"Because they recently conducted a June 2 primary election that had a number of delays and other problems," Jake answered.

"What is primary election?" Amir asked.

Jake gave Amir a simple course on U.S. election procedures. "Listen carefully, Amir. Someday, you'll take the exam to become a U.S. citizen. You'll need to know how this works."

* * *

ABELSON FIGURED THIS WAS precisely what Jake had speculated might happen. He didn't know Gancharov, but it was what and not who that Jake had nailed.

Gancharov explained why he was there. The GRU had taken his parents into custody. They would be sent to hard labor camps in the old Gulag, never to be seen again unless the son delivered what Turgenev wanted—information as to the whereabouts of someone by the name of Jake Klein. He had to deliver the information. Information that he was told Abelson had—or could obtain. Excuses would not count. His parents' lives were at stake.

"Come in," Abelson said. "I didn't know your name, but I was expecting you. I had to be sure you were the one."

"I'm afraid I don't understand. How could you have been expecting me, especially if you don't know me, didn't even know my name?" Gancharov asked.

"Oh, but I do know you, in a manner of speaking," Abelson replied. "You might say we've been introduced."

* * *

ABELSON OBTAINED THE FRIGHTENED Gancharov's contact information and assured him he'd be in touch. After Gancharov left, Abelson posted a three-word message on his Instagram account:

THREATENING STORM CLOUDS!

The three-word post was accompanied by an image of a threatening cloudy sky.

In less than an hour, his phone rang. It was another unknown caller. "You sure called it," was all he said. He listened. "Gotcha. I'll let them know."

CHAPTER 90
July 10, 2020, Two Days Later

JAKE SAT ACROSS THE conference table from the Pennsylvania Secretary of State. It didn't hurt that he said he had some information about their voting difficulties. Her name was Adele Manners. She was the senior administrator of all elections—local, statewide and federal—conducted in the State of Pennsylvania. He handed her copies of his driver's license and his student identity card. He didn't know how this meeting would go, and couldn't risk confiscation of the originals. Because he also couldn't rule out the possibility that he might be personally detained, the originals were not on his person either.

Amir was waiting in their car, parked several blocks away. He was under instruction to reach out to Abelson if Jake did not return in ninety minute's time.

"What can I do for you, Mr. Klein?" Ms. Manners inquired.

* * *

TURGENEV RECEIVED ANOTHER SEALED envelope through the daily pouch from the D.C. Russian Embassy. It looked exactly like, and was addressed identically to, the first one he had received on April 26, forty-eight days earlier. He dismissed his assistant and read:

7.08.2020

MR. PRESIDENT:

YOU'RE NOT PLAYING FAIR. I KNOW I SAID "FAMILY, FRIENDS, ACQUAINTANCES" IN MY ORIGINAL LETTER, AND I HAVE NEVER MET THE GANCHAROV FAMILY, BUT YOU ARE VIOLATING THE SPIRIT OF OUR ARRANGEMENT BY SEIZING INNOCENT THIRD PARTIES TO LEVERAGE YOUR HUNT FOR ME.

THANKS TO—HOW SHALL I PUT IT?—YOUR INTRODUCTION, I NOW COUNT EACH OF THE GANCHAROV FAMILY MEMBERS AMONG MY CIRCLE OF ACQUAINTANCES.

WITHIN 72 HOURS, A NONSTOP RUSSIAN AIRLINE FIRST IDENTIFIED IN WRITING BY ITS INTERNATIONAL CALL NUMBERS TO THE ISRAELI EMBASSY IN MOSCOW, AND CARRYING THOSE MEMBERS OF THE GANCHAROV FAMILY IN YOUR CONTROL, SHALL SAFELY SET DOWN IN TEL AVIV. THE FAMILY SHALL BE IN POSSESSION OF VALID RUSSIAN PASSPORTS AND SHALL BE IN SOUND HEALTH.

NO LATER THAN 24 HOURS BEFORE THE SAFE ARRIVAL OF THAT FLIGHT, A WIRE TRANSFER OF 250,000 U.S. DOLLARS MUST BE DELIVERED AND RECEIVED IN GOOD FUNDS IN ACCORDANCE WITH WIRING INSTRUCTIONS THAT WILL BE PROVIDED TO YOU BY THE ISRAELI EMBASSY. THESE FUNDS ARE TO FINANCE THE RESETTLING OF THE GANCHAROV FAMILY IN THEIR NEW HOME.

EVERY DOG GETS ITS FIRST BITE. YOU HAD YOURS WHEN TWO OF YOUR AGENTS, USING FALSE IDENTIFICATION, INTRUDED ON MY COLLEGE ROOMMATE AT HIS RESIDENCE ON 6.03.2020. THE REQUIREMENTS OF THIS LETTER ARE SOLELY OF YOUR OWN MAKING. IF YOU CHOOSE NOT TO COMPLY, I WILL HAVE NO CHOICE BUT TO PROCEED ON THE BASIS THAT YOU HAVE KNOWINGLY AND INTENTIONALLY VIOLATED OUR ARRANGEMENT.

PERSONALLY, I WOULD PREFER TO PLAY OUR MATCH FAIR AND SQUARE, WITHOUT ANY MORE NONSENSE. YOU? ARE YOU UP TO THE CHALLENGE? YOUR TREATMENT OF THE GANCHAROVS SUGGEST THAT YOU ARE NOT.

JAKE KLEIN

Goddamn kike Jews! To them, it's always about the money. Thieves, every one of them! The money is not important to me, especially since we can always get more where that came from—our workers. If Klein were as smart as he thinks he is, he would have insisted on even more. It was worth every penny to pin down with certainty that Israel is in fact backing Klein, as I suspected. Klein is living on borrowed time. So is Israel.

* * *

JAKE WAS NOT SURE what to make of Secretary Manners. *Her "What can I do for you, Mr. Klein?" seemed stiff. Did she recognize my name? If she did, was that good or bad? Was she just being polite? He felt like saying, "It's more a matter of what I can do for you," but that would have come across as way too arrogant. That they were each masked didn't help either of us read the other.* "I'm a computer sciences major, and I'm writing a paper for one of my classes. It's about the 2020 election. I was hoping I could interview you, and get your take on how your June 2 primary election went."

"Your reputation precedes you, Mr. Klein. Thanks to the *Red Crier,* it's not a very favorable reputation. Of course, I don't think much of the *Red Crier,* so their opinion of you may be a badge of honor. Still, you'll understand that I need to be very circumspect and guarded."

"I understand completely, Madam Secretary. I also have to be somewhat circumspect and guarded, strange and arrogant as that may sound for some-one in my modest position. If you'll permit me, I'll give you the shorthand version of my true story, and why I'm here—starting with the admission that I know how your June 2 primary election processes struggled, and how confidential strategic files of the Pennsylvania Democratic Party were hacked and leaked in advance of the 2016 election. I had to politely introduce myself in the most tactful way that I could, even if not fully candid." He proceeded to tell his story. It took him about twenty minutes. He was tracking the time on his smartphone as he spoke because he knew Amir was doing the same, that he was on the clock.

"That's a fascinating story, Mr. Klein. I'm honestly not sure what to make of it. Why don't we start by you calling me Adele, and my calling you Jake? By the way, are you in a hurry? Why do you keep glancing at your phone? May I remind you that you are the one who requested this meeting, unscheduled to boot?"

"Deal, Adele, although I answer most comfortably to JK. Also, my family really enjoys the television show, and I kind of enjoyed calling you Madam Secretary. As for my nervously checking the time on my phone, that's for two reasons. One, I don't want to monopolize your time. And two, as I've explained, there are some unsavory people looking for me. I have to keep moving. That's why I said a few minutes ago that I also have to be circumspect and guarded. I'm not stuffy. I'm . . . frightened." *I could have been more macho, but I'm guessing this plays better.*

"On your first point, JK, why don't you let me worry about my time? As far as your time, I'm sorry that you find yourself so vulnerable."

She had a number of additional questions. Jake tried to answer them as best he could. Finally, she said, "Okay, I think I understand you, at least, as best as I'm presently able. I need to kick this can down the road a bit with some folks who are smarter than I am." She handed him two of her business cards. "Not everyone gets this card. My private cell phone number is on there. You can reach me any time, literally. How about if you write your cell on one of those cards and hand them back to me?"

"Hmm, I hope you understand that I'm not directly reachable these days. Do you have an Instagram account?"

"I do."

"Just post something innocuous that I'll see on there, and I'll promptly get back to you. Apologies in advance for all the cloak and dagger. I can't be too careful."

"No worries. I have a silent alarm under the table here. Had I been interested in detaining you, I would have pushed it several minutes ago, and you would now be wearing handcuffs. But at least we offer you as many calls as it takes for you to reach your lawyer." Adele stood and escorted Jake out the door. "I'm not sure we'll be able to work together. Either way, please take good care of yourself, JK, and stay safe."

Jake made it back to Amir with barely ten minutes to spare.

* * *

AMIR LOOKED AT JAKE. "Mr. JK, okay? Look funny. But not laughing funny. Something wrong?"

"Not really, just a difficult meeting. I'm not honestly sure how it went. But what I do know is that we need to get moving. Fast."

"Where to, JK?"

"Atlanta, Georgia."

"Not know. How far this Atlanta, Georgia?"

"Turgenev is still looking for us. Probably now more than ever. In a direct straight route, Atlanta is around 700 miles from here. But we need to drive back roads that don't go in a straight line—much safer for us. Maybe close to 1,000 miles the way we'll go. We'll give ourselves several days to get there, and spend each night in small out of the way towns."

Amir started the car and eased into traffic. "Have question."

"For now, get on the freeway up ahead going south." Jake was already plotting their route. He had identified the town where they'd stop tonight, and the name of a small roadside inn. "Give me another minute, and I'll have the GPS directions for you to follow for our drive today."

"Okay, but Amir question different."

"Oh, sorry." Jake activated the GPS. "Alright, what's your question?" he asked Amir.

"Read news story to practice English while you in meeting. About expected Democratic candidate for president, Mr. Logan Sullivan. He make big speech against shareholder capitalism. Not sure understand. Sounds more like yesterday Russia than today America. You can explain?"

"Sure. Maybe this is another subject for you to know when you take the exam to become a U.S. citizen." Jake knew this was a complicated subject, combining economics and politics—the fundamental policy differences between the two major political parties in the U.S. concerning the services that each party believed the government should provide to the public, and how the government should impose taxes on the public to raise the funds to pay for those government services. *This would be difficult to discuss if Amir and I both spoke the same first language. But at least it might take our minds off things while we drive.*

Jake did most of the talking, so Amir did most of the listening. "Republicans want less tax. Mean less service. Democrats want give more service, need make more tax. Ending shareholder capitalism just fancy way say more tax. Which way think better, Mr. JK?"

Jake had registered as an Independent because he didn't think either the Republican Party or the Democratic Party really served the public interests, as opposed to their own interests—the perks that went with being a public representative, particularly as a member of the political party in control. He also believed that it was important that elections be free of undue influence so that the voters could genuinely determine which political party they wanted to be in control at any moment in time. "I don't know which party and system is best, Amir. I understand computers better than I understand government."

Jake wasn't sure that what he had explained to Amir as they drove was all that helpful, to either of them. What he did note was that Amir was a good listener and seemed to understand things a lot better than he could convey, at least in English. And it had for sure made the drive go by more quickly.

"Have headache thinking, Mr. JK. Is time eat. Know good Kazakhstan restaurant in this town?"

Some things were always important—food, for example. The thought of a good meal sounded appealing to Jake too. *How did that old saying go, "the condemned man ate a hearty last meal."*

CHAPTER 91
July 11, 2020, One Day Later

TURGENEV HAD SUMMONED BAROVSKY to his office. While Barovsky was not among those who were pursuing Klein's whereabouts for Turgenev, he had sent word to Turgenev that he had some news about where Klein *was*. "So, are you just here for some fine caviar and vodka, or do you have something useful to tell me about Klein? If you do, it may be worth a good deal of food and drink."

"I don't know where he is today, Mr. President, but I do know where he was yesterday."

"Well, it goes without saying that I'd rather know where he is today or, better still, where he will be tomorrow, but where he was yesterday is more than the dolts I have looking for him have been able to ascertain, and it may be a good start on figuring out where he will be tomorrow. Tell me already what you know."

"As you will recall, in 2016, we were able to hack into many local Democratic Party computers. We caused the Democratic Party considerable difficulty by leaking many of their confidential files."

"I remember. That was four years ago. What do you have for me now about Klein?

"One of the local Democratic computer systems we hacked into in 2016 was the computer system of the Pennsylvania State Democratic Party. We still have backdoor access into that computer system."

"And?" Turgenev motioned to Barovsky to get on with it.

"Yesterday, Klein had a meeting in person with the Pennsylvania Secretary of State in Harrisburg, Pennsylvania. Her name is Adele Manners."

"You say he met with Manners in person, not just by telephone?" Turgenev asked.

"Yes, absolutely," Barovsky answered.

"And how do you know this?" Turgenev pressed.

"Someone in Manner's inside circle relayed the existence and subject manner of the meeting to the Pennsylvania State Democratic Party. We intercepted the email."

"Very interesting. And what was the subject matter of the meeting?" Turgenev asked.

"It seems that Klein visited Manners because he knows the difficulty the Pennsylvania Democrats had with us in 2016, and the well-publicized problems Pennsylvania had with its primary elections last month. He met with Manners to offer his services with the November elections."

"What kind of services?"

"The email we accessed did not specify."

"You said that Klein was with Manners yesterday. How do you know he's still not in Harrisburg today?"

"Because the email said that Klein was leaving Harrisburg right after the meeting."

"Did the email say where he was going next?"

"No. It merely said Manners would consider Klein's proposal and had a secret way to get in touch with Klein. It did not say what that secret arrangement was."

"Do we have a way to hack into Manners's computer?"

"Unfortunately, no, not right now. Her computer system is highly secure. We can get past their security, but it will take some time. We cannot do it quickly enough to be of any practical use to you in tracking Klein."

"Too bad, but perhaps all is not lost. I can't imagine that Klein had any unique interest in Pennsylvania. I believe a number of U.S. states held primary elections earlier this month. Many of them had delays and various other difficulties. Let me know if you come across anything further regarding our elusive Mr. Klein."

* * *

Turgenev buzzed his assistant.

"Yes, Mr. President."

"In no more than one hour's time, I want a list on my desk of every U.S. state that has conducted a primary election in the last four months. Please see that this list includes a special notation of every one of those states that suffered any troubles or complications in conducting those elections. I also need to know the cities in each of those states where the election officials are located. Finally, I need maps of each of those states, and a map of the U.S. showing each state. Never mind Hawaii or Alaska."

"Right away, sir."

* * *

Bianchi hosted a belated July 4 holiday barbecue meeting with her DNC convention planning committee. Their agenda was extensive. She had a printed list of topics the committee needed to review. She was not distributing copies to the committee because she didn't want to risk the possibility that the agenda would somehow be leaked to the opposition or the press. She had the one-page agenda on her clipboard as the meeting got under way.

CONFIDENTIAL 2020 CONVENTION AGENDA

Presidential Nomination
Vice Presidential Vetting, Selection and Nomination
Convention Considerations
Pandemic
Party Platform
Social Unrest
#Me Too
BLM

POLICE DEFUNDING
BAKER
    TAX RETURNS
    CRONYISM
    2016 ELECTION FRAUD
    DACA
  2020 ELECTION FRAUD

The meeting ran true to form, until they came to the subject of election fraud. "Hey, Betty, we know that Russia's going to try to control the election in Baker's favor, even more than it did in 2016. How do you plan to deal with that?"

"One word, 'mail-in,'" Bianchi answered. "It will be hard for the Russians to manipulate the vote if we keep it off the internet from start to finish."

"Isn't that two words, Betty?"

"Very funny. I used a hyphen, so it's only one word."

"More seriously, how are we going to deal with everything that Baker is going to do to sabotage a massive mail-in vote? Won't he try to completely destroy the election?"

"He can make a lot of noise, but what's he really going to do? The Supreme Court won't back him—even if Baker gets to appoint another member of the Court before the election—and the Constitution makes me the next president if the election is still in doubt on January 20. He'll step down before he lets me become president."

"Gee, Betty, is that why you're pushing for a mail-in vote? Tell the truth, now."

"Haha," was all that Bianchi answered.

CHAPTER 92
July 12, 2020, One Day Later

THE MATERIALS TURGENEV HAD called for yesterday in one-hour's time had arrived right on schedule. And he would have dealt with them with equal haste had other responsibilities of even greater urgency not intervened. But he was now focused on the objects spread out in front of him on his office conference table.

He realized almost immediately that he had a problem he had not anticipated. The number of stops to which Klein might now be headed were far greater than he had imagined. It wasn't that Turgenev couldn't assemble the manpower to promptly take on the task at hand. Rather, the problem was he couldn't count on those numbers going unnoticed and, if discovered, it would appear as if Russia were invading America. He was reminded of the 1966 movie *The Russians Are Coming, The Russians Are Coming*. It would set off a notorious international incident that would prove counterproductive. That simply wouldn't do.

The movie was a comedy; his objective was anything but. However, the movie did give him an alternative way to proceed that he thought would work.

Within an hour, he arranged for the necessary encrypted text to be sent describing the situation and what action was needed. Within still another hour, he was in receipt of an encrypted reply that said the matter would be handled.

* * *

JAKE AND AMIR LEFT their first stopover, and were on the way to their second. Jake enjoyed Amir's company. Not only was it reassuring—even if falsely—not to be alone, but Amir was full of interesting questions about social studies and civics that really put Jake's mind to the test. And wasn't it ironic to be discussing these subjects on the fourth of July?

He had not thought about these subjects since high school, when they had struck him as totally boring. They now appeared to be of much greater immediacy and real-world concern. The U.S. seemed to be approaching a critical moment in its history of a magnitude not seen since the Civil War. *At least then, we had Abraham Lincoln to lead us back from the brink. Today, all we have is Baker or Sullivan—neither of them is an Abraham Lincoln.*

They reached their second stopover. Tomorrow night, they would encounter one more hideaway before finally arriving in Atlanta. Jake hated all of the delays, but he knew that discretion was the better part of valor. He had traveled too far—literally and figuratively—to lose his discipline and become reckless now. *I wonder what the next few days will bring.* Little did he know, it would be a lot more than just a few days.

CHAPTER 93
July 14, 2020, Two Days Later

ABELSON CALLED THE NUMBER Fyodor Gancharov had given him. Gancharov picked up on the first ring. "Fyodor, it's Gali. Your parents are fine—perhaps a little tired, but fine. Right now, they are getting acclimated to a new home. It's just temporary. Extreme circumstances called for extreme measures. We were not able to consult with them in advance. But know that they—and you—are safe. When they are ready, the three of you will decide where your permanent new family home should be, courtesy of the Russian government."

"Gali, I don't understand."

"When I hang up, you will hear a click. Stay on the line. I will be gone, but your parents will be on the line. Just the three of you—no one else. I know you will have lots of questions, but I figured it would be nicer for you to hear your parents' voices, and for them to be the ones to tell you how the past few days have transpired."

"I still don't understand, Gali, but I'm most grateful. Thank you."

"I'm not the one to thank. And you can always get ahold of me with any further questions later. There's no rush. Because of pandemic travel restrictions, you will not be able to join your parents now, but please rest assured that there's no need for that. They will be well taken care of until the three of you can be reunited." Abelson would have liked to listen in, but he respectfully hung up. Besides, he understood very little Russian. He didn't

266

hear the click, but he knew that Fyodor had; a first step to hopefully a better life for his family.

* * *

JAKE AND AMIR REACHED Atlanta. Jake had selected Atlanta as his next target because Georgia had reported terrible results with the use of its touted new voting machinery in its statewide June 9 primary elections. Georgia voters had been forced to wait upwards of three hours to cast their ballots. Atlanta, where the offices of the state election supervisor were located, had experienced particularly long lines, and serious delays.

They found a small, clean motor court on the outskirts of the city. After arranging their lodging, and with a map of the city in hand, courtesy of the front desk of the motor court, they spent almost two hours casually driving around downtown Atlanta where the seat of the state government was located—including the election supervisor, as well as the surrounding residential areas, which Jake and Amir found to be totally charming.

Jake hadn't yet heard back from Manners, the Pennsylvania election supervisor. Tomorrow, he would seek to meet with the Atlanta election supervisor to see what level of interest Georgia might have in his software program, if any.

As they returned to the motor court following their Atlanta outing, Jake checked Manners's Instagram account. He found a short post:

ALWAYS LOVE TALKING WITH MY FRIENDS.

The post was accompanied by two emojis, one a happy face and the other a heart. Followed by the words "Madam Secretary."

* * *

JAKE PULLED HIS LAST burner phone out of his backpack and dialed the cell number on the card Manners had given to him.

"Adele Manners," the soft voice answered.

"I always love talking with my friends too," Jake said.

"Happy to hear from you, JK. I trust and hope your travels are going well?"

"So far, so good. Tomorrow's another important day."

"Good luck with it, whatever it is. I'll come right to the point, JK. My technology colleagues want to put your software through its paces. If it passes muster, Pennsylvania would like to use your software in November."

"Wow, that's wonderful. I'd be delighted to work with your engineers and show them how the software works. I can also work with them on any custom tweaks necessary to make the software work seamlessly with your systems. I also have a user guide I've created and a few 'how to' white papers."

"Awesome, when can you return to Harrisburg?"

"Two to three days. Will that work for you?"

That'll be fine. If everything checks out, we would propose to obtain a non-exclusive license agreement for a term of one year. Does that sound okay?"

"Sure."

"Do you have a form of license agreement? If not, we have a form we use."

"My sister's a lawyer. Name's Leah Klein, she's in D.C. I'll be happy to have her put together a license agreement for your lawyers to look at."

"Great. What about your fees for the one year, including your consulting with us as needed?"

Seriously! I'd do it for free. The first deal is always the toughest one to come by. If Pennsylvania uses and endorses my software, I'll be golden. I also understand from Leah's mentor, Judge Brooks, that whomever goes first in negotiations loses. I tell you what, Adele, when we get to that point, you can tell me whatever the State of Pennsylvania thinks would be fair and would fit its budget. I'm sure we won't have any problems."

He was so excited he wanted to dance, maybe even with Amir. *Well, not quite.* He thought of Anya. That brought him back to terra firma.

CHAPTER 94
July 15, 2020, One Day Later

JAKE AND AMIR CHECKED out of the motor court. All of their worldly traveling possessions were in the trunk of Amir's car—that included all four of Jake's laptops, but not his smartphone, which was in his jacket pocket.

They found a two-hour parking space three short blocks away from the Georgia election supervisor's office. "Same drill as before, Amir. If I'm not back in ninety minutes, take off. Get the hell out of town and head home."

"Understand, Mr. JK, same as in Harrisburg, but not like. Supposed to be team."

"If I'm detained, there's nothing you can do for me. Historically, Georgia is a red state. I'm going into less friendly territory than in Harrisburg, which was more neutral. If I don't return, you have to protect yourself."

"Red state? What mean?"

"Republican. Probably in favor of Baker. Good chance they won't like what I'm trying to do."

* * *

JAKE WALKED INTO THE Georgia State Election Supervisor's office, Alistair Dobbs. "Is Mr. Dobbs available?" Jake asked. "Name's Jake Klein. It really is me under this mask."

The masked receptionist looked in her calendar. "Don't see your name here, son. Can I tell him what the purpose of your visit is?"

"Sure. I'd like to talk to him about security for Georgia's election software," Jake answered.

"Have a seat. I'll see if he's interested, and available." She disappeared through a door behind her desk.

Ten minutes later, the receptionist returned, followed by a non-descript man with an inquisitive look on his face. "That's him, Mr. Dobbs," the receptionist said, pointing a finger at Jake. She withdrew to her desk as Dobbs walked over to Jake. He was not wearing a mask.

"Was told you might be comin' here, boy. Under different circumstances, I'd frankly be interested in sittin' with you a spell, hearing your story, especially whatever it was you did to piss off POTUS and EBCOM so mightily. But today, I ain't in the market of buyin' what you're a sellin'. You didn't hear it from me, boy, but you oughta beat it outta here, lickety split. In about two minutes, you won't be able to." He turned and walked away before Jake could answer.

* * *

JAKE DID EXACTLY AS he was told, only faster. He hit the streets, saw nothing untoward, and walked as fast as he could to where Amir was parked. "Trouble, Amir, take off fast and don't stop 'til you're back home." Jake was gone before Amir could object.

He saw a traffic officer a block away. He approached the officer and asked whether there were any nearby car rentals, "just to do a little sightseeing, and then leave it at the airport."

The officer turned and pointed down the street. "Two blocks ahead, first signal, turn right, and it's one block down on the left side of the street."

"Much obliged, officer. Have a nice day." Jake walked off, trying to look relaxed. He was anything but.

He found the car rental, walked in, and told the agent he was visiting from out of town. "Flew in on a last-minute invitation to play Augusta. A lifelong dream. Came on such little notice, couldn't even pack my clubs. Was going to stay in Augusta, but wanted to rent a car to make the drive. I'll keep it for a couple of days and turn it back in at the airport."

"Holy fuckin shit, man," the agent said. "Lived here all my life and never been able to get on Augusta." He took pictures of Jake's credit card, driver's license, and insurance card. Jake was dying on the inside, but all smiles and happy talking about Augusta on the outside. Ten minutes later, he was in a fully gassed economy car, with a map of the area marked to show the way to Augusta, and the way to Hartsfield-Jackson Atlanta International Airport. It also showed the way north out of town, but that wasn't marked.

* * *

JAKE DROVE OUT OF the car rental and found the route out of town headed north. He pulled over into a mall parking lot, and sent two emails to Leah.
The first read:

> DEAR SIS!
> HOPE YOU'RE WELL. WE NEED TO CATCH UP.
> HUGS,
> JAKE

The second read:

> BUKAR ABCIM U-

* * *

JUST AS JAKE WAS about to finish the third word, hit send, and drive off, four unmarked black SUVs screamed into the mall lot and surrounded Jake's car. No sirens. No lights. Each SUV had two occupants—eight of them, and only one of Jake. Not very good odds.

Four huge white males in unmarked military fatigues rushed Jake's car with guns unholstered and pointed at Jake. He was barely able to add a dash to the last letter he had typed and hit send. They didn't ask him who he was, but they seemed to know.

"Turn off the engine, boy. Slowly hand me the car keys, and that phone of yours."

"Who are you gentlemen? May I see some identification? Have I done something wrong?"

"Don't make me repeat myself, boy. You won't like what'll happen if I have to."

Jake did as he was told.

"Outta the car and down on your knees. Hands behind your back. Now."

"Lucky I'm not black, huh." *Can't believe I said that. Just kinda slipped out.*

"Might as well be, far as we're concerned—smart-ass." The one who made that remark slapped Jake along the side of his head. Hard.

Jake was cuffed and thrown in the back seat of one of the SUVs. Pain shot through his shoulders as his hands were forced together behind his back. His cuffs were hooked to the side door. Two of the men got in the front seat of the SUV and one got in the back, alongside Jake. Two other men got into Jake's car and pulled in behind the lead SUV occupied by Jake.

"Where are you taking me?" Jake asked.

No one answered him. It was like he didn't exist.

He broke out in a cold sweat. He could feel his heart pounding. He could hardly catch his breath. He felt lightheaded, like he might pass out. *Oh shit! Not good. Definitely not good. But nothing to be gained by saying anything more for now.* The procession headed off. In the rearview mirror of the SUV, Jake could see his rental car, and the other three SUVs bringing up the rear. *Wonder if they'll turn in my rental car for me.* They drove with no regard for any local speed limits—but still no sirens, and still no flashing lights.

What little perception Jake had turned a hundredfold worse when the man sitting next to him, without warning, suddenly slipped an opaque hood over his head. *At least the KKK hoods had slits to see and breathe.*

* * *

It seemed a lot longer, but it was only ninety minutes since Leah had first read Jake's two emails—especially the first one that had put Leah on high alert, set her wheels in motion. *More like spinning in mud, going nowhere!* Leah's emotions vacillated back and forth between fear for her "kid" brother and irritation with her husband, who she had repeatedly, but unsuccessfully, been trying to reach every few minutes since Jake's two emails had arrived.

When Leah had married Frank, a half-dozen years earlier, she had adopted his two young children, Charlie and Madison, who had survived the hit-and-run death of their mom, Frank's first wife. It was a package deal. Leah became Mom. She couldn't have been more pleased. Probably Jake either, no doubt, because he assumed Leah's instant family responsibilities would have left her precious little time to mother him quite so much. Of course, he should have known better.

All Frank had to do was love, cherish, and obey—and always be telephonically available in the event of any family emergencies. First, Jake—missing and apparently in some kind of serious trouble. And now, Frank—who was also nowhere to be found.

* * *

TURGENEV READ THE UNSCRAMBLED message. *Finally. About fucking time!*

He arranged for the following text to be sent:

IT'S OVER. RETURN HOME SOONEST.

* * *

FIRE SHOT OUT OF Leah's eyes. "Where the hell have you been?" Leah said to Frank as he barely set foot through the front door of their well-sized home, and handed him the spray bottle of disinfectant sitting on the entryway table.

"Well, hello to you too," Frank said, as he discarded his mask and gloves. "My day was okay; thanks for asking. Yours, not so much, I'm guessing. Anything in particular?"

"I'm pissed," she answered.

"Could've fooled me. Pissed at who? Something I said? Did I say something wrong?"

"At *whom*. And not something you said, but something you *didn't* say. More importantly, something you didn't *do*. You didn't tell me where you've been. What if something had happened to Charlie or Madison? What if I needed you? What if *we* needed you?"

"It's not even dinnertime," he said. He quickly stole a peek at his watch for moral support. "Where do you *think* I've been? Like, maybe at work? Since you said 'what if', do I trust nothing's in fact up with Charlie or Madison? Aren't they still off visiting their grandparents for a few days, helping them stock up on groceries and taking care of some other household chores made a bit more complicated by the pandemic sheltering rules for older folks?"

"No, nothing's *up* with the kids, or your parents, they're all fine. But I'm always supposed to be able to reach you. I tried your cell—you didn't pick up.

273

I called your office—all they knew was that you were 'out in the field.' And you didn't call back! What if Charlie or Madison *did* need you?"

Frank looked sheepish. "Sorry, I know the drill. Turned out, I was in a bad patch, didn't have reception. And was out longer than I expected."

Leah took a couple of breaths. *Point made. Time to move on.* Her thoughts returned to Jake. She had managed to hold her emotions together—barely— until Frank arrived. *One problem down, one more to go.* The room started spinning. She clutched Frank's forearm to catch her balance, and took a deep breath.

"What is it?" Frank asked.

She took his hand, grabbed her purse and keys from the table where they had been standing in the front hallway, and ushered him out of the house.

* * *

ANYA READ THE TEXT. *It's over. Return home soonest. What does that mean— it's over?*

* * *

LEAH QUICKLY LED FRANK down to the street in front of their home and continued pulling him along the sidewalk for about a hundred yards or so before she halted. "It's Jake. He's in trouble," she finally said.

Frank looked into Leah's eyes. "What kind of trouble?" he asked, firmly but softly.

"I don't know. I got an email from Jake, actually two," she said. "I tried to call him. His number rolled over to voicemail. He hasn't called back. First Jake, and then you. No one was taking my damn calls! I sent Jake an email too. He hasn't responded to that either."

"Why are we standing here in the middle of the street?" Frank asked.

"I think our house might be bugged," Leah answered.

"What?" Frank stared at her. "Do you have Jake's emails? Can I see them?"

Thinking that her smartphone might also be bugged, Leah had printed out Jake's two emails, and intentionally left her phone behind in the house. She reached into her bag and pulled out the printed copies of the emails and handed them to Frank.

Frank read Jake's emails, and then stared at Leah. "The second email's a bit cryptic and strange, perhaps written by someone who's had one too many drinks, but the first email seems perfectly bland. What trouble do you think Jake's in? He doesn't say anything about trouble. Do you think he might be ill? Can you explain to me what's bothering you?"

All of a sudden, Leah's emotional dam burst. She let out a whimper and started to fall. Frank caught her, pulled her into him, and held her close for several moments, until her shaking subsided. "Whoa. Easy. Just catch your breath," he said to her.

She tried to speak, but couldn't.

"Leah, I'm right here. Take your time. There's no need to rush."

She pushed him away, put her arms around her shoulders, and took several slow exaggerated breaths. She closed her eyes. "I think I'm gonna be sick." She took more deep breaths.

"Breathe slower, less deeply," Frank said. "You're hyperventilating. If you're not careful, you'll pass out." He put his hands gently back on her shoulders.

She slowed down. "What do you mean there's no need to rush? I'm a mother, a sister, not a damn homicide investigator like you. First, I was all alone for almost two hours with Jake's emails. No idea where he is or what to do. Then, I started worrying someone may be watching *us*. I can't take it anymore." Her panic welled up all over again.

"Leah, stop. I understand. I got you. That's what I'm trying to tell you. You're not alone. We're in this together. We're a team, you and I. We'll figure this out. Together. We'll get through this."

"Frank, Jake's young, he feels invincible, independent. But now he's scared. And I don't know where he is. I can't reach him. I can't help him. I need to help him. Tell me, Mr. Detective, what am I going to do? I'm his big sister. I'm his mother. Tell me, please, what the hell am I going to do!"

"What are *we* going to do." He held her close once more. "We need to sort this out, but not here in the middle of the street." Still holding the emails, Frank guided Leah back to his car, and drove them to a nearby restaurant they frequented.

* * *

Turgenev looked incredulously at Lebedev's handler. "What do you mean there's no answer?" he asked.

"I mean, she hasn't responded to my instructions," the handler answered.

"Find her! And be fast about it, if you know what's good for you."

"Yes, Mr. President." The handler scurried out of Turgenev's office.

* * *

Leah hurried to a corner booth at the rear of the restaurant. The waitress brought them two glasses of water. They each ordered coffee, nothing more. They waited a couple of minutes until the waitress brought them their drinks.

Frank spread the two emails out in front of them on the table, facing him. He again said to Leah that he didn't get it.

"It's all over the email!" Leah all but shouted.

"Babe, I hear ya, but you gotta help me out a little here. *What's* all over the email?"

"For starters, the email begins **Dear Sis!** That's a dead giveaway, especially the exclamation mark."

"Because?"

"Because that's Jake's code for **Dire SOS!** He's in trouble—dire trouble." Leah was trying to calm down, but not succeeding.

"What code? Tell me about the code."

"You know how Jake's a techie? When he was a kid, he made up a code for fun, kind of like Pig Latin, but a little more tricky. In his code, which we named 'JK's Code', **Dear Sis!** becomes **Dire SOS!**"

"*Whoa.* Slow down. Walk me through the ground rules of how JK's Code works. One step at time, would ya please."

"Okay. First, you need to concentrate on the vowels, **A E I O U.** When you have two words, in this case, **Dear Sis!**, you have to take one word at a time, starting with the first word, **Dear.** Got that?"

"Kind of like charades. *Two words. First word. First clue.* Keep going."

"You take the first vowel in the first word, and you increase it by one—meaning, you change the **E** in **Dear** to an **I.** You still with me?"

"Hold up," Frank said. He removed his ever present old-fashioned pocket-sized detective's notepad and pen from his jacket and turned to a fresh page.

It amused Leah to no end that Frank refused to transfer his thought processes from his caveman era notepad to his 21st century smartphone.

On the first line, Frank wrote **DEAR**. On the second line, he next wrote **DEAR -> DIAR**. "So, **DEAR** is now **Diar**. I'm looking right at it. **Diar**. That's gobbledygook. There obviously has to be more than that. Right? What's next?"

"Stay with me. I told you JK's Code is a little tricky. When the *resulting* first word, **Diar**, also has two vowels in a row, one after another, **I** and **A**, which are in turn followed by a consonant, **R**, you now take the *second* vowel in the first word, and increase it by one—meaning, you change the **A** in what is **Diar** to an **E**, *and* you then move that resulting **E** to the *other* side of the consonant **R**. Therefore, **DIAR** becomes **Dier** and **Dier** becomes **DIRE**."

Leah looked for some sign that Frank was still following her.

Frank shook the apparent cobwebs out of his head. "I think I got it, but give me a sec," he said. On the third line of his notepad page, he wrote **DIAR -> Dier**. On the fourth line, he wrote **Dier -> DIRE**. "So, under JK's Code, you're telling me, bottom line, **DEAR** becomes **DIRE**. Right?"

"Exactly!" Leah said.

"What if the first word has another vowel in it, but it is not in succession with the first vowel?"

"Just repeat for the second vowel the rule I just gave you for the first vowel."

"Got it. Okay. Let's move on. **SIS!**, what do we do about the *second* word?" Frank asked.

"That's easy," Leah answered. "You go back to Jake's first rule and increase the vowel **I** in the second word by one vowel, in this case from **I** to **O**. So, **SIS!** becomes **Sos!** Taking a little literary license, **Sos!**, as a matter of emphasis, becomes **SOS!** Even with my slight embellishment, that should be pretty straightforward."

On the next two lines of Frank's notepad, he wrote **Sis! -> Sos!** and **Sos! -> SOS!** Frank bobbed his head, barely, but affirmatively.

On a roll, Leah charged on. "As a result, **DEAR SIS!** becomes **DIRE SOS!** Jake was signaling me that he's in trouble, not just some run-of-the-mill inconvenience trouble—*dire* trouble."

"I guess I follow you, but you still seem to be making quite a leap of faith," Frank said.

"Not really. When you're as used to JK's Code as I am, it's a snap. Besides, there's more in Jake's first email, a *lot* more," Leah urged.

"Show me," Frank replied, a bit more receptive, but still not yet convinced.

"One. Jake's emails are *always* . . . dry. His salutations never begin with **DEAR**. I'm lucky if I get a **HEY**, let alone a **HI**, but certainly never a **DEAR**. *Never*. And never any exclamation marks."

Frank nodded. "Anything else?"

"Yes. Look at the body of his email: **HOPE YOU'RE WELL. WE NEED TO CATCH UP**. You know Jake. He's quiet, understated. He never makes small talk like that. He never shows any sign of warmth. He always has to *look* tough, macho, even though I know better. Whether he realizes that or not. He'd never sign off with something like **LOVE** or **HUGS**. And he wouldn't *ever* say **JAKE**. All I ever get at the end of an email, if I get any personalization at all, is **JK**. He wouldn't sign off with **JAKE**. Everything about this email spells trouble—serious, serious trouble."

Frank glanced at what he had written on the seven lines of his notepad.

> DEAR.
> DEAR –> DIAR.
> DIAR –> DIER.
> DIER –> DIRE.
> SIS! –> SOS!
> SOS! –> SOS!
> DEAR SIS! –> DIRE SOS!

And what about the second email? Frank looked at it for a few minutes and jotted onto his notepad.

> BUKAR –> BAKER
> ABCIM –> EBCOM
> U- –> A-

He showed Leah what he had written down. "If, under your rules, the **U** loops back around to an **A**. Does it?"

"It does," Leah answered.

"So, you're the one who plays around with upper case and lower case, and editorial extrapolations about what Jake might have meant in between the actual words. Is it **BAKER** or **BAKER**, with an upper case B?"

"I have no idea, Frank. Jake typed it as lower case. I'm guessing he would have typed it as upper case if that's what he meant. Except, if he was in a hurry, he might not have had time to hit the upper case key, even if that's what he meant."

"And the second word, I'm guessing it's an acronym, as to which the case wouldn't matter," Frank said. "He might have typed it in lower case simply because it was faster and easier."

"Plus, people often don't bother with upper case in emails and texts," Leah said.

"Finally, the third word—or character—is even more vague," Frank said. "Is it just the letter, or is it some kind of an abbreviation, given the dash that follows it?"

"To me," Leah responded, "the dash suggests that Jake intended something more than just the letter. Why else would Jake have taken the time to add a dash? Also, this suggests, again, that Jake was in a hurry and ran out of time. What was rushing him?"

"So, the first word could mean someone who bakes cakes," Frank said, "which doesn't make a whole lot of sense. Or, it could also mean the name of a person—coincidentally, including our current president—which again is not very helpful, and is even more intriguing if, for some reason, Jake did mean our president. Do you have any idea? Do you know what the acronym in Jake's second email stands for?"

"I have no idea," Leah responded.

"Could the acronym possibly have anything to do with our president?" Frank asked.

"I told you, I have no idea!" Leah repeated, raising her voice again.

"And why do you think our house and your phone might be bugged?" Frank asked.

"That's easy. Jake hadn't used JK's Code with me in years. He would have had no reason to do so now, unless he was concealing what he was trying to tell me from someone he thought would intercept or see his emails. It would have been easier and quicker for Jake to just tell me what he wanted me to know. If he thought someone was watching him, it stands to reason that someone may also be watching me."

Frank nodded ever so slightly.

"Out in front of our home, you said the second email might have been written by someone who had a couple of drinks too many," Leah said. "In that same light, it could have been written by someone who was having a stroke."

"Hon, I just said what I did to try and keep things light," Frank replied.

"I know, but when I think more about it, I rule out both of those possibilities. JK's Code requires too much precision. I don't think a drunk, or one in the midst of having some kind of a stroke or a seizure, could have put those two emails together. I think Jake's trouble is coming from a third party."

"That does make sense," Frank said.

Leah got the impression that Frank might finally be coming around. That wasn't a solution, but at least it was a start—to have someone on her side. And Jake's.

* * *

JAKE TRIED TO KEEP track of how long the car ride was. *One thousand one, one thousand two.* He kept counting as best he could, but it was hard to concentrate. As near as he could tell, it was around thirty minutes when the car came to a stop, and the engine was turned off. He listened for conversation, anything that might help. Nothing. *Who the hell are these guys? Alistair Dobbs, the Georgia election official guy, mentioned POTUS and EBCOM. Ala Jake's Code, maybe that will mean something to Leah. Wanted to add my code for Atlanta, but it was either code for A- and hit send, or there wasn't going to be any second email. Hopefully, it will help. Half a loaf . . .*

The captors unhooked him from the SUV door, but kept the handcuffs and hood on. They led him somewhere through a succession of doors. There was a little talking, but lots of electronic noises and clicks.

Finally, he was given a shove, and thought he was being knocked to the ground—until he felt some kind of a cot break his fall. He was shivering. He couldn't tell if it was just him, or because it was cold. "Do I get a blanket?" he yelled out to no one in particular. No one answered, and no one brought him a blanket. "Don't I get my one phone call?" he again yelled out.

"Haha," someone shouted back. "Ain't you the comedian." *Nice to know I'm appreciated. And not alone. Rather have a hot shower, a change of clothes, and a glass of warm milk. Wonder if Leah got my emails, the closest it seems I'm going to get to my one call.* He was *trying* to think positive.

He heard his hosts depart, whispering something among themselves he couldn't make out. He was still cuffed and hooded, lying there uncomfortably on the cot, the cuffs digging into his wrists. The springs of the cot poked against his side. The ache in his shoulders grew worse, thanks to the handcuffs pinning his arms behind his back. He couldn't find a more comfortable position. It was hard breathing under the hood. Wherever he was, it was dank, but he couldn't tell if it was the hood or the room he was in, or both.

They weren't just holding him captive. They were also going out of their way to intimidate him. He was doing his best not to panic, but it was against long odds.

Sometime later, he couldn't tell exactly when, he sensed that he was no longer alone. Suddenly, he felt a sharp pinch in his shoulder, like the sting of a wasp he remembered from more otherwise pleasant summer days in his past. He felt dizzy and then everything went black—blacker than it already was under his hood.

CHAPTER 95
July 16, 2020, One Day Later

AMIR HAD CONTINUED DRIVING nonstop through the night. He was tired, but he knew that receiving no calls from Jake was not a good sign. He had to get to Jake's sister. He didn't remember her name, but knew she lived somewhere around D.C. and was a lawyer. She had given Jake some immigration information that Jake had passed along to him with her contact information in case he needed her help. He hoped she would be able to help Jake.

The contact information was in his apartment in New Haven. He would have to go there first, find her contact information, and then drive to D.C. It would not be good for him to call her because she didn't actually know him, and his poor English wouldn't help.

He heard the sirens behind him. Sirens were a bad thing in Kazakhstan. He was frightened. The cop, who was wearing a mask, pulled alongside him on a motorcycle and motioned for him to pull over onto the shoulder of the highway. He did as he was directed, and turned off the engine. Amir hurriedly put on his mask as the officer walked over to the car. He could see the officer's hand on his holster. *Definitely not good.* The cop signaled him to lower his window. He did.

"Where's the fire?"

"Sorry. No see fire."

"Did you know you were doing 80 in a 65-mile limit?"

"Sorry. Not know."

"Where are you from?"

"From New Haven, Connecticut, USA."

"Before that?"

"Kazakhstan."

"Never heard of it. Where's it at?"

"Europe." *Not say Eastern Europe. Better?*

"Do you have permission to be in America?"

"Yes. Am asylee. Have papers."

"Asylee? Let me see them papers."

Amir reached toward his glove compartment."

"Whoa. The officer pulled his gun from his holster. Keep your damn hands where I can see them!"

"Yes. Sorry. Papers in glove compartment."

"Okay. Slowly." The officer waved his gun toward the glove compartment.

Amir held his left hand in the air and moved his right hand to open the glove compartment. Slowly. He pulled out his passport with the asylum form and handed them to the cop. Slowly.

"Asylee? What the hell is that?" the cop asked.

"Means right to be in U.S. of A. Very pleased be here."

The cop looked at the picture in the passport, and then looked at Amir.

"Are you sick?"

"No."

"Do you have a fever?"

"No. Not cough either. Not tired. Taste and smell good."

The officer nodded. "Take off your mask."

Amir did as he was told. Slowly.

The officer looked at the passport photo and then at Amir again. "Not a very good picture."

"Yes. Mother say same." *Try be funny. Make friend.*

"Why are you sweating?"

"In Kazakhstan, stop by officer, very scary."

"You sure you don't have a temperature?"

"Sure. Yes. No temperature."

"Is this your car?"

"Yes. Drive for Uber in home town, New Haven, Connecticut, USA."

"Let me see your driver's license and registration."

"In glove compartment. Okay?"

"Slowly. Very slowly." He tightened the grip on his gun.

Amir handed his license and registration to the officer.

He looked at them and checked them on a handheld device. After a few minutes, he returned all of Amir's papers to him. "Okay, I'm going to let you off with just a warning this time because you seem like a nice guy. Keep it under 65."

"Yes. Thank you, Mr. Officer." Amir wiped his dripping forehead with the back of his hand as he drove off, slowly, relieved that the officer hadn't asked him why a man from Kazakhstan was traveling on a Bermuda passport.

* * *

POTUS, BAKER, JR. AND AUSTIN stood around on the driving range. "It really pisses me off to have to come over here to get away from those goddamn mandatory official White House recording devices. Like those cops now having to wear body cams. I'm the goddamned President of the United States. People shouldn't be trying to record what I say. And they shouldn't be wasting tax dollars trying to get my tax returns. What I say in my tax returns is nobody's business but my own. All this nonsense isn't going to continue much longer."

Austin and Baker, Jr. smiled knowingly.

"Okay, what's the poop on this schmuck, Klein?" Baker asked.

Austin proudly responded, "We got him. Locked up tighter than a walnut held between two butt cheeks."

"Where?" POTUS asked.

"United States Penitentiary, Atlanta," Austin answered.

"Visitors not permitted, right?" POTUS asked.

"Right, because of COVID-19 risks," Austin said.

"Hmm, would be too bad if he came down with that. How long can we hold him incommunicado?"

"Actually, Dad, we don't have the right to hold him incommunicado at all," Baker, Jr. said.

"Who the fuck says? I'm the goddamned President of the United States. If I wanna hold him incommunicado, I can. Period! The son of a bitch is a treasonist. That's a capital offense."

"You mean he's guilty of treason?" Austin asked.

That's what I said, didn't I?"

And who says I can't hold him avocado if I want? You didn't answer me about that, Junior."

"Your Attorney General does," Baker, Jr. said. "And you did mean incommunicado, right?"

"Yeah? Well, you tell the Attorney General I appointed him, I made him, and I can fire him. Tell him he better do some more research because I'm thinking of doing the same to all of these asshole protesters—the ones in Portland, Los Angeles, and Chicago. And around the White House. They're treasonists too. Why the hell do you think I'm egging them on? You think I don't know what I'm doing? And how come you don't laugh at my jokes, Junior? I made you, and I can fire you too."

Baker, Jr. laughed—sort of—POTUS didn't.

* * *

LEAH WOKE UP FROM a restless night's sleep, mostly past her anxiety, and ready to confront the task before her. Frank had a security firm he worked with sweep their home earlier that morning to verify there were no bugs planted anywhere in their home. He also bought Leah a new laptop computer and smartphone that she could use without having to worry about any planted backdoor hacking entrances.

Steaming coffee mug in hand, Leah was all over the internet looking for any sign of something or someone called EBCOM. A- was not even worth a try. *Maybe it will mean something if I can first find EBCOM.* Once again, directly typing EBCOM into her browser produced nothing, not through Google, not through Wikipedia, not through YouTube, and not through any other search engine.

She decided she would try searching on Dustin Baker to see if that brought up any references to EBCOM. The theory might have been good, but there were dozens of pages of entries under Dustin Baker.

Next, she searched on the White House Chief of Staff, the White House legal counsel, and all other White House executives. Again, nothing referring to EBCOM. *Can't give up.*

She went through each member of Baker's cabinet. Nothing after nothing after nothing. Until a little glimmer cropped up when she searched on the Secretary of Defense. On the eighth page of Google, she found it. A link that included the word EBCOM. There was no indication of what the letters stood for, but it was apparently some kind of committee on which the Secretary of Defense was a member.

The brief article appeared in a nondescript D.C. blog. The byline attributed the story to a journalist by the name of Regina Liu. The subject of Liu's blog was whether it was appropriate for White House cabinet members to sit on private for profit committees. In her blog, Liu said she tried, but was unable to obtain an interview of the Secretary of Defense or to find out anything about what EBCOM was or does.

* * *

ANYA WAS NOT HAPPY returning home to Russia without knowing what Jake's fate was, what exactly "it's over" meant. It was not likely that she would learn more under Turgenev's need-to-know philosophy. If she didn't return home soon, she knew her handler would send someone after her.

Anya's long blonde hair was now short, dark and cropped, made possible by the scissors and bottle of dye hidden away among the bare essentials packed into her roller bag. She omitted her laptop and smartphone, which she intentionally left behind in her Cambridge apartment. She stopped at a nearby computer store and purchased a new laptop and smartphone.

She made the purchases using a credit card in a name unknown to her handler. She set up her new devices using credentials that matched the credit card she used to make the purchases.

She called an Uber, again using the credit card with which she made her electronic purchases, and headed for the train station. She used cash to purchase her train ticket.

* * *

LEAH SAT IN THE coffee shop opposite Regina Liu.

Frank had wanted to accompany her. "Remember, we're a team," he'd said. "Besides, interrogations are what I do."

Leah had overruled him. "I'm afraid two of us might prove intimidating. Furthermore, I know how to take a deposition, too, if it comes to that."

Liu seemed quite nice and forthcoming, and they quickly dispensed with formalities and last names.

"I want to thank you again for meeting with me, Regina, especially on such short notice."

"My pleasure. You're the first one besides me who has shown any interest in EBCOM. Plus, I'm also curious to know exactly what your interest is."

Leah was afraid that if she explained her true motives, she might scare Liu away. *Also, Cyrus always tells me whoever goes first loses.* "Curious is a good choice of words. A friend of mine asked me if I had ever heard of EBCOM. I Googled it, but I couldn't find anything. That made me curious. Then I stumbled across your article, and here we are."

"I think you're probably the only one who's ever read my article. How in the world did you find it?" Liu asked.

"I honestly don't recall," Leah lied. "I was just looking around here and there, and stumbled across it somewhere." She paused and hoped that would do the trick—it did. Liu actually seemed quite pleased to have someone with whom to share her EBCOM journey.

Liu explained that her editor, an ardent Republican and Baker fan, had assigned her to do a puff piece on Baker's cabinet. In researching the Secretary of Defense, she came across an obscure reference to EBCOM and wondered what it was. She couldn't find any other references to the name, including in the Secretary's public bio. She guessed it was a committee or association of some kind, and wondered whether cabinet members generally sat on private committees or associations.

She called the Secretary and tried to set up an interview. In passing, she mentioned EBCOM to the Secretary's assistant. He professed not to know what it was, but said he would get back to her on the interview time. When he called back, he said that the Secretary did not do interviews. Liu found that odd. If the Secretary didn't do interviews, why wasn't that explained to her initially? She wondered if it had anything to do with her inquiry about EBCOM.

Liu decided to try a less direct approach. The Chairman of the Joint Chiefs of Staff is the ranking U.S. military officer. He runs the Pentagon and reports to, and advises, POTUS, the Secretary of Defense and the National Security Advisor, who is the head of the National Security Council. While the National Security Advisor is not customarily a member of the White House Cabinet, membership on the cabinet is essentially a matter of presidential discretion and pro-military Baker includes the National Security Advisor on his cabinet.

Liu had gotten nowhere with the Secretary of Defense. She thought maybe she could get there with the Chairman of the Joint Chiefs, given his close relationship with the Secretary of Defense and the National Security Advisor.

Liu was able to secure an interview with the Chairman of the Joint Chiefs. When she showed up at the appointed time, the chairman's assistant greeted her in the reception area of the Pentagon. She apologized profusely, but said the chairman was called away to an emergency meeting of EBCOM. The assistant rescheduled her interview.

When Liu returned for the rescheduled interview with the chairman, she was greeted by a new assistant. She asked about the assistant she had previously met. She was told that the former assistant was a temp, pinch-hitting for the woman speaking with Liu, and was now gone. Liu commented that she had enjoyed a pleasant chemistry with the temp during their brief exchange, and wondered if she might be given her name. The regular assistant responded that releasing that information would violate Pentagon privacy rules.

During the course of the interview with the chairman, Liu said she inquired about EBCOM, but was told that he had never heard of that name, and that Liu must have misunderstood the temp.

Liu interviewed the other cabinet members, and asked each one of them about EBCOM. Without exception, each denied ever having heard of EBCOM. However, the demeanor of the Chairman of the Federal Communications Commission changed noticeably after Liu inquired about EBCOM. He terminated the interview midstream a few minutes later, saying he had to prepare for his next meeting.

"Wow, that's quite a story," Leah said. "It's fascinating. You could probably write a bestselling book about it."

"I haven't even told you the most interesting part of the story," Liu replied. "When I shared the story with my editor, and proposed doing a deeper dig and blog, he dismissively told me he had another blog for me to pursue, and to just wrap up this one with a pablum piece on the Secretary of Defense. He redlined everything interesting I wrote. I think it was inadvertent that the one circumspect reference to EBCOM I included slipped through and made the cut.

* * *

ABELSON WAS WORRIED. NOT only was Jake still not answering his phone, he was no longer responding, even by burner phone, to his repeat Instagram posts. *I think it's time to meet the family.*

* * *

LEAH RETURNED HOME AND found Frank waiting there to help in any way he could. She filled him in on her meeting with Liu.

"For starters," Leah said, "hard as it is to imagine, we definitely now know that Jake was telling us the BAKER he cited in his second email was none other than U.S. President Baker. This has to be true because EBCOM is apparently some kind of highly secret organization in which at least two members of Baker's cabinet are involved—his Secretary of Defense and his Chairman of the Federal Communications Commission. In addition, the Chairman of the Joint Chiefs of Staff is also somehow involved in EBCOM. Moreover, Liu's boss, who she says is a staunch Baker supporter, did all he could to put the kibosh on any reference to EBCOM in Liu's otherwise benign blog.

Incidentally, Liu had no idea what A- could represent. And I still don't have any idea either."

"A private eye as well as a lawyer," Frank said. "Obviously, Jake was trying to tell us something more when he typed U-—meaning A- in JK's Code lingo—but was then interrupted and prevented from finishing what he was trying to add. No doubt, he barely was able to add the dash to signal us there was more, and then hit send before his phone was snatched away from him. We're going to have to press harder on EBCOM."

The image of what must have happened to Jake at that precise moment sent Leah spiraling back down into the dark place from which she was trying to rise up.

Just then, the front doorbell rang.

* * *

ANYA MADE HER WAY from the ticket machine to her private compartment in the first class section of the train. She was suspicious of everyone who passed her, no more than half of them wearing masks and gloves. COVID-19 was nothing to sneeze at, but her greater concern was any agents her handler may have dispatched to find her.

No sooner had she taken her seat than a man in his late thirties entered the compartment and took a seat opposite her. Moments later, an older woman—but not *that* old—entered the compartment, sat down, and pulled out a partially knitted sweater, two knitting needles, and a ball of yarn from a large bag. The needles could be lethal weapons, if intended.

Her mind was working overtime. Either or both of them could be care packages sent from her handler to bring her back home—or worse. At least they were both wearing masks and gloves. And their seats were socially distanced, sort of. Under the circumstances, that really didn't put her mind that much at ease.

She opened her laptop with an exaggeration to send a subliminal message that she was not interested in making small talk. Anya attempted to compose and reduce her thoughts to writing on her recently purchased laptop, keeping one eye on each of her compartment mates at all times. She didn't get very far.

* * *

AMIR FINALLY REACHED NEW Haven and went straight to his apartment. *Blessed be, roommate not here. No time for talk small.* He searched high and low, until he found what he was after—the handwritten note from Jake with his sister's name and contact information. Thirty minutes later, he brushed his teeth, took a quick shower, put on a fresh change of clothes and was off for D.C. and Leah Klein.

* * *

FRANK PEERED THROUGH THE peephole in the door. He didn't recognize the man who stared back at him, but he looked harmless enough. He was wearing a mask and gloves. "Hang on a minute." Frank reached into the entry hall table drawer and put on his own mask and gloves. He opened the door. "Hello," he said, "can I help you?"

"Are you Frank?" Abelson asked. "We obviously haven't met. My name's Gali Abelson. I'm a friend of JK's from SCSU." He stood back from the door in order to socially distance.

Frank wasn't sure what to expect. The man seemed polite and went out of his way to show he knew Frank's name, Jake's nickname, and where Jake went to school. He also looked pretty well built. Frank was mindful that he was all that stood between this stranger and Leah. *Would hate to get in a shoving match with this guy.*

"Look," Abelson said. "This is awkward for both of us. Let me try to get us past that as quickly as possible."

"I'm listening," Frank said. He did not yet invite Abelson into the house.

"I know you're a homicide investigator. I'm sort of in the same business." He pulled out a laminated identity card and handed it to Frank.

Frank looked at Abelson's ID. "You're shitting me, right? Mossad?" What the hell interest does Mossad have in Jake?"

"I know it seems a little funky, but even more so than you might think. I'm not here in the U.S. as a Mossad agent. I'm here as a foreign exchange student. Like Jake, I'm a computer sciences major. Jake and I have a couple of classes together, so we became friendly. Jake's a lot smarter than I am, but thanks to Mossad, I have access to some pretty high-powered technology Jake was interested in."

"Still listening." And the two men were still standing at the front door.

"Bottom line, starting last November, with my Tel Aviv boss's permission, I made some of our technology available to Jake. At least until recently, I knew pretty much what Jake was up to. A few days ago, Jake went completely off the grid. I haven't been able to reach him, not even using our clandestine way of communicating. I'm afraid Jake may be in some kind of trouble. I feel at least partially responsible—maybe more than partially. I'm here because I didn't know what else to do. I want to help you and Jake's sister get things sorted out, and hopefully get Jake back home, safe and sound."

Frank had heard enough. He handed Abelson's ID back to him. "Sorry for being so guarded and stiff. C'mon in. Let me introduce you to my wife, Jake's sister. Can I offer you something to drink?"

"Maybe a little later. For now, I'd just like to meet your wife and put our heads together and compare notes, so to speak. Or, at least our thinking, as quickly as possible. Not to sound melodramatic, but I'm afraid Jake's life may genuinely depend on what we can accomplish."

* * *

Leah had heard every word Frank and the man talking to him had exchanged. *Under the circumstances, would Frank have expected otherwise?* Before Frank could usher the man into the study where she and Frank had again been scrutinizing Jake's two emails, Leah intercepted them in the entry hall. She did not want to be perceived as some helpless victim, even though she wavered between thinking of herself as just that, versus a warrior on the attack.

"Hello, Gali," she said, now wearing her own mask and gloves, "I'm Leah. Please come in. For sure, let's put our heads together. As urgently—"

The doorbell sounded.

"—and quickly as possible."

The three of them froze, as if caught in the middle of some illicit act. Like someone had just tapped on the pause button to send some video back to play, Frank looked through the peephole for the second time in a matter of minutes.

* * *

Frank did not recognize the man at the door, also in a mask and gloves. What he did recognize was the duffel bag and backpack he was holding in each hand. Jake's. No quizzes through the door this time. Those items were the only admission pass the stranger at the door required. Frank opened the door. "Yes?"

"Am—"

"Where—"

"—Amir.—"

"—did you—"

"—Friend of Mr. JK."

"—get those bags?" The notion of social distancing seemed lost in the moment. Frank took custody of Jake's duffel bag and backpack.

"Yes, Amir," Leah intervened. "I'm Jake's sister, Leah Klein Lotello. I remember Jake telling me all about you. This is my husband, Frank Lotello, and this is our friend, Gali Abelson. Please, come in. But please tell us first where you got those bags."

"Yes, yes. Been on trip with Mr. JK. And bags. Many stops. Last stop Atlanta, Georgia. USA. Afraid big trouble. Not see. Mr. JK tell me run fast. Drive fast. Bags in car. Bring here."

Leah looked at Frank and beat him to the punch. "Atlanta! As in A-."

"We still don't know who or what, or even exactly why, but we sure as hell know where and when," Frank said.

Belatedly, at Leah's prompting, they all moved to the family room.

Frank superficially examined the contents of Jake's bags—nothing out of the ordinary, some clothes and a lot of laptop computers. *Typical Jake.*

Abelson was the first to pick up on Frank's last remark. "May I?" he asked Frank, reaching for Jake's bags without waiting for an okay. He pulled out the four laptop computers and lined them up on the coffee table around which the four of them were assembled. "I think I might be able to shed some light on the who, what, and why, but I need to open these laptops and they're each password protected. I can get past those, but it will take a little doing." He reached for his shoulder bag and removed his own laptop, and a thumb drive. He set them on the coffee table in front of him.

The other three in the room watched in intrigued silence as Abelson went to work.

"Jake and I kidded about what I am about to do. Kind of like James Bond's Q, the guy with all of the gadgets and widgets. You didn't see me doing what you are about to see me doing. I have some colleagues who might criticize me if they learned otherwise. Kind of like, 'if I show you, I have to kill you.'"

"Looks like we're going to be here awhile," Leah said. "I'll get us some snacks. Frank, can you please bring some ice and drinks, water, soft drinks, beer, nothing harder. We have to keep our wits." She also pointed out the powder room to Abelson and Amir.

Frank and Leah soon returned with the drinks and food.

"Frank, can you please call Charlie and Madison at your folks and make sure they stay put there a few extra days. We're going to need to commandeer their rooms for our guests. I'll put out fresh linens, towels, and toiletries." She briefly explained to Abelson and Amir that their two teenagers were doing pandemic duty with Grandpa and Grandma, replenishing groceries and sundries, so the more at risk grandparents who were just fine could stay responsibly hunkered down, while still practicing social distancing with their grandkids.

"Easier said than done, General," Frank said. "No way they are going to accept being told we are having houseguests in the middle of a pandemic without an explanation."

"Well, we sure can't lie to them," Leah said. "Or sugar coat it. They're not babies anymore. And Jake is too important to them. You'll have to tell them the truth and promise to keep them in the loop. Good or bad. They won't settle for less. And we can't expect otherwise."

Frank knew it was often wise to let Leah have the last word, even when she was wrong. Perhaps, this time she wasn't. Perhaps.

CHAPTER 96
July 17, 2020, One Day Later

ABELSON HANDLED THE GRAVEYARD shift while the others got some sleep. He was able to sidestep the passwords on each of Jake's laptops, but that was the easy part. He spent most of the night digesting what was on the computers, and figuring what to share with the others in the morning without violating Jake's privacy any more than necessary. He had also managed to get a couple of hours sleep, figuring that he would need at least a short nap if he were to remain on his toes.

He was still up ahead of the others. He roused Amir while the others were still sleeping. He wanted to find out how much Amir could supplement the contents of Jake's laptops with the time he had spent traveling with Jake. Amir was quite helpful in filling in what Abelson had learned from Jake's computers.

* * *

LEAH GENERALLY ENJOYED PLAYING hostess, even when her law practice was on overdrive. This was one time she was prepared to compromise. She needed to stay focused on the task at hand. The local deli and staff were pinch-hitting. The four of them were congregated, once again, in the family room. Everyone was doing their best to enjoy the brief culinary respite before the expected monsoon would soon hit.

* * *

FRANK WAS KEEPING HIS own thoughts when the doorbell rang once again. *My God, another day, another visitor. Wonder who this one is.* He got up and quickly went to the door. He returned just as swiftly, looked at Leah and said, "I think this one is for you to handle."

* * *

LEAH LOOKED OUT THROUGH the peephole in the front door. *Is that Anya? Oh my God. What happened to her hair? Where's her makeup? Look at the dark circles under her eyes. She's so drawn.* She opened the door. "Hi, Anya. Are you okay?"

"Hello, Leah. I'm sorry to disturb you. I didn't know where else to go. Where to turn."

"What's the matter?"

"Is Jake here? Is he okay? Do you know where he is? He's not been responding to my texts or emails. I just get service-canceled messages, and he hasn't been sending me any texts or emails of his own. I'm very worried."

Leah paused. She wasn't sure exactly what to say. She stared into Anya's eyes. "Jake's missing, Anya. We have no idea where he is or how he is."

Anya hesitated for a moment. "I was afraid of that," she finally said. "I came here because I may be able to help."

Anya was masked and gloved. So far, they were socially distanced. Leah broke pandemic protocols and stepped forward. She reached an arm behind Anya and softly placed her hand on the small of Anya's back. "Come with me." She guided Anya into her study, closed the door behind them and motioned for Anya to take a seat. She did not tell Anya about the others who were in the family room with Frank.

* * *

FRANK WONDERED WHAT WAS going on. Leah had been gone for almost ten minutes. He had expected her to bring Anya into the family room. *Does Anya know something we don't?* He would give Leah another few minutes.

* * *

JAKE HAD BEEN AWAKE for several hours, although he couldn't be sure how long. No one had come to see him, but at least he wasn't being abused—at least, not physically. All four walls of his cell were solid, there were no windows. There was one light on the ceiling. It had been on when he first discovered it. At some point, it went off, accidentally or by design. Maybe it was their way of telling him it was time to go to sleep. Sometime later, the light came back on. Maybe that was their way of telling him it was time to wake up. Shortly after the light came back on, a slot in the bottom of the door opened, and a tray of food was slid into the cell. He tasted it. *Not very good, but it could be worse. Probably should eat, keep my strength up. If they were going to kill me, it probably wouldn't be with poison in my food.*

He wondered what Leah was doing, whether she had received his emails and remembered JK's Code. *Been a long time since we played it, but didn't want whoever has me to know what I was trying to tell her.* He had wanted to say "Atlanta," but ran out of time. *Hope Amir gets to her. He doesn't know where I am, but at least he knows it's probably near Atlanta.*

* * *

LEAH WATCHED ANYA WRINGING her hands in her lap. She tried to connect to Anya through her eyes, but that didn't work because Anya was looking down at her hands. "It's okay, Anya. Whatever it is, you can tell me."

Slowly, Anya lifted her head and looked squarely into Leah's face. "I work for Russia." She paused, as if to let the words resonate with Leah.

"I know that," Leah replied. "You've been here studying English to work as a translator for Russia."

"No. I work for Russia *now*. I am not a translator."

"I don't understand. What are you saying?"

"I am a Russian spy. I was sent here by the Russian government to spy on Jake."

"*What?* Why? Why would Russia have any interest in Jake?"

"They do not tell me, but I can guess. I think it has something to do with the November election. You know, there are lots of rumors that Russia interfered with the 2016 U.S. election. One of the ways was with computers. There are rumors that Russia is going to do so again this year. I think Russia believes Jake has been investigating Russian computer technology to stop Russia from interfering again this year."

"Do you know that for sure?"

"No. I just heard rumors. Like Americans hear rumors."

"What exactly did the Russian government ask you to do?"

"To spy on Jake. Report whatever I see him doing."

"What else, Anya?"

"You know. To . . . to become close with Jake. Encourage him to tell me what he's doing, and then report that information to my handler."

"Who is your handler? Does he have a name?"

"Yes, of course. But I don't know what his real name is. Like me, I have a real name. But not the name on my passport that you and Jake know."

"What does your handler think you're doing now?"

"He sent me a message one day ago saying 'it's over. Come home to Russia now.' He thinks I am wrapping up loose ends and returning to Russia. In maybe one more day, he will become suspicious, and send someone to find me."

"Why did you come here to my home now?"

"Because I care for Jake. If he's still alive, I want to help him. I would like to help you help him."

"I want to believe you, Anya, but how can I? How can I possibly trust you? Are you the beautifully made up Anya with the long blonde hair, or this new plain Anya with short dark hair and no makeup? Are you the Russian spy who preyed on my brother, or the woman who says she now cares about my brother?"

"I understand. All I can say is that if I wasn't telling you the truth, there was no reason for me to come here today and risk going to a U.S. prison, instead of returning home. And I changed my looks because I was afraid Russian agents might follow me and prevent me from reaching you."

"Or, because you are now here to spy on me, as you spied on Jake, to advise your handler what I know, and what I'm now trying to do to help Jake."

Resigned, Anya looked back down at the hands in her lap. "I understand," she said softy.

"Please wait here." Leah pointed to an internal door in her study. "There's a bathroom through there if you need one."

* * *

LEAH LEFT ANYA IN her study, and closed the door behind her. She went into the family room, and reported to Frank, Abelson, and Amir what Anya had said. "What do you think?"

"Hard to tell," was all that Frank said.

Abelson offered a little perspective. "When Jake first told me he had a Russian girlfriend who just happened to sit next to him on his delayed flight home from Europe, I told him it was highly suspicious, too much of a coincidence. I encouraged him not to trust her, and to distance himself from her. That said, and while I don't know for sure, I can't see her handler sending her here to spy on Jake's family. The odds of her getting anything new from you are pretty slim. I think her handler would be far more likely to want her back in their grasp in Russia—or worse. She is a loose end. Potentially dangerous now to Russia because of what she knows."

"Amir know many similar situations with Russians. Many pretty Russian girls taken from poor background, have nothing, then educated and given nice life to help Russian government."

"It occurs to me," Frank said, "that she has very little to offer us that we don't already know at this point."

"Maybe yes, maybe no," Leah replied.

CHAPTER 97
July 18, 2020, One Day Later

LEAH AND FRANK TOOK the first flight out the next morning from D.C. to Atlanta. Abelson, Amir, and Anya remained at their home. Holding down the fort one might say, although there wasn't really much more they could do just yet. Abelson and Amir had agreed to double up in Charlie's room, so Anya could have Madison's room to herself.

Anya had wanted to get a hotel room nearby, but Leah had insisted that she stay at their place. *There would be time enough later for recriminations. Besides, this way, Gali and Amir can keep an eye on her.*

It was the first flight either Leah or Frank had taken during the pandemic. Leah found it irresponsible to see passengers sitting next to one another, even though the plane wasn't full, and the airlines could have imposed more socially distant seating. She was also upset that not all passengers were wearing masks, in spite of the closed loop cabin air conditioning system. She might have found a way to register her feelings with the airline if her plate was not already full.

Frank had insisted on accompanying Leah. She objected but he prevailed. She didn't know whether to be grateful that he cared, or insulted that he perhaps thought she couldn't handle things on her own. *Actually, it is reassuring to know that I have my own personal security detail,* and *that Frank wouldn't have it any other way.*

She hadn't decided yet whether she was going to tell him how much she actually appreciated his protection and his company in the midst of all this stress. She wondered if the Klein family stubborn streak explained why Jake was in such a predicament. *Hopefully* still *in such a predicament. Can't accept the alternative. Just can't.*

It was also nice to have someone with whom to think things through out loud on this mission. *Imagine someone seeing me talking to myself.*

Leah had used Google to put together a list of federal and state detention facilities in the Atlanta area while they waited to board their flight. For several reasons, she had decided to begin with the federal institutions first. One—there were fewer of them. Two—there were simply too many state and private establishments to cover. Three—her instincts told her that the entire EBCOM scheme, and what had apparently happened to Jake, reeked of a federal attitude and substantial federal resources.

There were only six federal detention centers in the greater Atlanta area. This kind of an operation seemed beyond the capabilities of five of them. They started there in order to quickly eliminate them. Those five were quite forthcoming, and quickly confirmed her suspicions—they had nothing to hide, and nothing to offer. The two of them were hurriedly in and out of each of the five.

The sixth—the United States Penitentiary Atlanta—was a different story altogether. The physical presence of the penitentiary was ominous and foreboding. The head of the establishment had a massive attitude. When Leah told him why they were there, he smirked, and said she was reading too many conspiracy novels. When she asked if she could tour the facilities, he responded, "Sure, when you get a court order."

The odds were, if Jake was being held somewhere, this was probably the place. However, even if Leah obtained a court order allowing her to make an inspection, she would need a full team of persons to carry it out to avoid being defeated by a game of musical chairs. Unless she could blanket the entire campus at one time, the warden could move Jake around from one cell to another quicker than she could cover them all. *The good news is, Jake must be alive, or this jerk would have told me to knock myself out when I said I wanted to inspect the place. Unless he's just too arrogant. Or stupid.*

For now, Leah thought they had what they came to find out. It was time to head back to D.C., but they made one more stop first.

* * *

BAKER FLEW INTO A rage. The warden had immediately called Austin. Austin summoned Baker, Jr. to a local park bench. No time for a couple buckets of balls. Baker, Jr. was now meeting with POTUS on the White House grounds.

"No surprise that this asshole Klein's sister is an obnoxious bitch," Baker said. "We have to stop her dead in her tracks because I think our confiscation of Klein is a seminal moment."

"What do you mean, Dad?"

"First—I don't want Klein to see the light of day until after the election, when it will be too late, no matter what the outcome is. Second—I'm planning to do to tons of obnoxious protesters what we've just done with this treasonist Klein. Third—"

"There are a lot of protesters, most of them pretty peaceful. How many arrests do you have in mind?"

"Don't interrupt me when I'm speaking."

"Sorry, Dad."

"These protesters come in a lot of shapes and sizes. We have to pick our battles carefully. I want to get the ones who we can argue we are undertaking an insurrection, even if peacefully. For example, I have a mind to arrest some of these professional athletes who are taking a knee and disparaging our flag and our military. Absolutely treasonous. Unacceptable. To me, and, I'm told, to many of my core supporters. I have to protect them—show them I am worthy of their support. You need to let Austin know to be prepared."

"Yes, Dad, I will. You can count on me."

"Also, you need to tell Austin that our White House communications people are about to release a series of trial balloons over the next week or so that I'm going to soon sign a number of Executive Orders. Austin needs to know."

"What kind of Executive Orders, Dad?

"Different kinds. For example, Congress isn't working out the right kind of pandemic relief legislation. I plan to suspend payroll taxes to fund more relief money to the unemployed. We want these people in my corner at the time of the election. And their employers who don't like paying taxes. I am also thinking about outlawing the use of any kind of mail ballots for the election. They invite chaos and election fraud, such as ballots sent to people who have moved. These ballots can be completed and sent in by fake people who will vote for my opponent. We can't have that. If mail-in ballots are used to any extent, I may have to order them tossed out."

"That's good stuff, Dad."

"Of course it is. I'm just getting started. There will be more steps, I just haven't thought of them all yet. But I am also going to start pardoning those who my enemies have put behind bars for nothing more than supporting my just causes. You just make sure Austin's ready for what's coming."

"Will do, Dad. By the way, is a pardon the same as an Executive Order?"

"Beats the shit out of me. It's whatever I say it is. I'm the goddamned president. I just call it whatever I want, whatever my lawyers say to call it. I don't care. It's all the same to me. We just give it a name, and have the photographers take a picture of our supporters standing behind me with smiles on their faces while I hold up the document with my beautiful strong large signature on it. Have you seen my signature? I just love it. It lets everyone know they're in good hands under my rule."

CHAPTER 98
July 19, 2020, One Day Later

LEAH SPOKE TO FRANK in their master bedroom before meeting with the three other members of Team Jake resident in their home. "We need to introduce the two new members of our team to Abelson, Amir, and Anya, but I arranged for you and me to speak with Cyrus first, so we can bring him up to speed. I spoke with him when we returned last night, after you were down and out, but only briefly. Can we go into my home office and get him on a videoconference?"

"How about if I get us some coffee while you hook Cyrus into the desktop in your study?" Frank suggested.

"Five minutes?" Leah responded.

"Yep," Frank confirmed.

* * *

FRANK WALKED INTO THE study with a cup of steaming coffee in each hand, using his elbow to close the door. "Morning, Judge," Frank said.

"Morning, Frank. I'll take mine black, thanks for asking."

Frank could see, literally, that Cyrus was already starting with his shtick. It was his way. Frank knew not to bite. It did bring a smile to his face to see Cyrus in his sweats and cross-training shoes, already tracing the perimeter of the rug in his home office. No doubt, he would keep that up for as long as they spoke."

"Enough banter," Cyrus said, ready to take over the conversation in his customary style. "Seriously, Leah, I have the big picture you gave me last night. Helluva story, helluva mess. How are you holding up?"

"You know me, Cyrus," Leah said. "I'm for shit, on the verge of going down for the count. I'd be a complete puddle if I didn't know I was all Jake has."

"That *we're* all Jake has," Frank corrected Leah. He saw Cyrus overlook Leah's blunder. He knew Cyrus wouldn't mind in the slightest, even under less distressing circumstances. *Leah's his favorite. He'd never let me get away with a faux pax like that.*

"Okay, so now give me the details, Leah," Cyrus said, cutting to the chase. "Let me know what I can do, how you think I can help." *No doubt, the bugger already knows how he thinks the matter should be handled.*

Frank admired how Cyrus was making the conversation all about Leah, wanting to prop her up and make sure she understood that she was in charge. He and Frank had worked together even more than Cyrus and Leah had. He was secure in the knowledge that Cyrus respected his judgment, and would lean on him when he was ready for it.

Leah walked Cyrus through all of the background, from soup to nuts, including a rundown on the other members of Team Jake—Sam Townsend, her old law school classmate and friend who was now practicing law in Atlanta, and was more than willing to do everything he could, and Abelson, Amir and Anya holed up in Leah and Frank's home. She didn't skip a beat, and Cyrus listened patiently, even if it was more than he actually needed to hear.

"That's some story, and that's some team. So, what do you want to accomplish here, Leah?" Cyrus asked.

"I want Jake outta there, home here with us."

"And how do you propose to accomplish that?"

"Petition the U.S. District Court in Atlanta for a *Writ of Habeas Corpus.* You know, some kind of an order compelling the penitentiary to turn Jake loose, or at least expeditiously charge him with some kind of crime and give us a shot at bail."

"Right. How long does that take?" Cyrus probed.

"I have no idea. I know what a *WHC* is, but I've never handled one."

"I've never handled one as a lawyer for a client either, but I've had to adjudicate several Petitions for a *WHC* back when I was sitting on the U.S. District Court here in D.C. They're reasonably straight forward and logical, but tons of them are filed every day, they're usually denied, and they take thirty to sixty days for a *Writ* to issue, if they do."

"*Thirty to sixty days!*" Leah shouted. "*That's unacceptable!*"

Frank thought Leah was on the verge of being reduced again to her infamous puddle.

"And why is that?" Cyrus gently probed Leah.

Frank was well acquainted with Cyrus's style. As Leah's decibel level rose, Cyrus would speak more and more softly.

"Because I have no idea how he is, what's being done to him! I can't stand the thought of him being locked up for that long. I have to know he's safe. That warden jerk we visited was absolutely frightening."

"Can we promptly find all that out through a *WHC?*" Cyrus asked Leah.

Frank suffered for Leah. Sometimes "Professor" Brooks could prove to be agonizing. But there usually was a method to his madness. *Thank goodness he didn't ask me that question.*

"I don't know, Judge. Can we?" Leah asked.

"Do you know what *habeas corpus* means, Leah? By the way, feel free to chime in anytime, Frank."

No way Frank was going to stick his nose under this tent and get it chopped off.

"Not really," Leah answered.

"It means 'produce the body,'" Cyrus said. "It doesn't say anything about what kind of shape it has to be in, or when it's to be produced, or what's to be done with it until or after it's produced."

"Well, what the hell good is that then?" Leah asked.

"C'mon Leah," Cyrus said, "you need the body produced, but what else?"

"I wish you'd quit talking about Jake's body. I need to know Jake's okay. Right away. And that he'll be okay until he is produced."

"Precisely. So?" Cyrus asked.

"How about we file some kind of civil rights lawsuit," Leah said, "that his civil rights are being violated?"

"I was wondering when you'd use your noodle and get there," Cyrus said. "Give the girl a kewpie doll! And?" he added.

"We file an application for a temporary restraining order, a TRO, under Rule 65 of *FRCP*, the *Federal Rules of Civil Procedure*, compelling that Jake's captors not harm him or otherwise violate his civil rights simultaneously when we file the lawsuit!"

"Bingo!" Cyrus exclaimed. "Couldn't have got there without you, Frank."

Frank knew there was no way he was going to come through this conversation unscathed. He wanted to add "if they haven't already done so," but Leah would not have been able to deal with that.

"All right, my dear, prepare the lawsuit and the application, and email them to me and I'll do a little editing, if need be. You and Townsend are all the lawyers we need to formally name in your papers as counsel of record, but I have a couple of old buddies on the Atlanta District Court bench. Let me know the minute Townsend is going to file the papers, and I'll make a couple of off-the-record calls and see if I can't grease the skids, just to make sure your papers don't slip through the cracks."

Leah sighed with relief. "Thanks, Judge. I couldn't possibly have thought this through without you."

"Sure you could have. And you'll do a great job on the papers, just as you did when you defended Cliff Norman in my court, and as you did when you second chaired *Congress vs. Nopoli* with me in the U.S. Supreme Court."

"Hey, what about the *Writ* Petition?"

"First things, first. We need to make sure Jake's okay. The petition is much more involved. We don't want its preparation to muddle or delay our lawsuit, and the application for a temporary restraining order. There is one other thing we need to discuss before I put my mask on and take my power walk outdoors."

"What's that?" Leah was almost afraid to ask.

"Anya Lebedev," Cyrus answered.

* * *

TURGENEV LOOKED AT ANYA's handler in disbelief. "What do you mean you *still* haven't been able to find her?" he asked the handler.

"After you and I spoke when she didn't immediately return to Moscow, I sent her another text. She still didn't answer. I then sent agents to her apartment in Cambridge. She's gone. Her phone and laptop were there, and a lot of clothes, but her travel bag was gone. Our agents found some hair in the bathroom sink. They think she has disguised her appearance and ran."

Turgenev pounded his desk. "Last warning, for both of you. Find her. Dispose of her—permanently. The last thing *you* need are any loose ends. You do understand what I'm saying, do you not?"

Anya's handler nodded solemnly and exited Turgenev's office.

* * *

LEAH PEEKED INTO THE family room, and motioned to Abelson to join her and Frank in the entryway. "Good morning," Leah said to Abelson. "I want to fill everyone in on what we're going to be doing today, but I first want to get your take on how Anya spent the day yesterday while Frank and I were in Atlanta, as well as any other news you might have for us."

"I spent most of the day on Jake's four laptops, trying to figure out exactly what he's been up to." Abelson gave her a non-technical summary of what he had found. "As for Anya, she spent a little time getting to know Amir better, but was mostly quiet and kept to herself. I suspect she has me sized up as not being in her corner. She's right about that. She looked at the books on your bookshelf and glanced through some of them. She also watched the news on TV. I think she was just really waiting for you to return. In the evening, she went to Madison's room pretty early."

Leah nodded and told Abelson what was going to happen next.

He nodded and went back into the family room. Leah and Frank exchanged a few words, and then entered the family room a couple of minutes after Abelson.

* * *

LEAH SAID GOOD MORNING to everyone. She next made sure her guests had everything they needed. She then turned to the business at hand. "I want to outline what we're going to be doing today. But I need to borrow Anya for a few minutes first." Leah turned and led Anya from the family room into her study and invited Anya to be seated. "How are you getting on?" Leah asked Anya.

"As you might expect under the circumstances, not so great. Everyone is being nice to me, or at least polite. Amir is friendly, Abelson not so much. I don't blame him. It's awkward, but that's of course my fault. Do you have any news about Jake?"

"I think Jake is alive, and is being held in a prison facility that we were able to identify yesterday. We don't know what his condition is, or what their plans are for him. The head of the prison would not even confirm that he knows who Jake is, or that he's there. It is quite possible that Jake will be relocated since they know we now suspect he's there."

Anya listened attentively. "Is there anything I can do?"

"That's what I want to discuss." Leah gave Anya a short discourse on the legal steps they would be taking. First, the filing of a lawsuit and a request for an order that Jake be treated decently, and after that a filing of papers to request that Jake be released pending any criminal charges asserted against him."

"These are very different concepts than anything I know in Russia. But can't you begin with the last step first?"

Leah explained why not. "The first steps can be filed with the court in Atlanta in one day's time, and should result in a court ruling within a few hours, maybe even less. The last step is more complicated paperwork, and won't result in a ruling for probably a month or longer. That is why we have to do it in the sequence I just outlined."

"Again, what can I do to help?"

"There is something you can do, but it involves some risks for you. It would be helpful if you signed a document for the court reciting certain facts of which you have personal knowledge. However, if you say anything false in the document you might agree to sign, you could get into serious trouble with our court. Also, while I would try to have the document you sign seen only by the court, it is possible that the court will not agree to that, and the document would likely then be seen by your Russian superiors."

"I'll sign whatever you would like me to sign. I don't care about the risks."

"Anya, I think you should hire a lawyer to advise you before you make a decision."

"You're a lawyer. You can advise me. You already have."

"It can't work that way. My duties as a lawyer are to my brother. What's best for him is not what's best for you. Therefore, our laws don't allow me to advise you when I'm already representing Jake."

"I understand, but is it necessary for me to hire a lawyer before I can sign the document?"

"No. No one can force you to hire a lawyer, but I am obliged to tell you that I think you should."

"I mean no disrespect to what you are telling me, but I will only tell the truth, so I am not worried about your court. And I don't want to delay helping Jake while I hire and speak with a lawyer. As for my Russian superiors, I can't get into more trouble with them than I already am."

"Maybe so, but right now, any Russian agents looking for you have no idea where you are. They'll have a good idea where to start looking if the court doesn't agree to seal the document you sign. Are you really sure you wanna do this?"

"I am."

"Okay, then, here's what I'd like to prepare for you to sign, and here's what I also need you to do."

* * *

LEAH LISTENED TO CYRUS'S few comments on her civil rights complaint, the accompanying application for a temporary restraining order, and the five declarations under penalty of perjury appended to the application for the TRO.

"Nice work, quickly put together."

"Thanks, Cyrus."

"Your and Frank's declarations are short and sweet," Cyrus said. "They'll nail down that it is more than speculation that Jake is in the respondent warden's possession, and that he was obnoxiously stonewalling you. That casts doubt on his trustworthiness to protect Jake's civil rights of his own volition."

"That was precisely my thinking too" Leah said.

"Amir's declaration shows that Jake feared for his and Amir's safety and well-being. His testimony may be hearsay, but it should be admissible to show Jake's state of mind, one of the many exceptions to the rule against hearsay. Abelson's declaration as to what Jake's computers showed he was and was not doing is also hearsay, but the declaration establishes that Abelson is an expert. Experts are permitted to offer hearsay testimony."

"Again, my sentiments exactly."

"The pièce de résistance is, of course, Anya's declaration, and it's two attached exhibits— the original Russian text she received to return home, and her English translation of the original for the court's convenience. The ominous words 'It's over' should have the intended profound effect on the court, ambiguous as they may technically be."

"I hope so. I'll make your suggested changes, email the final copies to Townsend, and ask him to file them first thing in the morning."

"Under the circumstances, service on the respondent warden is not required as a condition to the court ruling on our application for the temporary restraining order. With any luck, Townsend should be able to serve the order before the warden has any opportunity to hide the ball."

"That's the plan," Leah said.

"Under *FRCP* 65, Cyrus continued, that should give us two weeks to file the follow-up motion for preliminary injunction to extend the temporary restraining order through the trial of the civil rights lawsuit itself, if that even proves necessary. You should also be able to file your petition for a *Writ of Habeas Corpus* simultaneously with your motion for the preliminary injunction. I'll get on the horn as soon as we hang up and make sure at least one of my colleagues on the Atlanta District Court bench has the background, and will hopefully help assure that the TRO is promptly processed by the court. Keep me informed."

"Will do. Thank you again, Cyrus."

"You're welcome, but it's all your doing, Leah."

"Maybe so, but having you in my corner is incredibly reassuring."

* * *

JAKE WAS ANXIOUS. IT must have been nighttime because the solitary light in his cell was off. It was pitch black again, and he was tired, but he couldn't sleep.

He had lost track of time, but the faint marks he had managed to scratch out on the wall adjacent to his cot suggested that it was July 19. If that was correct, four days had elapsed since he was seized. *Arrested? Is that what I was . . . arrested?* No one had reached out to him, neither his captors nor Leah. *Either my emails had not gone through to Leah—two emails, that's what I sent, right?—or she had no idea what to make of them.*

"POTUS and EBCOM," those were the words that Dobbs, the Georgia election official, had said to me. *POTUS I know, President of the United*

States. But EBCOM, what does that stand for, and what does it have to do with POTUS?

Wish I had my laptop and access to the internet. And a light switch. Will have to do without, distract myself, take my mind off matters until sleep comes.

In his mind's eye, he saw the letters E B C O M and started listing the possibilities. What could the letters stand for? The name of some kind of business enterprise? A company? Probably not a company, because isn't that abbreviated CO rather than COM? If it were a company, wouldn't it be EBCO?

Maybe COM stands for committee or communication? That makes more sense. More sense than what? Concentrate!

What about EB? Someone's name? First initial E, second initial B. Hmm, POTUS. Baker. Maybe B stands for Baker? But his first name is Dustin.

If COM stands for committee, then maybe EB relates to committee. Executive Committee? Then what is the B for? Not Executive Committee.

B? B? Board! That's it. Executive Board. Executive Board of some committee. Some committee having something to do with POTUS. What to do with POTUS?

Crazy. Am I going stir crazy? Or just crazy, period?

Sleep finally came.

CHAPTER 99
July 20, 2020, One Day Later

LEAH HAD TO SUFFER through the longest July 19 ever. Or so it seemed. While Jake's team was willing to work weekends, the court was not. Finally, after what seemed like forever, Leah read out loud the TRO Townsend had emailed to her only moments earlier—on Monday. Amid a round of applause from the tiny but mighty anxious audience, she quickly told the members of the group gathered in the family room where things now stood.

As Townsend had elaborated to Leah, he had personally served the order, and the underlying papers, on the warden that morning. Pursuant to the order, Townsend had been allowed to visit Jake and had arranged for independent health care providers who had accompanied him to the prison to thoroughly examine Jake. He was frail and unnerved, but relieved to know that his emails had been received, that JK's Code had been deciphered, with a boost from Amir, and, most importantly, that he was not alone.

According to Townsend, Jake said that he had been moved to more humane quarters, allowed to shower and given a fresh change of clothes and a hot meal before Townsend was allowed to see him. As co-counsel of record along with Townsend, Leah would also be allowed to visit Jake in accordance with customary visiting rules of the facility.

"We don't yet officially know who physically abducted Jake—and on whose orders—but we'll get to the bottom of that in due course," Leah added.

Leah then turned to Anya. She paused. "Anya, I'm afraid there was one bit of bad news that Townsend reported to me. The court declined to seal your declaration, ruling that the first amendment, freedom of the press, and the public importance of this case and these events, prohibited the court from sealing your declaration."

If Anya were at all concerned, Leah couldn't detect it on her face or in her body language.

She wanted to be sure that Anya understood. "This means those who would do you harm will now be able to figure out where you went when you left Cambridge, and where you may now still be. However, Frank assures me that his Metropolitan D.C. Police Department will assign several undercover officers to protect you around the clock. At least for the time being. I also plan to hold a press conference to draw attention to President Turgenev's tactics. He will, of course, deny all of that, but even he should not be brazen enough to bother you any longer once we expose him."

Leah was still unable to detect any reaction on Anya's part.

"Now that we know Jake is safe, we will turn to the prospect of pursuing his release, and allowing him to accomplish what he was meant to do from the very beginning—when a young boy first conceived of Jake's Code."

Finally, Leah thought she detected a slight smile cross Anya's face.

CHAPTER 100
July 21, 2020, One Day Later

TURGENEV WATCHED THE LIVE video feed of Leah Klein's press conference. "This bitch is an even bigger pain in my ass than her younger brother." He turned to the man sitting in his office with him. "We have no choice. Call the dogs off of the Kleins, and Lebedev. They're too hot to handle now. But we will live to fight another day. And we will still pursue our election goals and helping Baker's reelection."

CHAPTER 101
August 3, 2020, Thirteen Days Later

THE COURT HEARD THE publicly noticed and scheduled matters by video conference. First, the petition for the *Writ of Habeas Corpus,* and then the motion for a preliminary injunction to assure Jake's safety pending the trial of his civil rights lawsuit, which would not occur for at least a full year.

In the actual courtroom were the presiding judge and his clerk, both masked and socially distanced. A number of other interested parties had electronically registered with the court clerk to attend the proceedings virtually.

Jake had already been formally charged and indicted for treason in the criminal court. He pleaded not guilty, but was still incarcerated because the criminal court had denied bail on the grounds that he was a flight risk. He was allowed to view these proceedings from his prison cell by means of a laptop computer brought into his cell.

Leah Klein appeared by video conference from her D.C. office. Present in her office, and watching the proceedings from off camera, were Cyrus and Eloise Brooks, Frank Lotello, Charlie and Madison, Amir, and Anya, all socially distanced and masked. Charlie and Madison were now graciously sharing their rooms at home with Amir and Anya.

Sam Townsend appeared by video conference from his office in Atlanta.

Abelson viewed the proceedings from his New Haven school apartment.

The Attorney General of The United States appeared by video conference from his D.C. office.

The Russian Ambassador to the United States viewed the proceedings from his private office in the Russian Embassy in Washington, D.C.

Rupert Austin viewed the proceedings from his home office. He would promptly report the outcome of the hearing to his fellow EBCOM members.

No doubt, other interested parties from various locations around the world also watched the proceedings by video conference. Just possibly the leaders of a country or two.

At a signal from the judge, the clerk called the case. The judge welcomed everyone, and commended all who were masked and socially distanced. He invited counsel for Mr. Klein to argue the writ petition.

By agreement with Townsend, Leah presented the argument for her brother. In essence, that he was not a flight risk, and should be released on his own recognizance pending his criminal trial. She also argued that supporting documents filed by her and co-counsel made it abundantly clear that the case was a witch hunt, exacerbated by the circumstances of Mr. Klein's seizure and treatment prior to the court's issuance of the temporary restraining order, and that he would ultimately be vindicated and found innocent, and awarded damages at trial for violation of his civil rights.

"Thank you, Ms. Klein. We'll now hear from the Attorney General. We acknowledge the importance of this matter to the federal government by virtue of your presence, Sir. We are honored to have your appearance in our courtroom, Mr. Attorney General."

"Thank you, your honor." The Attorney General then argued passionately that the accused was guilty of the capital offense of treason in seeking to control the upcoming elections, and that he should remain behind bars without bail pending his criminal trial.

"Thank you for your outstanding arguments, counsel," the judge said. "The court is prepared to rule from the bench. Subject to surrendering his passport to this court, Mr. Klein will be immediately released on his own recognizance pending his criminal trial. Mr. Klein will be confined to his home pending his criminal trial, and will be required at all times to wear a GPS monitor. He will, however, be permitted to leave his home as scheduled in advance with the clerk to meet with his counsel and for reasonable and necessary medical appointments.

While this court is not required to explain its thinking, I do wish to point out that I was heavily influenced by the circumstances underlying Mr. Klein's original arrest, if we can call it that, and the nature of his detention prior to the issuance of this court's temporary restraining order. Such behavior on the part of the government was indefensible, and cannot be countenanced. In light of the court's ruling today, the motion for a preliminary injunction to safely continue Mr. Klein's incarceration is moot, and dismissed without prejudice to renewal should circumstances warrant. The clerk shall give notice. Court is adjourned.

* * *

CYRUS TURNED TO LEAH. "Well done, Ms. Klein," he said. "I think you just might have a promising career as a lawyer," he added dryly, as only Brooks could.

"Enough of your humor, Cyrus," Eloise said.

Leah laughed. It was not clear whose remarks had elicited her reaction, Cyrus's or Eloise's.

"Mr. JK come home now?" Amir asked.

"That's right," Leah said to Amir, and perhaps to everyone in the room.

* * *

POTUS WAS OUTRAGED. AGAINST advice of counsel, he immediately tweeted "Terrible decision. Terrible judge. Klein guilty of treason. But I will fight for America. And I will win for America."

CHAPTER 102
September 28, 2020, Eight Weeks Later

JAKE REMAINED CONFINED TO Leah and Frank's home under the court's remand order. *Not so bad, but it would be nicer if it were voluntary.*

He had been watching all of the news, in particular any number of President Baker's public actions and remarks from time to time—including his continuing arrest of protesters in Portland and other cities—in similar fashion to the way Jake had been seized—in violation of their civil rights, his pardoning and commutation of his friends and supporters, his increasing disregard for the law, including his multiple violations of the Hatch Act at the GOP convention, his interference with the postal system in an attempt to prevent mail voting at the upcoming elections, his nomination of a Supreme Court justice less than six weeks before the November presidential election in an attempt to tip the Court in his favor, and his several vague implications on national television that he would not honor the results of the upcoming election if the results weren't what he wanted, perhaps emboldened by his latest Supreme Court appointment.

"What the hell does that mean, that he might not honor the results of the upcoming election?" Jake asked Leah and Frank.

"He might be able to go to court to stall the outcome of the election of his opponent, Sullivan," Leah answered her brother. "But to what end? Under the Constitution, Bianchi, who would presumably continue as Speaker of the House if Sullivan arguably wins the election, would become President on January 20."

Jake thought about what Leah had said. "I really don't get it, there doesn't then appear to be any way for Baker to win, unless he does so in conventional fashion, by the counted vote of we the people."

Jake was doodling on his ever present smartphone, not seeming to pay attention to the news, their conversation, or even what he was fiddling with on his phone. "You know, I'm so not into politics," Jake said, "but doesn't it come down to who the military backs, and who controls the communications systems?"

All of a sudden, Leah stood up, and bolted for her desk.

"What the hell?" Frank asked.

Leah returned in two minutes. "I've got it!" she exclaimed.

"Got what?" both men in the room asked.

"EBCOM," Leah shouted. "Our Secretary of Defense and our Chairman of the Federal Communications Commission are both members of EBCOM. The Chairman of the Joint Chiefs of Staff possibly is as well. Or at least he's working with it. Is Baker lining things up for a coup to take over the country if he's not reelected? What the hell do we do? Who would believe us?"

"I would," Jake said. He recalled his lonely jail cell examination of the possible meaning of the acronym EBCOM. "When I sat in the dark in my cell, I mentally went through all of the combinations and permutations of EBCOM. I came up with—and then discounted—Executive Board of some . . . committee. Such as the committee to reelect the president. And then it finally occurred to me: it "COM" wasn't short for committee; it stood for . . . command, as in military command. The Executive Board of the Committee to Reelect the President was code for The Executive Board of The Command to Take Over the Country—if Baker doesn't win the election. Others might still not believe us, but I do," Jake added.

CHAPTER 103
September 30, 2020, Two Days Later

JAKE OPENED HIS EMAIL. It was an email invitation from Yvgeny Barovsky inviting Jake to click on the link to video conference with him. Jake didn't recognize the name, and assumed it was some hacker or phisher. He was about to hit delete when he saw the words at the bottom of the email, almost an afterthought, "It's about EBCOM."

He instantly hit the link. And there he was, face-to-face with Barovsky.

"You don't know me, Mr. Klein, but perhaps you want to. I know a lot about you, and EBCOM. I believe I can help you, and I believe you can help me."

"How do you mean?" Jake asked. "Who exactly are you?"

Barovsky explained his background to Jake. More importantly, he explained that he was in D.C. on Russian business. "Perhaps I should say, Turgenev business. I have decided to defect. I have information that would be very important to the U.S. I would like you to ask your sister to consider representing me."

CHAPTER 104
October 2, 2020, Two Days Later

JAKE EMPLOYED THE SAME tactic as Barovsky had with him, an email invitation to Rupert Austin to join him in a videoconference. The email included a conference link, and the following short passage, "EBCOM, Executive Board of Command, Barovsky."

Austin obviously clicked on the link. "Although we've never met, I know who you are, Mr. Klein," Austin began. "How did you get my private email address? What is this nonsense? This is harassment, plain and simple—and ugly."

"I'll plead the 5th on harassment, but I assure you this is no nonsense, as you obviously know by virtue of the fact that you accepted my invitation to videoconference. I know what EBCOM is, and what it's planning to do if Baker loses the election. I also know that you are the chairman of EBCOM, and your membership includes our Secretary of Defense and our Chairman of the Federal Communications Commission."

"I joined you in this call purely out of curiosity, Mr. Klein. Now I know you're crazy, spouting pure nonsense, things about which you know nothing. You are, however, getting in way over your head, Mr. Klein. I assure you of that."

"Have I been in over my head so far, Mr. Austin? Have I been stopped so far? I've only scratched the surface. I have someone here with me who is intimately familiar with EBCOM and its purposes." Jake put on a mask.

Barovsky stepped into full view of the camera. He also was masked. "Hello, Rupert," Barovsky said.

"Yvgeny?" Austin said. "What are you doing?"

"I've defected. Decided I like the NBA games and don't want to wait for Turgenev to buy a team and move it to Moscow. I've also decided that my future will be a lot brighter and safer here in the U.S., given all that I know about Turgenev and his deeds. And yours, Rupert. To answer your question, this is how I'm going to pay my entry fee to my new home. Mr. Klein and I want to give you a chance to tee it up with us—before we take it public."

Austin had no comeback. He just ended the videoconference.

* * *

Two hours later, the headline story went viral. "Rupert Austin dead at age 72. No signs of foul play found. Suicide suspected." EBCOM died with Rupert, whether or not Baker agreed with that outcome, and to his great dismay.

CHAPTER 105
October 7, 2020, Five Days Later

JAKE HAD LEFT SCHOOL behind. At least for now. He was fully ensconced in his new venture, JK's Code, a D.C. limited liability company.

Leah had recently filed the papers for the new company. Its managing member was, of course, Jake. The other governing members of the company were Leah Klein, Frank Lotello, Cyrus Brooks, Amir, and . . . Anya Lebedev.

Anya would be dividing her time between handling public relations and marketing for JK's Code, and also tutoring American students studying Russian to help make ends meet.

JK's Code already had its first two cybersecurity clients, the States of Pennsylvania and Georgia. They would be using Jake's software to block any attempt by Russia to use Molloy's software program to interfere in the registration, voting, and tabulating of Pennsylvania and Georgia residents. Anya was going to be working with Jake and Barovsky to develop computer technology to identify fake news planted by Russian bots to mislead and influence American voters.

Based on the number of inquiries JK's Code was receiving as a result of all of the continuing disparagement Baker was still unleashing on Jake, the future of JK's Code looked bright. Anya might not have much more time, or need, to be tutoring students wanting to learn Russian.

When Jake had told Leah that he wanted to include Anya as one of the governing members of JK's Code, Leah responded that she was pleased that

Jake and Anya seemed to be working things out. Jake was still getting used to the real Anya, as opposed to the Anya he once thought he knew.

One subject in particular that still troubled Jake was how Anya would maintain her relationship with her parents back home in Russia. "Aren't you worried that Turgenev will harm them to get back at you? And force you to return?"

Leah looked away. "I'm sorry, JK, that was one of the many fabrications of the old Anya. My parents died in a car crash when I was five. I was living in an orphanage outside of Moscow when the GRU found and conscripted me into its service. I am afraid that is not uncommon. There is nothing Turgenev can do to hurt my parents now, or to use them to extort me. I always regretted not having any sisters or brothers or other relatives. It turns out, that was a blessing in disguise. America is now my home—and my future."

Like he said, Jake was still getting used to the new Anya. He thought about that. "Maybe one day, that future will include a new family for you."

EPILOGUE
October 2022, Two Years Later

As the CEO of JK's Code, Jake was about to call the second annual meeting of the governing members of the company to order. He thought about all that had happened in the past two years.

The 2020 elections had come and gone, and the country was still standing—more or less. Sadly, Democrats and Republicans still seemed more focused on what was wrong with the other party—and what was in it for themselves, rather than their constituents—instead of what they could and should be doing to effectively address the challenges still facing the country, and the world. Too bad they can't learn anything watching the grace, dignity, and sincerity of the NBA players and other professional athletes, and their willingness to sacrifice—the archaic opinion of Baker to the contrary notwithstanding.

Charlie and Madison were both in college, and doing very nicely. Cassie was taking the professional golfing world by storm, and also taking a part-time course of college classes. Even Jake was now taking a couple of college classes every semester, if only to please Sis Leah. With age comes a modicum of wisdom.

Abelson had finished his studies at SCSU a year ago, and returned home to Israel. His stature in Mossad was on the rise. He was even beginning to think about a role in Israeli politics.

Fyodor had earned his undergraduate degree at SCSU, and relocated to Israel to join his parents, who had decided to settle permanently there—comfortably so, thanks to Turgenev. Fyodor was now in graduate studies at the University of Haifa. They had adjusted nicely to their new home. Life, and pain, in Russia was a fading memory.

Amir was the head of a new transportation company that was giving Uber and Lyft fits. Jake had put together the technology for Amir that had made this possible. And Amir had recently been granted permanent U.S. residence. He was counting the days until he could take his citizenship exam. From time to time, Jake and Amir would argue about principles of U.S. government. They wondered how the 2024 U.S. election would play out. Thanks to Jake, and JK's Code, the election would at least be devoid of any fraud.

Oh, yes, and Anya was expecting.

NOTE FROM JK

As I MENTIONED IN *JK's Code*, I'm hardly a politician, or an economist. It's all I can do to keep up with computer science. Nonetheless, my fellow characters in *JK's Code* have asked me to forward this brief (?) note to you from them. Here goes.

Barak wants to be an author. Well, he is an author, but he wants to be a respected and branded author, kind of like I set out to become a respected and branded cybersecurity maven. As such, he's vulnerable to the wishes and advice of his developmental editor. I haven't met her, but Barak speaks highly of her, as you'll note in his acknowledgments in the back pages of this novel.

There were three scenes in particular that Barak included in his original draft of *JK's Code* (among many others—it seems one of her favorite words in the English language is "cut") that his developmental editor advised him to delete. She argued that these three scenes weren't relevant and harmed the otherwise pace of the novel.

The characters of *JK's Code* disagreed, arguing that, taking into account EBCOM, as well as the more obvious election fraud subject matter of the novel, the passages in question were at the very least relevant. That said, for the sake of our integrity, the characters of *JK's Code* were obliged to admit that there was some merit to the position that the scenes in question did distract from the pace of the novel.

Barak insisted that he had to pay homage to the long-standing craft principle that requires any responsible author to be willing to "kill his darlings", words that authors really liked, but couldn't professionally defend. (While I have researched the matter, any number of renowned authors are credited with this oft recited phrase, but it appears that they, at best, repeated it.)

Here, then, is the highly negotiated compromise, the three darling scenes, or sets of words, that were killed in the preceding *JK's Code,* or at least mortally wounded. These scenes are here replicated, not in the order they appeared in the earlier draft of the manuscript, but rather in the sequence the characters chose by majority decision.

#1
Almost All Politicians (and Media and Lobbyists Too) Are Created Equal. It Matters Not On What Side Of The Aisle They Reside (Or Support)

LEAH AND FRANK WERE sharing the cleanup detail after an enjoyable dinner for two. Leah was washing, and Frank was drying.

"Now that you've managed to help solve all of the problems of our immediate and extended families," Frank said, "I wonder if you might give me your solution for the broader social problems facing our country today."

"Something simple," Leah retorted.

"Let me narrow my inquiry a bit. I'm not asking you to find a vaccine for COVID-19, or to resolve the climate and environmental threats to our planet. What I'm after is your take on the narrower social issues deriding our country. I'm growing weary, having to cope with all of the social confrontations and protests increasing every day. They seem to be getting worse and worse. More and more noise, but less to show for it. How do we make things actually improve?"

"For me," Leah said, "I think the solution to what you're talking about boils down to three root ingredients, possibly only two."

"And those would be?" Frank asked.

"Politics, lobbyists and the media."

"By my count, that's three pieces to the puzzle. How do you characterize them as possibly only two?"

"Lobbyists might just be a subset of politics. I might even get it down to just one ingredient that transcends these two or three components: Integrity."

"I'm all ears," Frank said.

"Okay, let's talk politicians first, including lobbyists. The problem is, politicians think their primary commitment is to their own interests, rather than the interests of their constituents. Lobbyists fuel this and—sadly—too many of our voters accept this lack of integrity as acceptable par for the course, in spite of the growing social protest and unrest."

"Do you think this political impropriety is worse on either side of the aisle?" Frank asked.

"Not at all," Leah said. "Give or take, at any moment, I think the political dishonor is equally bad on both sides of the aisle."

Give me some examples," Frank said.

"We don't have that many dishes left to clean up," Leah responded. "I'll give you one on each side. Ignoring Baker's reelection misdeeds, which Jake thwarted, Baker has no respect for the law, no integrity, whether it's flaunting the Hatch Act about not mixing government and politics, or the Foreign Emoluments Clause, set forth in Article I, Section 9, Clause 8 of the U.S. Constitution, that prohibits foreign gifts to members of the federal government, including POTUS. Baker violated the Hatch Act when he staged reelection events at the White House. He violates the Foreign Emoluments Clause every time foreign dignitaries coming to visit him at the White House stay in one of his hotels, even though closer accommodations are available."

"And the Democrats?" Frank asked.

"Consider Sullivan, the Democratic nominee for president. Back when he was vice president, he made a trip to China on Air Force Two. Ostensibly, he was there on government business, and the cost of the trip for air travel, security, etc. was on the taxpayers' dole."

"What was wrong with that?" Frank asked.

"When the plane landed, photos all over the media showed Sullivan disembarking in the company of his adult son."

"What's the big deal about that? It's not like the son's presence increased the public's expense. Air Force Two was making the trip anyway."

"At a minimum, the appearance of the son hitching a free ride looked bad," Leah said. "Why was the son along for a free ride? If he had reason to travel to China, why didn't he buy a commercial plane ticket and travel there on his own—like you and I would do if we had reason to go to China?"

"Sounds ticky tack to me."

"There's more. When the son returned home from China, he and a small group of associates formed a private equity fund that was capitalized with $1.5 billion dollars, provided by the Chinese government or Chinese companies controlled by the Chinese government. Sullivan's son was a director of the fund and owned 10% of the fund. Under common "2-20" fee structures, the managers of the fund received an annual 2% of fund assets management fee, and 20% of the increase in asset value. Sullivan's 10% share of the 2-20 fee structure is a lot of money."

"That does seem more than ticky tack," Frank said.

"It gets worse. When the son was there, he met with a Chinese individual who went on to become president of the U.S. private equity fund."

"Why is that worse?" Frank asked.

"When asked about the matter, Vice President Sullivan said that was his son's business, not his business, and he and his son never discuss his son's business. If that doesn't strike you as unlikely, I have some Nebraska beachfront property I'd like to sell you. Moreover, when Sullivan was further probed, he acknowledged that his son introduced him to the Chinese president of the U.S. fund while father and son were in China. It sounds like the son traded on his father's federal government position for his own personal gain."

"That sounds like another Federal Emoluments Clause violation to me," Frank said.

"Among other possible violations of U.S. law. If Sullivan is now elected POTUS, will that mean we have a president who is beholden to China?"

"Are you sure these facts are reliable?" Frank asked.

"As to the underlying facts, that the son hitched a free ride on Air Force Two for no public purpose that you or I couldn't have done, that Sullivan says he never discusses his son's business with his son, that the son introduced his father, the then Vice President of the United States, to the Chinese individual who became the president of the U.S. private equity fund capitalized with $1.5 billion dollars out of China, that the son became an owner and director of the fund, yes. Whether Sullivan and his son ever discuss the son's business or whether the father used his federal government position to garner business for his son, and how much the son made off of this venture, and whether any of that directly or indirectly found its way to the father, no. Both the *Wall Street Journal* and the *New York Times* reported the underlying facts, but the *Journal* put an anti-Sullivan spin on it and the *Times* put a pro-Sullivan spin on it. Who knows what the truth is, but it sure looks bad. And it segues into the issue I related about the media being a serious part of the problem."

"How so," Frank asked.

"The *Journal* and the *Times* virtually never see the same story in the same light," Leah said.

"Well, that doesn't seem like a bad thing," Frank replied.

"I'm not so sure. All this talking has made my sweet tooth kick in. The dishes are done. Give me a couple of scoops of ice cream and I'll explain my concern about the media."

"Deal," Frank said.

"Bob Woodward, The Washington Post's syndicated columnist of Woodward and Bernstein, All The President's Men, Watergate, and "Deep Throat" fame, just released his latest book, *Rage.*"

"The book reporting on some eighteen hours of taped interviews with POTUS recorded with POTUS's consent?" Frank asked. "I've skimmed it. What's wrong with it?"

"Woodward presents himself as an objective "reporter" of the facts, but I don't believe that's true. Aside from "reporting" that Baker is not fit for the office, Woodward is guilty of precisely what he accuses Baker of doing."

"How so?" Frank asked.

"In a February 7 recording, Baker admitted that he knew COVID-19 was much more dangerous that he let on to the public. He said it was because he didn't want to create panic among the American public. Whether that was the reason or the reason was that Baker thought being candid might hurt his reelection chances, Woodward said that Baker should have trusted the American public to handle the news."

"So?"

"So why didn't Woodward use his branded syndicated column to do what he said Baker should have done?" Leah asked. "When asked about that, Woodward said he thought Baker's taped admission spoke only to the pandemic as it existed at the time, only in China. That might explain Woodward's silence in February, but not in March by when the pandemic had spread all across the U.S."

"Good point. Why do you think Woodward didn't come forward in March, if not February?" Frank asked.

"For me, the answers are obvious. One, the publisher of *Rage* didn't want the news to break until they were ready to release the book on

September 15. It would have been yesterday's news by the time the book came out if Woodward were the objective reporter he claims to be and had told what he knew back in February or March. That looks like greed, plain and simple. The publisher's greed and Woodward's greed. Two, Woodward does not appear to be an objective reporter as he claims. He strikes me as clearly anti-Baker as does his employer, *The Washington Post*."

"Interesting. You've downed the ice cream I gave you. What's the answer to my original question, how do we resolve and diffuse all the social unrest?"

"Unravel the greed factor and pave the way for integrity, both in the media and in politics. If we can reduce the greed factor, then both the media and our politicians will have less temptation to stray from integrity."

"Won't that take an amendment to our Constitution?" Frank asked.

"Yes. The amendment has already been written. It appears in a novel I think you know something about. It's titled *The Amendment Killer*. You can find it on Amazon."

#2
The 2020 Political Agenda Of The Democratic Party
(The 2020 Political Agenda of the Republican Party Is The Baker Agenda, Which Is Difficult, At Best, To Identify)

CONFIDENTIAL 2020 CONVENTION AGENDA
Presidential Nomination
Vice Presidential Vetting, Selection and Nomination
Convention Considerations
Pandemic
Party Platform
Social Unrest
Me Too
BLM
Police defunding
Baker
   Tax Returns
   Cronyism
   2016 Election Fraud
   DACA
2020 Election Fraud

"Let's skip the selection of Sullivan as our nominee. It's done and beyond our control at this point. He might not be a strong candidate, but we're stuck with him. As to the procedural details, we can leave those to staff. Let's focus on the substantive subparts of the agenda.

Bianchi ran through the list. "Let's take them one at a time. The first one I wrote down is Hashtag Me Too."

"That's simple, Betty. We all know that. We're on the right side of the argument. Baker has to agree, which makes him look weak to his own core, but the more he might resist, the weaker he hurts himself."

"I agree. Besides, his core will forgive him. Like he says, he could shoot someone on Fifth Avenue, and his core would still vote for him. The next subpart is Black Lives Matter."

"Much trickier," one of the committee members said. "This is a much more difficult issue than it appears to be on the surface. When people are cornered publicly, they all speak out for BLM because it's so politically correct. That doesn't mean that everyone feels that way privately. All those rioters breaking into stores and stealing everything in sight isn't really helping the cause. And all them damn athletes taking a knee every time the national anthem is played is alienating a lotta people. So are our wuss local officeholders who are so willing to pander to the protesters and support defunding the police. Personally, I think that's outright nonsense. That's how I also feel about the protesters who are rallying in front of the homes of local politicians 24/7, playing loud music and shining bright lights in the front windows of those homes to intimidate local politicians to do whatever the protesters want, no matter how absurd."

"Maybe so, but pandering to the protesters is exactly what we have to do," Betty said. "It's a numbers game and we need those black and brown votes, as well as those white votes who feel they're racist if they're not anti-racist."

"I'm not so sure, Betty. I think we may be more at risk regarding these extremists than we realize. Again, what people say and how they really feel may be more different than we realize."

"You get no argument from me, but the die is cast."

"What about defunding police, Betty?"

"That's largely just a subset of BLM."

"Agreed. Right or wrong, we have to push it, because that's what our core supporters want."

"This brings us to the final social unrest subpart, which is Baker himself, and which I actually have four sub-subparts, at least today. Baker gives us new items every single day. As of today, we're talking about Baker hiding the ball on his tax returns, the 2016 election fraud, all of his cronyism and then his latest for now, Deferred Action for Childhood Arrivals, DACA."

"Let's be sure we're on the same page here, Betty. We don't want any screwups of our own, and we don't want Logan botching up any of this."

"Sure thing. Baker's tax returns issue is simple. The more he digs in and resists disclosing what every other president has basically disclosed, the more it looks like he's got something to hide. I hope he keeps stonewalling us."

"What's the play on the cronyism? The fact that some of his supporters have crossed the line doesn't mean that he has."

"The cronyism is another subject for us to play up. No president has had more cronies convicted of crimes than Baker. We need to continue to press this and the fact that he and his Attorney General lackey are interfering with the legal process in order to put all his crooked friends above the law. It's just another example of Baker making clear that he thinks he's above the law, and entitled to do whatever he wants."

"And the 2016 election?" asked one of the committee members.

"The 2016 election fraud is pretty much the same as the tax returns. It's clear the Russians messed with the 2016 election to help get Baker elected. They deny it. So does Baker. No one believes either of them. Baker's own intelligence community says this is beyond question. We have to just keep making all the hay out of this we can, especially as Baker keeps pressing not to have mail-in voting, so the Russians have an easier time to come to his rescue again."

"What's your point on DACA, Betty? I thought the Supreme Court ruled against Baker on DACA and he jumped on the bandwagon and said he'd respect their decision."

"Typical Baker bullshit. That's what he said, but that's not what he's doing. The damn Supreme Court left him somewhat of an opening, and he's driving a Mack truck through that opening. The Supreme Court actually sent the case back to the lower courts for some more specificity, and Baker is still opposing relief for the DACA youngsters, even though he talks out of both sides of his mouth and denies it."

"Hey, Betty, we know that Russia's going to try to control the election in Baker's favor even more than it did in 2016. How do you plan to deal with that?"

"One word, 'mail-in,'" Bianchi answered. "It will be hard for the Russians to manipulate the vote if we keep it off the internet from start to finish."

"Isn't that two words, Betty?"

"Very funny. I used a hyphen, so it's only one word."

"More seriously, how are we going to deal with everything that Baker is going to do to sabotage a massive mail-in vote? Won't he try to completely destroy the election?"

"He can make a lot of noise, but what's he really going to do? The Supreme Court won't back him—even if Baker gets to appoint another member of the Court before the election—and the Constitution makes me the next president if the election is still in doubt on January 20. He'll step down before he lets me become president."

"Gee, Betty, is that why you're pushing for a mail-in vote? Tell the truth now."

"Haha," was all that Bianchi answered.

Geez, Betty, you sure you don't want to raise a bunch more points and keep us here all night?" someone asked. "We have July 4th family plans."

Don't shoot me, folks, I'm just delivering the mail. We have an election to win. We have to do whatever it takes, the merits and the best interests of the Happy Fourth."

#3
Shareholder Capitalism And The Dirty T Word, Taxation

"Okay, but Amir question different."

"Oh, sorry." Jake paused long enough to hit "Go" on the GPS. "All right, what's your question?" he asked Amir.

"Read news story to practice English while you in meeting. About expected Democratic candidate for president, Mr. Logan Sullivan. He make big speech against shareholder capitalism. Not sure understand. Sounds more like yesterday Russia than today America. You can explain?"

"Sure. Maybe this is another subject for you to learn for when you take the exam to become a U.S. citizen." Jake knew this was a complicated subject. He thought about how best to explain it in simple terms. At least it would help take his mind off things while they drove. Maybe Amir's too.

"Let's say you want to start a restaurant business. Maybe to cook and introduce Kazakhstan food to Americans."

"Okay," Amir nodded. "Good idea. Like."

"Say you rent some space in a mall and put a kitchen and appliances in part of the space, and tables and chairs for customers in the remainder of the space. You hope customers will pay you more money for the food you prepare than what you have to pay for rent, equipment, and the food you will cook for your customers. If you earn more than you spend, the difference is called profits. Understand?"

"Mr. JK. English bad. Business thinking okay. Many businesses in Kazakhstan. Have friend with good restaurant business in Kazakhstan. Had business in Kazakhstan. Made profits. Brought to America with me."

"Sorry, Amir. I know you understand. But what if you don't have enough money to pay your beginning expenses before you have customers?"

"No problem. Go to rich uncle. He loan money to begin."

"Okay. And when do you pay him back, and how much do you pay him?"

"Depends on how smart uncle is. Pay back loan plus something extra, maybe share of profits from restaurant. Uncle smart man."

"But what if your restaurant does not make profits? What if instead the customers don't pay enough to cover your expenses, and you have losses instead of profits? Who has to pay the unpaid bills?"

"Amir must pay."

"What about your uncle? Must he pay the unpaid bills too?"

"No. Uncle loaned certain amount of money. Not have to pay more."

"Now, we are coming to the question you asked me and what the Democratic candidate for president said that you read. In America, if your uncle loaned you money in exchange for a share of any profits your restaurant business might earn, he would have to pay unpaid bills like you, unless special steps were taken to assure otherwise."

"What steps, Mr. JK?"

"Special documents prepared that say the restaurant is owned by a business organization. Usually the organization is called a corporation. You and your uncle receive ownership of some portion or shares of the corporation instead of direct ownership of the restaurant business. You and your uncle are then called shareholders. In that case, unless you or your uncle agree otherwise, you may lose what you originally invested, but nothing more. This is called limited liability, and it's intended to encourage investment in businesses, both large and small. You might agree to pay any losses if the restaurant business fails and closes and has unpaid bills, but your uncle would not."

"Amir understand. Same in Kazakhstan, but not need corporation."

"Okay. So now I can try to answer your question. In America, as elsewhere in the world, governments charge their citizens—both individuals and business organizations, such as corporations—fees to raise money in order for the government to provide services to its citizens."

"What kind services?" Amir asked

"Many kinds. For example, providing schools for our youth, building and maintaining roads and airports, creating militaries to protect our country from foreign enemies, and medical and living expenses for our elderly."

"Understand. Same in Russia and Kazakhstan."

"We have two major political parties in the U.S., Republicans and Democrats. They each compete in elections to control our government. They have very different economic and social philosophies."

"Read about Democrats and Republicans, but not understand well."

"The Republicans generally like less government services and less taxes. They feel the citizens should keep more of what they earn and provide some of the services that might otherwise be covered by the government. The Republicans want to impose less taxes on corporations, and believe that the money corporations make should go only to their shareholders. That is called shareholder capitalism. The Republicans believe the shareholders and other wealthy individuals who are taxed less will spend more of the money that is not taxed in ways that will benefit our society."

"And Democrats?"

"The Democrats generally like the government to provide more services, and therefore want more taxes. They believe the government will do a better job of benefitting our society than our individual taxpayers will through the voluntary spending of their capital. The Democratic presidential candidate you read about wants the money corporations make to go not only to their shareholders who invested in the corporations but also to cities and needy people in general and not just shareholders.

"Which better, Mr. JK?"

"I don't know, Amir. I understand computers, not government. Besides, both political parties seldom speak truthfully. It is very difficult to understand what they genuinely want. For example, the word taxation is often thought to be a negative word so politicians avoid saying that word whenever possible. The Democratic candidate running against President Baker to be elected POTUS—President of the United States—in November, former Vice President Sullivan, says shareholder capitalism is no longer a good thing instead of saying what he really wants to do—which is to raise taxes on corporation. Republicans think this is just a hidden way of reducing limited liability which will discourage investment. If your uncle couldn't limit his liability, and the taxes on his profits, he might not be willing to invest in your Kazakhstan restaurant."

"Very difficult subjects, Mr. JK. Amir has seen Democrat style in old socialist Russia. Not work well. Think government should charge taxes only enough to make necessary services and help individuals unable to work to support themselves because old or ill. Have headache thinking. Is time eat? Know good Kazakhstan restaurant in this town?"

Jake agreed politics was a very difficult subject. He registered as an Independent because he didn't think either the Republicans or the Democrats really served the public interests. He also wasn't sure his remarks were particularly helpful to Amir, but at least it made the drive less boring, and it took Jake's mind off what always seemed to be on his mind at the moment.

ACKNOWLEDGMENTS

WRITERS DO THEIR THING in what can only be described as a "lonely place."

Fortunately, there are some exceptions. I'd like to thank a few of them, whose support means more to me than I can express (writer that I purport to be).

In no particular order, and with apologies to any I may inadvertently overlook:

The writers—T.F. Allen, Lee Child, Anthony Franz, Barry Lancet, Jon Land, Bill McCormick, Brad Meltzer, Christopher Reich, James Rollins—who already know how to do it. Read their books if you haven't already done so, and you'll see for yourself. Writing is an incredibly busy profession. For those who generously and graciously took time out from their demanding schedules to read my manuscript and favor me with their praise, encouragement, and fraternity, there is little that could make them more noble, and me feel more welcome and grateful.

The editors—Charlotte Herscher and Stephanie Cook, and others informally as well—who beat me up, over and over, and who put up with me when I resisted. Through it all, they have made me a better writer—and *JK's Code* a better story.

The loyal members of my beta readers team who toiled over multiple drafts of *JK's Code*—Todd Allen, Barbie Barak, Mark Barak, Hollace Brown, Larry Callagy, Cheryl Deariso, Stephen End, Lew Henkind, Larry Lugash, Mike Lurey, Marla Markman, Bill McCormick, Jaye Rochon, Sonny Wallensky, and Chuck Yarling—and made it better for their efforts.

The professionals—Cindy Doty, Sue Ganz, Jared Kuritz, Marla Markman, Jaye Rochon, Gwyn Snider, and everyone at Gander House Publishers—who have helped get my message out and make sure *JK's Code* looks like a book, inside and out. They have made sure you know this story exists, how and where to find it, and why you might want to read it. And, finally, they have ensured my website and newsletters are informative and entertaining and are worth visiting and reading. While I'm unequivocally grateful for the help and support of everyone mentioned, the contributions of the magnificent Js—Jared Kuritz, publicist extraordinaire and co-founder of Strategies PR, and Jaye Rochon, social media and graphics specialist extraordinaire and founder of Clever Unicorn—are especially invaluable because without them you might not know I exist!

And last, but certainly not least, the members of my family—the Wife, Barbie; the Brother, Gregg; the Son, Mark, who never ceases to amaze his mom and dad that he can do whatever he wants, and do it well; and the Granddaughters, Madison and Peyton—all of whom have provided me with their own special kind of love, support, and sustenance.

AUTHOR NOTE

THANK YOU FOR READING *JK's Code*. I hope you enjoyed it. If you did, I think you'll also enjoy three more in the Brooks/Lotello thriller series, *The Amendment Killer, The Puppet Master* and *Payback,* each on sale wherever books are sold. Pick your poison: hardcover, trade paperback, ebook or audiobook. Hopefully, enticing samples of each appear for your reading pleasure at the end of this work.

If you are not among my growing reader community who have already done so, please sign up for my newsletter at www.ronaldsbarak.com to learn everything exciting about me (well at least my writing), including when and where my books can be purchased. Hey, what's an occasional additional email in your inbox?

If you enjoyed *JK's Code,* I will be eternally grateful if you will spread the word wherever and however you can. Please tell a friend, or ten, and post a brief online review wherever you look for good books. It's easy (honest) and exciting (well, at least for me it is). Simple instructions on how to post online reviews can be found at www.ronaldsbarak.com/how-to-leave-an-online-review. Besides growing my fan base, it will impress my family and friends, who still aren't convinced why I do all this.

Thanks for connecting and for all your support.

ABOUT THE AUTHOR

RON BARAK, Olympic athlete, law school honors graduate, experienced courtroom lawyer, is uniquely qualified to write this suspenseful novel that will appeal to all political and legal thriller aficionados. Ron and his wife, Barbie, and the four-legged members of their family reside in Pacific Palisades, California.

To learn about preorder availability, new book launches, and limited-time discounts, please connect with and follow Ron by visiting:
www.bookbub.com/authors/ronald-s-barak
www.ronaldsbarak.com
www.facebook.com/ronaldsbarak
www.twitter.com/@RonBarakAuthor
www.instagram.com@RonBarakAuthor

To book Ron to speak, please contact info@ganderhouse.com.

MORE . . . BROOKS AND LOTELLO

Want more of Brooks and Lotello? Please read the following samples of *The Amendment Killer*, *The Puppet Master* and *Payback*, each on sale now wherever books are sold.

THE AMENDMENT KILLER

A BROOKS/LOTELLO THRILLER

RONALD S. BARAK

WE HAVE YOUR GRANDDAUGHTER. Here's what you need to do.

Thomas T. Thomas III reviewed the language. Again. He closed the phone without hitting send. Yet.

He stared through high-powered binoculars from atop the wooded knoll. As always, the girl hit one perfect shot after another.

Cassie Webber. Age 11. He'd been tailing her for three months. It seemed longer.

She was chaperoned everywhere she went. Two-a-day practices before and after school. Her dad drove her in the morning. He watched her empty bucket after bucket and then dropped her off at school. Her mom picked her up after school, ferried her back to the practice range, and brought her home after daughter and coach finished. Mom and daughter sometimes ran errands on the way, but always together. Even on the occasional weekend outing to the mall or the movies, the girl was constantly in the company of family or friends. *Having someone hovering over me all day would have driven me batshit.*

His childhood had been different. When Thomas was her age, he walked to school on his own. And he lived a lot farther away than the girl. His daddy had never let his driver chauffeur him around. Wasn't about to spoil him. *Spare the rod, spoil the child. Didn't spoil me that way either.*

He kept telling himself patience was the key. But his confidence was waning. And then, suddenly, he'd caught a break. The girl's routine had changed.

She started walking the few blocks between school and practice on her own. Dad dropped her off at morning practice and Mom met her at afternoon practice instead of school. Only a ten minute walk each way, but that was all the opening he needed.

Everything was finally in place. He would be able to make amends. He would not let them down.

This time.

She completed her morning regimen, unaware of Thomas's eyes trained on her from his tree-lined vantage point. No doubt about it, he thought to himself. She was incredibly good. Driven. Determined.

And pretty.

Very pretty.

He relieved himself, thinking about her. A long time . . . coming. *Haha!* As the girl disappeared into the locker room, he trekked back down the hill, and climbed into the passenger side of the van. He returned the binoculars to their case. He removed the cell from his pocket, and checked the pending text one more time.

Moments later, the girl emerged from the locker room, golf bag exchanged for the backpack over her shoulders. She ambled down the winding pathway, waved to the uniformed watchman standing next to the guardhouse, and crossed through the buzzing security gate. She headed off to school.

Without taking his eyes off her, Thomas barked at the man sitting next to him. "Go."

* * *

CASSIE LEFT THE PRACTICE range, looking momentarily at the clock on her phone. School began at eight. She had plenty of time.

She strolled along the familiar middle-class neighborhood route to school, sticking to the tree-hugged, concrete sidewalk. Well-kept houses on modest-sized manicured lots, one after another, adorned both sides of the paved street that divided the opposing sidewalks.

Mouthing the words to the song streaming through her earbuds, she made a mental note of a few questions from her morning practice to ask Coach Bob that afternoon.

Using her ever present designer sunglasses—a gift from her grandparents—to block the sun's glare, Cassie texted her best friend Madison:

Hey, BFF, meet u in cafeteria in 10. Out after 1st period to watch ur mom & my poppy in S Ct—how dope is that? 2 excited 4 words!

As she hit "Send," she was startled by the sound of screeching tires. She looked up from her phone and saw a van skid to the curb a few houses ahead of her. A man in a hoodie jumped out and charged straight at her.

She froze for an instant, but then spun and raced back in the direction of the clubhouse. "Help! Help!! Someone help me!!!"

As she ran, she looked all around. No one. She saw no one. The guard kiosk was in sight, but still over a block away. *Does he want to hurt me? Why? Why me?*

Hearing the man gaining on her, she tried to speed up. *If I can just get close enough to the gatehouse for someone to help me.* She glanced back, shrieking at the top of her lungs, just as the man lunged. He knocked her to the ground, shattering her glasses in the process. "What do you want?! Leave me alone! Get off me!!!"

She saw him grappling with a large syringe. "No!" She screamed even louder, clawing and kicking him savagely—until she felt the sharp stab in the back of her neck. Then nothing.

* * *

THOMAS GLANCED AROUND TO make sure there were no witnesses. He yanked the girl's limp body and attached backpack into his arms. He stumbled to keep his balance. Her backpack opened and spilled its contents to the ground, a bunch of books and papers. *Shit! Not so fucking easy.* He hauled her to the back of the van. As if on cue, his accomplice, Joseph Haddad, opened the rear doors. Thomas managed to lift the girl up to Haddad, who pulled her into the cargo area. Thomas ran back and gathered up the books and papers from the sidewalk. He returned to the van and stuffed them in the backpack. He made sure its latch was now secure.

His breathing had become labored, but Thomas was more interested in the girl's vitals than his own. He climbed into the van and checked her pulse. It was a little weak, but she seemed stable. He'd done his homework and opted for more of the drug than less. He wanted her out of sight as quickly as possible.

Thomas preferred to keep her alive. For now. Might help him control the grandfather. *But if she ODs, so be it. Just a matter of time anyway.*

He took stock of his wounds, acknowledged to himself how tough the brat was. He taped her mouth shut, placed a hood over her head, and hand-cuffed her to the inside of the van.

He downloaded the contents of her phone to his, verified the transfer completed, and then used the butt of his revolver to demolish her phone. He stored the remains in a plastic bag partially filled with rocks.

"Damn, Thomas," Haddad shouted from the driver's seat. "The hell you doing? We need to get the fuck outta here."

Thomas ignored Haddad. He climbed outside the van with the plastic bag in hand and looked around again to make sure no one was watching. He hurried back to where he'd knocked the girl to the ground. He scooped up the scattered remains of her sunglasses, added them to the plastic bag, and returned to the van.

Satisfied that he had removed all evidence and that there were no onlookers he needed to eliminate, he scrambled into the passenger seat and stored his gun and leg holster in the glove compartment.

"Take the route I gave you," Thomas said to Haddad. "Make sure you stay under the speed limit."

Five minutes later, they crossed the Potomac. Thomas directed Haddad to pull over and stop. He rolled down his window, tossed the weighted plastic bag into the river, and watched it sink below the surface. *Let's see what anyone does with her damn Find Phone app now.*

He looked over his shoulder and observed the girl. Nothing.

"Okay, let's head to the cabin. Mind the speed limit."

"When this is all over, you oughta think about renting yourself out as an echo."

Thomas scowled at Haddad, but said nothing further.

* * *

THOMAS REMOVED THE HOOD, tape, and handcuffs, and the girl's backpack.

She'd be dead in a week no matter how the Court ruled, but she'd be less of a nuisance in the interim if she didn't know the fate that awaited her. Nicer digs would give her false hope. Besides, he'd had some time to kill—so to speak—before he grabbed her. And putting his design and construction skills to work while he waited beat working on crossword puzzles and was . . . oddly therapeutic: a stocked mini-refrigerator beneath a small open cabinet with two shelves and a microwave sitting on top of the cabinet. The air-conditioning system he'd installed was working fine. He'd also rigged a portable bathroom in the corner, fully equipped with toilet, sink, shower, and even a second, larger cabinet with a few changes of clothes and toiletries. *Always like my ladies to smell nice.*

Written instructions for her if she woke up were on the table next to the bed. He really did hope she was just sleeping it off. The grandfather might insist on some form of evidence that she was alive. And well. He took out his phone, snapped a few pictures of her. Live video would, of course, be a lot more convincing. But she wasn't moving. The pictures would have to do if necessary.

* * *

As THOMAS SHOT THE still pictures of the girl, he noticed a small device protruding from her pant pocket. He froze, scared he might have missed a second GPS monitor in addition to the one destroyed with her phone. He had an involuntary urge to turn and look behind him. *At what?*

Cautiously, he pulled whatever the object was away from her body, spotting an almost invisible, clear, miniature plastic line coming off one end of the gadget and disappearing under her T-shirt. Now more curious than cautious, he peeled back the girl's top and saw the other end of the thin line—disappearing into her belly, no less.

His mind was racing. One question after another. *What the hell is that? Steroids? Is this why she plays golf so well? Does she have health issues? Does she play golf like she does despite a medical problem? Is this thing sending messages somewhere?* He wondered what would happen if he removed it.

He had to decide. If he left it in place, the girl was in control. If he removed it, *he* was in control. He grabbed the line where it entered her stomach, and pulled. It popped right out. Nothing. Just a couple drops of blood. Quiet. No alarm bells. At least none that he could hear.

Not happy. He hated loose ends. *Literally.*

He'd had no time to examine the contents of the girl's backpack when it opened and spilled out on the street. He emptied it out on the bed next to her and sifted through the contents. He found a bunch of school items, including those he had previously spilled and retrieved when he'd seized her. And a zippered canvas bag. He unzipped the bag and peered inside.

* * *

"WE'VE ACTUALLY HAD TWO prior constitutional conventions, Anne. The first in 1781, when the thirteen states adopted and ratified our first Constitution, the Articles of Confederation. The second in 1787, when the Articles of Confederation were repealed and replaced by our second Constitution. The one we still have today. The NoPoli convention last July 4th was actually the country's third constitutional convention."

"And the details of the convention?"

"A great deal of planning and work went into structuring our convention, but its conduct was fairly straightforward—and democratic. You reported it.

Delegates participated from all fifty states—50,000 in number, plus another 20,000 alternates. Selected by the respective NoPoli chapters in every state, they assembled in the New Orleans Superdome and enacted the amendment by a two-thirds super-majority vote of each state delegation."

Elliott made a living as a wordsmith, but Nishimura observed that Kessler was the stronger speaker. "Gentlemen, this would probably be a good time to take a moment to show our viewers exactly what this amendment looks like. Chris, would you please walk us through its provisions displayed on the giant electronic screen on the wall behind us?"

* * *

THOMAS LAUGHED OUT LOUD. Mystery solved. Not some kind of GPS.

The unzipped bag contained a partially used vial of insulin, a couple of syringes, and some other paraphernalia. What he'd just yanked out of the girl's stomach was an insulin pump. He'd read about those somewhere. *Geez, she's a diabetic.* Maybe she can reinsert the pump, he thought. If not, she'll have to use those backup syringes. That's obviously what they're for. He wondered how long this insulin supply would last.

He returned everything to the backpack, including the pump he'd removed from the girl's body—and perhaps irretrievably damaged. He dropped the backpack on the floor near the table with his note. He was on a tight schedule. No more time to admire his handiwork.

He locked the basement door, double-checked that it was secure, and ascended the stairs. He expected to find Haddad in the front room where he'd told him to wait and keep a lookout.

But Haddad was gone.

* * *

THOMAS LOOKED OUTSIDE AND saw Haddad leaning against a tree, smoking a cigarette, in full view of any hikers who might happen by.

Thomas was livid. He went out the front door and locked it behind him, again double-checking that it was secure.

"Thought I told you to stay put. Indoors. Out of sight."

No response.

"Did you not hear me?"

Haddad glowered. "Needed some fresh air. And a smoke. What's the fucking big deal? No one around here anyways. Just like we planned it."

Thomas shook his head. "Like *I* planned it. Let's go."

Haddad turned and stepped toward the van. With lightning speed, Thomas reached across Haddad's left side with his own left arm and latched onto Haddad's right shoulder. He pulled hard on the right shoulder as he simultaneously grabbed and jerked down on a fistful of Haddad's long hair just above the right ear. The loud snap of the man's neck told Thomas his accomplice was now his *former* accomplice—even before the released body slumped to the ground.

* * *

THOMAS LOOKED DOWN AT Haddad's body lying motionless on the ground. "Cigarettes are hazardous to your health, fool. So was your long, ugly mop of hair. You woulda done better with a buzz cut."

Thomas knew that discarding Haddad had only been a matter of time, but it frustrated him that the timing turned out not to be of his own choosing. Especially when some of the work in the days ahead would have been easier spread over two backs.

The last time Thomas had dropped his guard—just a little—it had almost cost him his life. It was during the *Norman* case, in Brooks's court. When Brooks was still on the bench. Brooks was the impetus behind Lotello going after Thomas. Even though neither one of them then realized it was Thomas. If they do even today. There was a shootout. Thomas escaped, just barely. He was lucky. Lotello wasn't. He caught a bullet.

Although Thomas managed to get away, it cost him everything he'd been working for. This was now Thomas's last chance. He could not fail this time. *No more mistakes. No more misjudgments. Haddad was unreliable. Insubordinate. A fool. Should have known better than to select him. Had to reassert myself. Had to get rid of him. No choice.*

Thomas threw Haddad's corpse in the back of the van, and drove off. He stopped along a quiet stretch of the Potomac, miles away from where he had dumped the bag with the remains of the girl's phone and sunglasses. He stuffed each of Haddad's pant and jacket pockets with rocks collected from the riverbed, dumped the body into the water, and watched it sink.

He chemically wiped down the inside of the van, and then burned the cleaning materials along with the latex gloves he'd been wearing all day. He sprinkled the ashes into the water and watched them float away. He would also soon dismantle and destroy the van. And everything else. In the meanwhile, he was confident no one could connect the van with him, the girl, or his ex-associate.

He hurried off to Court, again sticking to the speed limits. It was going to be close. He really wanted to monitor the girl's grandfather—and the results of all his planning and efforts—in person. If necessary, he had another cell phone ready to go and would watch the proceedings by television from a nearby bar he had already selected. Just in case. Control was everything.

* * *

GROGGY, HEAD POUNDING, EYELIDS so heavy, Cassie fought to break free of the cobwebs that were not yet ready to let go. No sense of time or place, muddled, she sought to gain some solid footing.

The day—if it were still the same day—had started like any other. Up at five every morning, the cost of wanting to be the best woman golfer in the world—not the best *diabetic* golfer, but the best golfer, period. And not *one* of the best, but *the* best. Her steady run of victories on the juniors' circuit demonstrated this was no fantasy.

She tested her blood sugar that morning, programmed a supplemental bolus through her insulin pump to cover her slightly elevated glucose level, threaded her orthodontic braces, organized her curls just so, put on her favorite earrings, and finished getting dressed. She fed Whitney, the family pup, next.

When she said, "C'mon, Whit, let's go potty outside," he looked at her curiously and hesitated. Hair too frizzy. Face full of freckles. Too skinny, the tallest in her class, even taller than the boys. Now, because of the ginormous lisp caused by her new braces, even her dog didn't know who she was anymore. In spite of her tough self-assessment, Whitney followed her out the door.

She remembered her dad driving her to morning practice. He answered emails and watched her hit until he left for work. Her parents still wouldn't let her walk to and from school on her own, but they'd finally caved in and allowed her to walk the few blocks back and forth between practice and school.

Cassie continued to retrace the morning. She'd finished hitting, was on the way to school, listening to music on her latest playlist, thinking about how practice had gone. She had also texted Madison that she would meet her in the cafeteria in a few and was looking forward to their trip to the Supreme Court.

Suddenly, it all came rushing back to her.

* * *

JUST AS CASSIE HAD sent the text to Madison, that dirty old van had screeched up alongside her. Guy in a hoodie jumped out and ran toward her. She tried to make it back to the golf course. He was too fast. Knocked her to the ground. She had tried to fight. Saw the large syringe in his hand sailing toward her. Something sharp stabbed her in the neck. That was it. Until now.

She began shaking, crying. Her knees were scraped and throbbing. Her neck was sore. She was trembling from head to toe, but she wanted to be brave. *He's a real perv, a big bully. He should pick on someone his own size. See how he'd like it then.*

Trying to be brave wasn't working. And then it dawned on her what was happening.

* * *

OH MY GOD. I'VE BEEN kidnapped!

Cassie began shuddering uncontrollably.

Not good. Why me? What did I do?

Tears again spilled out of her eyes and swamped her cheeks and T-shirt.

Her mind raced in all directions. *Mom and Dad. Nanny and Poppy. Whitney. Will I ever see any of them again? What about my golf? Michelle Wie tweeted she wanted to play with me. I so want to. And Madison—Madison—she's going to be so ticked at me for not showing.*

And then—as if things couldn't get any worse—they did.

* * *

CASSIE COULDN'T BREATHE. *My pump! Where's my pump?*

* * *

THE UNIFORMED SUPREME COURT security officer shouted over the clamor of echoing voices and shuffling feet beneath the high-vaulted ceiling of the courthouse lobby: "Empty your pockets and bags, place the contents in one of the free bins, and put the bin on the conveyor belt. Cameras, cell phones, and other electronic devices are not permitted in the courtroom and must be checked before entering. You'll be given a claim check and can retrieve your items when you leave."

"Nothing in my pockets, Officer," Thomas said. "Just my billfold, a notepad, and a couple of pens in my shoulder bag."

"Step ahead, stand on the marks, raise your hands above your head."

He did exactly as he was told.

"Come through," the security officer motioned.

Thomas entered the courtroom gallery, looked around, and limped over to the left aisle seat, one row forward from the rear. He stood there staring at the woman occupying the seat until she finally acknowledged his presence.

"Excuse me, ma'am. Any chance I could trouble you to find another seat? It's this darn stiff leg of mine. I sure could use an aisle seat near the exit."

She stared at him. He could almost see the wheels turning in her head. If she refused his entreaty, he had another couple seats nearby he'd try. If all three attempts fell flat, he'd have to revert to Plan B: Leave the courtroom, grab one of the other phones he'd hidden outside the courthouse, along with three extra SIM cards, each one barely the size of his thumbnail, and hurry to the bar down the street, where several wall-screen televisions would be carrying the coverage.

Finally, after what seemed like an eternity, the woman occupying his preferred spot nodded silently and moved over to one of the few remaining gallery seats. "Thank you kindly, ma'am," he called after her. Plan A it was, at least for this initial half-day session.

With an exaggerated effort, Thomas slumped down into the seat the woman had vacated, unlatched his shoulder bag, and placed it on the floor between his legs. He surveyed the courtroom in front of him with a mixture of admiration and amusement. The gallery was filling in quickly. Given the seminal importance of the case, Thomas knew the courtroom would soon be packed.

He leaned forward and coughed. He deftly removed one of the two phones and three of the six extra SIM cards he had two-way taped under each of the three-aisle gallery seats over the course of the prior week. He slipped the items into his bag.

So far, so good. It had been surprisingly easy for Thomas to get a night shift custodial position at the courthouse. Of course, it probably hadn't hurt his chances that two custodians—one was enough, the second was just for good measure—mysteriously went missing without notice only days earlier. Or that Thomas had been able to hack into the Court computer system and move his application to the head of the waiting list for custodial positions. *Not likely the incinerated bodies of those two janitors will ever turn up, or be tied to this case before the Court rules.*

Creating an employment history and references had required the fabrication of a handful of modest-sized custodial companies in several small easterly Virginia towns. Each with manufactured owners and phone numbers leading to additional prepaid cells Thomas had purchased. Of course, no one was there when calls came in to verify the references. But Thomas always promptly returned the voicemail messages left by the Court's human resources office. Using voice alteration software, he provided bona fides in sufficiently unique voices to accredit his fictitious applicant.

The interview had been a mere formality. Two weeks after he had sent in his application, Thomas's new job allowed him undisturbed access to the very courtroom where today's proceedings would take place. Over the course of several nights, he'd managed to sneak in six cell phones and extra SIM cards and taped them to the bottom of the three targeted seats. Including the one he now occupied.

Using three separate Craigslist ads, Thomas had surreptitiously hired three different people to stand in line this morning and get him a seat while he tended to more urgent priorities. He had paid each through a joint "Pay After Delivery" PayPal escrow account.

As for the phones, in addition to his personal smartphone for the possible rare occasion when he would need capability not included on burners, Thomas had purchased forty "burner" phones for cash over a period of several weeks. No identification was required. Each purchase was made at a different drugstore, electronics shop, or telecommunications carrier retailer. Fifty dollars bought a phone already loaded with one full month of prepaid service. The cost was a pittance.

It would have been easier, cheaper, and more efficient if he had purchased just a couple of phones and downloaded the latest burner apps to them that all the drug dealers, pimps, and hackers were using these days, but Thomas didn't trust the vulnerable security of that approach. He was far too cautious for anything that risky.

The extra effort expended was well worth it. So long as he meticulously followed his simple protocol, neither his identity nor his location could ever be traced: Employing a new SIM card for each text sent, removing the phone battery and old SIM card immediately after their use and breaking the old SIM card in half, and then reinserting the battery and a new SIM card at the time of the next use.

Each of the hidden burner phones, including the one now resting safely in the bag at his feet, contained the same unsent text message—the one he'd prepared before abducting the girl.

As the courtroom wall clock marched toward ten, Thomas basked in the grandeur of the chamber, its high ceilings, and its majestic finishes. He even admired the way everyone present had their respectively assigned places: Courtroom staff adjacent to the Justices, attorneys and their clients just beyond the staff, and, finally, the gallery of spectators. The buzz among the spectators was growing. They were there to see how the 28th Amendment would fare, but he wondered how specifically they would each be affected by the Court's decision. Perhaps he should say *his* decision.

Thomas's eyes settled on the three of them: Brooks, Klein, sitting next to Brooks, Lotello, seated behind Klein. He recalled bitterly his prior dealings with each. He knew that Lotello and Klein had married. Klein had also adopted Lotello's two kids, the brood sitting next to Lotello. *How I'd love to take the lot of them down right now. But no time for such whimsy now. First things first. Their time will come.*

As Thomas watched them, Lotello reached over and gave Klein an obvious last minute good luck squeeze on her shoulder. Klein turned and seemed to acknowledge the gesture with a preoccupied smile. Suddenly she glanced back, her line of sight intersecting Thomas's. Her smile transformed into a brief, puzzled expression. She returned her attention to the papers in front of her.

Thomas smiled. Sneered might be more precise. *Stare all you want, bitch. By the time you recognize me, it'll be too late. It already is. About 170 minutes to be exact. But who's counting?*

* * *

THE NINE SUPREME COURT Justices marched into the regal burgundy and gold hall right on time, exactly at 10 o'clock. Thomas respected that. He always sought to be on time too. Several cracks of the gavel, not unlike a staccato of gunfire, followed the Justices's entrance, reverberating throughout the courtroom. Momentarily startled out of his reverie, Thomas belatedly joined the remainder of the gallery in rising.

The Justices huddled and ceremoniously shook hands, demonstrating a lack of personal animosity despite whatever judicial differences they perhaps harbored. Thomas thought it played like a well-choreographed Broadway musical. As if on cue, they then took their places behind their assigned seats, the Chief Justice of the United States at the center and the eight Associate Justices alternating right and left of center in descending order of seniority, accompanied by the grand opening proclamation of the Court Marshal:

"The Honorable, the Chief Justice and the Associate Justices of the Supreme Court of the United States, Oyez! Oyez! Oyez! All persons having business before the Honorable, the Supreme Court of the United States, are admonished to draw near and give their attention, for the Court is now sitting. God save the United States and this Honorable Court."

That was Thomas's cue. As everyone throughout the courtroom resumed their seats, he reached into his bag on the floor and discreetly removed the phone. Hunched over, as he had practiced countless times without having to look, Thomas quickly opened the app and hit "Send." And just as quickly and discreetly, he returned the phone to the bag.

Showtime.

* * *

ASSOCIATE JUSTICE ARNOLD HIRSCHFELD's cell phone started vibrating just as Chief Justice Sheldon Trotter began his opening remarks. Few people had Hirschfeld's number. He reached inside his robe, removed the phone, and opened the text.

We have your granddaughter.

His eyes widened. His knuckles turned pale. Remembering where he was, he tried to regain his composure. He took a deep breath, and continued reading.

We have your granddaughter. Here's what you need to do.

Chief Justice Trotter's opening remarks seemed to come from a far-off place. "As many of you watching today have learned from the media, this is the first time we . . ."

Hirschfeld pushed Trotter's words to the recesses of his mind as he hurriedly skimmed the balance of the text.

If you don't follow these instructions exactly, your granddaughter dies.

Trotter rambled on ". . . are televising the proceedings of this Court . . ."

Hirschfeld half-rose from his leather chair and all but gave way to his urge to rush from the courtroom. He caught himself. And go where? Do what? *Are they watching me? Am I telegraphing my anxiety? What'll they do?* He tried to swallow. He couldn't.

The kids had given Cassie a cell phone on her last birthday. It was always with her. As nonchalantly as possible, he managed to tap in and send a text.

hey baby girl r u having a good day? luv u

He closed his eyes. The few unfilled seconds stretched to infinity.

Gazing vacantly out into the courtroom and the whirring cameras that glared back at him, the next text he fired off was to his daughter, Jill.

chk if cassie @ school NOW

All the while, Trotter prattled on. "For the benefit of those looking on from your televisions . . ."

Hirschfeld's phone vibrated. *Cassie? No. Only Jill.*

What r u saying dad? ur scaring me!

He fired back: *no time chk NOW*

He felt certain everyone in the courtroom was staring at him. He remained painfully aware that someone was.

He strained to be unobtrusive, natural. As if he were concentrating on Trotter's remarks. His phone vibrated again.

dad shes not at school! FOR GODS SAKE WHATS GOING ON?

He could no longer process what Trotter was saying. He put his phone on the leather notepad in front of him, pretending to be making notes. He tapped out and sent still another text.

someones got cassie call school back say she just walked in not feeling well came home b4 reaching school DON'T SAY ANYTHING MORE get mark home. DO NOTHING MORE! NO POLICE! wait for me 2 call @ 12 they r watching me on tv and in crtrm 2 b sure I do as told I WILL GET HER BACK

No sooner had he sent the message then his phone vibrated for the third time.

u no by now this is no joke. we r ur worst nightmare. u r starting 2 draw attention. put ur damn phone away. NOW! do exactly as we say or no more sweet little girl. on u grandpa.

No doubt the bastards were watching him. Hirschfeld quickly scanned the courtroom. Nothing seemed out of the ordinary. Just a sea of faces. Among them his longtime friend and law school classmate, Cyrus Brooks. Sitting in the Court well with the other lawyers in the case. *Is Cyrus staring at me?*

Hirschfeld had to stop broadcasting his terror. Do as they instructed. Calm down. His left eye twitched uncontrollably. He willed it to stop. He tried to focus on Trotter. *How am I ever going to make it to the noon recess?*

* * *

THOMAS STARED AT HIRSCHFELD. *Get it together, asshole. We have a lot riding on you. So does the girl.*

* * *

CASSIE WOKE SUDDENLY. AT first, she couldn't find herself. As if she were in some long, dark tunnel. She was confused. Her head hurt. Her knees ached. She struggled to remember what had happened. And then it came rushing back to her, along with the sheer terror she'd felt when the man attacked her, slammed her to the ground, thrust that scary needle at her. *But why me? Where am I? What time is it? And, where is my pump?*

Like tearing something sticky off her skin, she opened her eyes. *Ow! Burns.* She rubbed them and tried again. Lying on a bed. She struggled to sit up, look around. She was in a dingy room. Not much light. Just one hanging bulb. No windows. Stuffy. Cold. Walls dirty.

What kind of a room doesn't have windows?

A basement.

She spotted a door at the end of the room. She stood, but felt dizzy. She managed to cross the cellar. She grabbed at the doorknob. Locked. She listened for any sounds on the other side. "Hello? Is anyone there? Can you hear me? Please, can you help me?"

Silence. Now more afraid than ever, she returned to the bed. For the first time, she noticed a little table in the corner. She made her way over to it. She found the note addressed to her: *You have everything you need. You're going to be here for a while.*

THE
PUPPET
MASTER

A BROOKS/LOTELLO THRILLER

RONALD S. BARAK

PROLOGUE
Undated

HE DIDN'T THINK HE was a bad person. But he acknowledged how that could be open to debate. How others might disagree. Maybe it all comes down to the definition of "bad."

The window shades were drawn. What scant light there was came from a single lamp sitting on the desk.

It was quiet. Just the two of them. In the one room. He wondered how the prowler had missed him, sitting right there at the desk? His desk. *It is my desk, damn it. In my room. Looking at my computer. Right there. The words I had chosen to read right there on my computer. How could this trespasser be so fucking brazen? So damn impudent?*

A lesson needed to be taught. For sure. And he would be the teacher. Starting right now.

Without warning, the man stood and charged the intruder. Startled, certainly now aware of the man's presence, if he hadn't been before, his adversary seemed surprised now and hurriedly sought to withdraw. Realizing there was no avenue of escape, the interloper turned and confronted the man. *Mano a mano.*

They stared at each other. This was not going to take long. It was not going to be a happy ending. Not for the villain it wasn't. The man edged forward, backing his foe into the corner. Now perched on one leg, the other elevated, ala the black belt expert that he was. Poised like a rattle snake ready to strike.

Trapped, sensing the misfortune about to find its mark, the invader made one last desperate attempt to dart away, beyond the man's reach. But it was too late. The blow squarely found its target. A second assault would not be necessary.

These insufferable parasites just don't get it. Understand there's a price to be paid. A lesson to be learned. Right from wrong. I will be the one to teach them. Someone has to do it. Now. And as often as required.

The man bent down, grasped the smashed cockroach between his thumb and finger, and deposited it in the wastebasket. His wastebasket.

No. Everyone might not agree. But he didn't think he was a bad person. Not at all.

* * *

THERE WERE 117 ACTIVE trial court judges comprising the Washington, D.C., Superior Court infrastructure. Their primary task was to *impartially* assure a fair and balanced system of justice, the kind of justice that was supposed to be at the heart of every civilized society.

In the criminal courtroom, "fair" generally meant the avoidance of surprises. And "balanced" meant equal respect for the interests of all concerned, the accused, the victim, and the public. Without "impartiality," the ability to distinguish between accused and victim often proved unclear. As did maintaining the civilized character of our society.

Judge Cyrus Brooks always thought of himself as among the best of them. Those 117 active D.C. trial court judges charged with dispensing a fair and balanced judiciary. Lately, however, he was beginning to wonder whether he was still up to the task.

If a man was arrested for robbing a convenience store, it was clear who the accused was, who the victim was, and that what the public craved was upholding peace and order. Simple and straightforward. Easy for any disciplined and competent judge to impartially manage his courtroom to achieve the "correct" outcome. Right?

But what if the accused had been down on his luck? Destitute? Try as he had, not able to find a job. What if all he had been doing when caught was stealing a loaf of bread and a carton of milk to feed his kids? After he had already exhausted his food stamps for the month? He wasn't carrying a weapon when he had entered the convenience store, but the store proprietor was. And hadn't hesitated to use it.

Once upon a time, if you were unhappy about things, you wrote your congressman. If he ignored you, then you didn't vote for him the next time around. You voted for the other guy. Maybe, you even campaigned for the other guy.

But what if the problem you were unhappy about *was* your congressman? What if you thought he wasn't doing his job? Worse. What if you thought he was on the take? Corrupt? And what if the other guy was just as bad? Then what?

Brooks knew you couldn't just take matters into your own hands. Go out and shoot someone just because you were unhappy. Let alone shoot a *bunch* of people. People you didn't even know.

Or could you?

More and more, there were those today who seemed quite willing to do precisely that. To kill complete strangers just . . . because.

That was the crux of what had been troubling Brooks of late. What if one of those killers was arrested, and assigned for trial to his courtroom? Could he still—today—assure the accused, the families of the victim—or victims— and the people of Washington, D.C., that he remained able to impartially administer a fair and balanced trial? Could he genuinely suppress his personal views in the face of everything going on in our society today? Easy to frame the questions, right? But not so easy to answer them.

Once upon a time, Brooks had no trouble doing precisely that, remaining impartial and objective at all costs and under all circumstances, subordinating his own personal views when inside his courtroom. No matter what. Of late, however, he was finding it more and more difficult to achieve that vital impartiality.

Brooks wondered if his recent doubts and concerns meant it was time for him to step down. To retire. To pass the baton to someone else.

But he waited too long.

BOOK ONE
THE CRIMINALS
FEBRUARY 5–8

CHAPTER 1
Thursday, February 5, 7:20 p.m.

U.S. SENATOR JANE WELLS had been wondering whether tonight might be the night.

Her last two companions had been disappointing, downright boring, in *every* respect. Almost as boring as her political constituents, and having to pretend that she actually cared about them.

Being single again definitely had its benefits. No longer back home in dull, sedate Kansas—first the wife and then the widow of former U.S. Senator Arthur Wells—but things were still pretty boring. Maybe she had just found it more exciting sampling the other merchandise when still married. She hoped tonight would prove more fulfilling.

Wells glanced in the mirror opposite her desk, making sure everything was in order. *Not too bad for a fifty-year-old strawberry blonde in a bottle. Well, admittedly with a little help from Dr. Nip N' Tuck.* Looks had never been her problem. Or maybe that *was* her problem. Tall and curvaceous, she still managed to fill out her power suit in all the right places. Wells closed her briefcase and walked from her oversized private office into the also spacious and well-appointed reception area. She carried herself in a way that was not easy for anyone to miss.

"Night, Jimmy," Wells said to her Chief of Staff, boyishly good-looking James Ayres. When her husband had died suddenly, most Kansas locals had expected Ayres, her husband's Chief of Staff, to be tapped to fill her husband's remaining term. But the Kansas Governor had concluded that picking the distraught, martyred widow made more political sense. For him. It was rumored that it made more personal sense for him as well. Disappointed, Ayres nevertheless agreed to stay on as her Chief of Staff.

Wells considered Ayres's sandy brown locks and piercing hazel eyes— kind of a younger, chiseled version of Robert Redford—imagining for more than just a second what a frolic in the hay with Ayres might be like.

Probably a lot more virile than my somewhat more successful, but also older, recent partners. Hard not to visualize that hard body of Ayres gliding back and forth across mine. Certainly one way to get better acquainted with the staff! She'd had no luck with her not so subtle outreaches to date, but she still kept that image tucked away in the recesses of her mind. For further consideration.

Wells's mind drifted unintentionally from Ayres to her parents, how disappointed they would be if they knew her real interest—like that of most of the other members of the Senate Wall Street Oversight Committee —was not to manage Wall Street, but to be rewarded by Wall Street for *not* really managing it at all. She also couldn't help but wonder how her parents would feel if they also knew about her fast and loose lifestyle. Actually, she didn't really wonder at all. She knew precisely how they'd feel. She didn't feel much better about herself.

"Goodnight, Senator," Ayres replied, bringing Wells back into the moment. He summoned the elevator for her. "Robert's here to drive you home. He'll pick you up again in the morning at nine o'clock and get you to the WSOC hearings on time." Wells nodded absent-mindedly and stepped into the elevator.

* * *

AYRES STOOD THERE, STARING at the closing elevator door. He had agreed to stay on as Chief of Staff to the *new* Senator Wells following her selection. He just couldn't fathom how a low-life empty suit like Wells had been chosen over him to succeed the *real* Senator Wells. He quietly shook his head in dismay, turned away from the elevator bank, and walked back into his office.

* * *

AS ALWAYS, GOOD OLD dependable Robert Grant was right there, waiting for Wells as the elevator deposited her into the underground parking garage. "Evening, Senator. How are you tonight?"

"Okay, Robert, bit of a long day. You?"

"Fine, Senator. Thanks for asking. Let's get you home, then."

That was pretty much how it was with Grant every night, just a warm and fuzzy ride home, someone harmless with whom to make small talk. Wells had occasionally confided in Grant about her dates, but he just listened; didn't judge.

Riding home, Wells thought about tomorrow's hearings, to consider whether possible Wall Street malfeasance had contributed to the country's economic collapse. She knew the hearings were not going to be any fun. With increasing pressure and hostility from both the media and various public interest groups, it was becoming more difficult to keep up appearances without actually *doing* much of anything. Lately, she felt as if it were she—rather than Wall Street—who was under the microscope and being scrutinized.

The job was taking a greater toll on Wells every day. *What do people expect of me? Why are they so damn naïve?* Life was a lot easier when she was just a Midwestern farmer's daughter looking to find herself a rich husband and settle down. Maybe that simple life was not so bad after all. *Maybe I should return to that after my term is up.*

Wells' mind returned to the present. She had a premonition that someone was watching her. She glanced back over her shoulder but saw nothing out of the ordinary. Just a lot of cars on the road. Nothing unusual about that on the crowded D.C. roadways.

Wells tried to convince herself that she was just being silly, imagining that someone was following her. But she couldn't help herself. Her anxiety wasn't a matter of logic. It was what it was. Her heart was beating faster, and her breathing was becoming more labored. She'd take an Ativan when she got home. That always did the trip.

A few minutes later, Grant pulled his car into the rotunda outside the townhouse project where Wells lived. "Here we are, Senator. Let me walk you to your townhouse."

Somewhat calmer, Wells resisted giving into her anxiety any further. She was far more worried about the awkwardness that would ensue if Grant saw her guest for the evening, possibly already waiting at her front door. "No need, Robert," she said as she slid out of the limo. "I'm good, thanks. See you in the morning."

* * *

GRANT WATCHED WELLS WALK off through the outside lobby entrance to the townhouse project. He shrugged, and peeked at his watch. *Still time to make it home before the Lakers–Wizards game comes on.*

* * *

HE WATCHED WELLS ENTER the lobby, punch her identification code in the interior lobby security door, pass through the released door and start down the attractively landscaped path toward her individual townhouse unit. He wasted no time.

Being a former engineer had its advantages. One tap on the device in his hand and an alert on the lobby security console built into the security desk sounded. The security guard glanced at the console, and swiftly headed outside to find whatever it was that had set off the alarm.

The man smiled at the security guard's anticipated reaction. Two more taps on the device and the network of surveillance cameras immobilized and the interior lobby security door lock was deactivated. The man rapidly passed through the disabled door and briskly moved down the path he knew led toward Wells's townhouse.

He watched Wells enter her townhouse and close the door behind her. He carefully surveyed the surrounding environs as he inconspicuously approached her unit. He didn't see anyone.

Outside the entrance to her unit, the man paused and removed a pair of latex surgical gloves from his shoulder bag and snapped them onto his hands. He tried the door. Locked. No surprise there. He hurriedly withdrew a tiny instrument from his pant pocket and inserted it in the door lock. In a few seconds he had the door unlocked.

He tried again to see if he could open the door. Still no luck. It opened a little, but was held fast by a chain lock. The man was becoming agitated. Every second he remained outside the unit increased the likelihood of someone coming along the path and bearing witness to his presence.

He had to get inside the unit. Now.

He grasped the gun and attached suppressor from inside his shoulder bag, removed the safety catch, inhaled, and let fly a desperate kick at the door. He wasn't sure which would give way first, the chain lock, the door itself, or perhaps neither. But he had no choice. He had to try. He had to break this impasse. If not his foot as well. He couldn't risk standing around outside the unit any longer.

* * *

FORTUNATELY, THE CHAIN LOCK proved less sturdy than the door. And his foot. He was inside the unit. And had closed the undamaged door.

Hearing the noise, Wells rushed into the entryway of her townhouse when she heard the loud noise of the man's foot meeting the door. She looked right at him. She appeared momentarily confused. "What the hell? I thought . . ."

Before Wells could finish her exclamation, two bullets only partially muffled by the suppressor attached to the man's gun screamed through her chest. Cutting off any chance for *her* to scream. She involuntarily reached for her chest, where the blood was already spreading, but it was too late. She collapsed to the floor.

He checked for a pulse. There wasn't any. No reason to fire any more shots.

He lifted the body, carried it into the bedroom, and spread it out on the bed, face up, stripped it naked, and scattered the articles of clothing on the floor. He then opened his shoulder bag, removed a tube of Crazy Glue and a Monopoly make believe $100 bill. He applied an ample amount of Crazy Glue to the entire back side of the Monopoly bill and pressed it firmly against the forehead of the dead body. *Let the shrinks figure out the meaning of that signature marker.*

Despite the brief delay in gaining access to the unit, the man was quite pleased with the scene—his constructed body art as it were—and how smoothly things had generally gone. He allowed himself a moment to gloat over how well he had executed this first step in his plans. *Just the first step. More to follow. Soon. Very soon. Until they learn. Until I teach them. I will prevail. I must prevail.*

He quietly left the townhouse unit—intentionally choosing not to lock the door on the way out—and discreetly made his way back nearby the glass security door separating the townhouse grounds from the lobby. He paused the stopwatch feature of the smart phone clipped to his pants. Less than eleven minutes had transpired since he had first passed through the security door.

The security guard was back at his desk in the lobby. The man clicked the device in his hand. He watched the security guard momentarily stare at his console in apparent disbelief, utter something the man couldn't quite make out, and leave his post unattended for the second time in less than fifteen minutes, no doubt in search of whatever was setting off the repeated false fire alarms.

The man waited another minute for good measure. He then entered and walked through the lobby and back out into the world desperately in need of his services. He clicked on his device once more to reset the security feature on the interior lobby door. He didn't reset the surveillance cameras. There was no reason to leave a roadmap as to when the cameras had not been working. That would not be an issue with the security door lock.

Once again, the man reflected on how well things had gone.

* * *

AND HE WOULD HAVE been right, if not for the pair of eyes that had peered out at him from the nearby shadows as he had exited Wells's townhouse.

CHAPTER 2
Friday, February 6, 5:30 a.m.

FRANK LOTELLO WAS ALREADY awake when the alarm went off. He had not been sleeping well since that day, almost six months ago, when he lost his wife, Beth, to the carelessness of a drunk driver. Beth was his love, his best friend. She was the person Lotello had always discussed his cases with, *every* one of them, large or small, simple or complicated.

On extended bereavement leave, the department shrink they made him see said to be patient. Give it time, he said. The ache would lessen, he said. *Hey, I know I need to get past this. I do. But the thing is, I'm not sure I want to. Without you, Beth, I don't know who I am. What I am. I can't touch you—hold you, hug you—anymore. I can't feel you—hear you—anymore. It's even becoming harder for me to remember what you look like. I'm so afraid the ache is all I have left of you. If I let go of the ache, I'm afraid you'll disappear completely. Then what?*

Lotello's bereavement leave was now officially over, but he had not yet been assigned any new work through his on-call rotation. He wondered how much longer they would continue coddling him. Without saying as much, his homicide department was unofficially cutting him as much slack—and additional time—as they could.

He had spent years working his way up to homicide. Watching the needle on the scale and the inches on the tape measure climb as he put in the time. At least he still had an enviable full head of hair.

He loved homicide. Almost as much as he loved Beth. He hated the thought of possibly having to give it up. But—as a single father of two young kids, eleven-year-old Charlie and nine-year-old Maddie, who had just lost their mother—he wondered if he could balance the 24/7 on demand protocols of a large urban city homicide department with the always on demand requirements of single parenthood.

Of course, his first priority would have to be the kids.

People were always telling Lotello that his kids looked just like they had been lifted out of Mark Twain's novels, Charlie, the spitting image of brown-eyed, red-haired Tom Sawyer, and Maddie, the perfect clone of blue-eyed, blond, freckle-faced Becky Thatcher. But whenever Lotello looked at them, all *he* saw was Beth.

It was just the three of them now. It was up to him. Lotello was painfully aware his priorities needed to change. *I have to get past this all-consuming funk, feeling sorry for myself. Thinking about myself. I need to concentrate on Charlie and Maddie, not on myself.*

Nevertheless, he had told the department he wanted to give remaining in homicide a try. He explained that he had suitable primary and secondary parenting backup from his housekeeper and the next-door neighbor. The housekeeper was primary. The next-door neighbor was secondary. Both the housekeeper and the neighbor loved Charlie and Maddie and would do anything for them. They could be trusted. Completely.

Even with these arrangements theoretically in place, Lotello wondered if he was truly ready for a "big leagues" *real* case.

* * *

ALMOST AS IF ON cue, the telephone rang. "Lotello."

"Hey, Frank, it's me, Jeremy."

Jeremy Barnet was Lotello's younger homicide partner. "No shit, J. Who else would be calling at 5:30 in the morning? While the kids were still asleep. What's up?"

"You know Jane Wells? *Senator* Jane Wells?"

"Sure, make it a point to have lunch with *Jane* at least once every other week. How many senators do *you* know?"

"Funny. Don't really need your sarcasm right now. It's just as early for me. Do you know *who* Wells is?"

"I see her on the news now and then. *So?*"

"Dead, murdered in her townhouse. We drew next on the wheel. The case is ours. I'm on the way to her townhouse now. Just texted you the address. How soon can you get there?"

"Not supposed to text and drive, J. To early for the housekeeper. Gotta get the kids up and out and over to the neighbor's. Make sure she'll get the kids to school. I'll call when I'm on the way."

"Drive'll take you about 30 minutes at this hour. See ya there."

Lotello's question about how much longer they were going to shelter him had been answered. In spades. It was not lost on
Lotello—or his pride—that the first case back he'd caught was this high pro-
file. No way that was on his young partner. "Wait up, J. When did all this
supposedly happen?"

"I'm not sure. I got the call a few minutes ago. I was anxious to reach you
and get going."

"What's the rush? Where'd you think I'd be at this hour? Find out who
called this in, and when. I'll meet you at Wells's place as fast as I can."

Barnet hung up. Lotello knew Barnet was not happy with his answer; that
he probably was tearing out to Wells's townhouse on a Code 3 emergency
response, lights and siren, and wanted assurance that Lotello would be doing
likewise. *Barnet is such a fuss budget. Not necessary. Maybe a Code 3 for the patrol cars, but not for homicide. Not like it's going to bring Wells back to life.*

Lotello dragged himself out of bed, pulled the covers up over the pil-
lows, threw on some sweats, and bent down to stroke Beau, the youngest
member of their family, a German shepherd rescue pup, one of Beth's many
thoughtful acts. Lotello went out front, grabbed the newspaper, glanced at
the headlines while waiting for Beau to piddle, and then went back inside
and into the kitchen. He opened the refrigerator and took a few sips from
the carton of orange juice as he quickly skimmed the remainder of the
newspaper to see if there was anything about Wells. If there was, he didn't
see it. He did notice that the Lakers had pummeled the Wizards the night
before.

Lotello put some food and water down for Beau, who needed little coax-
ing. He also put out some dry cereal, milk, and fruit for the kids, and confirmed their lunch pails were in the refrigerator ready to go from last night.

He knew he had to get out to Wells's townhouse. But he needed to take a
couple minutes on the treadmill in his combination home office and exercise room to get the kinks out and to get his juices flowing. It was going
to be a long day. He spent two minutes in the shower—one of his favorite
thinking spots—and drying off. He thought it odd that someone reported
the Wells body around 4 or 5 in the morning. *What do you think, Beth?*

If Wells had already been missing for any period of time, wouldn't that have made the morning newspapers? You know I read the papers every morning. There were no such reports. If the murder happened last night or early this morning, who—other than the killer—would have known about the body, and called it in so early this morning? This means the killer probably made the call. Why would he do that, especially at that hour?

Beth didn't answer.

* * *

NO MORE STALLING, THEY had to get going, but he needed to ease in the next-door neighbor. Just this first time.

"Dad," said Maddie, as he gently woke her, "what are you doing? It's still *way* too early."

"Morning, Pussycat," Lotello said, kissing both of her sleepy eyes. "It's not *still* way too early. Breakfast's out and your lunches are in the 'fridge. I've already fed Beau. You and Charlie need to get up, brush your teeth, get dressed, eat breakfast, and take Beau with you next door to stay with Mrs. Schwartz 'til Elena gets here. Mrs. Schwartz will get you and Charlie to school. C'mon, get a move on it! And remind Charlie that Elena'll pick you up after school. I gotta go. See you tonight, Princess. Love you."

"Love you too, Dad," Maddie parroted back.

Beth had been right about Beau. It was good for Charlie and Maddie to have some responsibility, and a friend who would watch out for them. Maddie seemed to be adjusting to Beth's death okay, at least as near as Lotello could tell, but Lotello wasn't so sure about Charlie, who was a lot quieter than he used to be, and a lot more moody. He needed to keep a closer watch on both of them, especially Charlie.

* * *

AS LOTELLO DROVE OFF in the "family-safe" Volvo, he inconsistently snuck an unsafe peek at his text messages to see exactly where Wells lived— where she used to live. *Not supposed to text and drive, but, hey, I'm just reading. And I may have broken protocol by about seven minutes. So I'll break a few speeding rules and make up half of that on the way. Not gonna matter.*

CHAPTER 3
Friday, February 6, 7:35 a.m.

HE SAT THERE IN the dark, all alone. Things weren't like they used to be. He had lost *so* much, but he was going to get even. They would be sorry.

So far, so good, it had all gone much easier than he had imagined. The first call was a little dicey, but he was off the phone in a flash, well before the cops could have thought to trace it. If he had called 911 instead, the call would have been recorded, if not traced, before he could have hung up.

The timing of the second call, to the reporter, also went pretty easy. The story would soon make the media outlets and begin drawing attention. He wondered what she would say to explain how she got her information.

He knew the next murder would also be easy, but they would then start becoming more difficult to pull off. He didn't care. *I have to shake things up, bring about some real change.*

He liked the dark. It was quiet, peaceful. No one bothered him. Not anymore. It allowed him to think, and to plan.

CHAPTER 4
Friday, February 6, 8:47 a.m.

GRANT ARRIVED AND PARKED in the rotunda of the Townhouse complex at 8:45 a.m., fifteen minutes before Wells was to meet him there at nine o'clock. When she still hadn't shown at 9:10 a.m., he tried to raise her on her cell phone. There was no answer.

He entered the lobby and told the security guard sitting at the desk what was going on. Or more precisely what was not. The two of them hurried to Wells's unit. The front door was closed, but looked as if it had suffered some recent assault. Grant grimaced and absently pulled at his throat. The guard knocked on the door. Nothing. He knocked again. Louder this time. Still nothing.

Grant called out, "Senator?" No response.

The security guard tried the door. It wasn't locked. He opened it and entered. Grant was right behind him. Grant called out again. Nothing. It was only two seconds later until the guard entered the bedroom, Grant right on his heels. Beads of sweat appearing on his brow.

They both gasped at the same instant. And at the same sight. Wells lying face up on the bed, naked, looking very still, although certainly not peaceful. And then there was the fake $100 bill stuck to her forehead.

Grant unsuccessfully attempted to swallow a cry of despair: "Senator. Oh my God." He reached for his cell phone, dialed James Ayres, Wells's Chief of Staff, and frantically described to him what he was looking at. The guard, professionally a bit more stoic, but just barely, used his cell phone to call 911. Ayres said he would be there as quickly as traffic would allow. 911 said both a patrol car and ambulance were already on the way.

Grant walked toward the body. The guard grabbed him. "What are you doing?"

"I want to cover her up. She's entitled to that."

"I don't think we should touch anything until the police and the ambulance arrive. They're on the way. It should just be a few minutes. We need to let them take charge of things."

Grant didn't agree, but he deferred, sat down on a lone ottoman against the wall, put his head in his hands, and softly said, "No, no, no. No."

Neither man said another word until the authorities entered the townhouse.

* * *

WHEN LOTELLO ARRIVED, THE multi-residential townhouse complex in which Wells's townhouse unit was located looked more like Grand Central Station than the upscale multi-residential community that it was. People seemed to be coming and going everywhere. But Lotello knew that was not quite so.

He first walked from outside the complex to the center of the crime scene, Wells's townhouse unit. He then reversed his course and slowly walked back to the rotunda outside the interior lobby, taking it all in. He then retraced his steps back to the Senator's unit.

In keeping with standard custom and practice, the first patrol car to arrive at a possible crime scene would have first gone inside to verify that no persons were lurking or hiding in wait. Only then would they have "yellow tape" secured the immediate crime scene perimeter to assure no unauthorized entry.

Given the layout of the overall complex, one of the two patrol officers would have remained at the unit to enforce its integrity while the other patrol officer would have established second and third yellow tape perimeters—one around the grounds just inside the interior lobby and the other around the grounds just outside the interior lobby. Because of the secure perimeter of the complex itself, this was perhaps somewhat of an overkill, but this also was a U.S. senator. Lotello knew that crime scene protocol would have been be strictly enforced.

While the several perimeters were still being secured, ambulance personnel would have arrived, and been permitted to enter the unit to confirm that the body was dead. They would then have departed. Additional patrol cars would have been assigned to prevent the breach of any of the yellow tape perimeters—inward bound or outward bound.

One of the first patrol officers to arrive at the scene would also have reported in to dispatch, which would in turn have notified the medical examiner, crime lab officials, the homicide department, and the district attorney's office. Lotello and Barnett were next up on the wheel and homicide department seniors had obviously decided that Lotello's bereavement was now in fact over.

* * *

LOTELLO SILENTLY CAUGHT BARNET'S eye, but his arrival didn't seem to offer Barnet any solace. "Damn, Frank, what took you so frigging long? Place's a madhouse. This case is gonna be nothin' but trouble."

"Lighten up, J. Wells isn't going anywhere. What do you have so far?"

"Already *two* people here from Wells' office. First one's her limo driver, a Robert Grant. Here to drive Wells to some senate committee hearing this morning. Along with the security guard, they found the body when Wells was a no show."

"Who put the call into 911?

"Grant and the security guard. Grant also called Wells's Chief of Staff, a James Ayres. Grant's quiet. Not much of a problem. Ayres is an absolute piece of work, a real *prima donna*. Acts like *he's* in charge."

"Where are they now?

"One of the patrol officer's babysitting Grant and the security guard in the lobby entrance to the complex. Ayres wanted access to the Senator's townhouse, ostensibly to see the body. Went ballistic when he was told he would not be allowed to enter the crime scene. He's been threatening to call in everyone he *supposedly* knows—from the FBI Director to the U.S. Attorney General, even the President—if he's not afforded the respect to which he thinks he's entitled."

"I trust all that got him was an assignment of his very own patrol officer—outside the outer perimeter."

"Exactly."

* * *

LOTELLO CHECKED OUT the body and looked around the townhouse. *Nice digs. Nothing surprising about that. Nothing out of the ordinary about the body, except for the chest wounds and that phony hundred-dollar bill glued to Wells's forehead.*

Barnet followed after Lotello. He started in again. Lotello understood Barnet's apprehension. This was obviously going to be a high-profile case, lots of attention, lots of pressure. He didn't want to add to Jeremy's anxiety. "J . . ." Lotello paused for effect. "Calm down. I'll take the security guard and Grant. And then the high and mighty Mr. Ayres. You should stay with the lab guys and photographers. Don't let anyone *else* in. Let's not compromise the crime scene any more than it already has been."

* * *

LOTELLO WALKED INTO THE free-standing lobby area. He saw two men sitting together off in one corner of the room, both in uniform, one dressed like some kind of a security guard, the other dressed like a limousine driver. He approached the two men. "Would you two be Mr. Robert Grant and Officer Thornton Smythe?" Granted nodded yes but didn't speak. Officer Smythe said his name was pronounced the same as Smith, but added that most folks call him Smitty.

Opening his wallet, Lotello handed each of the two men one of his cards. "Detective Frank Lotello, Metropolitan D.C. Police, Homicide. Sorry to be meeting under these circumstances. Mr. Grant would you please sit tight, give me a few minutes to briefly talk to Smitty?"

"Sure, I guess. Is this going to take long? I'm not feeling too well."

"Just a few minutes. I'll be back as quickly as I can."

* * *

LOTELLO LED OFFICER SMYTHE over to the desk at the other end of the lobby. He wanted to separate Smythe and Grant.

"How long have you been in charge of security at this complex, Smitty?" Lotello knew Smythe was not in charge, but it never hurt to gratuitously elevate a witness's status. Make them feel important.

"Oh, I'm not in charge of anything, Detective, just one of the security staff. This is my second year on the job."

"How many security folks are there?"

There's eleven of us, not counting Joel Kirst, who's kind of the security boss around here. I don't know who Joel reports to. We provide onsite security 24/7. Always two of us on duty, one here for unit owners, tenants, and guests and another one slightly down the road for employees and trades. That's also where trucks come in and out."

"So, how are people allowed to come and go?"

"Identification cards are issued to owners and tenants and project employees. Guests and other workers are admitted by the security guard on duty only if an owner, tenant, or employee calls in their names in advance. They have to show a matching photo ID as well."

"Sounds like you guys run a pretty tight ship."

"We try to."

"What about all this fancy equipment?"

"Not really all that much. We have a video surveillance system that covers the entire complex. We also have a fire alarm system. And then of course we have electronic control of the secured admissions at each entrance. Exits are not controlled, although they are picked up by the surveillance cameras."

"Did you know Senator Wells?"

"Just a little. To say hello, chit-chat for a moment here and there. She was always polite. That was about it."

"So, I'm going to need to go into all of this security business in some detail, but I think we should do that down at the station, but probably not today." Lotello knew that Smythe would have to come when they were ready for him, but there was no reason not to appear as accommodating as possible. "When's your day off?"

"Probably best if you talk to Joel about that." Smitty wrote down Joel's telephone number and email address on a card and handed it to Lotello. "My day off floats; it would be hard for me to know what day to schedule with you. Besides I don't know much about the technical side of our equipment. I can use it, but I don't really understand it very well."

I'll talk to Joel, Smitty. But please keep my card, hold yourself available, and give me a call if you think of anything more to tell me in the interim."

"Okay."

"By the way, let me ask you one question on the equipment side for now. Did you happen to have any technical difficulties last night?

"Funny you should ask. For the last week or so, we've had several false positives with our fire alarm system, maybe once every couple of days. But last night we had two false positives in about fifteen minutes."

"Back up a second, Smitty. What do you do when a fire alarms goes off?"

"I have to run out and check to see if there's a fire that actually set off the system."

"How long does that take you?"

"About ten minutes."

"And it happened twice last night?"

"Yep. I was back less than five minutes after verifying a false positive and resetting the system when we had a second false positive. First time that happened twice in a row like that."

"And when that happens, you're away from your desk here?"

"Yes, like I said, for at least five or ten minutes."

"And while you're away, an intruder could just walk through the security door here?"

"No, not really, because it still requires a permanent or temporary identity card passcode."

"If someone somehow bypassed your passcode system, would we have anyway to know?"

"We should still be able to spot the person on our surveillance cameras, including the ones directed at the entrances."

"Smitty, I have to go visit with Mr. Grant for a few minutes. He's been waiting patiently while you and I talked. Could you check your surveillance system for last night to see if it was working properly? And, if it was, whether there were any people wandering around on the grounds last night who were not unit owners or tenants or other guests or workers you recognize?"

"Sure, it'll take me a few minutes."

"That's perfect. It'll give me time to talk with Mr. Grant. When I'm done I'll come back over here to see what you've found."

* * *

LOTELLO WALKED BACK ACROSS the lobby where Grant seemed to be a bit anxious. "Sorry Mr. Grant, that took a little longer than I expected. I'll be quick. What brought you out here so early this morning?"

"I'm Senator Wells' driver. I was here this morning to pick her up, like I always do when she's in town."

"What time did you arrive?"

"Around 8:45, maybe a few minutes earlier."

"How long have you been driving the Senator?"

"About four months."

"And before that?"

"I drove for a local limo service."

"For how long?"

"About eight years or so."

"How did you become the Senator's driver?"

"I got a call one day from our dispatcher to pick her up. I gave her a ride. She asked me if I could drive her again the next day. I did. After that, she said she'd lost her prior driver and wondered if I would be interested in driving for her on a regular basis. It sounded good to me, I said sure, and that was that."

"What will you do now?"

"I'm not sure, I'll probably go home. I don't mind telling you that I'm more than a little upset."

"No, no, not today. I mean now that you won't be driving the Senator any longer."

"Oh, sorry. Don't really know. Probably go back to driving for a limo service."

"What was the name of the limo service you worked for before?"

"Tri-Star Limousine Service."

"Can you go back there?"

"Don't know why not."

"By the way, did you drive the Senator home last night?"

"Yes, around 7:45."

"Do you know what plans she had for the evening?"

"Nope. She didn't mention any to me."

Lotello sensed some discomfort on Grant's part with that last question. His denial seemed a little too quick. "Would you have driven her last night if she was going out for the evening?"

"Sometimes, but I didn't last night."

Again, Lotello thought Grant was holding back, but it could just be the shock of Wells' unexpected and grisly death. In the meanwhile, he caught Smythe's return to his desk out of the corner of his eye.

"Okay, Mr. Grant. I may have some follow-up questions for you, but that's it for now. Do you have a number where I can reach you?"

Grant gave Lotello his cell phone number. "Can I go now?"

Lotello made a mental note not to forget Grant's visible agitation when Lotello had asked about Wells's plans last night. If Wells had any strange goings on, there was a good chance that Grant would know about some of them. "Sure. See you."

* * *

LOTELLO WALKED BACK OVER to Smythe. "Any luck, Smitty?"

"Yes and no. The first false positive fire alarm last night was at 7:50. Our camera system went down as well last night at 7:51."

"When did it come back up?"

"It didn't. It's still down."

Lotello thought about that. "How about the passcode lock on the interior lobby security door? Anything unusual with it last night?"

"I thought you might ask. So I checked. It was turned off at 7:52 last night."

"Who has the ability to turn the passcode system off?' Besides me, no one that I know could have done that last night."

"And is it still off?"

"Nope. It was turned back on at 8:10."

"And let me guess: You don't know of anyone who could have done that last night other than you and you didn't do it."

"Exactly."

"Okay, Smitty, you've really been helpful. If you think of anything further, please do call me. In the meanwhile, please let Joel know I'll be in touch with him."

"Will do, on both scores."

* * *

LOTELLO WALKED OUT THROUGH the lobby to the rotunda, looking for Ayres. Before Lotello could figure out who was who, a man in an obviously expensive dark pinstripe business suit came bustling up to him. "Are you in charge here?"

Opening his wallet, Lotello responded, "Detective Frank Lotello, Metropolitan DC Police. Can I help you, Mr. . . . ?"

"Ayres, James Ayres, Senator Wells's Chief of Staff. What happened here?"

"Sorry for your loss, Mr. Ayres, but I understand you've been here longer this morning than I have. Not much information I can share with you yet. Are you usually at the Senator's townhouse this time of day?"

Ayres seemed taken aback, exactly the effect Lotello had intended. "No, of course not." Pausing, he added, "The Senator's driver arrived to pick her up earlier this morning. She didn't show. He and the security guard went to her unit and found her body. He called me and I came as quickly as I could. Isn't there something you can tell me?"

"Aside from the fact that Senator Wells is dead, no, I'm afraid not. Why don't *you* tell *me* where the Senator was supposed to be this morning? And where she was supposed to be last night?"

"She left her office last night a little after seven. Her driver brought her home. Then went home himself. No idea what plans she had for the evening. She was supposed to be at the WSOC hearings this morning. That's the Senate Wall Street Oversight Committee."

"Her driver? That's Robert Grant?"

"Right."

"How long did Grant work for the Senator? How well do you know him?"

"About three months. I met him when he started working for her. Seems like a nice enough guy. He cleared the government security check okay."

"How is it you know Grant went home last night after he dropped the Senator off?"

Ayres thought about that for a moment. "Guess I don't. I just assumed it."

"Assumptions aren't very helpful, Mr. Ayres, especially ones you keep to yourself. Do you know anyone who might have wanted Senator Wells out of the way?"

"No, but she is on the Senate WSOC. They deal with lots of contentious and inflammatory issues concerning the economy. No shortage of kooks out there, but I don't recall any out-of-the-ordinary threats against her."

"Okay, Mr. Ayres. Thanks. You can be on your way. I'll speak to Mr. Grant. We may release a statement later this morning. I'll be in touch."

Lotello watched Ayres turn around and leave. Ayres didn't seem to like being told what to do.

* * *

LOTELLO WALKED BACK TO the townhouse and found Barnet. "Finish up here as we discussed. I'll see you back at the station."

* * *

LOTELLO WALKED OUTSIDE THE townhouse complex, stretched, looked around the exterior of the complex once more, and headed back to his car. He was surprised to see one of the local beat reporters, Rachel Santana, already at the scene. Santana wasn't a bad looker, Lotello thought, if you liked the flamboyant, ostentatious, over the top look, heels too high, skirt too short, top too tight, too much make up. "Hey, Rachel, what brings you out here so early?"

"Missing your pretty face, Frank. You know, when the boys and I have nothing better to do, we just start following you around. Figure sooner or later something interesting will pop."

"Yeah, *right*. Suppose it wouldn't do me any good to ask you for a more serious answer?"

"Probably not. Any chance you might have something for me?"

"Probably not."

"C'mon, Frank, give me *something*. I will tell you I got an anonymous voicemail message earlier this morning saying Wells was caught without her panties one too many times, that it would be worth my while to stop by her place. Couldn't pass that up. So what gives, Frank?"

"Nothing yet. Hey, Rachel?"

"Yeah?"

"You still have that voicemail message?"

"Not sure, Frank. Guess I could check."

"I can get a search warrant for it. Anonymous calls aren't protected."

"No point, Frank. You know how I am with technology. All thumbs. Voicemail's probably long gone."

"Never learn, do you, Rachel? See you around."

"Right, Frank."

Frank drove off, mired in thought. *Okay, that's two mysterious telephone calls this morning, one to the station and one to Santana. Who's making all these damn calls? And why?*

CHAPTER 5
Friday, February 6, 10:00 a.m.

FIRST CAME ANGER. THEN anger turned to rage. Then rage led to confusion. He was becoming more and more confused. It was all becoming more and more confusing. He had not always been this way. Things had not always been this way. *But I will prevail. I must prevail.*

* * *

THERE SHE SAT, ONE week earlier, frightened, miserable, and all alone, in the lobby of the psychiatric ward of that local Washington, D.C., hospital. Paige Rogers Norman wondered how all of this could have happened so quickly, in the blink of an eye one might say.

Blink once. There was Paige, with husband Cliff and their young son Ryan. It was early 2008. They were on top of the world, happily married for twelve years, the owners of a highly successful local electronics business they had toiled together for more than a decade to build. Paige was now retired from the business and in charge of all family matters, including Ryan and their beautiful Georgetown home. Originally an engineer, Cliff now ran the business and was in the midst of merger negotiations to sell their company to a large national electronics chain. They were both looking forward to more family time together, and hopefully an addition or two to the Norman family.

Blink again. It was still 2008, but a few months later. The economy had come crashing down around them. Paige first thought the economy was just a problem for others, not for the Normans. But then their business began suffering too. Company accounts began drying up. Cliff was forced to lay off employees that were like family to him, and to Paige as well. If that was not enough, the merger fell through and their business failed altogether. The low teaser rate on their home mortgage expired, and the value of their home fell below the amount of their mortgage, making a sale all but impossible. The bank foreclosed on their home. They were now living in a tiny one-bedroom apartment, depleting what little savings remained while Cliff looked for a job to sustain their family—His success had proved unsuccessful. There were no jobs to be had.

When it seemed like nothing more could go wrong for them, something else *did* go wrong. Terribly wrong. Ryan had become ill. They had found a tumor. It was malignant. Ryan's only chance was a prohibitively expensive new course of treatment. The Normans had a healthcare policy, one of the few remnants left over from their failed company, but the insurer wouldn't cover the procedure because they said it was "experimental."

Cliff had no family to help. Paige had only her parents, retired in Flagstaff, Arizona, barely making ends meet. Frantic, Cliff went to New York and tried to meet with senior executives of the insurance company, but they were in the midst of a weeklong corporate "retreat" at some fancy island golf and polo resort. And unavailable. His messages went unreturned.

Conventional treatment had proved inadequate. Ryan died barely two months later.

Blink once more. Cliff had all but died with Ryan. The Normans were hardly functioning, or even speaking. Paige would watch Cliff go off in the morning without a word, not returning until late at night, again completely silent and withdrawn.

Still grieving the loss of Ryan, Paige worried more and more about Cliff. He wasn't eating. He wasn't sleeping. He had nothing to say, except on rare occasion when he barely muttered to himself. Paige begged Cliff to let her take him for medical help. He just quietly stared back at her.

Then, one night, Cliff didn't come home. Not that night. Not the next day. Not *any* time thereafter. Paige went to the authorities. They said there was nothing they could do, which was exactly what they did. Nothing.

Weeks went by. Nothing changed. Paige finally decided there was nothing more she could do. Heartbroken, she gave the authorities a forwarding address and reluctantly went to live with her parents in Arizona.

One more blink. Ten days ago, DC authorities contacted Paige. Cliff had finally turned up, on the steps of the Capitol Building. He was physically and emotionally disheveled, ranting at the top of his lungs. "It's all your fault. You did it. You killed Ryan. Now I'm going to get you."

The police were quickly summoned. Cliff was committed to a local psychiatric facility. The authorities contacted Paige. She returned overnight to D.C., all to no avail. Cliff was completely unresponsive, to the doctors and to Paige. After expiration of the short mandatory confinement procedures under D.C. law, the hospital was forced to release Cliff. He vanished all over again.

* * *

On the same day Cliff was released, a short story appeared in one of the back pages of *The Washington Post* under the headline:

LOCAL MAN TRAGICALLY LOSES FAMILY, IS ARRESTED

Anger turned to rage. Rage turned to confusion. He read the words again. *It's all your fault. You did it. You killed Ryan. Now I'm going to get you. Am I crazy? Who knows? But I will prevail. I must prevail.*

PAYBACK

A BROOKS/LOTELLO THRILLER

RONALD S. BARAK

PROLOGUE
Ten Weeks Before

I REMEMBER WHEN I first had the urge to kill someone. Not just *anyone*, mind you. After all, I'm not capricious. Or uncouth. I'm just . . . me.

To be sure, my deadly urges were not the first of my social . . . anomalies, you might say, but they were, no doubt, a natural and foreseeable evolution of my earlier . . . irregularities.

But I'm getting ahead of myself, something I often do. Digressing, you might say. Allow me to rewind and start at the beginning, at least as I know it. Hmm, rewind. I like that word because, at the end of the day, that's what we're talking about, how I'm . . . wound. Hah! *I am dark and stormy even if the night wasn't.*

I was probably always the way I am. I just didn't know it. I'd always thought it was *them*. Until it finally dawned on me. *I* was the one who was . . . different, don't you see? Who are . . . them, you ask? That's easy. Them is everyone. Everyone other than me.

To make things better, to fix things, I had to change . . . *me*. Not them. I had to change the way I was wired. The way I was wound. Don't you see?

But how, you ask? It's okay that you ask, because I asked too.

And so I did some research. I read some books. Actually, I read a lot of books. What I learned, according to all the shrinks, was that a good way to change, to fix myself, would be by writing things down. About me. Reflecting about myself. Sort of keeping a diary. This made sense to me too.

But if writing would help, why stop at writing about myself? After all, I'm not all that interesting. Writing about me was boring. Instead of dwelling on me, I decided I would dwell on others. I would write about . . . them. That way, I could *become* . . . *like* them.

But I didn't know many others. Actually, I really didn't know *any* others. At least not well. So I decided I would simply make them up. In my mind. I would write fiction. I would . . . become a novelist.

And so I began writing about others. Others I wanted to *be like*. Others I wanted to . . . *like me*.

I thought it was going to make a difference. In me. For me. Don't you see? A huge difference. But it didn't. Not at all. Why? I don't know. You have to ask *them*. But you had better not dally.

CHAPTER 1
Eight Weeks Before

ELOISE BROOKS HAD PLANNED the evening very strategically. Dinner at their favorite restaurant with her husband, Cyrus, and their two closest friends, Frank Lotello and Leah Klein Lotello, ostensibly to celebrate the Brookses' fifty-fifth anniversary, but actually to spring a surprise on Cyrus in a setting where it would be difficult for him to object. He was the only one at the table who had no idea what was coming.

Knowing Cyrus as she did, Eloise sensed the timing was right. After a distinguished 35-year career as a U.S. District Court Judge, Cyrus had voluntarily stepped down from the bench and retired about ten years ago. But retired was a weak euphemism for what still drove Cyrus. He remained passionately committed to the law, in one form or another.

And therein lay the problem, Eloise's not Cyrus's. Both on the bench and off, Cyrus was constantly finding himself in life-threatening situations, especially after he and homicide investigator Frank Lotello became so close. Cyrus seemed to relish all the danger, but Eloise did not.

Fortunately, as only Eloise really knew, Cyrus did have other interests: music, dance, and writing—to name just a few. But he couldn't sing or dance, and his few attempts at writing a novel ended unsuccessfully. Infinitely patient and disciplined when it came to matters of the law, and the heart, he lacked both when it came to his attempts to become a novelist.

But Eloise was not about to give up, especially as she observed Cyrus recently exhibiting some degree of restlessness. When Cyrus was a highly renowned jurist, people listened to him, looked up to him, admired him. His confidence and self-esteem were at a high. Once he stepped down from the bench, the attention visited on him diminished considerably. Sure, he was still respected, but it wasn't the same. It wasn't as noticeable. His self-esteem understandably waned. It was only natural.

She knew what the problem was. Cyrus was overcompensating, seeking to hold onto his recognition and standing. He couldn't say or admit that, and she couldn't raise it to him. He was proud. It would hurt him terribly to confront any of this.

But there were other ways. It was time to strike. "Happy Anniversary, dear," Eloise said, handing the previously concealed envelope to Cyrus.

Cyrus's face scrunched up as he stared at the envelope in mock discomfort. "I'm afraid you caught me unawares," he said.

"Oh, just open the envelope," Frank said to Leah's laughter.

"Hmm," Cyrus responded, "now I'm as curious as I am suspicious. Why do I feel like I'm the only one at the table who doesn't know what's coming?"

He opened the envelope and removed a brochure announcing a one-week writers' retreat named Thriller Jubilee to be hosted by TITO, The International Thrillers Organization, at Hotel Marisol on the "sun-bathed" island of Punta Maya off the coast of Spain. "What, pray tell, is this?" Cyrus asked.

"We're all going, the four of us, eight weeks from today," Eloise answered. "It's time for you to learn how to write one of those novels you're always been starting but never finishing."

"In eight weeks? That's impossible. My desk is piled high with pending chores. Besides, I'm not a writer. And my fair skin will never hold up for a week in all that sunshine."

"Nothing on your desk that won't keep, and who says you're not a writer?" Eloise countered. "And you'll use sunscreen like everyone else. Only now you'll be able to stalk *imaginary* murder and mayhem instead of the *real-world* murder and mayhem that always seems to stalk *you*, and how to write *about* judges and lawyers instead of *being* one. With all the stories in your head, you'll soon be writing with the best of them. You just need a little encouragement."

"Well, even if we assume I agree to this boondoggle, who or what the hell is TITO, and how do our dear friends Frank and Leah fit into all this?"

Leah had the answers to Cyrus's last two questions. "When Eloise showed me the brochures, I figured if you were in, Cyrus, so were Frank and I. We haven't had a vacation in I don't know how long. Besides, we have to be there to witness and support your nascent writing adventure. And Eloise will need someone to keep her company when you're off in all your classes. Knowing you as I do, I did a little research. TITO is headquartered in New York and is the largest and most prominent thriller organization in the world. It has a membership in excess of 10,000 thriller writers, readers, promoters, and fans. It's the real deal."

Frank looked at Cyrus and smiled. "No point fighting it, Judge. Sometimes you just have to let go and live to fight another day."

"Well, maybe just to accommodate the three of you. If they offer singing and dancing classes as well, I can cover my entire bucket list in one fell swoop."

Eloise ignored his attempted diversions. "It's settled then," she said to Cyrus victoriously. "I'm so looking forward to you not getting into trouble for a change. After all, what could possibly go wrong at a writers' conference?"

* * *

"WRITING IS JUST A thin version of doing," Brooks said to himself, as they shared a scoop of raspberry sorbet delivered to their table with four spoons. *How much harm could two small bites do to my waistline?* Truth be told, genuinely learning how to write a credible novel would probably be great fun, especially if anyone might actually want to read it. Besides, he knew, how could he possibly say no to Eloise after she went to all of this trouble and got her hopes up about taking me in this safer direction? *"Safer?" Pshaw! Just so long as everyone knows I'm only doing this for Eloise and not for myself.*

CHAPTER 2
One Week Before

"I'm back," I said aloud, to no one in particular. That made perfectly good sense of course—to no one in particular—because there was no one else there. *Besides me.* There never is anyone else there. *Besides me.*

"Well, let's see now what we have here, as if I don't know," still speaking aloud to no one in particular, while carefully removing the contents of the grocery bag and neatly lining up each item on the table: one small orange, one large watermelon, one vial of saline solution—"just saline solution for now," again out loud, to what end it was unclear—and, finally, one sealed package of six disposable syringes. "Amazing." The vial and syringes did not require a doctor's prescription. *Only my fake driver's license.* The pharmacist didn't seem the least bit interested.

"Practice, practice, practice." *What a busy little beaver I am. Because we all know that practice makes perfect, doesn't it? Don't you see?*

CHAPTER 3
Five Days Before

JAMES LLEWELLYN, THE HEAD of Gander House Publishers, one of the "big five" publishing houses, was sitting at his regular breakfast spot across the street from his midtown Manhattan headquarter offices, all five floors of them. He was on his second cup of coffee when her lips brushed his cheek.

Those lips belonged to Arianna Simpson, owner of book publicist extraordinaire Simpson Public Relations (SPR). She wore dark red lipstick, matching the color of her well-fitted Chanel outfit. Llewellyn couldn't decide which he liked more, her eye-catching, short, jet-black modern haircut or her provocative, musky perfume. She slipped into the seat opposite him, asking the waiter for a cup of hot water and lemon.

"And you, Mr. Llewellyn, your usual: a half grapefruit, two eggs over easy, bacon well done, and an order of wheat toast?" the waiter asked.

He nodded affirmatively, turned to Simpson and said, "That's it, lemon-flavored water? Didn't your mother impress upon you that breakfast is the most important meal of the day?"

"She also taught me that a girl has to watch her figure. I'm not lucky like you, tall and thin with your curly salt and pepper locks. Dressed to the nines in your navy three-piece pinstripe suit, you look almost good enough to eat."

"Ooh, I like your thinking."

"I said 'almost.'"

"Tease."

Married, but not to each other, Llewellyn and Simpson knew each other well. Publicly, they shared a number of author clients, published by Gander House and publicized by SPR. Privately, on occasion, when the opportunity presented itself, they also shared the same bed.

In high demand, they often also spoke at the same posh writing conferences, including Thriller Jubilee (TJ), hosted on Punta Maya every year by TITO. They were each members of TITO's board of directors.

"When's your flight to Punta Maya?" Llewellyn asked Simpson.

"Monday. My panel presentation's not until Tuesday. I have a lot on my table here. I can barely afford the time I'm giving it, but that's where I land new clients. When are you leaving?"

"Tomorrow. I have to spend a couple of days in our London offices first. I get into Punta Maya Sunday evening."

"'Have to'? Poor baby. I've tried to put together a London office for SPR. Unfortunately, the economics just don't pencil."

"Too bad. Wouldn't *that* be nice for us."

Simpson didn't take the bait. "This is your meeting, Jim. What's on your mind? Besides, that is, what's *always* on your mind."

"Wanted to give you a heads-up. Jonathan's not happy. Thinks he's not getting what he should for the five thousand a month he's paying you."

"Jonathan" was Jonathan Connor. Author of three *New York Times* bestsellers over the past three years. But none of them number one. Connor thought each should have made number one.

"What the hell does he expect?" Simpson asked. "The asshole's never satisfied. I've got each of his last three novels on the *Times* bestseller list."

"You mean *we've* got each of his last three novels on the bestseller list."

"Is Connor unhappy with you too?" Simpson asked.

"Not that I know of. But there's a difference. I *pay* him a pretty hefty guaranteed advance on his book sales. You *charge* him a pretty hefty monthly retainer fee. Every month. He thinks he should be receiving more media coverage than he is."

"Connor never owns it. It's always the other guy's fault. What he tells *me* is that it's *your* fault. If you didn't set the price on his books so high, he'd have far more sales and he would be number one."

"Yeah. Maybe. But if we hadn't been required to pay him such a whopping advance, we could afford to set his book prices lower. Our margins on him are too damn thin as it is. Maybe you *should* try to get him some more publicity."

"It's not us. We *are* trying. We're doing all the right things for him. Not to mention that I have other clients to tend to as well. Connor's just not that appealing to the media. His interviews are just so damn boring. Frankly, so's his writing. He's fucking lucky to be where he's at."

"I agree," Llewellyn said. "But we have a lot invested in him. Too much. Way too much. Lasko interested two other houses in Connor and was able to force us into a bidding war on his latest novel. We had to pay way too much to keep him in our catalog. I'm still pissed at her about that."

"C'mon, you have no one to blame but yourself," Simpson said. "You should have tied Connor down on a three-book deal at the time of his first novel when you had the chance. When you were in the driver's seat rather than his agent."

"You're probably right. The problem was we weren't sure back then that he wasn't just a one-trick pony, a one-and-done. But, hey, it is what it is. Too late for us to cry about it now. What we do need to do is to have lunch with Connor at TJ, blow some smoke up his ass, calm him down, make him feel better, make him feel *loved*."

"And also make him lower his sights. Enlighten him on today's business realities," Simpson added. "Unless his writing and speaking skills improve considerably, this schmuck is headed for a crash. Big time."

* * *

GENEVIEVE LASKO SAT THERE, staring ahead at the rubble in front of her, shaking her head. Her partner-sized stainless steel and glass desk—piled high with stacks of paper, too many in number to count and each of them one to two feet high—sat in front of her, painfully reminding her of all she had on her plate.

Suddenly, her junior partner, Allison Remy, stumbled awkwardly into Lasko's office with still more piles of papers precariously balanced across her hands and forearms. "Geez, Genevieve, I'm sorry for not knocking. Aside from the fact that I didn't have a free hand, I also didn't expect to see you in this early."

"No problem, Allie, don't sweat it. Besides, misery loves company."

"I'm guessing all those stacks may have something to do with your glum chum look. And here I come along making things worse. When are you finally going to start delegating more of that shit? Pardon my language."

Lasko ignored the not so subtle reminder that her life would be a lot more manageable if she would start delegating more of her work to Allie and their two other partners. "It's not just what you see sitting here. I have to leave for Punta Maya in just a couple of days. I'm so drowning here, and I haven't even started on all I have to do at TJ."

Lasko's presence every year at TJ was a must. Like all literary agents, she and her partners were compensated on a contingent fee basis. If they invested their time and money in a writer they couldn't sell to one of the traditional publishing houses, they didn't make a dime. In contrast to the thousands of individual query submissions they reviewed every year on an individual basis to come up with one or two possible new clients on whom to gamble, a highly visible presence at established writing conferences like TJ offered a far more efficient opportunity to meet and evaluate promising new talent in person. In one week, Lasko typically generated more worthwhile new clients than she did throughout the rest of the year.

Lasko chaired one of the most popular panel presentations at TJ every year: "What Literary Agents Want to See in an Effective Query Letter Submission Requesting Agency Representation." Several hundred rapt writers—hungry, if not desperate, for an agent to "rep" them—hung on Lasko's every word. And with good reason: in the literary world, Lasko's gatekeeper influence between writer hopefuls and the publishing houses was unparalleled. Year in and year out, no literary agent negotiated more successful deals between authors and publishing houses than she and her agency, Lasko Partners Literary Agency. But with that distinction came a price: the pressure of remaining atop the heap.

Lasko also participated every year in TJ's "Pitch Gala," a one-afternoon-long agent querying adventure, during which authors hungry to secure an agent lined up in front of approximately fifty literary agents *reportedly* looking for fresh blood in a large ballroom. While some agents were just there to be seen and to maintain their image, a three-minutes, in-person speed date-style presentation of their wares to those who truly were hungry for qualified new writers offered far better odds than an impersonal one-minute *possible* review of a written query submission. When a typographical error, a misspelled word, a poorly crafted sentence, the smallest deviation from the agent's website-posted submission requirements, or the absence of the coveted "Invited to Submit at Pitch Gala" often meant sudden death. The lines in front of Lasko were always the longest because of her known reputation, that she was always genuinely on the prowl for gifted new stars and knew how to land deals with the publishing houses.

This year, for the first time, Lasko was also invited to participate in TJ's Virtuoso program, a day-long writing class—actually ten such day-long classes—held the day before TJ's official opening date for all other TJ participants. In each class, a *New York Times* bestselling author is paired with ten pre-qualified, top-notch mentees to review 2,500 word samples submitted by each mentee. This year, TITO's board decided to select a literary agent as one of the mentors. That honor—and the opportunity to identify and corral a handful of top new writers—was bestowed on Lasko, ostensibly because of her standing as a top literary agent. She knew it didn't hurt that she also was a member of TITO's board and an active TJ speaker and Pitch Gala participant every year.

"By the way," Allie said to Lasko, "what's your take on those samples? Are your mentees showing as much promise as you hoped? And justifying the time you're spending on Virtuoso?"

Lasko pointed to the stack of samples in front of her, stifled an involuntary yawn, and grimaced. "Not based on my preliminary reviews. Hopefully, they'll look better when I give them a closer look on my flight. This may turn out to be just some more wasted time. Still, how could I turn down the chance to be a Virtuoso mentor?"

Just then, Lasko's interior line buzzed. "What's up, Heidi?" she said to her secretary.

"Jonathan Connor on line one," Heidi replied.

"Right, just what I need, Jonathan frigging pain in the ass Connor. Tell him I'm tied up and can't possibly break away right now. Try to soften the blow by telling him I said we'll get together on Punta Maya." *Or not.*

* * *

JONATHAN CONNOR CLICKED OFF his mobile phone. And exploded! "Ms. Lasko's tied up and can't be interrupted right now," he mimicked Lasko's secretary. "She said to tell you she'd get together with you at Thriller Jubilee."

* * *

Connor sat all alone in his home office, staring at the walls. "If she was so 'tied up' and 'couldn't possibly be interrupted,'" he fumed and shouted out loud to no one but those walls, "how was her secretary able to speak with her and relay Lasko's message to me? Well, Ms. Lasko can bet her sweet ass that 'we'll get together' on Punta Maya, a get together she won't soon forget!"

CHAPTER 4
Three Days Before

LISA CATE LEWIS, PROGRAM director of Thriller Jubilee, boarded the first leg of the two flights that would take her from JFK in New York to the sun-drenched island of Punta Maya, eleven miles off the coast of Spain. On either side of the ninety-minute layover in Barcelona to clear Spanish customs and immigration, her total flying time would be approximately eight hours, a little more than seven hours on the Trans-Atlantic jumbo jet into Barcelona and close to another hour aboard the small puddle-jumper that would carry her to her ultimate destination.

Every summer for as long as Lewis could remember, Hotel Marisol, the crown jewel and economic epicenter of Punta Maya, played host to Thriller Jubilee.

After nine successive years of volunteer service as TJ's program director, Lewis continued to enjoy her annual sojourn to Hotel Marisol. What was not to like? Great climes, where the dress code favored comfortable shorts and tee-shirts, a chance to shine and be appreciated for what she brought to TJ, and the opportunity to network and develop her own budding writing career, which was advancing at a record clip, thanks in large measure to her standing in the TITO community and the many perks that came with that, including, for example, her private access to and use of TITO's extensive membership email list. Word of mouth was the number one factor in book sales and email lists were the single most significant word of mouth vehicle.

Lewis was flying high, figuratively and literally.

Several hours into her cross-atlantic flight, Lewis suddenly found her first-class cabin a bit chilly. She zipped up the jacket of her Prada sweatsuit. In anticipation of the approaching layover, she pulled the makeup kit out of her carry-on, studied the reflection in her compact mirror, released her ponytail of long wavy blonde hair, and nodded in approval. *Never know who I might bump into in the lounge.*

* * *

SEATED ON THE CONNECTING flight into Punta Maya, Lewis removed the laptop from her computer bag and reviewed her daily TJ material one more time. She allowed her mind to fast forward to the daily retreat schedule. She was confident that everything was locked in and ready to go. All of the panels and programs were in place. More importantly, all of the choice speaking assignments had been meted out, and everyone who had received one or more of those assignments knew they were in her debt.

All at once, she sensed someone staring at her from the adjacent aisle. She looked up.

After a moment of awkward silence: "Lisa Lewis, right? Or should I say L.C. Lewis? Or Ms. Lewis? I'm Robin Donnelly. We met at TJ last year. I learned so much and love attending the event. I'm on my way to this year's. By the way, I've also read and enjoyed both of your novels. I'm a huge fan. You have really made the big time. I'm on your email list and looking forward to your third."

"Hi, Robin. Yes. Of course, I remember meeting you last year." *Yeah, right. Seriously?* "Nice to see you again. I'm so glad you've enjoyed my novels. Both of them, no less. Wow. And thanks for subscribing to my newsletter. How nice to have your support. And I'm still just Lisa. To my friends."

"Lisa, it is." Donnelly's eyes shifted to the laptop. "Working on your next one?"

"Not this week. Going over everything I still have to do for the retreat. Not much time left, I'm afraid." *How the hell do I get rid of this bore?*

Lewis returned her gaze to the laptop. Fiddled with the keyboard.

"Well, I should let you get back to it. Maybe we can get a drink sometime during the week. I'd appreciate the chance to show you what I'm working on. Get your thoughts."

"For sure, Robin. I'll look forward to that." *Zip-a-dee-doo-dah, I can hardly wait!*

* * *

CONNOR CLIMBED OUT OF the limousine as it stopped at the main entrance to the Hotel Marisol. He was greeted by a bellhop who said, "Checking in? Can I help you with your luggage?"

"That won't be necessary," he replied. "I'll handle them myself. They contain some very delicate items," he added. "I need the frig in my room as quickly as possible. Will appreciate if you can move me through check in ASAP, and get me my keys." He handed the bellhop a ten dollar bill.

"Yes sir, right away!" the bellhop responded.

CPSIA information can be obtained
at www.ICGtesting.com
Printed in the USA
LVHW040713280722
724561LV00001B/94

9 781734 539721